86

The Quilter's Homecoming

An Elm Creek Quilts Novel

Jennifer Chiaverini

SIMON & SCHUSTER PAPERBACKS
New York London Toronto Sydney

SIMON & SCHUSTER PAPERBACKS
1230 Avenue of the Americas
New York, NY 10020

First Simon & Schuster trade paperback edition January 2008

SIMON & SCHUSTER and colophon are registered
trademarks of Simon & Schuster, Inc.

For information about special discounts for bulk purchases,
please contact Simon & Schuster Special Sales at
1-800-456-6798 or business@simonandschuster.com.

DESIGNED BY LAUREN SIMONETTI

Manufactured in the United States of America

10 9 8 7 6 5 4 3 2 1

Library of Congress Cataloging-in-Publication Data
Chiaverini, Jennifer.
The quilter's homecoming : an Elm Creek quilts novel / Jennifer Chiaverini.
        p. cm.
1. Quilting—Fiction. 2. Quiltmakers—Fiction. 3. Quilts—Fiction. 4. Pennsylvania—
Fiction. 5. Domestic fiction. I. Title.
PS3553.H473Q57 2007
813'.54—dc22
2006050580

ISBN-13: 978-0-7432-6022-0
ISBN-10:   0-7432-6022-8
ISBN-13: 978-0-7432-6023-7 (pbk)
ISBN-10:   0-7432-6023-6 (pbk)

To Nan Bawn,
Quilt Maker,
Book Lover,
Friend,
and Honorary Elm Creek Quilter

Acknowledgments

I am very grateful to Denise Roy, Maria Massie, Rebecca Davis, Annie Orr, Aileen Boyle, Honi Werner, Melanie Parks, and David Rosenthal for their ongoing support for—and contributions to— the Elm Creek Quilts series throughout the years.

Many thanks to Tara Shaughnessy, nanny extraordinaire, who lovingly cares for my boys and gives me time to write.

I thank Lou Kirby and Susan Robb at the Stagecoach Inn Museum in Newbury Park, California, who generously provided historical details that helped shape two important settings in this novel; Ross E. Pollock of the B&O Railroad Historical Society for advising me regarding rail travel in the 1920s; and Jeanette Berard, special collections librarian at the Thousand Oaks City Library, who directed me to invaluable research sources. I am also indebted to Mary Kay Brown, a fine quilter and storyteller, for sharing her perspective of Southern California farm life, and to the late Patricia A. Allen, whose chronicles of life in the Conejo Valley informed the research for this novel. It was my great privilege to know Pat when we both worked at the Thousand Oaks City Library years ago. Her love for local history inspired my own.

Thank you to the friends and family who have supported and encouraged me through the years, especially Geraldine Neidenbach, Heather Neidenbach, Nic Neidenbach, Virginia Riechman, and Leonard and Marlene Chiaverini. My late grandfather, Edward Riechman, encouraged me until the end.

As always, I thank my husband, Marty, and my sons, Nicholas and Michael, for everything.

Chapter One

1924

As her father's car rumbled across the bridge over Elm Creek and emerged from the forest of bare-limbed trees onto a broad, snow-covered lawn of the Bergstrom estate, Elizabeth Bergstrom was seized by the sudden and unshakable certainty that she should not have come to this place. She should have stayed in Harrisburg, Pennsylvania, to help her brother run the hotel, even though business invariably slowed during the holiday week. Or she should have offered to help care for her sister's newborn twins. Even celebrating Christmas alone would have been preferable to returning to Elm Creek Manor. Her lifelong feelings of warmth and comfort toward the family home had suddenly given way to dread and foreboding. She would have to pass the week next door to Henry, knowing that he was near, and waiting in vain for him to come to her.

As Elm Creek Manor came into view, Elizabeth watched her father straighten in the driver's seat, his leather-gloved fingers flexing around the steering wheel of the new Model T Ford, an unaccustomed look of ease and contentment on his face. He never drank at Elm Creek Manor, nor in the days leading up to their visits, which made Elizabeth wonder why he could not abstain in Harrisburg as well. Apparently he craved his brothers' approval more than that of his wife and children, not that anyone but Elizabeth ever complained about his drinking.

"We're almost home," Elizabeth's father said. Her mother responded with an almost inaudible sniff. It irked her that after all these years, her husband still referred to Elm Creek Manor as home, rather than their stylish apartment in the hotel her father had turned over to their management upon their marriage. Second only to her father's flagship hotel, the Riverview Arms was smartly situated on the most fashionable street in Harrisburg, just blocks from the capitol building. It was a good living, much more reliable and lucrative than raising horses for Bergstrom Thoroughbreds. On his better days, George remembered that, but his insistence upon calling Elm Creek Manor home smacked of ingratitude.

But in this matter, if nothing else, Elizabeth understood her father. Of course Elm Creek Manor was home. The first Bergstroms in America had established the farm in 1857 and ever since, their family had run the farm and raised their prizewinning horses there, building on to the original farmhouse as the number of their descendants grew. They had lived, loved, argued, and celebrated within those gray stone walls for generations. But it was her father's fate to fall in love with a girl who loved the comforts of the city too much to abandon them for life on a horse farm. He could not have Millie and Elm Creek Manor both, so he accepted his future father-in-law's offer to sell his stake in Bergstrom Thoroughbreds and invest the profits in the Riverview Arms. Still, though he had sold his inheritance to his siblings, Elizabeth's father would always consider Elm Creek Manor the home of his heart.

And so would she, Elizabeth told herself firmly. Though Elm Creek Manor would never belong to her the way it would her cousins, every visit would be a homecoming for as long as she lived. She would not mourn for what was lost, whether an inheritance sold off before it could pass to her, or the love of a good man whose affection she had taken for granted.

Her father parked in the circular drive and took his wife's hand to help her from the car. Elizabeth climbed down from the backseat unassisted. A host of aunts, uncles, and cousins greeted them at the door at the top of the veranda. Uncle Fred embraced his younger brother while dear Aunt Eleanor kissed Elizabeth's mother on both cheeks. Aunt Eleanor's eyes sparkled with delight to have the family reunited again, but she was paler and thinner than she had been when Elizabeth last saw her, at the end of summer. Aunt Eleanor had heart trouble and had never in Elizabeth's memory been robust, but she was so spirited that one could almost forget her affliction. Elizabeth wondered if those who lived with her daily were oblivious to how she weakened by imperceptible degrees.

Suddenly Elizabeth's four-year-old cousin, Sylvia, darted through the crowd of taller relatives and took hold of Elizabeth's sleeve. "I thought you were never going to get here," she cried. "Come and play with me."

"Let me at least get though the doorway," said Elizabeth, laughing as Sylvia tugged off her coat. She had hoped to linger long enough to ask Aunt Eleanor—casually, of course—if she had any news of the Nelson family, but Sylvia seized her hand and led her across the marble foyer and up two flights of stairs to the nursery before Eleanor could even give her aunt and uncle a proper greeting.

Elizabeth would have to wait until supper to learn no one had seen Henry Nelson since the harvest dance in early November, except to wave to him from a distance as he worked in the fields with his brothers and father. Elizabeth feigned indifference, but her heart sank at the thought of Henry with some other girl on his arm—someone pretty and cheerful who didn't spend half her time in a far-distant city writing teasing letters about all the fun she was having with other young men. It was probably too much to hope Henry had danced only with his sister.

By the next morning Elizabeth had persuaded herself that she didn't care how Henry might have carried on at some silly country dance. After all, since they had said good-bye at the end of the summer, she had attended many dances, shows, and clubs, always escorted by one handsome fellow or another. Her mother worried that she was running with a fast crowd, but her father, who should have known better since his own hotel had a nightclub, assumed Elizabeth and her friends passed the time together as his own generation had—in carefully supervised, sedate activities where young men and women congregated on opposite sides of the room unless prompted by a chaperone to interact. Elizabeth's mother had a more vivid imagination, and it was she who waited up for her youngest daughter with the lights on until she was safely tucked into bed on Friday and Saturday nights.

Every summer, Elizabeth surprised her mother by willingly abandoning the delights of the city for Elm Creek Manor. Millie, oblivious to the appeal of the solace and serenity of the farm, always expected Elizabeth to put up more of an argument. Elizabeth certainly did about everything else. She wanted to bob her hair and wear dresses with hemlines up to her knee. She plastered her bedroom walls with magazine photographs of Paris, London, Venice, and other places she was highly unlikely to visit, covering up the perfectly lovely floral wallpaper selected by Millie's mother when the hotel was built. She chatted easily with young men, guests of the hotel, before they had been properly introduced. Millie shook her head in despair over her daughter's seeming indifference to how things looked, to what people thought. Why should anyone believe she was a well-brought-up girl if she didn't behave like one?

Yet every year as spring turned to summer, Elizabeth found herself longing for the cool breeze off the Four Brothers Mountains, the scent of apple blossoms in the orchard, the grace and speed of the horses, the awkward beauty of the colts, the warmth and affection of her aunts and uncles and grandparents. She felt at ease at Elm Creek Manor. Her meddling mother was far away. She was in no danger of walking into a room to find her father passed out over a ledger, an empty brandy bottle on the desk. There was only comfort and acceptance and peace. And Henry.

Once he had only been Henry Nelson from the next farm over, a boy more her brother's friend than her own. All the children played together, Bergstroms and Nelsons meeting at the flat rock beneath the willow next to Elm Creek after chores were done and running wild in the forests until they were called home for supper. They met again after evening chores and stayed out well after dark, playing hide-and-seek and Ghost in the Graveyard. One hot August night on the eve of her return to the city, Elizabeth, her brother Lawrence, Henry, and Henry's brother climbed to the top of a haystack and lay on their backs watching the night sky for shooting stars. One by one the other children crept off home to bed, but Elizabeth felt compelled to stay until she had counted one hundred shooting stars. Secretly, she had convinced herself that if she could stay awake long enough to count one hundred stars, her parents would decide that they could stay another day.

She had only reached fifty-one when Lawrence sat up and brushed hay from his hair. "We should go in."

"If you want to go in, go ahead. I'll come when I'm ready."

"I'm not letting you walk back alone in the dark. You'll probably trip over a rock and fall in the creek."

The darkness hid Elizabeth's scarlet flush of shame and anger. Lawrence never made any effort to disguise his certainty that his youngest sister would fail at everything she tried. "I will not. I know the way as well as you."

"I'll walk back with her," said Henry.

Lawrence agreed, glad to be rid of the burden, then he slid down from the haystack and disappeared into the night.

Elizabeth counted shooting stars in indignant silence.

"Thank you," she said, after a while. She lay back and gazed up at the starry heavens, hay prickling beneath her, warm and sweet from the sun. After a time, Henry's hand touched hers, and closed around it. Warmth bloomed inside her, and she knew suddenly that after this summer, everything would be different. Henry had chosen her over her brother. Henry was hers.

She was fourteen.

After that, whenever Henry came to Elm Creek Manor, Elizabeth knew she was the person he had come to see. They began exchanging letters during the months they were separated, letters in which each confided more about their hopes and fears than either would have been able to say aloud. Whenever they reunited after a long absence, Elizabeth always experienced a fleeting moment of shyness, wondering if she should have told him about her dreams to visit Paris and London and Venice, her longing to leave the stifling streets of Harrisburg for the rolling hills and green forests of the Elm Creek Valley, her shame and embarrassment when her father stumbled through the hotel lobby after returning home from his favorite speakeasy, her frustration when the rest of the family turned a blind eye. But Henry never laughed at her or turned away in disgust. In time, he became her dearest confidant and closest friend.

As the years passed, Elizabeth wondered if he would ever become more than that. He never drowned her in flattery the way other young men did; in fact, he was so plainspoken and solemn she often wondered if he cared for her at all. Sometimes she teased him by describing the parties she attended back home, the flowers other young men brought her, the poems they sent. She casually threw out references to the movies she had seen in one fellow's company or another's, the dances she enjoyed, how Gerald preferred the fox-trot but Jack was wild about the Charleston and Frank seemed to consider himself another Rudolph Valentino, the way he danced the tango. She hoped to provoke Henry into making romantic gestures of his own, or at least to do something that might indicate a hidden reservoir of jealousy.

In her most recent letter, she had described a Christmas concert she had attended with a young man whose determination to marry her had only increased after she declined his first proposal. She had worn a blue velvet dress with a matching cloche hat; her escort had given her a corsage with three roses and a ribbon the exact shade of her dress. They had traveled in style in his father's new Packard. The next day, their photo appeared on the society page of the Harrisburg *Patriot* above a caption that declared them the most handsome couple in attendance. Elizabeth included the newspaper clipping in her letter and asked Henry for his opinion: "Do you think this will encourage him to think of us as a couple? I should discourage him, but he's such a sweet boy I hate to seem unkind. I imagine many girls are eventually won this way. Persistence is admirable in a man. If he doesn't become impatient waiting for me, maybe someday I will come to think of him as more than a friend."

Satisfied, she sent off her letter and awaited a declaration of Henry's true feelings by return mail.

It never came.

As the days passed, she began to worry that instead of stirring him into action, she had driven him away. Henry was, after all, a practical man. He would not pursue a lost cause, and she had all but declared the inevitability of her marriage to another more persistent, more expressive man. Henry had endured her teasing stoically through the years, but to repay him with musings that she might fall in love with someone else might, possibly, have been going too far.

Henry had never said he loved her. He had made her no promises. He had never kissed her and rarely held her hand except to help her jump from stone to stone as they crossed Elm Creek at the narrows, or to assist her onto her horse when they went riding. She had it on very good authority that he had not sat around pining for her at that harvest dance. How dare he end a ten-year friendship and five-year correspondence when she quite reasonably asked his opinion about the man who seemed most interested in marrying her? He ought to be flattered that she thought so highly of his opinion, especially since he seemed to lack any romantic instincts whatsoever. She would have done better to consult Lawrence.

Henry had given up too easily. If he loved her, he would have written back. He would have been waiting for her on the front steps of Elm Creek Manor to demand that she turn down Gerald or Jack or any other fellow who came too close. He would have done something.

He hadn't, and that told her the truth she did not want to know.

Two days before Christmas Eve, Elizabeth tried to lose herself in the joyful anticipation of the holidays. She played with little cousin Sylvia, threaded needles for Great-Aunt Lucinda as she sewed a green-and-red Feathered Star quilt, and helped Aunt Eleanor and the other Bergstrom women make delicious apple strudel as gifts for neighbors. Perhaps she should offer to take the Nelsons' to them at Two Bears Farm on the chance that she might see Henry—but what then? How pathetic she would seem, hoping to win him back with pastry. It was very good pastry, but even so. She had her pride.

She was reading a Christmas story to Sylvia when a cousin came running to the nursery to announce that Elizabeth had a visitor. She almost knocked Sylvia out of the rocking chair in her haste to see who had come.

She hurried downstairs to find Henry in the kitchen talking companionably with her father and Uncle Fred. Her heart quickened at the sight of him, taller and more handsome than she remembered, fairer and slighter of frame than the Bergstrom men but with the hardened muscles and callused hands of a farmer. She was pleased to see he had since summer shaved off his seasonal mustache because she had never liked the way it hid the curve of his mouth. He smiled warmly at her, but she was struck by a new-found resolve in his eyes.

She knew at once that he had come to tell her he had fallen in love with someone else.

He invited her to go for a walk. Together they crossed the bridge over Elm Creek, passed the barn, and strolled along the apple grove, the trees bare-limbed and bleak against the gray sky. "What did you think of my last letter?" Elizabeth asked when she could endure exchanging pleasantries no longer. "You never answered, unless your reply was lost in the mail."

He was silent for a moment; the only sound was the crunching of their boots upon snow and the far-off caw of a crow. "I'm always glad to get your letters. I'm sorry I didn't have a chance to write back. I've been busy with . . . some business matters."

She smiled tightly. December was not usually a busy time around Two Bears Farm. "I asked for your opinion and I was counting on you to offer it."

"I wasn't sure what you were asking," said Henry. "Do I think this friend of yours considers you two a couple? I'd bet on it, if you haven't told him otherwise. Do I think you should discourage him? That depends."

"It depends?" Elizabeth stopped and looked up at him. "It depends on what?"

"Do you want him to think you're his girl or not? I never thought you were the type to marry a fellow because he wore you down, but if you are, maybe you should save him the time and trouble and marry him now."

"Thank you for the suggestion," said Elizabeth. She resumed walking, faster now, to put distance between them. "I'll consider it."

Henry easily caught up to her. "It wasn't a suggestion."

"Then what *do* you think?"

"Do you love him?"

"He asked me to marry him, and I refused, didn't I?"

Henry caught her by the elbow. "That doesn't answer my question. Do you love him?"

"No," Elizabeth burst out. "I don't love him, but at least I know how he feels about me, which is more than I can say about you."

She did not expect to see Henry again, but he returned the next afternoon. By that time, most of her anger had abated. Though the memory of her outburst and subsequent flight embarrassed her, she was determined not to apologize. She agreed to another walk, mostly out of curiosity. She had puzzled too long over the mystery of Henry's feelings to send him away when he had apparently decided to divulge them.

He waited until they had crossed the bridge, out of earshot of both the house and the barn—unless they shouted, which was perhaps not out of the question. "I thought you knew I loved you."

The gracelessness of his declaration sparked her anger. "How would I know, since you've never told me?"

"Would I write to you for five years if I didn't love you? Would I come to Elm Creek Manor and see you every day you're here?"

"I don't know. Maybe."

"No, I wouldn't," he said emphatically, and Elizabeth knew it to be true. Another man might, but not Henry.

"Well, say it, then," she told him.

He hesitated. "Why do I have to say it?"

"Because I need to know. Because you never lie, and if you say you love me straight out, I'll have no choice but to believe you."

He shrugged. "All right, then, I love you."

Elizabeth nearly laughed, incredulous. "Is that the best you can do?"

"What else do you want me to say?"

"I've received four proposals—five, counting yours—and I have to say that this one was by far the least romantic. It might very well be the least romantic proposal of all time."

"I wasn't proposing. I was only trying to tell you that I love you."

"Oh." All the blood seemed to rush to Elizabeth's face. "Oh. I didn't mean—"

"Elizabeth, wait." His voice was low and gentle, with a trace of embarrassment. "I'm coming to that part."

She took a deep breath, ducked her chin into the collar of her coat, and waited for him to continue.

Henry took a thick envelope from his overcoat pocket. "I know you want to see the world. I know you wish you had land to call your own the way your aunt and uncle have Elm Creek Manor. I know you're tired of your father's hotel and of Harrisburg." He thrust the envelope into her hand. When she just stared at it, he said, "Go on. Open it."

She withdrew several sheets of thick paper, folded into thirds, and three photographs of an arid landscape of rolling hills dotted with clusters of oaks. She unfolded the papers, and as she scanned the first, Henry said, "Yesterday I told you I couldn't answer your letter because I was occupied with some business. That's the title to a cattle ranch in southern California."

"The Rancho Triunfo," Elizabeth read aloud. "You bought a ranch?"

"With every cent I've earned and saved since I was twelve years old. It's about forty-five miles north of Los Angeles. They say it's like paradise, Elizabeth. Summer all year round, orange trees growing in the backyard—"

"It's so far away." And he had purchased the ranch without knowing whether she would want to go with him.

"Aren't you always saying you want to leave Harrisburg?"

"Well, yes, but . . ." She had wanted to see the world and then come home to Elm Creek Manor. She never meant to stay away forever. "It's on the other side of the country."

"That's the point." Henry took her hands, crumpling the papers between them. "If you'll marry me, I want to give you land of your own in the most beautiful part of the country I could find. If you won't marry me, I want to put a continent between me and the chance I might ever see you in the arms of another man."

Elizabeth felt breathless, light-headed. As far as she was concerned, the most beautiful part of the country was right here, all around them. "What about Two Bears Farm? What will your parents think?"

"They have my brothers and sister to help them work the place and take it over for them one day. If I go, there will be one less person arguing for a piece of the same pie."

And what of her family? Her mother and father expected her to marry a nice young man from Harrisburg who would come to work for her father in the family business. That was what her mother had done. Millie had shrieked in outrage when Elizabeth refused Gerald's proposal. Gerald, who would fit so neatly into Millie's plans for the hotel—and who drank nearly as much as her father and seemed constitutionally incapable of fidelity.

It was Henry Elizabeth wanted, although when she had imagined them together it had been at Two Bears Ranch, so close to Elm Creek Manor that it was almost as good as coming home. A ranch in southern California might be beautiful, but it would not be home.

But Henry was going, with or without her.

"Yes," she told him softly. "I'll marry you."

He kissed her. The papers and photographs fell to the snowy ground, forgotten.

As Elizabeth had expected, her parents were dismayed to hear of their plans to move so far away. Millie could not disguise her anger that they had come to inform them of a decision already made, and not to seek advice and permission. George did not share his wife's outrage, but admitted surprise that the prudent, steadfast Henry had acted so impulsively. "If you're tired of farm life, you can come and work for me," he offered. "I wanted to open a second hotel, and with you to help me, I could do it. It would be advantageous to both of us. Why go to the ends of the earth when you can make a decent living here?"

"I don't intend to make only a decent living, sir. I intend to make a fortune."

Henry spoke in such frank seriousness that Elizabeth could not help but believe him, but her father looked dubious. "A man doesn't become a farmer to get rich."

"Your grandfather did, sir."

Elizabeth's father smiled grudgingly. "That was a very different time. There are fortunes to be made every day, but not in farming, not anymore. The land isn't worth what it used to be. My brothers have prospered because they raise prize horses. They cater to wealthy customers, and I can tell you those customers aren't farmers. The place for an enterprising young man these days is business."

Henry shook his head. "I intend to raise cattle, sir, not corn, not oats. I'll be raising beef. All those wealthy businessmen who buy your Bergstrom Thoroughbreds want beef for their tables. Providing it will make me a rich man."

Elizabeth's father sighed, knowing the argument was lost before it had begun. "Farming is the only industry I can think of riskier than opening a new hotel across the street from your strongest competitor. If you come work for me, you'll still make your fortune. It may take time, but you'll get there."

"With all due respect, sir," said Henry carefully, "and I do value your opinion, but I could never live away from the land."

Elizabeth's father, who had given up his share of the Bergstrom land for a love that had not flourished with the passing of time, nodded and said no more, except to offer the couple his blessing.

When the family gathered for Christmas Eve supper the next evening, Elizabeth's father announced their engagement. Everyone but little Sylvia welcomed the news with great joy, which made it more difficult to announce their plans to move away. The family accepted the couple's decision with surprise, but steadied themselves with the knowledge that most Bergstroms who left the Elm Creek Valley eventually returned.

Henry's family was far less sanguine. His sister, Rosemary, broke down in tears and begged him to reconsider. His brothers, who had assumed he would always be there to help them run the farm, voiced cautious support, shot through with shock and betrayal. His father was concerned that his ordinarily prudent son had purchased land without examining it firsthand, but after he studied the documents and photographs, he admitted everything looked to be in order. If the land was indeed as the agent had described it, Henry had made a sound investment, a sensible purchase.

But Henry's mother took Elizabeth aside. "You can still talk him out of this," she beseeched in a whisper. "Henry adores you. He will stay here if he knows that's what you want."

"I'm afraid it's too late for that," Elizabeth told her gently. "I don't think he could get out of the sale even if he wanted to."

What she did not say was that despite the small seeds of doubt Henry's father had planted with his concerns about the sight-unseen purchase, Elizabeth had no intention of talking Henry out of it. She had become as eager as Henry to embark on their adventure, and in idle moments she would take out the photographs, search them for tiny details she had previously overlooked, and murmur, "Triumph Ranch." The very name rang with promise.

Elizabeth had little time for romantic musings, for there was much to do before the wedding. The Pittsburgh landbroker from whom Henry had purchased the ranch assured him that the former owners would be willing to remain on the ranch and tend the livestock until the end of April, but he could make no guarantees after that. At first, Henry suggested he and Elizabeth leave the week after New Year's and marry when they arrived in California, but Elizabeth firmly refused. Her family put great stock in propriety and tradition, and she would not deny them the pleasure of a traditional Bergstrom wedding.

The scant three months of preparations raced by in a blur of dress fittings, china pattern selections, and private lectures from all of her aunts, including her unmarried great-aunt Lucinda, about what she could expect from married life. Some of their advice was amusing, but when the lessons dismayed and alarmed her, she allowed her mind to wander. Hadn't she already learned everything she needed to know about being a good wife by watching her mother, grandmothers, and aunts?

When the time came to pack for their journey west, the enormity of their undertaking began to sink in. She felt almost as if she and Henry were among the early pioneers, setting out for the West with grand dreams to meet an unknown fate, uncertain whether they would ever return home. Silently she chastised herself for such foolish worries, for so much homesickness before they even left Pennsylvania, and this from the girl who all her life had longed to see the world. Once she and Henry were established, they would surely be able to leave the Rancho Triunfo in the care of trusted ranch hands long enough for a visit home. Still, she did not know how soon a return trip might come, and she had to swallow a lump in her throat every time she thought of spending years without seeing Elm Creek Manor and those who lived there.

She took comfort in the handmade gifts the Bergstrom women gave to her as the wedding approached. In addition to lovely new clothes, they made her several quilts to use in her new home. Great-Aunt Lydia doubted that quilts would be necessary in so warm a place as southern California, but Aunt Eleanor declared that they would be a beautiful touch of home nonetheless. One of Elizabeth's favorites was a bridal quilt in the Double Wedding Ring pattern, embellished with beautiful floral appliqués. All the women of the family had sewn together the arcs and wedges of the pieced rings, and whenever Elizabeth looked upon the quilt she recognized the work of individual quiltmakers: Great-Aunt Lucinda's precise piecing, Aunt Eleanor's intricate appliqué, Great-Aunt Lydia's painstaking stipple quilting, her grandmother's perfectly mitered binding. As the finest quilt Elizabeth owned, it should have been saved for company, but as soon as she saw it, she decided it must grace the bed she would share with Henry.

As lovely as the bridal quilt was, a second quilt was somehow more precious to her, even though it was only a sturdy scrap quilt meant for everyday use. Great-Aunt Lucinda had sewn it in the evenings after the day's work was done, rocking in her favorite chair in the parlor and hiding the pieces whenever Elizabeth entered the room. Elizabeth pretended not to notice since it was obvious Great-Aunt Lucinda intended the quilt to be a surprise, but her curiosity was piqued and she could not resist a little surreptitious observation of her aunt at work. One day a few weeks before the wedding, Sylvia gave Elizabeth the perfect opportunity. She had just been scolded by her father for some minor offense intended to prevent the marriage—telling Henry she hated him, perhaps, or pretending she had the plague so the house would be quarantined—and she had sought out the comfort of Great-Aunt Lucinda's lap for her sulk. Elizabeth listened just beyond the doorway as Great-Aunt Lucinda told Sylvia about the quilt, made in a pattern of concentric rectangles and squares, one half of the block light colors, the other dark in the fashion of a Log Cabin block.

"This pattern is called Chimneys and Cornerstones," Great-Aunt Lucinda explained. "Whenever Elizabeth sees it, she'll remember our home and all the people in it. We Bergstroms have been blessed to have a home filled with love from the chimneys to the cornerstone. This quilt will help Elizabeth take some of that love with her."

Silence prompted Elizabeth to draw closer and peek into the room. Sylvia was watching Great-Aunt Lucinda as she ran her finger along a diagonal row of red squares, from one corner of the block to its opposite. "Do you see these red squares?" asked Lucinda. "Each is a fire burning in the fireplace to warm Elizabeth after a weary journey home."

"You made too many," said Sylvia, counting. "We don't have so many fireplaces."

"I know," said Lucinda, smiling in amusement. "It's just a fancy. Elizabeth will understand. But there's more to the story. Do you see how one half of the block is dark fabric, and the other is light? The dark half represents the sorrows in a life, and the light colors represent the joys."

"Then why don't you give her a quilt with all light fabric?"

"I suppose I could, but then she wouldn't be able to see the pattern. The design appears only if you have both dark and light fabric."

"But I don't want Elizabeth to have any sorrows."

"I don't either, love, but sorrows come to us all. But don't worry. Remember these?" Lucinda touched several red squares arranged diagonally across one block. "As long as these home fires keep burning, Elizabeth will always have more joys than sorrows."

Little Sylvia's brow furrowed as she studied the quilt. Suddenly she brightened. "The red squares are keeping the sorrow part away from the light part."

"That's exactly right," Great-Aunt Lucinda praised. "What a bright little girl you are."

Pleased, Sylvia snuggled closer to her great-aunt. "I still don't like the sorrow part."

"None of us do. Let's hope that Elizabeth finds all the joy she deserves, and only enough sorrow to nurture an empathetic heart."

When Great-Aunt Lucinda gave Elizabeth the quilt the day before the wedding, she said nothing of the quilt's symbolism or how much Elizabeth would be missed. Lucinda had stitched her farewells and hopes for her grandniece into the quilt, and as Elizabeth held the soft folds of cloth to her heart, she understood everything Lucinda could not say. For a fleeting moment she feared that leaving Pennsylvania would be a terrible mistake, bringing down upon her all the sorrows that Great-Aunt Lucinda wanted the fires of home to protect her from. Then she thought of Henry, and how in all her hopes of future happiness, she imagined herself by his side. She knew she could not stay behind.

She wrapped their new china in the precious quilts for protection and placed them in her sturdiest trunk, a gift from Lawrence. Then, at last, all was ready.

The wedding itself passed in a blur. She had always heard that a wedding day was the happiest in a young woman's life, but she was sure she would remember hers only in glimpses: her mother help-ing her arrange her golden hair into long corkscrew curls swept back from her face by her headpiece and veil, her father walking her down the aisle of the same church her parents had married in, Henry's encouraging smile as she murmured her vows, a whirl of celebration back at the manor. She could not swallow more than a few bites of the delicious feast her mother and aunts had prepared, but her first dance with Henry as husband and wife filled her with the warmth of pure happiness. She knew with a certainty she could not explain that she and Henry would weather whatever storms came their way—not that they were likely to face many in sunny southern California.

∾

1875

Isabel ran up and down the length of the front porch, her bare feet padding on the smooth oaken boards, pausing only briefly when Mami and Abuelo crossed her path carrying boxes from the house to the wagon. Abuela waited on the front seat, holding Isabel's little sister on her lap. Her back was tall and straight, and she would not turn around no matter how often Isabel called out to her to look, to see how fast she could run.

Swinging her doll by the arm as she darted back and forth, Isabel stumbled and ran headlong into her mother's legs. "Will someone keep this child out of my way?" her mother cried. And she was crying. Horrified, Isabel watched as her mother struggled to balance a box of dishes on her hip while wiping tears from her eyes.

"I didn't mean to hurt you," said Isabel. She did not think she had struck her mother so hard. She had not hurt herself even one little bit.

"You didn't, *mija*." Mami forced a smile and continued down the porch steps to the wagon. "Go and play for a little while longer."

Worried, Isabel wandered away from their cabin home and into the backyard, wishing her brother would come and play, but he had gone with Papi up to the big farmhouse to collect Papi's pay. Her father would come home happy. He always did on paydays. Sometimes he brought her little treats, too—candy or a ribbon for her hair.

She sat on a rock drawing patterns in the dirt with a stick, listening to her mother and grandfather loading the wagon, unseen on the other side of the cabin. They had been working all morning, and everyone was sad except for the baby. Abuela had not started dinner, working the cornmeal with her hands and frying the tortillas as she usually did at this time of the day. Isabel was hungry. When were they going to eat?

She went to find her mother but found her grandfather first. "I'm hungry," she told him, slipping her hand into his.

He hesitated and looked back at the cabin. Mami was somewhere inside; Isabel heard a door open and close. "We're almost done," he said. "Can you wait?"

Isabel shook her head.

Her grandfather smiled kindly down at her. "Very well. Let's see what we can find."

Together they went around back to the pair of orange trees that grew side by side a few yards from the cabin. They searched the branches, but found no ripe oranges, only hard, green fruit too bitter to eat. Her grandfather thought for a moment. "We will have to search a little ways from the house," he told her. "Can you walk that far?"

Isabel nodded, although she was not sure how far he meant to go.

Hand in hand they walked up the hill, leaving the cabin behind. Before long Isabel's legs grew tired, but she did not complain. She was relieved when her grandfather finally halted, but surprised that he had chosen the apricot orchard for their rest. Isabel and her brother were strictly forbidden to play there, lest they accidentally harm the trees.

The branches were heavy with plump, ripe fruit. Already Papi and the other hired hands had stuck the posts deep into the ground where every year they set up the cutting shed. The harvest would start soon. Even Mami and Abuelo worked the apricot harvest. Someday Isabel would, too.

"Would you like one?" her grandfather asked, gesturing to the nearest tree.

"Mami says we aren't allowed," Isabel said, though the sight of the fruit made her mouth water. "She says we should never, never take the apricots without permission."

"On an ordinary day, I would say that is very good advice," her grandfather replied. "But today is a special day, and just this once, you may have any apricot you choose."

He hoisted her up onto his shoulders and moved so close to the trees that she felt hidden within the branches like a little bird. Giggling, she searched and searched until she found the perfect apricot—rosy and plump, without a single blemish. She plucked it, wiped it on the hem of her dress, and bit into the soft flesh. The sweet juice trickled down her chin, warm from the sun. Sometimes her father brought home the dried, cured apricot slices at the end of harvest, but Isabel rarely tasted the fresh fruit, and never straight from the tree.

She picked a second apricot for Abuelo, and then one for Mami, Papi, Abuela, and her brother. She took one for the baby, too; she could suck on it even though she didn't have any teeth. Isabel expected her grandfather to tell her to stop, to warn her that she was taking too many, but he let her continue until she could carry no more. Only then did he lower her to the ground.

They walked slowly back to the cabin. Isabel held up her hem to make a basket of her skirt, carefully cradling the fruit. Abuelo offered to help, but she insisted upon carrying the apricots herself. She had picked them; she would bring them home to the family.

"Abuelo?" she asked. "How long are we going away?"

His dark, graying eyebrows rose. "How long?"

"When are we coming home?"

He watched her for a moment, his rich brown eyes full of sympathy. Then he sat down and drew her onto his lap. *"Niña,"* he said, "we aren't coming back. You know that. Your mami and papi have found a new home for you and your brother and sister."

"What about you?"

"Abuela and I will be right next door."

"But I don't want to go." She loved the orange trees, the shady front porch, the cozy room she shared with her brother and baby sister. When her parents had taken her to see their new home on the western side of the valley near the grocery store, she never thought they were meant to live there forever.

Her eyes welled up with tears.

"Oh, no, we can't have tears," said her grandfather sternly. "You're a big girl and you mustn't cry. You must be proud. Remember that this land once belonged to our family, from those high hills to the east and as far as you can see to the west. The king of Spain gave all this to my grandfather as a reward for his courage. You must be as brave as he was."

Isabel gulped air and dried her tears. She understood now why her grandmother had turned her back upon the cabin where they had spent so many happy years. It was already a part of their past.

Chapter Two
1925

Elizabeth and Henry almost missed their train. They had planned to arrive at the Harrisburg station in plenty of time to make the 10:05 night train, but after the car was packed and the last farewells said, Elizabeth discovered that her shoes were missing. At first she thought she had merely misplaced them in the excitement surrounding the wedding, but little cousin Sylvia couldn't hide her grin of satisfaction, refusing to help in the search or give the grown-ups a single clue as to their whereabouts. Elizabeth had to bite the inside of her cheek to keep from laughing, but when Henry glanced at his watch and checked the car for the hundredth time, she took pity on him.

"I suppose those shoes are gone for good," she said, rising with a sigh and smoothing the skirt of her traveling suit, a gift sewn by her aunt Eleanor and great-aunt Lucinda. "They were my favorite pair, too. I'll suppose I'll have to do without until we reach California."

While Sylvia looked on suspiciously, Elizabeth bade farewell to each cousin, aunt, uncle, and grandparent in turn, exchanging hugs and kisses and promises to write. Last of all, Elizabeth said good-bye to her parents. Her father was too overcome to speak, but he hugged Elizabeth and held her so long she wondered if Henry might be forced to pry her loose. Her mother, tears filling her eyes, choked out a few last-minute warnings about the dangers of travel. Elizabeth nodded, but the words scarcely registered. Shoes or no shoes, she really was leaving.

She took Henry's arm and left Elm Creek Manor, chasing away thoughts that she might be crossing the threshold for the last time. Gingerly she picked her way across the veranda in her stocking feet, greatly exaggerating the discomfort.

"You can't go all the way to California like that," protested Sylvia.

"I could lend you my boots," said Henry.

Elizabeth raised her eyebrows at him, surprised that he had decided to play along. "I don't have any choice," she told Sylvia. "If Henry and I don't reach the ranch before the former owners leave, who will take care of the animals? They'll be hungry and lonely, the poor things."

Elizabeth knew Sylvia loved animals too much to bear the thought of one neglected. Sure enough, the little girl scowled, disappeared into the manor, and returned moments later carrying Elizabeth's black leather Mary Janes. "Here," she said sullenly, thrusting them at her cousin.

"Oh, you found them," exclaimed Elizabeth, slipping them on. "What a clever girl."

Sylvia did not smile at the praise. She flung her arms around Elizabeth for one last, fierce hug and ran back into the manor without a word.

Elizabeth held Henry's hand tightly as Elm Creek Manor disappeared behind them. She held her gaze on the photographs of Triumph Ranch, lingering over the beautiful landscape that she and Henry would soon call home. Yet Two Bears Farm would always mean as much to Henry as Elm Creek Manor did to her. Two Bears Farm had been in the Nelson family since before the Bergstrom family came to America, and its history was just as renowned. Henry's great-grandparents, Thomas and Dorothea Nelson, had run an Underground Railroad station out of the old farmhouse, and the Nelson children loved to retell the story of how Thomas had been shot defending the home from slave catchers. Dorothea had run the farm, raised a child, and edited an abolitionist newspaper while Thomas was off fighting in the Civil War. The farm had sustained Henry's family for generations. If only Triumph Ranch would prove as bountiful.

Because it was their honeymoon, Henry splurged on a compartment for the eighteen-hour-and-five-minute trip from Harrisburg to St. Louis on Train 17. The accommodations were small but well appointed, but most important, they were private—which was in Elizabeth's opinion essential for a newlywed couple. Their compartment boasted two facing seats, an ingenious washbasin that folded into the wall, and a covered toilet in the corner. Elizabeth immediately decided that she would send Henry out into the corridor whenever she needed to use it. Married or not, there were some activities she had no intention of sharing with him.

The night porter helped them settle in with their hand luggage and then converted one of the seats into a double bed, where Elizabeth and Henry snuggled beneath the covers. As Henry held her and kissed her to the swaying of the train, Elizabeth wished their wedding quilt was not packed away with their china in the luggage car. She had meant for them to sleep beneath it every night of their marriage.

The next morning she and Henry had breakfast in the dining car. Afterward they explored the train and settled in the observation car, where Henry wanted to enjoy the view as the forested hills of

Pennsylvania gave way to the low mountains of West Virginia and the flat farmlands of the Midwest. Elizabeth preferred to observe their fellow passengers. She was fascinated by the knee-high hemlines of the ladies' dresses, the dropped waists that gave their slim figures a boyish look, the lipstick carefully applied to mimic the effect of a bee sting. "Every one of them has her hair bobbed," Elizabeth whispered to Henry, envious. Her parents had forbidden her to cut hers. "They look like they stepped out of a Hollywood fashion magazine."

"I love your hair," said Henry. "Don't cut it off to chase a fad. You're prettier than any of these girls."

Pleased, Elizabeth rewarded him with a kiss on the cheek, glancing over his shoulder at a woman with a sleek, dark bob who held her cigarette holder elegantly as she pored over a recent issue of *True Story*. With a flash of inspiration, she rose and excused herself. She hurried back to their honeymoon suite, as they had nicknamed it, and unearthed her sewing box. The jolting of the train at first made it difficult to thread her needle, but she soon altered the hem of her dress with swift, deft stitches.

"Perfect," she declared, admiring the fall of the skirt and the daring show of leg.

As for her hair . . .

She braided it into two golden plaits, took a deep breath, and raised the scissors. Quickly, before she could change her mind, she cut off the braids and immediately shut her eyes, setting the scissors down as if the metal scalded.

Not that she regretted what she had done; she would look like a blond Clara Bow, only prettier. Henry would love it.

Elizabeth opened her eyes and peered into the mirror. Her gentle ringlets had given way to wild, uneven curls.

She gulped and pressed a hand to her stomach. Her hair would grow back. It would take years for it to regain its former length, but it would grow back. In the meantime, she would wear fashionable hats.

She left the sleeper and made her way back to the observation lounge, taking her time and rehearsing her entrance. With any luck, Henry would be so distracted by her higher hemline that he wouldn't notice her hair. Yet whom should she pass in the narrow corridor but the woman with the enviable, sleek, dark-haired bob.

"Jeez!" the woman exclaimed. "Didya forget your beautician's birthday or something? 'Cause it looks like she saved the dull scissors for you."

Elizabeth promptly burst into tears.

"Oh, hey, hey there, honey. I didn't mean nothing by it." She patted Elizabeth awkwardly on the shoulder. "You look fine. I mean—well, not fine, but it'll grow back, right?"

Elizabeth took out her handkerchief and tried to compose herself. "I was just trying to bob—bob—"

"Another bob gone bad," said the woman, shaking her head. "Well, I've seen worse. Do you want me to fix it?"

"Can you? I didn't think it could be fixed."

"Sure. It won't be as good as new, but it'll be swell. Don't you worry."

The woman, whose name was Mae, followed Elizabeth back to her compartment. "Nice digs," she remarked, glancing around as Elizabeth dug in her sewing box for the scissors. "You sure know how to travel in style."

"We splurged," Elizabeth explained, handing her the scissors. "It's our honeymoon."

"You don't say." Mae gestured for her to take a seat. "I guess the fun's over for you, honey."

"On the contrary, I think the fun has just started."

"You must've married one hell of a fella to feel that way." Mae studied Elizabeth's mangled locks. "Say, wait a minute. I saw you two in the observation car. That sandy-haired looker is your husband?"

"That's right," said Elizabeth, cringing slightly at the sound of the scissors snipping away near her right ear.

"He seems . . ." Mae paused. "Awful serious."

"I suppose he is, but he knows how to have a good time, too."

"Don't get me wrong, honey. A guy like that is the right sort of fella when you're ready to settle down." Mae sighed. "Sure wish I could fall in love with one of those. You don't know how lucky you are."

But Elizabeth did know, and she felt a surge of love and pride for her new husband. "Henry's one in a million, all right."

Mae snorted. "So's Peter, but I don't think I mean that the same way you do."

"Is Peter your husband?"

"No, and I tell him he won't be until he proves he can keep a job for more than two months running. And I mean a decent job, too."

"He probably just hasn't found his niche yet," Elizabeth said.

"Oh, he's found his niche all right. There's only one thing he's any good at." Mae thought for a moment. "Okay, two things, but he sure can't make any money doing the other. I would have to put my foot down, if you know what I mean."

Elizabeth had no idea what she meant, but she murmured a vague agreement. At last Mae handed the scissors back to Elizabeth. "It's not bad for a makeshift barbershop on a moving train," she remarked, looking pleased with herself. "You're a regular jazz baby now."

Elizabeth leapt to her feet and snatched up the mirror. "I can't believe it," she exclaimed, tossing her short curls. It was a perfectly shaped bob, light and carefree. "You're a miracle worker."

"I know," said Mae, "but I still don't want to be around when your husband sees you for the first time."

Elizabeth tugged on her cloche and returned to the observation car, where Henry's eyes widened as they traveled from her raised hemline to her bobbed hair. In that instant, she knew exactly how to play it. "Like it?" she asked, snatching off her cloche. She shook her bobbed curls, sat down beside him, and smiled.

"Your . . . hair," Henry managed to say. "And . . . your dress."

"Enjoy the view?" she asked playfully, crossing her legs at the knee and swinging her foot in his direction.

"Of course I enjoy it." He lowered his voice. "I just don't know if I want everyone else to enjoy it."

Elizabeth laughed. "Don't be silly. Don't you think I'm pretty?"

"Of course. You're beautiful. You'll always be beautiful. But . . ." He struggled for words. "Why?"

Elizabeth shrugged. "I thought it would be more practical. It's going to be hot in southern California, and we're going to be awfully busy on the ranch. Bobbed hair is cooler and easier to care for. I don't want to waste a minute on my hair that could be spent helping you run the ranch."

Henry looked as if he didn't quite believe her, but she smiled and settled back with a copy of Willa Cather's *A Lost Lady* someone had abandoned on an adjacent seat. Later, back in their compartment, she would alter another dress or two before they repacked their bags and changed trains in St. Louis. By the time they reached California, she could make over her entire wardrobe.

A few hours later as they were sitting down to lunch, Elizabeth spotted Mae entering the dining car on the arm of a red-haired man in a finely cut double-breasted wool flannel suit. He was a few inches shorter than the willowy Mae, with a small mouth, a pencil-thin mustache, and a large mole on his left cheek.

Elizabeth caught Mae's eye and beckoned her to join them. Mae hesitated before speaking quietly to her companion, whose glance in the newlyweds' direction, Elizabeth had the distinct impression, took in more than it seemed, down to guessing within a dollar the number of bills in Henry's wallet.

Mae and Peter strolled over to their table. "You don't have a black eye, so I guess he liked the hair," Mae greeted her. She extended a hand to Henry. "Hi, Henry One-in-a-Million."

Startled, Henry rose slightly from his chair to shake her hand. "Hello."

"Henry, this is Mae," said Elizabeth, "and I assume you're Peter?" When he inclined his head in acknowledgment, Elizabeth smiled and gestured to the two empty seats beside her and Henry. "Will you join us for lunch?"

"We don't want to intrude on your honeymoon," Peter demurred.

"That's all right," said Henry. "It's a long trip. I don't want Elizabeth to get bored with only me to talk to."

Mae laughed and pulled out the chair beside Henry.

"How long a trip?" asked Peter as he sat down beside Elizabeth, across from Mae.

"All the way to California," said Elizabeth. "We're changing trains in St. Louis."

"Well, what do you know?" said Mae. "We're on our way to California, too. Peter goes at least twice a year, but this is the first time he's taken me. And it's not even my birthday."

"Maybe we'll be on the same train," said Elizabeth.

"Unlikely," said Peter, as the waiter approached to take their orders. "We're stopping over for the night in St. Louis on business."

"But once that's out of the way, we'll be on our way to Los Angeles," said Mae. "Orange groves, palm trees, Hollywood— Say, why are you going to California, anyway? It's a long way from Pennsylvania even for a honeymoon."

Surprised, Elizabeth said, "I never mentioned that we're from Pennsylvania."

"No, but you got on in Harrisburg and you have those accents."

Elizabeth and Henry shared a look of amusement. It was Mae who had the accent—a thick New York accent just like an actor playing a big-city cabbie on a radio program. Peter didn't, Elizabeth suddenly realized. His accent was more polished, as if that same actor had taken elocution lessons from the man who sold the sponsors' products between programs.

"We're not going only for a honeymoon," explained Elizabeth. "We're staying. Henry's bought a ranch."

Peter regarded them, intrigued. "You don't say."

"One hundred and twenty acres of prime southern California ranchland," said Elizabeth. "Over two hundred head of cattle, the farmhouse, a bunkhouse, and even a stream, a tributary of the Salto Creek."

"Never heard of it," said Mae.

Peter seemed more impressed, and he looked to Henry for confirmation. Henry's pride won out and he explained, "It's called the Rancho Triunfo. It's about forty-five miles north of Los Angeles in the Arboles Valley."

"Actually," added Elizabeth, "the proper name is 'El Triunfo del Dulcisimo Nombre de Jesús,' but we're going to call it Triumph Ranch."

"Or we'll just stick with the Rancho Triunfo, since that's what it says on all the maps," said Henry good-naturedly.

"Triumph Ranch," said Mae. "That sounds like a sure thing, doesn't it?"

"There's no such thing as a sure thing," said Henry. "I have every intention of succeeding, but our only guarantee is that we're in for a lot of hard work."

"You don't say," said Mae, with a glance for Elizabeth that

inquired if she still believed the fun was just beginning, because it certainly didn't sound like Henry thought so.

To change the subject, Elizabeth asked, "What line of work are you in, Peter?"

"Sales and distribution."

Mae choked on her water. She set down her glass, wiped her lips delicately with her napkin, and nodded to the table behind Elizabeth and Peter. "Don't make a big show of it, but take a look."

As inconspicuously as she could, Elizabeth glanced over her shoulder at the middle-aged man in a black pinstriped suit and bowler hat, dining alone. He had unscrewed the brass handle of his walking stick and was surreptitiously pouring a clear liquid into a glass of tomato juice.

"I'm shocked," remarked Peter in a low voice, shaking his head. "Absolutely shocked."

"Because he's flouting the law so publicly?" asked Elizabeth, not at all shocked. She had seen worse in the hotel back in Harrisburg, in the dining room as well as her father's private study.

"No, because he's drinking that rotgut. By the cut of his suit, he can clearly afford something smoother, as well as a decent flask to carry it in. That wooden cane can't be doing much for the taste."

The waiter arrived and set their plates before them. "You must really know your liquors to be able to tell rotgut from the best Russian vodka at this distance," said Henry.

"It's the most obvious conclusion. If it were the finest Russian vodka, he would either make a show of drinking it to impress everyone with his wealth and connections, or he'd drink it at home, alone, in the privacy of his study. He wouldn't ruin it by storing it in a cane."

"It's hard to argue with that logic," said Henry.

"Tell me, Henry." Peter paused to taste his pork chop. "What is your opinion on the issue of Prohibition?"

Henry thought for a moment, sparing a glance for Elizabeth. "I think it was well intentioned, but it's created more problems than it's solved. From what I've seen, it hasn't done much to stop people from drinking."

"What do you expect?" said Mae. She sounded almost pleased. "Booze is forbidden fruit now. If you want to make something seem a lot more fun, make it illegal."

"Oh, I agree completely. Back in Harrisburg, girls who would never set foot in a saloon sneak off to speakeasies every Friday and Saturday night and drink nearly as much as their dates." At a surprised look from Henry, Elizabeth quickly added, "Not that I have any firsthand knowledge of such places."

"Of course not," said Mae. "Me, neither."

"Back where we come from, most of the farmers have been making their own home brews just as their German ancestors did generations ago," said Henry. "Who am I to say they should stop?"

"The law says they should," said Peter.

"Maybe it's a misguided law."

Peter smiled. "Then I gather you're not planning to turn in the gentleman seated behind me?"

"No. Live and let live, I say. He's no danger to anyone as far as I can see." Henry regarded Peter curiously. "Why, are you planning to report him?"

"Of course not. It's none of my business." Peter picked up his fork and continued eating. "Besides, he'll drink away the evidence before the authorities meet the train in St. Louis. It would be our word against his and a waste of everyone's time."

Henry merely shrugged and finished his coffee.

After lunch, the two couples went their separate ways. Elizabeth and Henry went to the observation car, where Elizabeth altered the hemline of a poplin housedress and Henry read a farming journal. The flat farmlands of central Indiana sped past the windows, the first early shoots of corn and wheat wafting a light green haze to the horizon.

"I wonder," said Henry suddenly, in a voice too low for anyone else to overhear, "what it is exactly that Peter sells and distributes."

Elizabeth looked up from her sewing. "What do you mean?"

"He said he was in sales and distribution. I'm just curious what his product is. He seems to know a lot about alcohol."

Elizabeth smothered a laugh and resumed her work. "You're right, he did. He also seems to know a lot about canes. That must mean he's either a cane salesman or a bootlegger."

"You can laugh," said Henry. "But don't you think it's interesting that he noticed we got on in Harrisburg? Out of all these passengers, he remembered that about us?"

"All that means is that he's observant. Doesn't a salesman have to be? And anyway, it wasn't Peter who said that but Mae."

"Right. Mae." Henry brooded in silence. "I bet she knows a lot more about speakeasies than she lets on."

"Well, obviously."

"Maybe you should steer clear of her for the rest of the trip."

Elizabeth set down her sewing. "Henry Nelson, you might be my husband now but you can't tell me who my friends should be. Mae was kind to me when I needed someone to salvage my hair and I'm not going to give her the cold shoulder just because you're suspicious of her boyfriend."

"Salvage your hair?" Then her words fully sank in. "You mean they're not married?"

"Oh, for goodness sakes. So what if they aren't? That doesn't mean anything. Didn't you suggest that we should wait to get married until we arrived in California?"

"I'm glad you talked me out of it. I wouldn't want anyone to get the wrong idea about you."

"Just like you're probably getting the wrong idea about Mae and

Peter." Elizabeth hated to argue with Henry on their honeymoon, so she gave him a fond smile and said, "They're getting off in St. Louis, so it doesn't matter anyway. After a few hours, we'll never see them again."

Henry nodded and raised her hand to his lips in apology, yet it seemed the train could not reach St. Louis soon enough to suit him.

About an hour outside of St. Louis, someone rapped on their compartment door. Thinking she was admitting the porter, Elizabeth was startled to discover Peter standing in the corridor, hands in his pockets. "May I speak with your husband?"

Elizabeth nodded, beckoned to Henry, who joined Peter outside, leaving the door ajar. "I wondered if you might be amenable to a business proposition," she heard Peter say, while she pretended to be intent on her sewing.

"All of my savings went into the ranch," said Henry. "I can't afford any other investments right now."

"I'm not asking for money. I'm offering you the chance to earn some. A good amount, in fact, with little or no effort on your part."

"Sounds too good to be true."

"I assure you, it's not," said Peter. "I have friends in southern California who are interested in expanding their business. Your ranch lies in an area that is of particular interest to them."

"I've been told there's little in the Arboles Valley besides ranches and farms."

"Its location makes it important," said Peter. "The valley lies between Los Angeles and the cities of Oxnard and Santa Barbara. My acquaintances have had . . . let's call it distribution problems conveying their wares from Los Angeles to cities farther north. The route through those hills can be treacherous—and I'm not speaking only of the terrain but of highwaymen and other unsavory types. Entire shipments have been stolen along the way, or the shippers have been forced to abandon their cargo to preserve their own lives."

"I've been warned about highwaymen," said Henry slowly. Elizabeth resisted the urge to shoot him a sharp look. He had said nothing to her about such dangers. "What would your acquaintances need from me?"

"They need a place where they could store their shipments in case of emergency. They need an honest fellow willing to allow them to use a remote corner of his property and not ask any questions. In exchange for a regular fee, of course. We can call it rent."

"I see," said Henry.

"At lunch I discovered that you're not a man to meddle in another's business. I saw that you're willing to look the other way. That's what my associates want. I assure you, they're discreet. You'd never even know they were there, except for the payments delivered to your door on the first of each month, in cash. They can also offer you . . . protection, should these highwaymen or anyone else cause trouble around your ranch."

"Your associates will protect *me*?" asked Henry. "They seem to have trouble protecting themselves."

Peter gave a low chuckle. "I wouldn't worry about that. They know how to handle people who cross them. So tell me, what's your price?"

"Sorry, but I can't help you." Henry stepped back into the compartment.

"You're passing up a great opportunity," Peter cautioned, blocking the door with his foot. "Regular cash payments, powerful friends, and your hands stay clean. Think about it."

"I don't need to think about it. I've made up my mind. Thanks, but no thanks."

Henry stood firm until Peter retreated.

"What do you think he was talking about?" said Elizabeth when they had shut and locked the door. "Bootlegging? Guns?"

"I don't know and I don't want to know. Whatever it is, I don't want any part of it on our ranch." Henry held Elizabeth's gaze, apprehensive. "Elizabeth, I don't want to make an enemy of Peter, but I think we should avoid your new friends for the rest of the trip. I also think we should keep our business in California to ourselves from now on."

"I won't breathe a word of it until we reach the land office," said Elizabeth shakily.

They remained in their compartment until the train reached St. Louis. As they pulled into Union Station, Elizabeth glanced through the window and spotted a dozen uniformed police officers lined up along the platform. "Is this a typical Missouri welcome?" she asked Henry as they gathered their bags.

"I doubt it," he said grimly.

They were about to disembark when suddenly Elizabeth felt a whiff of perfumed air on her cheek as Mae came swiftly up from behind them and linked her arms through theirs. "Let me leave with you," she said in a low, urgent voice. "Just until we cross the Midway. Act natural. We're old, dear friends traveling together."

Elizabeth was too surprised to say anything, Henry, too reluctant to make a scene, so they allowed Mae to lead them off the train, down the platform, and past the waiting policemen. After they rounded a corner and ducked out of sight between a cigar shop and a newsstand, Mae released their arms and breathed a deep sigh of relief. "Thanks, kids," she said. "That was a close one."

"Listen," said Henry, his voice stern but too low to draw attention. "If you're in trouble with the law—"

Mae's eyes went wide. "Me? I haven't done anything. It's Peter they want. I'm just afraid of getting dragged down as an accomplice."

"*Are* you his accomplice?" asked Elizabeth.

"Of course not," said Mae reproachfully. "But that's not what it looks like, and that's all the Feds care about. I'm his girl, aren't I? That's enough to condemn me right there."

"What did Peter do?" Henry quickly shook his head. "Never mind. I don't want to know. If you say you weren't involved, we'll take your word for it."

"Thank you."

"What are you going to do?" asked Elizabeth.

"I can't go back for my luggage, that's for sure," said Mae, regretful. Then she smiled. "Don't worry about me. I have a little money tucked away—" She patted her leg, close to where her garter probably was. "I'll find work and earn the fare back to New York. With any luck, they'll spring Peter soon and he'll come home to me."

"Are you sure you want him to?" asked Henry. "Whatever he's done, he's obviously trouble."

"I know it doesn't make any sense." For a moment, Mae's mask of surety slipped and a more wistful, vulnerable woman looked back at them. "But Peter's the only man for me." She touched Elizabeth's shoulder and gave her a quick kiss on the cheek. "Good luck to you both. I hope California suits you." She darted off and lost herself in the throng of people passing to and fro on the covered transfer area.

After a moment, Henry took Elizabeth's hand. "Come on," he said. "We don't have much time before our next train."

As they crossed the Midway, they passed within two yards of Peter being led away in handcuffs. His gaze slid past them as if he had never seen them before.

1885

Isabel was fifteen when illness forced her mother to quit her job cleaning rooms at the Grand Union Hotel. The lump beneath her arm had become so swollen and sore that she could not sweep or scrub floors without pain. Isabel's father insisted upon taking her to the doctor in Oxnard, who told them that she had a cancer of the breast and less than three months to live.

The doctor gave them medicine for the pain and sent them home with little hope. Friends and neighbors brought food and said prayers. Isabel's father wept on the back stoop at night while he thought the children were asleep.

A day came when Isabel's mother called her to her bedside, gripped her arm, and told her to visit her cousin in San Mateo. She was a *curandera,* a healer, and she would know what to do. She would know more than that doctor, a man, how to treat a woman's illness.

Isabel hitched a ride to San Mateo and found the address of the *curandera.* Her mother's cousin, an old, wizened woman with long gray hair and gnarled hands, offered her coffee and listened intently as Isabel described her mother's symptoms. "Your mother's cancer is caused by grief and longing," she said. "Has she lost a child? Has her husband strayed?"

"No," Isabel told her.

The *curandera* said she could prepare a remedy, but unless they could figure out what secret grief festered in her mother's heart, the cancer would return.

The *curandera* sent Isabel home with a list of ingredients she must gather: a bottle of holy water blessed by her mother's confessor, wild raspberry leaves from a plant growing no more than a hundred paces from where her mother slept at night, and fifty seeds from fifty freshly picked, unblemished apricots.

Two weeks passed while Isabel waited for the harvest to begin, two weeks while her mother's pain increased until even the doctor's medicine could not abate it. "What did my cousin say?" she demanded. "Has she nothing for me?"

"She says you must not ask questions or her cure will not work," Isabel lied. "She's working on a poultice. In the meantime you must keep saying the rosary twice a day, at morning and at night."

When harvesttime came, Isabel slipped into the line of men and women seeking jobs at the orchard. To her surprise, the hired hand who issued her a punch card did not react when she gave him her name. Yes, she had expected to be compelled to explain, I am Isabel Rodriguez, whose parents once owned all the land you see from the eastern hills to the Salto Canyon. But the hired man either was not paying attention or he had never heard the story of how her father had sworn that neither he nor his descendants would ever again toil for those who had stolen their land. He merely waved Isabel toward the cutting shed and told her to take a place at one of the tables.

A girl she knew from school glanced at her in surprise as Isabel took an empty place at her table, but she said nothing. Isabel took up her knife as a man left a box of apricots beside their table. Isabel worked in silence with her eyes downcast, unwilling to draw attention to herself as she carefully chose unblemished fruit, swiftly cut out the seed, and placed the apricots cut-side up on the table. A bag sat on the table for collecting the seeds; Isabel brushed the bag with her hand as if she were dropping the seeds within, but instead she tucked them into her apron pocket.

Suddenly a hand closed around her wrist so hard she dropped the knife. "What are you doing?" a young woman said in her ear.

Isabel jerked her arm free and stepped back. "Nothing." She recognized the brown-haired girl, although she wasn't sure Hannah knew her. They had played together as young children, in the cabin as well as in the yard of the farmhouse where Hannah lived with her family.

"I saw you put something in your pocket," Hannah said in a low voice. Her discretion came too late; already the other cutters had stopped working to watch them. "Are you stealing apricots?"

"Of course not."

"Then why are your pockets bulging?"

Slowly, aware of all the eyes upon her, Isabel reached into her apron and withdrew a handful of seeds. When she opened her palm, Hannah barked out a laugh. "What in the world are you going to do with those? Plant your own orchard?"

"Of course not," said Isabel. "My family has no land for an orchard."

Hannah flinched. Perhaps she recognized Isabel after all. "You can't eat the seeds, you know," she said sharply. "They're poisonous."

No, Isabel thought. They are medicine. "That's what I need them for," she said. "Poisoning rats. We grind up the dried seeds and sprinkle them on the floor, in the corners."

"I never heard of that."

"You probably never needed to know. I doubt that you have to worry about rats in your home."

Hannah fixed her with a hard stare for a moment before looking away. "Take all the seeds you want. If you need food, ask first."

Isabel nodded and resumed cutting fruit, her face hot with shame. She needed no charity from Hannah or her family. She had only taken what was needed to save her mother, something that otherwise would have been discarded.

At the end of the day, she collected her wages and told the hired man she would not be back.

The next morning, Isabel returned to the *curandera* and waited while she prepared the medicines for her mother. Others waited in the parlor—an old man with a pain in his chest, an angry mother with a nervous girl not much younger than Isabel, a sad woman with the first streaks of gray in her hair and no wedding band on her finger. The old man, wheezing and spitting, told Isabel that she was lucky—*muy afortunada!*—that the *curandera* had agreed to help her. "Her power never fails," he confided. "You will see, my girl. All will be well."

The *curandera* returned from the back room with two parcels wrapped in cheesecloth for Isabel, one large and one small. The first was a poultice for her mother to wear upon the skin between her arm and her breast. It would draw the cancer to the surface, roots and all, where it would be expelled by the body. The smaller parcel was a tea. Isabel's mother should drink a strong brew of it every morning upon waking, then take the leaves from the bottom of her cup and mark a cross upon her heart.

"How long until she will be better?" Isabel asked. A month, perhaps two. If the cancer had not been expelled by the end of the second month but her mother yet lived, Isabel should return for a stronger poultice.

That evening, Isabel helped her mother tie the poultice to her arm to keep it in place while she slept. For the first time in weeks, her mother smiled. "The poultice has a familiar smell," she said as Isabel drew her favorite quilt over her. It was one Isabel's grandmother had sewn as a young bride-to-be, and it seemed to remind Isabel's mother of more hopeful times.

Her mother slept well. In the morning Isabel brewed her a cup of the tea and brought it to her in bed. Her mother sat up, thanked her, and sipped from the steaming cup. A slight frown clouded her face. "What do I taste?" she asked, inhaling deeply.

"It's better not to ask," said Isabel. "As long as it works, it doesn't matter how foul it tastes."

"It tastes of raspberry leaves," said her mother. She brewed a similar tea to ease her monthly pains. "But also of apricots. I haven't tasted apricots in years."

Isabel busied herself with folding bedclothes that had fallen to the floor.

"Isabel," her mother said, her voice rising. "Are there apricots in this tea? In this poultice?"

"You would have to ask the *curandera*. She made them in a back room. I wasn't watching."

"But I know she gave you a list of ingredients to gather. I know you took them to her. What was in that bag you carried?"

"Just drink the tea, Mami. It will make you well."

"It was harvesttime that week. Were you there? Are these apricots from the ranch?"

Isabel could not lie to her so she said nothing.

Isabel's mother set the cup aside and tore off the poultice. "I want nothing from those people. Their apricots are poison to me."

"What does it matter where the apricots came from?" cried Isabel. "The apricots don't know who owns them."

"But I know. *I* know."

Isabel argued and fought with her mother until they were both in tears, but her mother was resolute. She ordered Isabel to carry the offending medicines far away and bury them deep within the ground.

Isabel obeyed, her heart brimming over with helpless anger. Without the *curandera*'s remedies, her mother would die.

If only they had never left the cabin. If only Hannah's family had not made them go.

If they lived there still, her mother never would have refused the gift of the land.

Chapter Three

1925

Henry gripped Elizabeth's arm tightly as they left the Midway for the Headhouse. "This way," he said, guiding her beneath the Grand Hall's gothic arches. Elizabeth marveled at the cathedral ceilings and stained glass windows. Her traveler's eye was drawn to a tableau of three train stations—the castle-like structure of St. Louis's Union Station framed by the New York and San Francisco rail hubs, all rendered in lead and glass. Her gaze continued upward until it settled upon the Whispering Arch she had heard tell of on board the train. A person could reputedly speak softly at one end of the arch and be heard with perfect clarity at the other end, nearly forty feet away. Elizabeth had intended to try it out for herself, but Henry looked determined to quickly and cleanly distance them from her new friends.

The Headhouse contained the ticket office, a hotel, and a restaurant, where Henry and Elizabeth joined the queue at the door. The brakeman had taken the passengers' orders earlier that day before they crossed the Mississippi and had wired them ahead to the restaurant.

"This is a marvel of convenience," Henry said as he sampled his dinner. "Tasty, too."

"It's quite good," said Elizabeth. They were the first words they had exchanged since leaving Mae, and purposefully innocuous, until she forged ahead. "I feel like Saint Peter at the high priest's palace."

"You can't be serious," Henry replied in an undertone. "Allowing them to face the consequences of their actions is hardly denying Jesus three times. If they've done something wrong, they need to face up to it. If Peter's innocent, which I doubt, he'll be released. If anyone asks, we'll tell the truth. We've done nothing wrong." He hesitated. "Except in letting Mae go. We probably should have turned her in."

After finishing their meal, Elizabeth and Henry hurried down the Midway to catch the *Pacific Coast Limited* to Los Angeles.

Their encounter with Peter and Mae had left them wary of other passengers, so they remained in their compartment throughout the trip except for visits to the dining car. Eventually their unease faded, but they had come to enjoy their comfortable isolation and ventured out only rarely. Elizabeth had to laugh one morning when she caught Henry tipping the porter extra to straighten their bed-covers but not fold the bed away.

As the train crossed the Central Plains, the flat landscape stretched and rolled into hills and mountains. Although Elizabeth relished the undivided attention they were finally able to give each other, she noticed that Henry grew more pensive the farther west they traveled. He seemed fully at ease only when he held her in his arms.

"What's wrong?" she asked him one evening as the train crossed the Arizona desert. "Are you still upset about Peter, or are you just sorry that our honeymoon's nearly over?"

Henry gave her a brief smile and laced his fingers through hers.

"As far as I'm concerned, the honeymoon is never going to end."

"Then what's wrong?"

"I just want the ranch to be perfect for you." He hesitated. "Maybe I should have come out to inspect it myself before buying."

She was reluctant to point out that he probably could not have afforded an additional round-trip, cross-country journey. "You saw the pictures, didn't you? You have the surveyor's map."

"It's not the same as seeing it with my own eyes. I'm also wondering how I'm going to manage the ranch crew. I've never farmed with anyone but my father and brothers and hired hands I've known all my life. Now I'll be giving orders to men who understand that ranch better than I do. Why should they listen to me?"

"Because you're their boss, that's why," said Elizabeth with more certainty than she felt. "You're a natural leader, and if you show them confidence, they'll cooperate. Consult them about their knowledge of the land and then make the best decisions you can. The men will respect you if they know you respect them."

Henry smiled. "Asking you to marry me was the best decision I ever made."

"I couldn't agree more. Don't you see? Once the hired hands meet me, everyone there will know you're a man of sound judgment. Of course they'll listen to you."

She was rewarded by Henry's rich, rare laughter, but even that could not put her own nagging worries completely to rest.

They reached Los Angeles by midafternoon the same day. Their last train would not depart until the following morning, so Henry had arranged for them to spend the night in a modest boarding-house not far from the station. Elizabeth was eager to see the ocean, though she was surprised and somewhat disappointed to learn that not every place in Los Angeles was convenient to the ocean.

"You could take the trolley to Venice," their landlady suggested.

"Venice?" said Henry, grinning. "That's for us. My wife has always wanted to see Venice."

"I meant Venice, Italy," said Elizabeth, amused. "Not Venice Beach, California."

"It was my Harry's favorite place," said their landlady. "He used to take me there on weekends. We always had a grand time—dancing under the stars, riding the roller coaster, poling along in a gondola. . . . But that was before our favorite pier burned down. And before the Great War." She made an abrupt gesture to a framed photograph on the mantel. A sailor in uniform regarded the camera with steady pride. Flanking the photograph were a folded American flag in a triangular wooden case and a smaller frame enclosing two medals.

Their landlady watched them hopefully, awaiting their reply.

"I didn't know they had real gondolas," said Elizabeth. "I wouldn't miss that for the world. Henry, please say you'll take me."

Their landlady brightened and gave them directions. From the station a few blocks away, they rode a Pacific Electric Red Car southwest out of the city, marveling at the sight of streets washed in sunshine and lined with palm trees. Elizabeth wished she had a camera so she could capture the scenes for the worried folks back home. Never had she imagined such a bright and promising place.

They disembarked at Windward Avenue. Following the breeze off the ocean, they strolled along canals filled with couples in gondolas and children paddling canoes toward streets of shops and restaurants. Elizabeth gasped at the sight of roller coasters looming above the amusements. "We have to ride one," she exclaimed, seizing Henry's hand and pulling him in the direction of the nearest.

"Hold on," said Henry, pausing at the entrance of the Great Dipper. "I thought you wanted to see the ocean."

"I do." She tugged at his hand when he did not budge. "We will. Let's try this first."

"Sweetheart, we're running low on money. It's ten cents apiece."

"We can spare twenty cents."

"Not if you want ice cream and lemonade on the beach."

"You just don't want to ride. You're afraid you'll sick up and embarrass yourself."

"How do you know *you* won't sick up?" he countered. "You've never been on a roller coaster."

Elizabeth considered, scanning the height of the lacy wooden structure. She jumped and clutched her hat in place as a car full of screaming riders hurtled overhead, swirling sand and debris in its wake. "All right," she said shakily. "You can have your way this time, but only because I love you and I don't want an upset stomach to spoil your day."

"Thanks," said Henry, struggling to hide a grin. "That's kind of you."

They strolled along Ocean Front Walk past cafés and beach houses, where the breeze off the ocean was strong and cool.

"I'm going in," Elizabeth declared.

Henry watched with alarm as she peeled off her stockings. "You're kidding."

"I'll only dip my toes in," she assured him. "I want to tell the folks back home that I set foot in the Pacific Ocean. Don't you want to be able to say that?"

"I'd rather have dry feet."

Disappointed, Elizabeth handed him her shoes and stockings. "Then you can watch these until I get back."

She marched unsteadily across the beach toward the water, then stood on the wet sand and let the ocean come to her. The first wave upon her toes shocked her with its coldness. She gasped from surprise, and then, as she grew accustomed to the cold, she waded in up to her ankles. A second wave swept up to her knees and tugged at her gently, beckoning her forward into the deeper water.

She laughed aloud and took a step back toward dry land, but a sudden wave rushed forward and seized her, knocking her off balance. A firm hand on her arm caught her before she fell. "Careful," said Henry, his voice carried away by the wind.

He had removed his shoes and socks, but the rolled cuffs of his trousers were soaked through. As he helped her regain her footing and led her from the water, sand collected on his cuffs in a layer that thickened as they crossed the beach.

When they reached the pavement of Ocean Front Walk, he tried to shake his cuffs free of sand. "I'm sorry," said Elizabeth. "It's my fault you're such a mess."

"Never mind." He handed her her shoes and stockings, which he had left beside his own on a bench. "I'm sure I'm not the first man to walk the streets of Venice covered in a good portion of the beach."

"It was sweet of you to come along after me."

He sat down and brushed sand from his toes. "I wanted to be there to witness it if you decided to dive in headfirst."

Elizabeth laughed. She had never been happier, not even on their wedding day. She had waded in the Pacific Ocean, something no one in her family had ever done. She had seen sights they had never seen. Every day of the rest of her life would be an adventure, with Henry nearby to steady her if she should stumble.

Walking out on the Venice Pier—past the Flying Circles aerial ride, the Dragon Bamboo slide, and the Ship Café—Elizabeth and Henry came upon two dozen couples in just that predicament. On the maple floor of a spacious dance hall, partners dragged their feet to a lively Irving Berlin tune. Some of the women slung their arms about their partners' shoulders and clung to them to keep themselves upright. Several of the men had apparently nodded off with their heads on the shoulders of their smaller partners, who struggled to keep them on their feet. Suddenly a woman appeared to faint; at first her partner grappled to catch her but then he too collapsed onto the hardwood floor. Three men rushed out to drag them out of the way while the other couples danced on, oblivious and glassy-eyed.

"How long have they been at it?" Henry asked a man who stood near the orchestra pit sipping a ginger ale.

"Three days," said the man, shaking his head in amazement.

"How do they stay on their feet?" marveled Elizabeth. "I'd want to pass out."

"Some of them do." The man indicated a man at least six feet tall dancing with a petite, red-haired woman. "See that couple over there? That's my brother and his girlfriend. They soaked their feet in brine and vinegar for two days straight beforehand. They'll be going strong for a long time yet, you just wait and see. They'll take home that thousand-dollar prize sure enough."

"A thousand dollars?" Elizabeth touched Henry's arm. "Isn't it a shame we didn't arrive in time to enter?"

"It's a shame, all right," replied Henry, sounding not at all disappointed. "Do you want to stay and watch the action, or see more of Venice?"

"Let's stay for a while. Maybe we'll see who wins."

"Probably not," said the man. "Some of these marathons last a week or more."

Henry, looking ever more pleased they had arrived too late to compete, offered to get them some drinks while Elizabeth found a place to sit and watch the marathon.

"I bet you could dance circles around them all," a man spoke close to her ear. Startled, she drew back as he pulled out the chair beside her and sat down. "You look like a girl with energy to spare."

"Not that much," she admitted. "I like dancing, but in smaller doses."

"I'd ask you to dance, but the floor is reserved for the marathon."

"I'd have to refuse," she told him. "I'm married."

He made an exaggerated show of looking around. "I don't see any husband. If you were my wife, I wouldn't let you out of my sight."

Elizabeth laughed politely and watched as a dancing woman frantically waved smelling salts beneath her partner's nostrils. She shrieked and burst into tears as he staggered into a table at the edge of the dance floor, sending glasses of lemonade and ginger ale flying.

"That'll disqualify him," the man remarked. His hair was parted down the middle and combed down neatly. When Elizabeth nodded, he suddenly peered at her curiously. "Say, aren't you that actress, the one from that movie—what was it? No, don't tell me. *The Thief of Baghdad?*"

Elizabeth smiled. "No, that wasn't me. I'm not an actress."

"Are you sure?"

"I think I would know."

"You're pretty enough to be an actress. Have you ever thought about being in the movies?"

"No, I can't say that I have," said Elizabeth. "But I've been in California only a day."

"Well, let me tell you, sister, girls not half as pretty as you are making movies every day." He reached into his breast pocket and pulled out a business card. "I'm a producer myself, always on the lookout for new talent. Where are you from? Ohio? Indiana?"

"Pennsylvania."

"Same difference. You've got that wholesome, midwestern look the camera just loves. I have half a dozen scripts on my desk with roles you'd be perfect for."

"But I've never acted before," Elizabeth said, fingering the business card. "I wouldn't know the first thing to do."

He shrugged. "We have an acting coach on staff. It's easy. You're a smart girl. You'll pick it up. My number's on the card. Just call me at my office—"

"My wife won't have time to be in your picture," said Henry, directly behind them. "We're ranchers, not movie stars."

The producer jumped up in surprise, nearly knocking over his chair. He eyed Henry's strong farmer's build before taking a step back and saying, "She looks like a girl who can answer for herself."

"I can," said Elizabeth quickly, as Henry glowered. "And my husband's right. I'm going to be much too busy to be an actress. I'm sorry, but thank you anyway."

"Suit yourself." Grumbling, the man walked off and disappeared into the crowd of observers lining the dance floor.

"You didn't have to be so rude," said Elizabeth as Henry took the vacant chair and set two glasses of lemonade before them. "He might have put me in a movie. It would have been fun."

"I doubt he was a real producer."

"He had a business card." Elizabeth held it up. "See? Grover Higgins, Golden Reel Productions, Hollywood, California."

Henry jerked his thumb toward the entrance. "Back out on the midway, I can buy a copy of *Life* magazine with my picture on the cover. I don't think a fake movie mogul would have any trouble making fake business cards."

Insulted, Elizabeth turned away from him and studied the exhausted dancers. When Henry reached over to touch her arm, she scooted her chair out of reach.

"Sweetheart, don't be like that," he said. "Even if he was the real thing, that's not the life for us. You never even thought about being an actress until he came along."

"Maybe it never occurred to me that it was possible," she retorted. "You know I love the movies. Why couldn't I be an actress?"

"Because the day after tomorrow, you and I are going to be in the Arboles Valley running the Rancho Triunfo."

Elizabeth had nothing to say. Why was it so impossible to believe that a genuine movie producer thought she had talent?

They sipped their drinks in silence until Henry abruptly drained his and stood. "Come on." He held out his hand, and by force of habit she took it and rose. "You want to go to Hollywood? I'll take you to Hollywood."

On the way to the door, Elizabeth tightened her grip on Henry's hand—and slipped the business card into her pocket.

On the way back to the trolley station, Elizabeth persuaded Henry to stop and allow her to shop for souvenirs. He owed her that much, she figured, for his unwillingness to consider the possibility that she could be the next Clara Bow or Mary Pickford. As she browsed through racks of purses and jewelry at a shop on Windward Avenue, Henry's willingness to please her despite their dwindling funds made her feel demanding and unreasonable, and ashamed of herself. She was a married woman now, not some Sheba with a string of boyfriends who only accepted apologies in gift boxes. If she told Henry she had changed her mind about choosing a souvenir, he would never believe it, so she settled for a postcard of the midway at Venice Beach with a view of the Giant Dipper roller coaster and the Bamboo Dragon slide to send to little cousin Sylvia and a silk scarf with the words *Venice Beach, California* printed upon it in curved letters that reminded her of the crash of ocean waves upon the sand.

From Venice Beach they took the Red Car trolley north to Hollywood, where they strolled along the sidewalks lined by shops and businesses built in an eclectic assemblage of Beaux Arts, Spanish Colonial Revival, and Art Deco architectural styles. They stopped at Sardi's on Hollywood and Vine for a soda, then continued down Hollywood Boulevard to Grauman's Egyptian Theater. The name alone prepared Elizabeth for the hieroglyphics and decorative carvings, but the front courtyard also boasted columns larger around than her favorite stately trees along Elm Creek back home. She and Henry marveled over the tiled murals and a fountain, enormous planters filled with exotic flowers, and a twelve-foot statue of an Egyptian idol with the head of a dog. "All this before we pass through the front doors," Elizabeth exclaimed. Henry laughed and squeezed her hand.

Halfway through the first feature, *Trouble at Rocky Ranch,* Elizabeth leaned over to Henry and whispered, "Do you think our ranch will be anything like this one?"

"Considering that we've already seen three men shot, a bank robbed, and two women kidnapped by Indians, I sure hope not."

Elizabeth smothered a laugh and settled back to enjoy the movie, savoring every bit of pleasure from the lavish theater and the company of her dear, wonderful husband. She knew this would be one last day of fun before the real work began. In the morning they would take the train northwest into the Arboles Valley, or at least as close as they could come to it. Henry had shown her on the map how the railroad actually ran through a valley to the east, where they would disembark and hire a cab to take them the rest of the way. They would spend one night in a hotel, but the next morning they would go to the land office and take possession of Triumph Ranch.

After so much waiting and planning, only the last stage of their journey still lay ahead of them. They were almost home.

1886

After her mother's death in late summer, Isabel left school to care for her younger brother and sister and keep house for her father. Her closest friends did not forget her. Every day after school, they gathered on her small back stoop to gossip and help Isabel with her chores. Isabel's heart lifted when her friends were near, but all too soon summer came, and her friends' visits ceased. She soon discovered the reasons for their absence. Most had to work their family farms; others had taken summer jobs in the sugar factories in Oxnard. If they had forgotten her, it was only because they had become as busy with responsibilities as she.

Even her father had taken a second job delivering milk. Every morning he rose well before dawn to walk to the dairy farm two miles away. Before the sun rose, he was crisscrossing the Arboles Valley in a wagon loaded with milk and butter and cheese. Isabel would have his breakfast waiting for him when he returned. He would bolt down whatever she put in front of him, thank her, and give her sleeping brother and sister quick, gentle kisses before leaving for his regular job as a handyman at the Grand Union Hotel. He returned home in time for supper, exhausted, with little to say. The children crept quietly around the house when their father was home, heeding Isabel's warnings to let him sleep. Although her father had never raised his voice to them, Isabel slowly came to understand that they were fearful of the stoic, silent man who worked so hard to provide for the family. She wished they had known the father she remembered, the man he had been before her mother died.

On her birthday, Isabel's father gave her a dollar to spend as she pleased, so she decided to take her brother and sister to the Arboles Grocery for ice cream. She bought them each an Eskimo Pie, pocketed the change, and took them outside to enjoy their treats in the shade of the live oaks.

As her brother and sister chattered happily, Isabel heard through the open store window a conversation in Spanish. "Who's the beautiful widow?" a young man not much older than herself asked.

"Who?" another man replied.

"The pretty widow who just left. You saw her. She bought ice cream for her boy and girl."

The second man laughed. "Widow? Are you crazy? That's Isabel Rodriguez. She went to school with us. She was in the same class as your sister."

"That's not Isabel Rodriguez. She's much prettier than Isabel."

"I'm telling you, that's her. She's a friend of my cousin. That was her little brother and sister with her, not her kids."

The men argued good-naturedly as they left the store and approached the three siblings. Isabel pretended not to see them, but they strolled over, all too casually. *"Buenos días,* Isabel," her friend's cousin greeted her. "Do you know my friend, Miguel Diaz?"

Miguel, whom she recognized as a boy a few years ahead of her in school, smiled in a friendly, hopeful way, but Isabel returned an icy glare. "Only by what one overhears."

Miguel winced, but his friend grinned.

"It's Isabel's birthday," her younger sister piped up. "You should tell her happy birthday."

"Feliz cumpleaños, Isabel Rodriguez," said Miguel, with a regretful look that begged for an apology. She was only sixteen, but the past year had not been kind to her. Someone she barely knew thought she looked old enough to have children ages ten and thirteen. Isabel hardened her heart, gave her friend's cousin a curt nod, and took the children home.

She sent her brother and sister out to play while she put beans on to soak and made tortillas. She ached for her mother. She longed for her to walk through the front door, smile in her fond and gentle way, and tie on her apron. She wished her mother could be beside her, teaching her all the treasured family recipes she had learned from her own mother. On Christmas, Isabel had tried to make tamales the way her mother had always done, but her brother complained that they tasted nothing like Mami's and her sister left hers untouched on her plate. Nothing was right without their mother. Nothing had been right since they had left the little cabin on the ranch so many years before. She wished she were still that five-year-old girl, safe and happy within the lie that all would be well in her world, that she would always be loved and protected and happy.

Chapter Four

1925

Elizabeth woke in the middle of the night, shivering. She groped around at the foot of the bed for the comforter that she had folded out of the way when she first climbed beneath the covers, certain she would not need it, not in California. She drew it over herself and snuggled closer to Henry, who put his arm around her and slept on. The landlady had told them she kept extra quilts in the cedar chest at the foot of the bed, but Elizabeth was too cold to climb from beneath the covers to find one. She wished again for her wedding quilt, still tucked away in the trunk her brother had given her, bundled protectively around their fine china. Elizabeth puzzled over the curious cold snap until she grew warm enough to fall back asleep.

It was still early when she woke again. Henry had already risen and was sitting on the edge of the bed, pulling on his shoes. He saw that she was awake and leaned across the bed to kiss her. "Good morning," he said. "Better get up soon if you want breakfast before we go to the station."

Elizabeth would have gladly done without breakfast if it meant reaching the Arboles Valley sooner, but their tickets were for the midmorning train and it wouldn't do them any good to wait on the platform for hours. She threw back the covers and quickly washed and dressed. It took only moments to repack her suitcase, and soon they joined several of the other guests in the dining room, where their landlady was serving breakfast.

"You folks leaving so soon?" inquired a traveling salesman seated across the table. "You won't find many places on the road as hospitable as this."

"Flatterer," scoffed the landlady, but Elizabeth noticed that she added an extra pancake to his stack.

"If we weren't expected elsewhere, we'd be happy to stay another night," said Elizabeth, with a smile for her hostess. "We're on our way to the Arboles Valley."

The salesman turned an inquiring look upon Henry. "What do you plan to do all the way out there? The most popular tourist attractions are around the city. I hope you didn't buy a bogus map. You have to be careful around here. People take advantage of tourists."

"We're not tourists," said Henry. "We've come to stay. We're farmers."

"Farmers?" The salesman smiled at Elizabeth. "You're much too pretty to be a farm wife. If you want work, you should get into the movies."

"You're not the only one to think so," said Elizabeth, deliberately avoiding Henry's eye. "Perhaps someday."

"Not likely," said Henry. "I don't think you'll be running into many movie producers in the Arboles Valley."

"You'd be surprised," remarked their landlady. "Movies shoot on location up that way all the time."

Elizabeth threw Henry a triumphant grin. Perhaps the movie producers would come to her. Besides, as long as she had one producer's card in her pocketbook, she didn't need to meet any others.

"We'll be too busy," Henry reminded her. "Don't get your hopes up."

"I won't, but I also won't dismiss the possibility entirely," said Elizabeth. "Isn't California the land of opportunity? Anything can happen."

The salesman nodded in approval of her optimism. The landlady beamed, and why shouldn't she? Someday she might be able to brag to her friends that she had hosted the famous Elizabeth Nelson on her first night in California. Henry merely scowled and continued eating.

"Take care on the route north," cautioned an older guest, who had introduced himself as a civil engineer visiting Los Angeles to study the aqueducts. "It's a dangerous road through those hills. Highwaymen stop automobiles, wagons—anyone traveling alone. They'll steal anything of value they can find and they're not above roughing up women. Begging your pardon, miss."

Elizabeth gave him a quick smile to reassure him that his words had not upset her, although they had, a little. After what Peter had said, the engineer's warning carried more weight than he knew.

"The Sheik Bandits have been at it again," said the landlady. "It's in the paper this morning. They robbed a bank and left the poor cashier tied up in the vault. They were last seen heading north."

"The Sheik Bandits?" echoed Elizabeth.

"A gang of three or four men, always sharply dressed," said the salesman. "A couple of years ago, they held up a post office just over the Los Angeles County line. They bound and gagged the postmistress and made off with nearly five hundred dollars cash."

Elizabeth shuddered. "My goodness. The poor woman."

"Anyone can disappear in those rugged hills," said the engineer. "Rumor has it the bandits hide out in the old Indian caves. No one should drive that road without a loaded firearm at his side. You're not safe until you're within the Oxnard city limits."

"It's not that bad," said the salesman, but unconvincingly. "The

Arboles Valley is perfectly safe. It's just getting there that's the trouble. You young folks won't be traveling after dark, will you?"

"We're traveling by train to the Simi Valley and driving over the grade from there," said Henry.

Around the table, the other guests visibly relaxed. "In that case, you'll be fine," said the engineer.

Elizabeth managed a brief, shaky smile, wondering what other plans Henry had made without explaining their imperative to her. She had assumed he had chosen the train for its speed and directness, not because their lives depended on it.

For the relatively short trip to the Simi Valley station, Henry had purchased two seats in coach and paid an additional fee for their excess luggage. Their seats were quite a change from the comfortable private compartments they had enjoyed on the first two legs of their journey, but Elizabeth was so eager to reach their final destination she did not mind.

At last the conductor called out the Simi Valley station. Almost before the train halted, Elizabeth and Henry leaped to their feet to collect their bags. As they waited for their trunks to be unloaded from the luggage car, Elizabeth paced along the platform, taking in the sights and unfamiliar smells, breathless from excitement. The station lay in a broad, flat valley surrounded by low, arid mountains. Just over the ridge was the Arboles Valley.

Henry set Elizabeth to counting their pile of trunks and suitcases while he went to hail a cab. She sat down on the largest trunk and watched arriving passengers being met by family as outgoing passengers climbed aboard the train. The conductor called out his warning; shortly after, the engine started up again and the train chugged out of the station. Elizabeth sat alone on the platform.

She rose, shaded her eyes, and looked around for Henry, but all she saw was a man working inside the ticket booth. In a moment, even he disappeared from view. Elizabeth began pacing again, but did not stray far from their belongings. Finally Henry appeared. "There's not a cab anywhere."

"Well, we *are* out in the country."

"Sure, but this is a train station. We can't be the only passengers who arrive here without anyone to pick them up."

Elizabeth glanced around the platform but decided not to point out that they certainly seemed to be, at least for that train. "Could we send word to the ranch? If they know we've arrived, I'm sure they'd send someone for us."

"If we had someone to send word to the ranch, we'd have our ride."

"Of course," Elizabeth murmured. She sat down on the trunk again, planted her elbows on her knees, and rested her head in her palms.

"I'll find us something to drink," said Henry in a kinder tone, as if to apologize for his impatience. He went off again and returned with two paper cones of cool water. Elizabeth drained hers quickly and wished for more, but Henry was in such a sour mood she didn't want to inconvenience him.

A few minutes passed and Henry went off to try again to find a cab. Elizabeth wished him good luck with more cheerfulness than she felt. Nearly an hour had passed since their arrival, and a trickle of people had begun to gather on the platform to await the next train. Before long Henry hurried back, grinning. "I helped a farmer unload his cargo in exchange for a ride," he said. "Our hotel for tonight is out of his way. Let's hurry so we don't delay him any longer than necessary."

Elizabeth quickly rose and took two of the lighter suitcases in hand while Henry hefted a trunk onto his shoulder. She followed him off the platform and around the corner, where a tall, thin man in faded overalls and a plaid shirt waited beside a wagon, holding the reins of two draft horses. The weathered lines of his face spoke of hard times and disappointment, but his gaze was steady, though unsmiling. Henry hurried through introductions, and while Elizabeth shook Lars Jorgensen's hand, her husband returned to the platform for their remaining luggage.

"Can you hold a team?" Lars Jorgensen asked Elizabeth gruffly. When she nodded, he helped her up onto the wagon seat and handed her the reins. One of the horses stomped an enormous hoof and shook his shaggy mane. The farmer said something to him in a language Elizabeth did not recognize and went off to assist Henry.

The Nelsons' belongings took up nearly half of the wagon bed, much more territory than that claimed by the few wooden crates of supplies and cans of kerosene Lars Jorgensen had already stowed there. Lars took the reins from Elizabeth, who moved over to make room for him on the seat. Henry climbed into the back with the cargo. "Thank you for the ride," he said to their host. "We're obliged to you."

"Yes, thank you very much," Elizabeth added. Lars nodded and shook the reins to start the team forward. The wagon lurched and headed off down the road toward the west.

Elizabeth expected the farmer to be curious about strangers traveling with so much luggage, but he said nothing until the train station had disappeared behind them. "So you're a Nelsen?" he said, and then added a few words in the same language with which he had addressed the horses.

"Sorry," said Henry ruefully. "I know very little Swedish, barely enough to say hello and good-bye. My family always spoke English at home."

"That was Norwegian," said Lars dryly. "Many Norwegian families live in the Arboles Valley. Why did you say you were a Nelsen? You must be a Nel*son*."

Henry gave a small, baffled shrug. "That's right. Sorry."

"Norwegian settlers?" said Elizabeth. "I had expected Spaniards."

"We got some of them, too. Mostly Mexican, though, not Spanish." Lars fell silent for a moment, as if contemplating how much to tell them. "Most of the Arboles Valley belongs to five different families—the Olsens, the Pedersens, the Kelleys, the Borchards, and my people, the Jorgensens. Other families have smaller farms and ranches scattered thereabouts. We still got more sheep than people in the valley, but I expect that'll change in days to come."

Elizabeth wondered why he had left the former owners of Triumph Ranch off the list. "You have cattle, too, isn't that so? I understand this is an excellent region for raising cattle."

Lars shrugged. "Some folks have done all right with cattle. Sheep fare better here."

At the risk of alarming Henry by divulging too much of their secret, Elizabeth persisted. "You must know the Rodriguez family, I'm sure."

He gave her a sharp look. "Yes, I know them. Of course I know them. Their people have been around here for generations."

And yet he was not aware of the Rodriguez family who ran a thriving cattle ranch? Elizabeth wondered if the Arboles Valley was larger and more populous than Henry had led her to believe. She was about to jog the farmer's memory when Henry spoke up. "What crops do you raise on your farm, Mr. Jorgensen?"

Elizabeth recognized his attempt to change the subject and let the matter drop.

"I work my brother's farm," replied Lars. "He raises sheep, barley, and apricots. Sometimes he tries his hand at another crop just to see how it fares, but sheep, barley, and apricots are our mainstays. That was a load of wool bound for Los Angeles you helped me unload back at the station."

Suddenly the wagon pitched as a wheel rumbled over a pothole in the hard-packed dirt road. Instinctively Elizabeth gasped and clutched the seat. Lars glanced at her, and something that could have passed for a smile briefly appeared in the tanned leather of his face. "Road's a little rough in parts," he said. "It'll smooth out once we cross over the grade."

"I don't suppose there are any plans to improve the road?" asked Elizabeth, her teeth rattling with each jolt of the wagon. In the wagon bed, Henry muffled an exclamation as a trunk slid into him. China rattled. Elizabeth hoped fervently that the quilts the Bergstrom women had made would see the precious wedding gifts safely the remaining few miles of their journey.

"You're looking at the improvements," Lars replied. "Folks used to have to come over the Old Butterfield Road to the Camarillo Valley to haul our crops to the train. It was even steeper than this, and when it rained the wheels would stick in the mud so you'd lose half a day getting your wagon free. Everyone knew it was only a matter of time until a wagon overturned and someone got killed. So a farmer named Nils Olsen donated the land, and all the Norwegian families worked together in their spare time for two years to carve this route through the hills. They did it all on their own, with no help from the government except for the money the county gave them to buy dynamite to blast the boulders too large to move." Lars regarded the road before them with pride. "They call this the Norwegian Grade in honor of those families."

"They must be very proud," said Elizabeth faintly. If this were the safer pass, she prayed she would never be required to take the Old Butterfield route.

The team pulled the wagon over the grade. At the summit, Elizabeth forgot about the rough road as she gazed out upon the Arboles Valley, a patchwork quilt of green and brown bathed in warmth and sunlight and framed by mountains. Behind her, Henry rose to his knees in the wagon bed for a better look. Elizabeth beamed at him as he took her hand, but she quickly returned her gaze to the breathtaking sight. She wished she knew which of the patchwork farms and ranches was theirs.

"What's that?" asked Henry suddenly, indicating a shadow cutting into the gentle roll of the valley floor.

"That's the Salto Canyon," said Lars. "The Salto Creek runs through the bottom. Best source of water in the valley. The only reliable source when the rains don't come."

The description of their land included a creek; perhaps it was this one. Elizabeth shaded her eyes with her hands and eagerly searched the region around the canyon for landmarks from the photographs the land agent had given Henry, but from their vantage point, one cluster of oaks resembled every other. She wished Henry would take out his map and locate Triumph Ranch while they could still enjoy the view of it from above, but he would not risk divulging their secret too soon, even to one taciturn farmer.

They descended from the hills into the valley, and as Lars had promised, the road grew considerably smoother. They passed other farms and had a first glimpse of their new neighbors from a distance. Farmers labored in fields; a pair of dogs chased the wagon for an eighth of a mile before giving up and going home, tails wagging.

They had nearly reached the opposite side of the valley before the first real signs of a town appeared. They passed the Arboles Grocery, a modest, one-story wooden structure with a single gas pump out front. Farther down the road was the Arboles School, a newer, whitewashed building with a bell in a high cupola. Children played in the short, brown school-yard grass.

"Where's the post office?" asked Henry. Elizabeth knew he really wanted to know how to find the land office, which was located within the post office, not an unusual arrangement for a town this size.

"John Barclay runs it out of his front room."

"The post office is in his house?" asked Elizabeth.

Lars shrugged. "He is the postmaster."

"How do we get there?" asked Henry. "And how early does he open?"

"Take the El Camino Real north from your hotel, turn right at the first road east, and you'll go right past it. Barclay's likely up at daybreak to care for his livestock. If you go to see him that early, you'll find him in the barn. If you want him to leave his chores to take care of post office business, you should offer to help him or he's liable to take his own sweet time just to spite you."

"I gather Mr. Barclay's a difficult man," remarked Elizabeth.

"No more than any other man who's well acquainted with trouble. Some folks might say he's brought his troubles on himself— and I might be one of them—but what hurts him hurts his wife, and she surely doesn't deserve any more heartbreak."

Lars broke off and frowned deeply as if startled by his own frankness. Elizabeth wanted to ask him what manner of trouble and heartbreak had afflicted the Barclay family, but the set of his jaw made it obvious that he had said all he intended to say. She glanced over her shoulder at Henry, who was mulling over Lars's words in bemused concern. Henry would not be content until the deed of trust was in his hand, and if what Lars said was true, acquiring it depended upon the goodwill of a temperamental man.

Surely Mr. Barclay would fulfill his professional obligations, bad temper or not. Surely the citizens of the Arboles Valley would not have chosen him as their postmaster if he was the sort of man to disrupt official business on a whim.

The wagon topped a low rise and approached an intersection with a broader, more recently paved road. "There it is," said Lars, gesturing toward a two-story building on the other side of the street, high above them on a foothill of the scrub-covered mountains that rose dramatically behind it. "The Grand Union Hotel."

It was the tallest, most stately building they had seen so far in the valley, freshly painted, with a broad wraparound porch, tall windows, and a second-floor balcony with a railing of turned spindles. Tall, leafy oaks lined the cobblestone drive leading up to the hotel, where Mr. Jorgensen brought the horses to a halt. The front walk was neatly kept, and the garden boasted several magnolia trees in full bloom. Around the side of the hotel, Elizabeth spotted a grove of orange and lemon trees with a walking path and a gazebo. Suddenly she felt a sharp, painful longing for home. Somehow this hotel, smaller and so different in appearance from Elm Creek Manor, reminded her of that beloved place.

Henry jumped down from the wagon and assisted her to the ground. While Lars helped Henry unload their belongings, Elizabeth took in the view from the porch and tried to peek inside the curtained windows. Then Lars tugged on the brim of his hat, wished them well, and turned the horses back down the cobblestone drive.

Elizabeth's attention was drawn to the windowsill, which was pockmarked by many small holes. "What creature made these, do you suppose?" she asked Henry when he joined her on the porch. "An insect? A woodpecker, perhaps?"

Henry studied the holes. "That's buckshot."

"What?" said Elizabeth. "You mean someone shot at our hotel?"

"A long time ago," Henry quickly replied. "Those are old scars. This is an old hotel. I'm sure it's perfectly safe now."

"Perhaps, or perhaps some of Peter's business associates paid a recent call."

"It's safe." Henry opened the door and gestured for her to precede him inside. "I wouldn't put us up anywhere that wasn't safe."

"Not knowingly, you wouldn't."

"Elizabeth—" Henry waved her inside impatiently. "It's safe. Go on in."

She obeyed, reluctantly, and only because she did not think they had any other choice. Lars Jorgensen was long gone, and they had nowhere else to stay for the night.

Inside the lobby, the front desk was unoccupied, but Elizabeth heard voices and the clinking of glassware somewhere beyond. To her right was the doorway to a barroom, with a long bar that seemed to run the entire length of the building. Three or four men sat on tall bar stools, their backs to the lobby. Elizabeth wondered what they were drinking. If alcohol filled their glasses, they were making no effort to conceal it.

She looked to her left, through a second doorway leading into a Victorian parlor, which appeared to be unoccupied. Between the lobby and the parlor was a polished hardwood staircase spindled even more ornately than the balcony outside. The same small holes that marred the windowsill also riddled the banister. Elizabeth, hearing quick footsteps approach, gestured at the holes and raised her eyebrows at her husband to be sure he had taken note of them. Henry smiled weakly and shrugged just as a woman in her sixties entered through a doorway behind the desk. Her two dark braids threaded heavily with gray were coiled at the nape of her neck, her manner officious but cordial. "Welcome to the Grand Union," she greeted them. "Do you need lodgings for the night or shall I show you to the dining room? Or perhaps you'd like refreshments in the bar?"

"We'll be staying the night." Henry reached into his breast pocket and pulled out a letter. "I'm Henry Nelson and this is my wife, Elizabeth. I wrote to you last month."

"Oh, yes, of course. The newlyweds." The proprietress smiled briefly as she skimmed the letter. "I'm Gertrude Diegel. Your room is upstairs. Do you need help with your luggage?"

When they explained that most of their luggage sat outside on the front porch, Mrs. Diegel suggested they store the heavy trunks in the staff area off the kitchen. Elizabeth and Henry agreed, and after summoning a porter, Mrs. Diegel led them upstairs. The staircase divided at a landing; they followed Mrs. Diegel up the right-hand stairs to the east wing, down a narrow hall past several closed doors, and to their own room close to the end.

"It's a single bed," Mrs. Diegel warned them as she opened the door. "It will be cozy, but perhaps as newlyweds you don't mind. Or would you care to take a second room?"

Peering inside, Elizabeth saw that the room was only about eight by ten feet, with a narrow dresser, a ladder-back chair pulled up to a table scarcely large enough to hold the vase of flowers set upon it, and a bed no wider than a single berth on the *Pacific Coast Limited*. It was smaller than Elizabeth had expected, but she did not want to spend the last night of her honeymoon apart from her husband, especially since their funds were dwindling and they had barely enough left to pay for the single room. Henry must have been thinking the same, for they both quickly assured Mrs. Diegel that a second room would not be necessary. Mrs. Diegel nodded, reminded them that supper would be served at five o'clock, and left them alone in the small room.

Elizabeth promptly went to the washbasin and pitcher on a dresser near the window, eager to freshen up and explore the citrus grove before supper. With a creak of bedsprings, Henry sat down and unfolded the map on the quilt, smoothing out the creases. "I think this is an older map," he said after a moment. "None of the names of the families Lars Jorgensen mentioned are marked on any of the farms and ranches bordering our property."

Elizabeth dried her face and hands and retrieved her brush from her handbag. "Is the hotel on the map?"

"No, but that doesn't mean anything. This map only shows property boundaries, not buildings."

Elizabeth ran the brush through her bobbed curls, unconcerned. "Land changes hands. Families change names through marriage. We'll sort everything out at the land office tomorrow."

"I'd rather go today." Henry refolded the map, frowning. "I'd go this minute if I could."

"They aren't expecting us until tomorrow."

"But John Barclay will be there, won't he, if the office is in his house?"

"I suppose so, but if he's as cranky as Lars Jorgensen implied, he probably won't be happy if we show up early. What's your hurry? Triumph Ranch is already ours. Waiting half a day won't make a difference."

"The sooner I can see the place with my own eyes, the better I'll feel."

"Really, Henry, what are you so worried about? Say we show up at the ranch and the cattle are sickly and the barn roof is half caved in. We can fix whatever's wrong, and if we can't, we'll sell the land to recover our costs and go back home to Two Bears Farm. That's the worst that could happen, and you have to admit that isn't so bad."

He looked up at her with such unexpected bleakness that she immediately regretted her flippant tone. She sat down on the bed beside him and kissed him on the cheek. "I'm only joking," she said. "Everything's going to be fine. Cheer up, won't you? This is the last day of our honeymoon, we're almost out of money, and tomorrow the real work begins. Let's have fun while we still can."

Henry closed his hand around hers and gently stroked her cheek. "You're right," he said, but the worry did not completely leave his eyes.

❧

Elizabeth persuaded Henry to join her on a stroll along the walking path that wound through the orange and lemon trees. They found a stone bench beneath a shady oak and sat down to take in the view of the Arboles Valley, less dramatic than from the Norwegian Grade, but still lovely. Henry's old confidence returned as he pointed out the direction of Triumph Ranch and what he thought was the western boundary of the property.

"Tomorrow we're going home," he promised. "We'll have lunch in the kitchen of the Rancho Triunfo and sleep in a comfortable bed."

"And we'll sleep beneath our wedding quilt," Elizabeth promised in return. "It's too beautiful to save for only special occasions."

Henry laughed. "Any other woman would say that it is too beautiful to use every day."

"Things don't become more beautiful locked away in a trunk," protested Elizabeth. "I say if one can surround oneself with lovely things, one should."

Henry smiled and kissed her. "That's why you belong here in California. You are too beautiful yourself not to be surrounded by beauty every day of your life."

At five o'clock, they met Mrs. Diegel in the dining room just off the parlor Elizabeth had seen from the lobby. Beyond it lay the kitchen, from which delicious smells wafted. Elizabeth had not eaten since breakfast back in Los Angeles, so she eagerly sat down when Henry pulled out her chair. Six other guests had already seated themselves, four men traveling on business and another married couple about ten years older than the Nelsons. The guests introduced themselves and chatted while Mrs. Diegel served chicken and dumplings with a salad of sliced tomatoes and cucumbers. As they had in the Los Angeles boardinghouse just that morning, the Nelsons found themselves forced to be evasive when confronted by their fellow guests' friendly curiosity. This time, however, their usual reply that they were farmers who had come to the Arboles Valley to settle down met with puzzlement.

"You're planning to buy a farm?" asked one man, who, to Elizabeth's consternation, happened to be in the real estate business. "I wasn't aware that there were any farms for sale in the valley. Or should I say, farms for sale that are going to remain farms."

"Don't tell him what land you have your eye on," advised another man jovially. "Milton here will buy it out from under you and subdivide it into a dozen lots before you have time to grab your coat and hat."

"It's an honest living," replied Mr. Milton, apparently unoffended.

"We aren't looking to buy a farm," said Henry. It wasn't a lie; he had already purchased a ranch.

Mr. Milton regarded them with new interest. "Then perhaps you've come to look at Meadowbrook Hills? I apologize, but I don't remember a Mr. and Mrs. Nelson on my list of appointments. No matter. I have a few hours free tomorrow afternoon after I take the Crewes out." He nodded to the other married couple. "I'd be happy to show you the remaining lots after they have their turn."

"Maybe the Nelsons came to see Oakwood Glen," suggested Mrs. Diegel as she passed through the dining room with a pitcher to refresh their water glasses.

Mr. Milton frowned. "I never thought I'd say this about any plot of land, but that development would be better off plowed and seeded with alfalfa."

"You only say that because Mr. Donovan is your biggest competitor," said Mrs. Diegel airily. "I happen to know you tried to buy the Lindstrom farm, but Mr. Donovan made a higher offer."

"We're not interested in Oakwood Glen," said Elizabeth hastily as Mr. Milton's scowl deepened. She wished Henry had agreed to tell everyone that they were merely newlyweds on their honeymoon.

"What sort of development are you talking about?" asked Henry. "New businesses coming to town?"

"No, although I'm sure that will follow." Mrs. Diegel regarded the Nelsons with surprise. "All this time, I had you two pegged as another young couple looking to buy homes in these developments Mr. Donovan and Mr. Milton are building."

"Perhaps I can still persuade you," said Mr. Milton, passing Henry a business card. "I still have several half-acre lots with scenic views available."

"The views are scenic *now*," said Mrs. Diegel. "They won't be forever if you and Mr. Donovan have your way. Leave these young people alone and let them finish their dinner. They clearly aren't in the market for one of your homes."

To Elizabeth's surprise, Mr. Milton chuckled. "Say what you will, I know you're happy we're improving those empty acres of farmland. You'll thank me when you prosper from all the new residents. These developments will make up for everything the stagecoach and the train never delivered."

Elizabeth had no idea what he meant. She exchanged a look with Henry and knew that his thoughts mirrored her own: They were very fortunate to have purchased the Rancho Triunfo before Mr. Milton or Mr. Donovan heard the land was up for sale.

That night, hours after Henry had fallen asleep beside her, Elizabeth climbed carefully from the narrow bed and slipped a robe over her nightgown. Her thoughts were too full of their plans for the next day to allow her to rest. Lighting the lamp, she took paper and pen from her bag, wrapped a blue-and-white Nine-Patch quilt around herself, and settled into the ladder-back chair to write letters home. She wrote to her parents first, assuring them she was safe in California and describing their journey west in the best possible terms. Of Peter and Mae she said only that she and Henry had met an interesting couple traveling from New York on business, but she did not expect to see them again since they disembarked in St. Louis and she did not think to get their address.

She wrote to little Sylvia about the train ride west, wading in the Pacific Ocean at Venice Beach, and the glamorous Egyptian Theater. To Aunt Eleanor she wrote of all these things, but also described her encounter with Grover Higgins, movie producer, and how quickly her excitement had turned to disappointment when Henry chased him off. "Please don't tell my mother about the movie producer," she added in a postscript. "Henry disliked him at first sight (I think he was jealous) and I doubt my parents would approve. Still, wouldn't it be marvelous to have even a small role in a movie—perhaps with Rudolph Valentino as my leading man? I confess that as we sat in the dark of that sumptuous theater, I imagined myself up there, in a glamorous costume, enthralling the audience. Perhaps it's nothing more than a silly fantasy, but let's not forget that I never dreamed I would one day live on a ranch in California, or see any place lovelier than Elm Creek Manor, or visit a town any more exotic than Pittsburgh. Now I am a rancher's wife and I've seen the Pacific Ocean. Who knows what else the future might hold?"

She wrote a last quick letter to her brother Lawrence, telling him—almost defiantly—that she and Henry had arrived safely and were having a marvelous time. She finished up with envelopes and stamps—and glanced over at her husband, slumbering peacefully, while she felt not the least bit tired. Tomorrow morning, she would regret not following his example.

Her mother always recommended warm milk as a cure for sleeplessness, but Elizabeth had never heeded her advice. Privately, she knew that she would have tried it long ago if her aunt Eleanor, and not her mother, had offered the suggestion, so she decided to stop spiting herself and do as her mother instructed for a change. Her mother would never know. Elizabeth doubted any of the kitchen staff would be awake at that hour, but she didn't see anything wrong with helping herself as long as she tidied up afterward and remembered to tell Mrs. Diegel to add it to their account.

She descended the oak staircase in darkness. Her hand slid along the banister, polished to a glossy smoothness with age except where it was riddled with bullet holes and buckshot. A dim glow came from the parlor, and to her surprise she found Mrs. Diegel seated in a chintz armchair piecing a simple nine-patch quilt block by the light of a single lamp.

The proprietress looked up at the sound of Elizabeth's footfalls. "Good evening," she said, resting her sewing in her lap. She did not seem to think it unusual for a hotel guest to be wandering about at that hour. "Or rather, good morning. Did you need something? An extra blanket, perhaps?"

"No, thank you." Elizabeth had not been warm enough until she threw an extra quilt on the bed, but the room was comfortable despite the close quarters. "I couldn't sleep."

"Did the ghost wake you?"

Elizabeth felt a chill on the nape of her neck that had nothing to do with the unseasonably cool night—if it *was* unseasonable. She was beginning to suspect it was not. "Ghost?" she said. "You're joking."

Mrs. Diegel shrugged and resumed sewing. "His name is Pierre—Duval or Duvon, the stories aren't consistent. He was shot and killed in the barroom back in the eighteen eighties. I've never seen him myself, but some guests claim to have woken in the middle of the night to discover a man with a handlebar mustache staring at them from the foot of the bed and suddenly vanishing. He slams doors and rearranges the furniture from time to time, hides keys and hairbrushes when you most need them. He's more of a nuisance than a fright, as far as I'm concerned."

"I don't believe in ghosts," said Elizabeth firmly.

"Most people don't until they see one. Our postmaster didn't believe, either, until he saw the ghost of his dead mother-in-law wandering the mesa near the Salto Canyon. Or so he says. It nearly unhinged him." Mrs. Diegel looked up and smiled. "I don't suppose this sort of talk will cure what ails you. Would you like a glass of warm milk or a cup of tea?"

"A glass of warm milk, please. If it isn't too much trouble."

"Not at all." Mrs. Diegel set aside her sewing and left the parlor. Unsure whether she was meant to wait or to follow, Elizabeth hesitated a moment before trailing after her hostess to the kitchen. She sat down at a broad oak table while Mrs. Diegel poured milk from a glass bottle into a saucepan and heated it over a burner of the gas stove.

Mrs. Diegel stirred the saucepan with a wooden spoon, her expression thoughtful. "So you and your husband aren't in the market for one of Mr. Milton's houses," she remarked after a time. "You say you're farmers and that you've come to the Arboles Valley to live, when as far as I know—and I would know—there aren't any farms for sale in the valley at present."

She glanced over her shoulder at Elizabeth, who responded with an uncertain nod.

"I suppose it wouldn't do any good to ask you what your business here is."

"I can't tell you today," said Elizabeth. "Tomorrow afternoon I'll be able to say more."

"I can wait that long." Mrs. Diegel filled a coffee cup with steaming milk, stirred in a dash of vanilla, and set it before Elizabeth. She pulled up a chair across the table and regarded her speculatively.

Elizabeth thanked her, picked up the cup, and took a sip. The warmth of the milk and the fragrance of vanilla were soothing. "I hope you won't think I'm prying," she said. "But I've been wondering what Mr. Milton meant earlier today when he said that the neighborhoods he is building will make up for what the stagecoach and the train didn't deliver."

"So that's what's keeping you awake tonight?" said Mrs. Diegel, amused. "He was referring to the history of this old place. James Hammell built the Grand Union Hotel in 1876 and welcomed his first guests on July Fourth. It was a grand place, comfortable and beautifully decorated, an oasis for weary travelers taking the Coast Line Stage from Los Angeles to points farther north. He stood to make a fortune, but then the stagecoach line switched its route from the Arboles Valley to the Santa Clara and took his customers with it. He might have endured that blow if not for the terrible drought of seventy-six and seventy-seven. The valley saw only three inches of rain in all that time. James Hammell wasn't the only one to lose everything in those years. He was forced to sell, and my grandfather bought the hotel and about a thousand acres of farmland at a sheriff's auction." Mrs. Diegel sighed and shook her head, remembering. "There were rumors that a train connecting Los Angeles and Oxnard would run right through the Arboles Valley. My grandfather had a friend in the transportation department who assured him this was so. He was certain he would become rich from the travelers who had eluded Mr. Hammell. But as you know, the railroad companies chose the Simi Valley instead."

"So the stagecoaches and trains brought only disappointment," said Elizabeth.

"No, not only that. Enough travelers ventured this way for my grandfather to stay afloat, and our farmers benefited from the train as much as anyone. Still, when another drought struck years later, my grandfather was forced to choose between selling the hotel or selling the farm. He received a better price for the farm, so he sold it and kept the hotel. My family has run it ever since."

"What happened to the farm?"

"It's changed hands several times since, so I suppose my grandfather made the right choice." For a long moment, Mrs. Diegel cupped her chin in her hand and stared off into space. Then, suddenly, she fixed Elizabeth with a steady, appraising gaze. "For more than fifty years, my family has welcomed fortune-seekers to the Arboles Valley. Within a few years most newcomers pack up and leave—as soon as times get tougher than they expected. It takes a strong will and a good dose of luck to make it here. Many folks go broke, give up, and move away, while others stay, endure, and wait for better times. I wonder which kind you and your husband are."

Elizabeth, secure in the knowledge that Triumph Ranch awaited them, replied, "We're the kind to hang on."

"Everyone thinks that or they wouldn't come in the first place." With a sigh, Mrs. Diegel rose and carried Elizabeth's empty cup to the sink. "Only time will tell."

"Our families have always been farmers," said Elizabeth. Mrs. Diegel did not need to know that Elizabeth's experience was limited to a few summers of helping her aunt and uncle on their horse farm because her father had given up the land to marry her mother. "They've endured floods and accidents and every other imaginable hardship. I assure you, we're the kind of people to hang on."

Mrs. Diegel gestured to the doorway. "Then you'll need your rest."

Elizabeth followed Mrs. Diegel from the kitchen, through the dining room, and back into the parlor, where Mrs. Diegel paused to pack up her sewing. As she folded her Nine-Patch quilt block and tucked it into her sewing basket, Elizabeth glimpsed scraps of a familiar fabric.

Impulsively, she asked, "May I see that?"

"The quilt block?" Mrs. Diegel unfolded it and smoothed out the creases on her open palms. "It's just a simple Nine-Patch. I'm not much of a quilter, but I must keep my guests warm."

"It's very well done," said Elizabeth generously, sparing a once-over for the block before peering into the basket. "Would you be willing to swap scraps? I could bring my sewing basket to breakfast and let you take your pick of my collection."

"There's no need to trade." Mrs. Diegel folded back the lid of the basket and held it out to Elizabeth. "Take whatever you need if you can put it to good use."

Elizabeth took the basket, hesitant. "Are you sure? I wouldn't want you to run out."

"I have plenty of scraps already. These are too small for the quilts I make, but I'm too frugal to throw them out. I'm glad to find a better use for them."

"Thank you." Elizabeth took out two pieces each of three different cotton prints—a shirting fabric, a demure floral, and a cheerful blue-and-white check.

"You're very welcome." Mrs. Diegel closed the basket. "Now, don't stay up all night sewing this quilt of yours. I suspect you have a busy day ahead."

Elizabeth promised she wouldn't, an easy promise to keep because she hadn't nearly enough fabric to begin the quilt that a glimpse of Mrs. Diegel's scraps had inspired her to make. As soon as Elizabeth spotted them in the sewing basket, she knew they must be left over from the innkeeper's sewing for the Grand Union Hotel. The brown-and-white pinstriped fabric matched the shirtwaist dress Mrs. Diegel had worn when she welcomed the Nelsons in the lobby. The pretty chintz floral was identical to the pillowcases in the little room she and Henry shared. The blue-and-white check must have been trimmed from the tablecloth in the dining room where they had enjoyed their first meal in the Arboles Valley, sharing a delicious chicken and dumpling supper with the other guests. Each of those scraps held a special memory for Elizabeth. She would collect others—a piece from the silk scarf she had bought at Venice Beach, the trimmings left over from when she hemmed her skirts on the train west—and stitch them together into a patchwork of memories, a record of their journey. It would be only fitting for such a quilt to be the first she would make on Triumph Ranch.

∾❦

1889

It took Miguel Diaz three years to convince Isabel to marry him. The first year went to making up for the bad impression he had made on her sixteenth birthday. Once he persuaded her to tolerate him, he needed a second year to win her heart. He rejoiced the day she confessed she loved him, too, unaware that this did not mean she would agree to become his wife. One more full year passed in which he felt as if he were taking her by the hand and cajoling her to take small steps out her front door and into the sunlight.

Her father was no help. Whenever the couple brought up the subject of marriage, her father spoke of how much her brother and sister needed her. How would they manage without Isabel to care for them? How would *he* manage? He had no wife. He worked from daybreak to sunset to provide for his family. Without their mother, without Isabel, the family would fall apart.

Whenever her father spoke this way, Isabel reluctantly set aside any thought of leaving. Miguel wanted to admire her loyalty, but he was becoming impatient. Would he have to wait for the old man to die—God forgive him for such a thought—before he could make Isabel his wife? Miguel promised her they would live close enough that she could check on her father and sister and brother every day if she wished. He would welcome her father into their home if that was what he had to do. Isabel listened to his assurances and told him, wistfully, that they needed to wait, to wait and see. Perhaps someday the time would be right.

The day finally came on her sister's birthday. "She's sixteen today," Miguel remarked, watching from the kitchen chair as Isabel mixed up batter for a birthday cake. "She's the same age you were when I saw you buying ice cream at the Arboles Grocery."

Isabel smiled, remembering. "Yes, that's right." Then her smile faded.

"Maybe I shouldn't have reminded you," said Miguel ruefully. "After working so hard to make you forget it—"

But Isabel did not seem to hear him. "At her age, I was taking care of the whole family. I had left school. I was so lonely."

Not like her sister, who excelled at school, flourished in her circle of friends, and insisted that after graduating, she would go to college and become a teacher. Miguel wondered what dreams Isabel had cherished in her heart at sixteen, dreams that she had been unable to fulfill. Did she hope someday to make them come true, or had she abandoned them?

"Your brother and sister are old enough to take care of themselves now," he told her.

"Yes, but my father—" Her spoon clattered against the side of the mixing bowl. "Don't you see? If I leave, my sister will take my place. There will be no graduation for her, no college, no classroom of her own, no love of her own. I can't do that to her."

"Isabel, listen to me." Miguel took her hands. "Your father can look after himself. Your sister knows that. She won't fall into that trap."

Isabel tore her hands from his. "Is that how you see me? I'm not trapped. This is my choice. My family needs me. I can't walk away from my duties. This is what my mother would want."

"Would she?" asked Miguel gently. "You *are* locked in a trap, and you're carrying the key in your own pocket. Are you sure that's what your mother would want?"

Miguel's words haunted Isabel long after he went home. She

could not bear to think that he pitied her. She did not want him to think that caring for her family was a burden. It was not the life she would have chosen, but neither would her mother have chosen to die.

Isabel was so subdued during the family birthday party for her sister that her brother asked if she was feeling ill. "I am, a little," she said. "I think I'll go to bed early."

The next morning, she remained in bed long after she should have risen to fix her father's breakfast. She heard him moving around the kitchen but feigned sleep when he came to her doorway. Finally he rapped softly on the door. "Isabel," he whispered. "Are you all right?"

"I'm not feeling well." It was no lie. She had not felt well since Miguel told her she was trapped.

Her father hesitated in the doorway. "Can you make breakfast?"

Annoyance flared. "No," she said, a trifle harder than a sick woman should have been able to manage.

After a significant pause, her father shuffled off to the kitchen to find something to eat. Silently Isabel wished him luck, rolled over, and went back to sleep.

She woke to sunlight streaming through the windows. After stretching luxuriously beneath her favorite quilt, the one her mother had made as a young bride-to-be, she was struck by the realization that her brother and sister had allowed her to sleep in rather than waking her to fix their breakfasts, pack their lunches, and send them off to school. They would not have risen until after their father had left for the dairy, so he could not have told them Isabel was very sick. Perhaps they had assumed as much, because Isabel had never let illness keep her in bed before. Or perhaps— and this was a more troubling thought—they had let her sleep in because, like Miguel, they felt sorry for her.

She ate a light breakfast on the back patio and spent the rest of the day working on a Double Nine-Patch quilt she was making to use up scraps. It was bright, colorful, and cheerful, and when she had begun piecing the first blocks, she imagined spreading it over the bed she would share with Miguel after they married. How quickly she had sewn those first dozen blocks, as if that would speed her wedding day. Now she knew that unless she stood firm, she would have all the time in the world to complete her wedding quilt—all the time, and none of the necessity.

When she expected her brother home from school, she put the quilt away and hurried back to bed. He checked in on her, feeling her forehead and offering to bring her a glass of orange juice, as she always did for him whenever he did not feel well. He was so sweet and courteous that she felt guilty for deceiving him, but a sudden recovery would raise too many questions, so she stayed in bed.

Her sister came home soon after, toting an armload of books. She perched on the edge of Isabel's bed and asked about her symptoms, frowning studiously at Isabel's carefully worded, vague replies. She only wanted a day off, not a diagnosis that would alarm the people she loved.

Her father came home just as the sun was going down. Isabel listened to his footfalls from her bedroom and heard him come to an abrupt halt in the kitchen. The sight of an empty table where he had always found a meal waiting before had apparently confounded him.

When he came to her doorway, she pretended to be asleep. Rather than disturb her, he moved on to the front room, where her sister was curled up in a chair with a biology textbook on loan from her teacher.

"I'm home," he told her, somewhat mournfully.

"Hi, Papi. How was your day?"

"Good, good. Busy." He hesitated. "It's suppertime."

"I'm not hungry. I ate when I came home from school."

"Well, I'm hungry, and I'm sure your brother is, too," he said. "Will you make us something to eat?"

"Sorry, Papi, but I have to finish this book tonight. My teacher has to return it to her college's library tomorrow."

"Oh. Of course." Papi respected teachers and was proud of his bright daughter's achievements. He would never ask her to set a schoolbook aside. "Well . . . I guess I'll fix myself something."

Before long, Isabel heard the frying pan sizzling on the stove and her father call her brother to the table. They even washed the dishes afterward.

The next morning, Isabel was miraculously cured. She prepared breakfast cheerfully and sent her siblings off to school, then hurried off to see Miguel. By the time her family returned home to supper waiting on the table like always, she and Miguel were engaged.

They married three months later. Her father turned out to be a fine cook, and fairly good at keeping house and doing laundry. At Christmas, he prepared tamales from memories pieced together of his wife and mother and grandmother in their kitchens, taking two days to cook enough for the family and to share with friends. Isabel's brother swore they were much better than Isabel's and nearly as good as those their mother had once made.

Isabel, who had not finished her wedding quilt in time after all, was happy to agree.

Chapter Five

1925

The next morning Elizabeth rose at dawn full of anticipation and as energetic as if she had slept soundly the entire night. Henry had risen even earlier and dressed in his second-best suit. He sat on the bed going over their papers for Triumph Ranch while Elizabeth quickly washed and dressed. They were the first guests to the breakfast table and the first to finish eating. Afterward, Henry arranged for Mrs. Diegel's handyman, Carlos, to drive them to the post office. They would take their overnight bags with them and arrange to pick up the rest of their luggage later that day.

Cool mists shrouded the hotel grounds when the Nelsons met the handyman in the garage, but he assured them they would burn off by midmorning. "They always do," he said. "Except during the winter. Then they might linger all day—or turn into rain."

"You have winter here?" asked Elizabeth as she climbed into the car.

"*Sí*, we do." Carlos grinned. "Maybe not so bad as what you have back east, but we do have winter, even here."

"Does it ever snow?" asked Henry.

"Only on the mountaintops."

"Then it can't be too bad," said Elizabeth, hoping it was so. "Per-

haps California winters only seem cold to you because you're used
to Mexican winters."

Carlos was silent for a moment. "That might be so, except I was
born in the Arboles Valley. I am a sixth-generation Californian on
my mother's side."

"I beg your pardon," said Elizabeth, abashed. "From your
appearance and accent I assumed— Please forgive me. I have this
terrible habit of making a fool of myself by speaking on subjects I
know nothing about."

"I'm not offended," said Carlos, with a tolerant chuckle. "You're
not the first to make that mistake and I doubt you'll be the last."

The car rumbled over the cobblestone driveway and back onto
the road they had taken across the valley the day before. They
turned north at the intersection instead of heading back east
toward the Norwegian Grade. It was a smooth, gently descending
ride from the foothills though oak groves and past the outer pastures of farms. After a mile or two, Carlos turned east onto a dirt
road.

"Do you know Mr. Barclay well?" Henry asked.

Carlos shrugged. "He's married to my sister."

Elizabeth took it as a bad sign that he did not continue. "Is he an
able postmaster?"

"He fulfills his duties competently."

"I would have expected higher praise from a brother-in-law."

Carlos gave her a sidelong glance before returning his attention
to the road ahead. "You're right."

"About what?"

"You do have a terrible habit."

Henry let out a loud guffaw. Elizabeth was about to protest when
a small, one-story farmhouse, a larger barn, and several smaller
outbuildings came into view. Carlos turned the car onto a narrow,
dirt road in poor repair. Elizabeth saw his gaze leap from a broken

fence to a half-plowed field. "He plows later each year," Carlos grumbled softly, as if to himself. "And fewer acres."

He said nothing more as they topped a low rise and pulled up in front of a tidy wood and adobe structure. ARBOLES VALLEY POST OF-FICE proclaimed a signpost hammered in the ground beside a walk-way of worn wooden planks. Two little girls about four and twelve years old played jacks on the hard-packed earth near the front steps, where another girl of about eight sat watching them listlessly. Their floral calico dresses appeared handmade but deftly stitched, and their dark brown hair was neatly braided. The girls were a solemn-eyed welcoming committee, but they brightened at the sight of Car-los. Somewhere inside the house, a toddler wailed weakly.

"Your nieces are beautiful," said Elizabeth, and in his proud smile she saw that her earlier gaffe had been forgotten.

"I'll wait here with *mis pequeñas preciosas* while you conduct your business," said Carlos as the two jack players came running. He scooped up the youngest and swung her high in the air as the older girl flung her arms around his waist. On the steps, the middle girl sat up straighter and beamed at her uncle, barely registering the Nelsons' approach.

Henry rapped on the front door. "Papi's in the barn," said the middle girl, her gaze fixed on her uncle.

At that moment, the door opened and a woman holding a baby on her shoulder peered cautiously outside. "Yes?" she said, her wary gaze darting from Henry's face to Elizabeth's. With her dark lustrous hair and regal features, she looked to be no more than ten years older than Elizabeth, yet her eyes seemed to have witnessed all the grief of the world. She would have been beautiful if not for those eyes. The baby, a tiny bundle with a dark cap of black curls, lay limply upon his mother's shoulder.

"Good morning," said Henry. "We have business with the land office."

The woman did not seem to hear. Her gaze rested upon Carlos, playing with his two nieces in the dusty yard. "*Buenos días,* Carlos," she said to him, so quietly that Elizabeth doubted he would have heard.

But Carlos halted and turned to face her, his expression unreadable. "*Buenos días,* Rosa." His eyes fell upon the baby on her shoulder. "Miguel has fallen ill?"

His sister shrugged and attempted a smile, but it was a bitter grimace. "He is two. He had two blessed years."

Anger flashed in Carlos's eyes. He muttered something in Spanish but broke off abruptly at the sight of his nieces. Sick at heart, Elizabeth looked upon the tiny child with shock and dismay. At his age, Elizabeth's cousins had been twice his size, and his illness, whatever it was, had apparently not been unexpected.

"Have you called the doctor?" asked Carlos in a flat voice.

"Of course, but what good will that do?" Suddenly Rosa seemed to remember the Nelsons. "My husband is in the barn. If you care to wait here, I'll get him for you."

"That's all right," said Henry quickly. "We'll find him ourselves."

Rosa nodded, withdrew into the house, and shut the door. Elizabeth trailed after Henry to the barn, mulling over the short exchange between brother and sister, wondering why Carlos had not gone inside with Rosa.

They found John Barclay in the barn, wrench in hand, tightening bolts on a tiller. He looked up when the Nelsons entered and wiped his hands on a rag. Henry introduced himself and Elizabeth and explained that they had come to collect the deed of trust that was being held for them in the land office.

John Barclay looked puzzled. "I'm not holding any deeds of trust at the moment," he said. "What did you say your name was again?"

"Nelson. Henry Nelson. From Pennsylvania. Back in December, I bought the Rancho Triunfo from Vicente Rodriguez through J. T. Simmons, a land agent from Pittsburgh."

"Aw, hell, not again." John Barclay flung his rag down in disgust. "I suppose you have some documents to show me?"

Henry nodded and retrieved them from the pocket of his suit-coat. John looked them over, shaking his head. Elizabeth tried not to wince at the greasy fingerprints he left on the parchment.

"There's no good way to say this, so I'll just tell you straight out." John thrust the papers back at Henry. "You've been had."

Henry returned a blank stare. "What?"

"You've been had. There's no Rancho Triunfo, at least, not any-more. Vicente Rodriguez was my wife's great-grandfather. He died years ago. The land you paid for has been in the Jorgensen family for three generations."

"But . . ." Henry seemed to struggle for words. "We have a signed contract. A map. Photographs."

"Forgeries." John rustled the worthless papers. "Go on. Take them. They won't do me any good."

Numbly, Henry did.

"You said, 'Not again,' " said Elizabeth.

"This J. T. Simmons character sold this property to two others before you. First fellow was from South Bend, Indiana. Second was from Cleveland. I guess he's working his way east." John spat into the dirt and took up his wrench again. "I swear I'd throttle him if I could get my hands on him. Why he chose to make this my prob-lem, I surely don't know."

"Your problem?" echoed Henry in a strangled voice. "I gave every cent I owned to that man."

John Barclay hesitated, scratched the back of his neck, and frowned in what might have been sympathy. "I hate to say it, but you can kiss that money good-bye. Though I guess it's too late for that, since it's already gone." He eyed them for a moment. "Unless you folks have a letter to mail, I've got work to do."

With trembling hands, Elizabeth gave him the letters she had written the night before. John stuffed them into his pocket and was back to turning wrenches before the Nelsons left the barn. Outside in the yard, Carlos took one glance at their stunned expressions and shooed his nieces toward the house. "Are you all right?" he asked.

Henry said nothing. As if in a daze, he went to the car, climbed inside, and shut the door.

Carlos turned to Elizabeth. "What happened? Did you collect your letter? Was it bad news from home?"

"We weren't here for the post office." Elizabeth craned her neck to watch her husband, but all she could see was his head, slumped wearily in his hands. "I'm afraid we've had a shock. We thought we had bought a ranch, but our papers were forgeries. We've been robbed."

"*Dios mio.* Not El Rancho Triunfo again."

Elizabeth nodded.

Carlos scowled. "That swindler should be tried and hanged."

"He has to be caught first." Suddenly dizzy, Elizabeth pressed a hand to her forehead. "God help us. We've lost everything."

Carlos caught her by the arm and helped her to the car. The Nelsons sat wordless from shock as he started the car and left the Barclay farm behind. "Do you have family?" Carlos asked. "Someone who can wire money, enough to get you home?"

"No," said Henry shortly. "I won't go hat in hand to my father. It was my mistake that got us into this mess. I'll get us out of it."

Carlos glanced at Elizabeth to see if she might respond differently, but she would not humiliate Henry by contradicting him.

"What do you want to do?" Carlos asked her. "Should I take you back to the Grand Union?"

"I suppose." They had nowhere else to go. With a sudden jolt, Elizabeth realized that they could not afford a second night in the hotel.

They drove along without speaking until Carlos broke the silence. "The Jorgensens are decent people. Every farm in the valley is glad to have extra hands. They might offer you work, good work, until you can get back on your feet."

Henry said nothing.

"Henry?" Elizabeth prompted. "It would be a start. Just until we can make a better plan."

"All right," he said dully. "All right."

Carlos pulled the car onto another dirt road that gradually turned toward the east. It occurred to Elizabeth that they were crossing through the landscape they had admired from the citrus grove the day before, but its beauty was lost on them. Everything they had planned for and dreamed about for the past four months had vanished in an instant, burned away like the ocean mists beneath the brilliant California sun.

Elizabeth recognized the Jorgensen farm from the photographs of Triumph Ranch, although there were several additional outbuildings and the yellow farmhouse with white shutters had a new wing. Chickens scratched in the front yard. Petunias grew in window boxes; a young woman and a girl hung laundry on a line. Beyond the house, Elizabeth glimpsed row after orderly row of trees in full leaf, pink and white blossoms newly emerging. It was a cheerful, prosperous farm, as ambitious and industrious as the Barclay farm had been despondent.

It should have been theirs.

Henry's gaze followed a team of sowers laboring in a newly plowed field. Elizabeth wondered if he was imagining himself among them.

"Spring planting has just begun," said Carlos. "This is a good time to be seeking work. You have worked a farm before?"

"Since before I could walk," said Henry.

"Then the Jorgensens are fortunate you have come. I hear they pay a good wage, the best in the valley. They offer room and board, as well."

Carlos was doing his best to raise their spirits. Somewhere in the depths of his shock and disappointment, Henry must have recognized this, for he managed a nod and a tight-lipped smile.

Carlos parked the car outside a machine shed and called to a man inside working beneath the hood of a truck. They exchanged a few words in Spanish. "Oscar Jorgensen and his brother are in the barley fields," he reported. "My friend says they're short-handed."

"Then let's go meet him," said Henry grimly.

Carlos suggested that Elizabeth wait by the car; she was not sure if that was because her shoes were not fit for a trek through the mud or because it was not fitting for a man to ask for work with his wife by his side. She strolled around the front yard, keeping out of sight of the woman and girl hanging laundry. A mother and a daughter, she decided. They were laughing and talking as they fastened men's flannel work shirts to the rope line with clothespins. White sheets billowed in the breeze. Elizabeth felt a sudden, painful ache for her aunt Eleanor so intensely that she had to sit down on the fender and catch her breath.

Before long the men returned, Carlos beaming, Henry holding his head high though a muscle worked in his jaw. "They offered you a job?" Elizabeth exclaimed, relieved. She had not dared to think about what they would do if the Jorgensens refused.

"I can start immediately," said Henry. "Lars Jorgensen told his brother how I helped him unload the wool at the train station yesterday. Oscar hired me on his brother's recommendation."

"There's more good news," said Carlos. "Oscar said they need help around the house. There's work for you, too."

"I'll take it," said Elizabeth quickly. If she worked hard enough, the Jorgensens might never know she had been raised in the city.

"No," said Henry. "This is my fault. You don't have to work to pay for my mistake."

"We'll earn money twice as fast if we both work." Well, perhaps not twice as fast. She doubted she would earn as much working as a domestic as Henry would as a farmhand. "Besides, what else am I going to do all day? Sit around like a lady of leisure? I doubt even Oscar Jorgensen's wife can do that. I'd rather help with chores than die of boredom, so I might as well be paid for it."

She could tell from his expression that he didn't like it, but he couldn't come up with a reasonable argument against it. After unloading their suitcases from the car, Carlos took Elizabeth around back to the kitchen door while Henry found a place to change from his second-best suit into work clothes.

A sturdy, brown-haired woman in her late sixties answered Carlos's knock. "Yes, Carlos?" She gave Elizabeth a quick once-over but did not otherwise acknowledge her. "What can I do for you?"

"This is Elizabeth Nelson," said Carlos. "She's Henry Nelson's wife. Oscar just hired him as a farmhand and he thought that you might have work for Elizabeth."

"I could always use extra help around here." Mrs. Jorgensen folded her arms over her blue gingham apron and studied Elizabeth. "I need a girl who's a decent cook and can keep a house clean. Have you worked a farm kitchen before?"

"Yes, at my aunt and uncle's horse farm back in Pennsylvania. I've also worked at my father's hotel for many years."

Her eyebrows rose. "What brings you to the Arboles Valley if you have a family farm and a hotel back east?"

Elizabeth hesitated. "My husband's other plans for employment fell through."

"So working for us is not your first choice. Well, at least you're honest about it." Mrs. Jorgensen looked past the visitors on her doorstep at the approach of the younger woman and the girl carrying the laundry basket. "Mind you keep an eye on those clouds," she warned the eldest. "You should have had that laundry hung an hour ago. If it rains on my sheets you'll have to do them over."

The younger of the pair, a girl of about twelve, abruptly stopped smiling, but the elder tossed her head and laughed. "It's not going to rain, Mother Jorgensen. Look at that sky! It's a beautiful day. Hello," she greeted Elizabeth suddenly. "I'm Mary Katherine Jorgensen. This is my daughter, Annalise. And you are?"

"Elizabeth Nelson." Elizabeth shook her hand and flashed a quick smile at Annalise.

"Elizabeth and her husband have just hired on," said Mrs. Jorgensen. "Perhaps you can show her around while I get back to work."

Her eyes on Elizabeth, Mary Katherine said, "Have you settled on a wage yet?"

As Elizabeth shook her head, Mrs. Jorgensen said, "We don't have time for that at the moment. We can take care of it at the end of the day."

"Oh, let's just take care of it now, get it out of the way." Mary Katherine waved a hand dismissively. "What were you thinking of paying Elizabeth, Mother?"

"Twenty-five cents a day is a fair wage for a new kitchen helper."

"I agree completely, but as soon as Elizabeth finds out that the Russells are paying fifty cents, she'll quit and go work for them. I think we ought to pay fifty just to be safe, don't you?"

Mrs. Jorgensen frowned. "I suppose so."

"And if we would like her to help in the garden occasionally—" Mary Katherine touched Elizabeth lightly on the forearm. "You don't mind gardening, do you?" Elizabeth shook her head. "Then we ought to pay seventy-five. That's the going rate on the Kelley farm."

"This is not the Kelley farm."

Mary Katherine shrugged. "No, I suppose it isn't. Elizabeth, honey, do you have a place to live?"

"I'm afraid not," said Elizabeth.

"Then we'll have to provide room and board as well. And Sundays off."

"Of course she'll have Sundays off," said Mrs. Jorgensen, indignant. "But room and board will have to come out of her wages. Ten cents a day."

"Very well," said Mary Katherine. "Sixty-five cents a day plus room and board and Sundays off. But Elizabeth can't live in the bunkhouse with the men. We'll have to make other arrangements for her and her husband. How about the yellow room off the parlor?"

"You can't mean the guest room," said Mrs. Jorgensen.

"Why not? It's rarely used."

"I can't ask guests to sleep on the sofa because two hired hands have the only spare bedroom. We can fix up the quarters over the carriage house."

"It will take weeks to make that place habitable."

"Then I suppose they can have the cabin." Mrs. Jorgensen drew herself up and looked Elizabeth squarely in the eye. "It's small, but it has a kitchen and a front room and two bedrooms. There's no running water, but the well has a pump. Will that do?"

"It sounds fine. Thank you."

"Very well." Mrs. Jorgensen turned to go. "Change into more suitable clothes and meet me in the kitchen."

"Just a moment," said Mary Katherine. "Let's shake on it."

Mrs. Jorgensen halted and peered over her shoulder at her daughter-in-law. "What?"

Mary Katherine's eyes were wide with innocence. "Isn't that what Oscar does to seal a business agreement?"

Her mouth pressed in a sour line, Mrs. Jorgensen thrust a hand toward Elizabeth, who shook it. "Thank you," Elizabeth added for good measure.

"When you've changed, I'll take you through the house," Mrs. Jorgensen replied. She returned inside, the screen door banging shut behind her. When they could no longer hear her footsteps, Annalise let out a nervous giggle.

Mary Katherine gave her a warning look, but it quickly melted into a grin. "Go help your sister in the garden. I'll catch up," she said. As Annalise ran off, to Elizabeth she added, "Don't let Mother Jorgensen intimidate you. She likes to think she's still the lady of the house."

Elizabeth nodded. "My suitcase is outside. Could you show me where I can change?"

"Of course." Mary Katherine accompanied her outside for the suitcase and then showed her to a modest bedroom with yellow roses on the wallpaper and a yellow-and-white Grape Basket quilt on a bed with a cherry headboard. After Mary Katherine departed, Elizabeth swiftly changed from the traveling suit Aunt Eleanor had sewn for her into a cotton housedress and sturdy shoes. She was grateful to Mary Katherine for negotiating a higher wage and better room and board, but it was not lost on her that Mrs. Jorgensen had made the final decision—or that Carlos had taken Elizabeth to the elder Mrs. Jorgensen to ask for work, when it would have been easier to go to Mary Katherine, who was already outside. Perhaps Mrs. Jorgensen retained the role of lady of the house despite what Mary Katherine thought.

She met Mrs. Jorgensen in the kitchen, where she had time for a quick look around before her new employer sent her running downstairs to the root cellar for a bushel of potatoes, which she washed and sliced in preparation for lunch. Mrs. Jorgensen spoke little as they worked, issuing directions or asking for assistance, but not indulging in friendly chat. Elizabeth supposed that was just as well. She could not bear to be forced to explain how she and Henry had ended up in this state. She still could not believe they had fallen so low so quickly, although she had the waterlogged hands and frying oil splatters on her apron to prove it was no dream.

Henry came in at lunchtime with the men, as sunburned, tired, and hungry as they were, but with a stunned, disbelieving look in his eyes that set him apart. Lars Jorgensen offered her a nod of recognition and welcome, but said nothing to indicate that he thought it odd for the Nelsons to be respected guests of the Grand Union Hotel one day and hired hands the next. The men ate swiftly, barely pausing between bites to discuss the condition of the fields or to plan for the afternoon. Oscar Jorgensen did most of the talking, consulting his brother, who sat at his right hand at the long, redwood plank table that took up most of the kitchen. Despite his thinning blond hair, Oscar resembled his mother—sturdily built, serious, and direct of expression—and seemed years younger than weathered, somber Lars. His face broke into a smile whenever his gaze fell upon his daughters, and Mary Katherine regarded him affectionately as she served the meal. He grinned up at her as she passed the plate of fried chicken, and Elizabeth suspected he might have pulled her adoring face toward his for a kiss if there hadn't been so many people watching.

The men had barely cleaned their plates when Oscar gave the order for them to return to the fields. Elizabeth could not get Henry alone long enough to ask about his morning or offer encouragement. In the few words they managed to exchange in passing, he said stoically that the field work was no worse than back home in Pennsylvania, and that he hoped the Jorgensen women had been pleasant company for her. Elizabeth assured him that everyone had made her feel right at home, although that was not entirely true. Mrs. Jorgensen was not unkind or short-tempered, but she kept her thoughts to herself, making Elizabeth long for the warmth and cheerful banter of the kitchen at Elm Creek Manor, where her grandmother and aunts teased and gossiped and laughed as they prepared meals for the family.

After lunch, she washed the dishes while Mrs. Jorgensen dried them and put them away. Later Mrs. Jorgensen took her through the house, instructing her what to clean and how often. Elizabeth's spirits faltered as she learned about the house that she had meant to call home. She imagined her wedding quilt spread on the four-poster bed in the master bedroom. A smaller bedroom beside it would have made a perfect nursery. The comfortable chair by the window in the front room would have been a lovely place to sit and quilt after the day's work was done. On holidays, Henry could have sat at the head of the walnut table in the dining room. If little cousin Sylvia visited, she could have slept in the yellow guest room off the parlor—although she probably would have crawled into bed with Elizabeth in the middle of the night and nudged Henry farther and farther aside until he gave up and retired to the guest room himself. But it was not to be, none of it.

After the house tour, Mrs. Jorgensen sent Elizabeth out to help Mary Katherine, Annalise, and a younger daughter, Margaret, in the garden. The girls were so cheerful, their mother so friendly, that at last some of Elizabeth's heartache began to ease. She told them about her family back in Pennsylvania, Elm Creek Manor, and her parents' hotel in Harrisburg, but provided only vague answers to Mary Katherine's probing questions about how she and Henry had ended up in the Arboles Valley. Perhaps when she knew them better, if Mary Katherine became a friend and not just an employer, Elizabeth would confide in her. For now, she was too ashamed of their gullibility and foolish optimism to tell them about the reckless gamble that had cost them every cent they had to their name.

Later, Mrs. Jorgensen called Elizabeth back inside to help prepare supper. The meal passed much as lunch had, with ravenous men eating too quickly to allow for conversation. Afterward, Oscar instructed Lars to show Henry around the farm, to let him know how things were done on Jorgensen land. When the men left, Mary Katherine took her daughters off to play while Elizabeth stayed behind to clean up the kitchen.

When she had finished the dishes, Mrs. Jorgensen said, "You've put in a good day's work. If this is how things are going to be, and not just a show for your first day, you'll work out fine here."

"Thank you," said Elizabeth.

Mrs. Jorgensen nodded, opened the kitchen door, and called for Annalise. "You have your own place to fix up," she said as her granddaughter came running. "Annalise will show you the way. I'll expect you here tomorrow morning, five o'clock sharp, to start breakfast."

"Five o'clock," Elizabeth repeated, hoping the cabin had an alarm clock.

"Wait. Before you go—" Mrs. Jorgensen disappeared around the corner and returned with a mop, broom, and a bucket full of clean rags, a scrub brush, and a box of soap powder. "You'll need these."

"Thank you, Mrs. Jorgensen. I'll bring them back tomorrow."

"There's no need. We have others."

Annalise chattered happily as she helped Elizabeth lug the two suitcases and the cleaning supplies a half mile east of the farmhouse to the cabin. "It's been here forever, even before my great-grandfather came to California from Norway," she said proudly as they climbed a low hill from which Elizabeth first caught sight of her new home. "No one's lived in it for ages, not since Nana was a little girl. Sometimes my sister and I play there, but not so much anymore."

"Why not?" asked Elizabeth, wincing as the suitcase banged into her shin.

"Margaret doesn't like spiders."

"Well," said Elizabeth uneasily, "one could hardly blame her. Are there . . . many?"

"Loads," said Annalise enthusiastically.

For an abandoned cabin, it didn't look too bad from the outside. It was a square structure, only one story high but twice as wide as it was tall, with what looked to be a sound roof and a shaded porch running the length of the front of the cabin. There were glass windows, and to Elizabeth's relief, both a chimney and the vent pipe for a cookstove. She had envisioned herself cooking outdoors over an open fire.

The old wooden boards creaked as they climbed the three stairs and crossed the porch. When the front door stuck, Annalise shoved it open and darted inside; Elizabeth followed, but not before sweeping a cobweb from the doorway. It took a moment for her eyes to adjust to the darkness, for the windows, coated with years of grime, let in only feeble trickles of the fading daylight. As Annalise ran from here to there, exclaiming over forgotten treasures, Elizabeth stood in the center of the room, slowly turning, taking the measure of her new home. The front room took up half of the cabin, with the right side set up as a kitchen and the left as a sitting room, where a rocking chair and a three-legged stool stood before the fireplace. An old braided rag rug lay on the floor, so filthy that in the dim light Elizabeth could not tell what color it was. Cinders and soot from the fireplace spilled out onto the hearth, while on the opposite wall, a thick layer of black grease covered the cookstove. Spiderwebs were everywhere, and a rustling in the corners suggested that field mice had made homes in the walls.

Elizabeth pressed a hand to her stomach and took a deep breath. There were cupboards, she told herself firmly. There was a sink with a pump, so she would not have to haul water from the well. The roof—she glanced up at the ceiling to be sure, and felt a wave of relief when she could glimpse neither sunlight nor water stains. The longest wall, facing the front entrance, had two doors hanging ajar. Elizabeth crossed the room and gingerly pushed upon the door on the left. It creaked open to reveal a room half the size of the front room, with a window, a bed, a narrow wardrobe, and a faded steamer trunk. The other room was the same size, but contained two smaller beds, their mattresses sagging in the middle.

Elizabeth leaned against the wall for support, then quickly pushed herself away from it and brushed the dust from her shoulder, resisting the urge to flee. What would Henry say when he saw the accommodations she had arranged for them? She never should have agreed to take the cabin without seeing it first. Had she learned nothing from Henry's mistake?

"Nana says I can stay to help, but I have to come home before dark," said Annalise, who had followed Elizabeth inside the second bedroom.

Elizabeth closed her eyes and took a deep breath. Perhaps she could ask to see the loft above the carriage house and choose between the two. Perhaps Mrs. Jorgensen would agree to allow the Nelsons to share the yellow guest room until they could fix up the cabin. But this would not do. They could not live here, not in this state.

"Elizabeth?"

Elizabeth jumped. "Yes, Annalise?"

"Don't you like it here?" Annalise's smooth brow furrowed in worry. "I know it's messy but I'll help you tidy it up. Nana says . . ."

"What does your nana say?" Elizabeth prompted gently when the girl did not continue.

"She says one day's work doesn't make you a farmer. She thinks you and your husband came out here to buy a house in Meadowbrook Hills or Oakwood Glen like all the other city people but you lost your money and so you had to find work."

"That's not true," said Elizabeth. "We never even heard of Meadowbrook Hills or Oakwood Glen until last night. Henry and I come from farming families. We came to the Arboles Valley for the land."

"I knew it. Mama said so, too. She says no city girl knows her way around a garden the way you do." Then Annalise's smile faded. "Nana says if you turn up your nose at the cabin, you don't have the mettle to last a week on the farm."

"She said that, did she?"

"I probably shouldn't have told you."

"It'll be our secret." First Mrs. Diegel, now Mrs. Jorgensen. Elizabeth was growing impatient with these people who expected the Nelsons to fail.

Henry would be making his way to the cabin soon. She could not let him see the place like this.

"All right," she said briskly. "Let's start with the other bedroom first. My husband will be tired and he might want to go straight to bed. I must have it ready for him."

Annalise nodded and ran off for the cleaning supplies they had left on the porch. She swept the room while Elizabeth wrestled the thin, musty mattress outside and beat it with the mop handle. Her skin crawled when she thought of how long it had been abandoned in the cabin, what sort of creatures might infest it, but it would have to do until their first payday. She hoped their first week's wages would cover the cost of a new mattress.

When the mattress was as clean as she could make it, she wiped down the bed frame, brought the mattress back inside, and set it in place. Annalise had finished sweeping the floor and had turned to clearing the spiderwebs from the corners and the window frame. The window stuck, but with Annalise's help, Elizabeth managed to shove it open. Soon an evening breeze began to clear away the stale air.

Elizabeth searched the wardrobe for bed linens, but found only a small parcel of mothballs, a sock that needed darning, and something that suspiciously resembled mouse droppings. She pried open the rusted clasp of the steamer trunk and discovered a worn, grayed bedsheet and two faded patchwork quilts. Elizabeth took them outside and shook them fiercely, relieved to see that the trunk had kept them relatively clean. She thought longingly of the crisp sheets and pillowcases in one of the trunks she had left at the Grand Union Hotel, gifts from Great-Aunt Lydia. Mrs. Diegel surely must be wondering why the Nelsons had not returned for their belongings. Elizabeth would find a way to retrieve them as soon as she could.

Annalise helped her make the bed with the better of the two quilts, but the sun was slipping behind the Santa Monica Mountains to the west, and soon the girl had to run off for home. Elizabeth finished the master bedroom, shut the door firmly on the other bedroom to hide the mess, and started in on the kitchen. The pump groaned and complained when she worked the handle, but a spurt of rusty water splashed into the sink, smelling of iron. She pumped until her arms ached, but at last, clear water gushed forth. By then Elizabeth was so thirsty that she threw caution aside and drank from the stream of water, praying that it was clean. She would have preferred to boil it first, but she had no fire, no pot.

She filled the bucket with soapy water, seized a rag, and scrubbed the stove, stripping off layers of grease and decades' worth of caked-on dust. Twice she had to empty and refill the bucket with fresh water. As the gold-specked white enamel began to shine through, words in her mind echoed the rhythm of her strokes: *We should have known it was too good to be true. We should have known.* She wished Henry were there to put his arms around her and assure her that everything would be all right, that somehow they would find their footing again.

By the time Henry came in, exhausted and smelling of sweat and soil, Elizabeth was filthy and sore, but the cookstove was clean, inside and out, and the rest of the kitchen was tolerable. She quickly put away her scrub brush and washed her hands at the pump as Henry looked around at the cabin, expressionless.

"You should have seen it before I cleaned up," she said, forcing a smile.

"You can't stay here."

"Yes, we can. I know it's not what we expected but it's a home. Once I've cleaned it properly, once we've spread our own things around, it will be as cozy and comfortable as we could ever want." Elizabeth took his hand and led him to the armchair, but she had to push him into it. When he sat, she unlaced and removed his boots. "Are you hungry?"

He glanced at the kitchen. "Do we have anything to eat?"

"I saved some biscuits from supper." She took the biscuits from her apron pocket, unfolded the napkin she had wrapped them in, and placed them on his lap. "I'm afraid we don't have any plates or cutlery. Or drinking glasses. Tomorrow I'll ask Mrs. Jorgensen if she has a few she could spare."

Henry raised a biscuit to his mouth, staring straight ahead at the wall, chewing and swallowing mechanically until he had eaten the last crumb. "I don't want you to go begging for their castoffs."

Elizabeth was so astonished she laughed. "It's not begging, Henry, just borrowing a few necessities to get us through until we can collect our own things from the hotel. Honestly. Would you rather eat with your fingers and drink straight from the pump?"

Elbows on his knees, Henry leaned forward and buried his head in his hands. He was silent so long Elizabeth worried that he might have fallen asleep. "You will write to your parents," he said at last, wearily, without looking up. "You'll write to them tonight and ask them to wire you the train fare home."

"What about you?"

"I'll stay behind and work until I've earned enough to repay my debt to your family."

"And earn your own fare home," Elizabeth finished for him.

Henry said nothing.

"I don't think that's a good plan at all," she declared. "We'll earn the train fare to Pennsylvania much faster if we both work. Besides, I wouldn't dream of going back to Harrisburg without you. What would people think?"

Henry straightened, his mouth set in a grim line. "I've made my decision. You're going back. This is not what I promised you when I asked you to marry me. This is not what you agreed to. I won't have you living like this."

"You can't force me to get on a train," Elizabeth retorted, her voice shaking with anger. "I am not going without you and that's final."

Henry hauled himself to his feet. "I'm too tired to argue." He paused, looking from one of the bedroom doors to the other. "Is there a bed in this shack or do we sleep on the floor?"

"The door on the left is our bedroom. Our suitcases are in the wardrobe."

"Is it too much to hope that other door leads to a bathroom?"

"There's an outhouse in back."

Henry made a noise of disgust, shook his head, and went outside. Heart pounding, Elizabeth worked the pump, filling the sink with wash water for him. When he returned, she handed him a clean rag to use as a towel. Wordlessly, he took it and scrubbed his face, neck, and hands clean while she turned down the bed. When he finished, he undressed and dropped into bed without looking around the room, and she took his place in the kitchen, emptying and refilling the sink, washing herself as thoroughly as she could. She longed for the claw-footed iron tub back home. If she were there now, she would fill it and submerge herself in the steaming water until the weariness and filth that had worked into her skin melted away.

The cabin had grown dark. Elizabeth felt her way into the bedroom, slipped on her nightgown, and climbed into bed beside her husband. Bedsprings complained; the mattress sagged and gave off a faint, stale odor.

She knew Henry was bone-tired, but she also knew he wasn't yet asleep. "You never promised me a life of ease," she said softly. "We expected to work hard here. Nothing's changed."

"Everything's changed," retorted Henry. "We came here to work as owners of the Rancho Triunfo. Making decisions, supervising the hired hands, planning for the future of our own land. Now we work as hard as we planned to for ourselves, but for someone else."

Elizabeth lay silently listening to the crickets chirping outside, trying not to hear the whispery scuttling within the walls. "We'll go back to Two Bears Farm," she said. "But I won't go without you."

"Yes, you will," Henry said. "I can't face my family—I can't face *your* family—until I've earned back everything I've lost."

"Everything? Not just the train fare—"

"Every last cent I lost to that cheating, thieving liar. I won't go home worse off than when I left."

"But that was your life savings. It will take years to earn back."

"I know," said Henry. "If you don't think you can wait, if one of your rich boyfriends—"

"Stop right there, Henry Nelson," snapped Elizabeth. "Don't say it. Don't even think it. I am your wife, and I am going to stay your wife—unless you cheat on me, in which case you'll be in worse shape than you are right now. So don't suggest otherwise ever again."

"All right," said Henry, surprised. "I thought it was only fair to offer you a way out. But you're still going home as soon as your parents can wire the money."

"I can't go home yet. I can't face my family, either."

"Why not? You don't have anything to be ashamed of. It wasn't your idea to buy the ranch."

Elizabeth thought quickly. "My hair. Can you imagine what my mother will do when she sees how I've bobbed my hair? The sight of it will take years off her life. You've known my mother long enough to know I'm right."

"Then I guess you could—"

"Don't say I can just stay with Aunt Eleanor and Uncle Fred at Elm Creek Manor. You know someone will squeal."

Henry sighed heavily. "All right. You can stay until your hair grows out enough. Then you're getting on a train and going home."

"Promise? Not until then?"

"Yes. Fine. I promise."

"Then I agree."

Elizabeth pulled the worn quilt over herself and sank into a sleep of pure exhaustion, knowing that she had bought herself only a few months at best. As relieved as she was to know the haven of Two Bears Farm and Elm Creek Manor awaited them and that she would only have to endure the ramshackle cabin for a little while, she refused to set one foot on an eastbound train without Henry at her side.

1898

Rosa was born within a week of Isabel and Miguel's first anniversary. Carlos followed two years later. Money was tight, but Isabel was used to that. Miguel was so kind and good-natured that even the worst days, when the children were tired and cranky and she felt that it was all she could do to keep the house clean and get food on the table, she was happy.

But as the children grew, Miguel's wages stretched thinner and thinner over the costs of raising a family. Sometimes Isabel's father gave them money, but she did not tell Miguel, who would have been too proud to accept it. Sometimes they stayed up late talking about how to get ahead, how to save up enough money to set aside for the future, but they already lived as frugally as they could.

In the summer when Rosa turned eight, Miguel came home for supper and announced that he had taken a second job. Isabel was torn. She would be grateful for the extra money when it came time to buy school clothes for the children, but she remembered how her father had worked such long hours that he hardly came home except to eat and sleep. She did not want that for her family.

Miguel quickly assured her that this would be only a short-term job, three weeks or so, just long enough to earn something to put away for a rainy day. "As soon as the apricot harvest is over, I'll be back to my usual hours."

Isabel's breath caught in her throat. "You signed on to help with the apricot harvest? At the Jorgensen farm?"

She could not bear to call it El Rancho Triunfo anymore, even though her father still did. Every other Rodriguez did, but not Isabel. El Rancho Triunfo was gone. It has ceased to exist the day her family had been forced to leave the land.

"It's good money, Isabel."

"I don't care if it's good money. It's *their* money, and I want no part of it."

"Isabel—" Miguel spread his hands, half smiling, half pleading, as if he could not quite believe that she meant it. "Think of what we could do with those wages.

Isabel had thought of it. It would be so easy to tell him to take the job, take their money, and pretend she was not betraying her family, betraying every ancestor back to the great-great-grandfather whose courage and service to a king had earned him that land. But she hardened her heart against temptation and thought of her mother, on her deathbed, refusing the medicines that would have saved her life. Isabel had not understood her mother's choice then, but time had taught her well.

She took a deep breath and locked her gaze with Miguel's. "I will not have you going to them, hat in hand."

Her appeal to his pride failed. "It's a job, not charity. You're making our children pay for a feud that should have ended long ago."

"This is no simple grudge," snapped Isabel. "The Jorgensens cost my family our dignity and our livelihood. They cost my mother her life."

"Your father tells me the Jorgensens bought the ranch fairly," said Miguel. "Your family did not have to sell. The Jorgensens bought drought-stricken land at the best price they could get. They didn't know the rains would fall two months later any more than your family did. They took a chance and won."

"They took advantage of us when we were desperate. My father and grandfather only sold the land because they thought they could earn enough to buy it back someday, when the land value dropped lower."

She could not continue. Miguel already knew how the family had struggled for so long just to make ends meet. Saving enough money to buy back the ranch had been nothing but a wistful dream, an impossible promise they had made to themselves to ease their parting. Once they had sold the land, they had lost any chance of ever again calling El Rancho Triunfo their home.

Unlike the Jorgensens, the Rodriguezes had taken a chance and lost.

As Miguel watched her soberly, Isabel struggled to regain her composure. "I don't make demands of you, but in this matter, I must have my way. If you want to take on a second job, do so, but not this job. Not this job. Not for them. Not ever."

After a long moment, Miguel sighed. "I'll do as you ask. I'll find another job. But I want you to remember something, *querida*. Bitterness and hatred can kill you as surely as cancer does. Think of your mother and remember that."

Chapter Six

1925

Elizabeth dreamed she was on safari on the African savannah, armed only with a pair of sewing shears and a broom. She had lost sight of Henry. Calling out his name as she pushed her way through the long grasses, she stopped short at the sound of a low growl. Heart pounding, she whirled around but saw nothing. When the grass rustled on her left, she broke into a run. Suddenly a roar sounded in her ear, she felt hot, moist breath upon her neck—

She bolted awake, clutching the worn quilt and gasping. Beyond the filthy window, dawn had not yet broken and mists hung over the yard in an eerie calm. She shook Henry awake. "Did you hear that?" she said.

"Hear what?" he mumbled, rolling over onto his side.

"That roar. It sounded like a lion. It woke me up." Elizabeth took a deep breath to clear her head. "Are there lions in California?"

"No, sweetheart." Henry yawned and sat up. "You must have been dreaming."

"What about mountain lions? Maybe it was a mountain lion. Or a bobcat."

"It was a dream." Henry bent down to pick up his watch from

the floor beside his shoes. "It's ten minutes after five. I'll have to hurry or I'll be late."

Elizabeth's visions of Africa fled and she flung back the covers with a moan of dismay. She washed and dressed as well as she could manage at the kitchen pump, the cold water shocking her awake. She and Henry hurried to the yellow farmhouse together but parted at the door with a quick kiss, Henry striding off to the barn, Elizabeth darting into the kitchen, where Mrs. Jorgensen and Mary Katherine had already begun breakfast.

"You're late," said Mrs. Jorgensen. "Didn't the rooster wake you?"

"Something woke me, but it was no rooster." Elizabeth snatched from its hook the apron Mrs. Jorgensen had lent her the previous day. "Are there mountain lions living in the hills?"

"I doubt you heard a mountain lion," said Mary Katherine cheerfully, setting the table. "That was probably Charlie."

"Who's Charlie?"

"Charlie is a fourteen-year-old African lion." Mrs. Jorgensen motioned for Elizabeth to take her place at the stove. "Fry these potato pancakes until they're golden brown, no more."

Dumbfounded, Elizabeth took the spatula. "An African lion is stalking the Arboles Valley?"

"Of course not," said Mary Katherine. "He's in a pen. Except when his trainer brings him into the ring for a performance."

"Oh," said Elizabeth, relieved. "You mean he's a circus lion."

"Not at all. Charlie's a movie star."

"Retired movie star," Mrs. Jorgensen corrected. "A few years ago, an animal trainer from Hollywood bought land in the Arboles Valley for a lion farm, where he could raise lions and other wild animals and train them to be in the pictures. I believe they have six lions now, as well as other big cats, some camels, and bears. George Hanneman and his family put on shows on the weekends. I've never gone, but it's become quite a popular tourist attraction. Until those housing developments came, Safari World was the only reason anyone from Los Angeles visited the Arboles Valley."

Her tone suggested that, unlike Mrs. Diegel, she did not approve of the new construction. "I've heard that the developments will bring greater prosperity to the valley," Elizabeth offered.

"I can't imagine where you heard that," scoffed Mrs. Jorgensen. "The only folks who will prosper from these developments are the developers. They name those rows and rows of identical houses after the things they tear down and dig up to build them. In a decade, we'll look just like every other valley between here and Los Angeles: acres of cement and stucco where green growing things once flourished. Meadowbrook Hills and Oakwood Glen, indeed."

Mary Katherine sighed. "Now, Mother Jorgensen—"

"Don't 'Mother Jorgensen' me. I know you have your heart set on more neighbors so you can widen your social circle, but you should not put your own interests above those of future generations."

Mary Katherine planted a fist on her hip. "Whatever are you talking about?"

"Water. There won't be enough for all of those newcomers."

"But they aren't farmers. They aren't dependent upon rain for their livelihoods. We've always had enough water before."

"Not in drought years," said Mrs. Jorgensen. "We've had enough for the family and livestock, true, but that's because we have one well for one hundred twenty acres. What if we had one well for each acre?"

Mary Katherine considered that, then shrugged and turned back to her work. "I don't think it will be as bad as you say."

"Maybe you're right, but if I had my choice, I'd rather have lions and panthers for neighbors."

Elizabeth wished she had not brought up the subject. She

flipped the potato pancakes, which sizzled in the skillet and gave off an aroma that made her mouth water. "Are you ever afraid, with so many dangerous animals so near?"

"Charlie's loud voice is deceiving," said Mrs. Jorgensen. "Safari World is about four miles to the southwest."

"None of the animals has ever gotten loose," Mary Katherine reassured her. "Although there are rumors that a panther escaped years ago and now lives in the hills on the eastern edge of our farm. Whenever sheep or calves go missing, the rumors fly."

"Stirred up by the boys who were supposed to be watching the livestock, no doubt." Mrs. Jorgensen bustled between the oven and the table with platters of food as the men came in to eat. "It's more likely that the missing sheep and calves fell into the canyon when the boys weren't paying attention."

Mary Katherine touched Elizabeth on the arm in passing. "The shows at Safari World are lots of fun. The girls and I will take you someday, all right?"

Elizabeth agreed with a quick smile and carried the platter of steaming potato pancakes to the table as Oscar Jorgensen sat down. He and the men were more talkative than the previous day, planning the day's work as they ate. When they had nearly finished, Mrs. Jorgensen said that she had some letters to mail and wondered if Oscar could spare someone to take them to the post office.

"I'll let you know after lunch," Oscar promised his mother. "We'll see how the day goes."

"Lars could take your letters for you," remarked Mary Katherine.

"I'm sure Lars is too busy," said Mrs. Jorgensen.

Lars continued eating, apparently unconcerned. "I'm not too busy."

"Why shouldn't Lars go?" asked Oscar.

Mrs. Jorgensen looked at him as if surprised he would ask such a question. "He's your foreman. You need him here."

"This time of year, I need everyone."

Mrs. Jorgensen waved a hand dismissively. "You're right, of course. My letters can wait for another day, when I can take them myself."

"I'd be happy to take them for you, Mother," said Lars mildly.

"Well, you're not going alone," said Mrs. Jorgensen, a fine, sharp edge to her voice.

"I'll go," said Mary Katherine. "I could use an outing."

Her mother-in-law shook her head. "Not you. I can't spare you today."

"Can you spare her?" asked Lars, nodding to Elizabeth. "We could leave your letters at the post office and then go by the Grand Union to pick up the Nelsons' things. They stored most of their luggage with Mrs. Diegel."

Annalise looked up at Elizabeth in awe. "You stayed at the Grand Union Hotel?"

Elizabeth nodded, aware of everyone's eyes upon her.

"Was it pretty?" asked Annalise. "Daddy took me to lunch in the dining room on my last birthday but I've never been upstairs."

"It was lovely." Elizabeth felt a tug of longing for the clean, soft bed she had considered too narrow, the china pitcher and wash-bowl, the crisp, fresh sheets. What she wouldn't give for them now.

Mrs. Jorgensen gave her a speculative look, then nodded to Lars. "Very well. After lunch, if Oscar doesn't need you elsewhere, you and Elizabeth may go. Elizabeth, I hope you packed an alarm clock with your things. When I say be here at five o'clock sharp, I mean not a minute later."

Elizabeth pretended not to notice how Henry bristled at Mrs. Jorgensen's tone. "I do have an alarm clock, actually. It was a wedding present from my sister."

"Odd sort of wedding present," one of the hired hands said.

"Not from a concerned older sister," said Elizabeth, smiling. "This isn't the first time I've overslept."

Several of the men chuckled. Elizabeth glanced at Henry and was dismayed to see him frowning at Mrs. Jorgensen. Fortunately, the older woman's attention was still on her sons, and she did not notice the dark looks the newest hired hand shot her way.

After breakfast, Elizabeth and Annalise tidied the kitchen together. Annalise kept up a cheerful patter as they worked, telling Elizabeth about the farm, her many pets, and so many cousins and aunts and uncles that Elizabeth had no hope of keeping them straight.

"I can tell you have a close family," said Elizabeth when Annalise paused for breath. She thought wistfully of the family she had left behind in Pennsylvania. "Your grandmother likes to keep you near, doesn't she?"

"What do you mean?"

"She didn't even want your uncle Lars to leave the farm for a simple errand."

"Oh, no, it's not that." Annalise carefully swept the kitchen floor. "He goes on errands all the time. Nana just doesn't like him to go to the post office."

Elizabeth smothered a laugh. "Why not? What's wrong with the post office?" Then she remembered the curt postmaster. "Or doesn't your uncle Lars get along with Mr. Barclay?"

"No one really gets along with Mr. Barclay," Annalise pointed out. "I don't think that's it, but I don't know. I've never been to the Barclay farm, either."

"Never? But they have a girl right around your age."

"I know. She's in my class at school. I see her and her sisters there but Nana says I'm not allowed to play with them."

Elizabeth paused in wiping up a spill on the counter. "Did your grandmother give you a reason?"

"Maybe she thinks we'll get sick like the Barclay kids." Annalise opened the kitchen door to sweep the dirt outside. "Did you know that Mrs. Barclay had eight babies and four of them died? They start out okay but they all get sick. Well, not all of them. Marta, the girl my age, she's never gotten sick. Neither has her little sister, Lupita. But the rest of them all do sooner or later. Don't you think that's sad?"

"I can't imagine anything sadder," said Elizabeth. Her heart ached for the poor woman with haunted eyes she had met the day before, for the limp child exhausted from illness in her arms. To lose one child must bring such unimaginable pain, but to lose four, and then to watch as the other children succumbed—

At the sound of footsteps approaching, Elizabeth quickly resumed wiping down the counter. Mrs. Jorgensen entered, took the broom from her granddaughter, and sent her off to help her mother. She and Elizabeth finished cleaning the kitchen in silence, and despite her concern for the Barclay children, Elizabeth decided not to ask Mrs. Jorgensen about their tragic illnesses. Even if Mrs. Jorgensen had forbidden her grandchildren to play with the Barclay children out of concern for their own health, shunning them struck Elizabeth as so unfair, so cruel, that she doubted she could rely upon Mrs. Jorgensen for an accurate account of their circumstances.

After the kitchen was tidy once more, Mrs. Jorgensen instructed Elizabeth to clean the upstairs bedrooms. Elizabeth did as she was told, unsure whether to interpret her employer's silence in the kitchen to mean that she had overheard the conversation and disapproved, or if it was merely her customary reticence.

At least Mrs. Jorgensen hadn't scolded her—this time. Worry pricked Elizabeth when she remembered how Henry had glowered as Mrs. Jorgensen rebuked her for her tardiness. She knew he was likely to rush to her defense rather than allow Mrs. Jorgensen to reprimand her a second time, however deservedly—and get them both fired in the process. This was not Elm Creek Manor, where she was surrounded by loving aunts who doted upon her, who laughed off her mistakes and encouraged her to do better next time. It was not her parents' hotel, where she charmed the customers and her father thought she could do no wrong. She had never known how much her family had tolerated out of love for her. She had always felt so trapped in Harrisburg, bound by her mother's propriety and her father's expectations. Only from a distance did she see how much freedom she had truly enjoyed within the circle of her family's affection.

She worked alone upstairs until Mrs. Jorgensen called her to the kitchen to help prepare lunch. As the men came to the table, Elizabeth managed to pull Henry aside for a kiss, but he only shrugged and pulled away when she asked how his morning had gone. She pressed her lips together and busied herself with serving the corn fritters and ham so that no one would notice her disappointment. Henry was tired and hungry, and he had never been one to kiss her with other people watching, even in his best moods. Once he had eaten and rested, he would regret being so abrupt with her. When he apologized, she would forgive him—although he had better not let it become a habit.

When lunch ended, Lars reminded Oscar about their mother's letters, and the two brothers quickly concluded that Lars could be spared long enough to run the errands to the post office and the Grand Union Hotel.

"Mary Katherine and I are accustomed to working without Elizabeth, so she can be spared as well," said Mrs. Jorgensen as the men pushed back their chairs.

"I'm sorry, Mother," said Oscar. "I should have thought to ask you. I suppose Elizabeth doesn't have to go along."

"No, that's quite all right." Mrs. Jorgensen rose and began clearing the table. "Only Elizabeth or Henry would know if one of their bags was missing. We wouldn't want to make a second trip to pick up something that had been left behind."

Elizabeth tried to conceal her relief. Ever since breakfast she had been looking forward to a respite from the seemingly endless array of farm chores. She suspected occasions when she could escape from the drudgery of housework and see more of the Arboles Valley would be few and far between, and she meant to enjoy this one. She tried to catch Henry's eye so he could share in her pleasure, but he left the kitchen with the rest of the men without looking her way. Stung, Elizabeth vowed to speak to him as soon as they had a moment alone.

She helped Mary Katherine and the girls clean the kitchen—a mere few hours before they would make a mess of it again preparing supper—and met Lars outside the barn, where he waited with the wagon and horses. He helped her onto the wagon seat and chirruped to the horses.

"The car's too small," Lars said when they reached the main road.

"I beg your pardon?"

"I didn't think all of your stuff would fit in the car. That's why we're taking the wagon instead, though the car's more comfortable."

"I don't mind the wagon." In fact, today she rather preferred it. It was a beautiful afternoon, the sun warm and bright in a cloudless blue sky. She was in no hurry to return to sweeping floors and peeling potatoes.

"I guess not." There was a hint of amusement in his voice that suggested he knew what she was thinking. It occurred to her that she ought to thank him for choosing her to accompany him, although she suspected he would have preferred to go alone.

"You were right to warn us about John Barclay," she said. "I don't think he would had been as helpful if we had not approached him with the proper deference."

"He was helpful?"

Elizabeth smiled. "Not very. But it's not all his fault. There was very little he could do to help us. And . . . I think he might have been preoccupied with other things. His children."

"Well, that didn't take long," said Lars dryly. "I guess Mary Katherine told you."

"Annalise," said Elizabeth, hoping she would not get the young girl in trouble.

Lars shook his head, squinting in the sunlight. "It's a shame. Four little ones gone and no doctor can say why."

"Yes, of course, but I was referring to the two others who have fallen ill."

Lars gave her a sharp look. "What's that you say?"

"When Henry and I were there yesterday, two of the children seemed ill."

"Which two?"

His urgency took her by surprise. "I—I'm not sure of their names. Wait. Miguel. The youngest, the baby, his name was Miguel. The other was the middle girl. She sat on the steps, very weak, listless, while her sisters played."

Lars drew in a long breath. "Ana," he said, exhaling her name. "The middle girl's name is Ana. The eldest is Marta, and the youngest girl is Lupita. I knew Ana had gotten sick, but I didn't know about the baby."

"Annalise says she isn't allowed to play with the Barclay kids," said Elizabeth carefully, unwilling to seem critical of his mother. "Is Mrs. Jorgensen afraid she and Margaret might come down with the illness?"

"If she is, that's a mighty foolish fear," said Lars. "If it was catching, wouldn't Marta and Lupita catch it? Wouldn't Rosa and John?"

"I suppose so." Elizabeth hesitated. "No one knows what causes this disease?"

"Some folks say it's bad water on their place, too much alkali. Others say . . ." Lars shrugged. "Some blame one thing, some another. When folks don't have any facts, they imagine every kind of craziness."

"Have the children seen a doctor?"

"Only every doctor between Oxnard and Los Angeles. None of them can explain it. It always starts the same way. For the first year, the baby looks as healthy as any other. Then the illness takes hold and the child just wastes away. Sometimes it might take two years, sometimes four, but the end is always the same. Another child in the ground before the age of eight."

"Except for Marta and Lupita," said Elizabeth.

"Lupita is young yet," Lars reminded her. "But Marta—yes, it looks like Marta has been spared."

They drove along in silence the rest of the way to the Barclay farm. From a distance, Elizabeth spotted John Barclay plowing his fields. Marta and Lupita played in the shade of three live oaks near the house, but Rosa and the other two children were nowhere to be seen. Lars pulled the horses to a stop, jumped down from the wagon seat, and crossed the dusty yard to the front door. Rosa answered his knock, baby Miguel in her arms.

"I came to collect the mail," said Lars gruffly, his gaze fixed on Rosa's careworn and exhausted face. "And my mother would like to mail these."

Rosa shifted the baby and took the letters. "I'll give them to John when he comes in from the fields. There's no mail for your family this time."

"I hear Miguel has taken ill."

Rosa nodded and looked away. Elizabeth thought she saw tears in her eyes.

"Rosa—" Lars reached out as if to touch her shoulder, but let his hand fall back to his side. "What do you need? What can I do?"

"There's nothing you can do."

"But you have no one to help you."

Rosa straightened and regarded him almost defiantly. "I have Marta. She is a great help to me."

"But she's just a girl. What about Carlos and Lupe?"

Rosa gave a bitter laugh. "My brother and his wife want nothing to do with us. You know that." She glanced past his shoulder. "John is coming. You'd better go."

When Lars did not budge, she disappeared inside the house and closed the door. John shouted to Lars as he approached, crossing the newly plowed field at a fast pace. Reluctantly, Lars left the house and met him halfway.

"What's your business here?" demanded John, panting.

"Just mailing some letters for my mother. I gave them to Rosa."

John eyed him, squinting, then turned his attention to Elizabeth. "I got a couple of letters here for an Elizabeth Nelson at Triumph Ranch. There's no such place, so I wasn't sure what to do with them."

Elizabeth felt color rise in her cheeks. "I'll take them, thank you."

John Barclay grinned, enjoying her embarrassment. "You might want to tell folks to address your mail correctly or it might get misdirected."

"Don't be a fool, Barclay," said Lars. "She's the only Elizabeth Nelson in the Arboles Valley."

John scowled and spat into the dirt. "I'll get your letters," he told Elizabeth, and sauntered off to the house. Lars climbed back onto the wagon seat and took up the reins while they waited. From inside the house came the sound of raised voices, John shouting while a child cried. Lars stiffened and wrapped the leather reins around his fist. Another few minutes passed before John returned and placed two envelopes in Elizabeth's hand. Her heart lifted when she saw the Pennsylvania postmarks and the return addresses, one from her parents in Harrisburg, the second from Elm Creek Manor.

She thanked John, but he waved her off and headed back to the fields. Lars started the wagon and turned down the road toward the western edge of the valley. When the Barclay farm was well behind them, Lars said, "Triumph Ranch?"

Elizabeth could not look at him. "It's hard to explain."

"You didn't get taken in by that Rancho Triunfo scam, did you? Your Henry seems too smart for that."

"Don't tell anyone, please," begged Elizabeth. "I don't know what Henry would do if Oscar or your mother found out. It's such an embarrassment to end up working as hired hands at the farm we thought we owned."

"Your secret's safe with me," Lars assured her. "But you're not the first to be swindled. You ought to swallow your pride and contact the police. Maybe they can help you get your money back."

"As far as we know, the man who cheated us is on the other side of the country."

"Maybe so, but it's worth a shot."

"What did the others do, the others who were cheated? Did they go to the police? Did they get their money back?"

"No. They mostly slunk off with their tails between their legs the moment they found out they'd been swindled. You and Henry are the first to stay more than a day afterward."

Elizabeth sighed softly, fingering the precious letters from home. What did that say about her and Henry, that they had stayed when the others had departed? Were the Nelsons more resilient or simply more foolish?

Before long they reached the row of shops and offices that made up the town proper nestled in the Santa Monica foothills, and soon the wagon was clattering along the cobblestone road leading to the Grand Union Hotel. Carlos stepped from the carriage house at the sound of their approach. He called out a greeting to Elizabeth, a question in his eyes. No doubt he wondered how things had gone at the Jorgensen farm after he had deposited the Nelsons there. Elizabeth returned his greeting with a smile to assure him all was well, but when Lars acknowledged the welcome, Carlos gave him only a wordless nod and quickly disappeared back into the carriage house.

Lars did not seem surprised by the curt welcome, so Elizabeth pretended not to notice it. As Lars helped her down from the wagon seat, it occurred to her that if John Barclay was the most unpopular man in town, Lars seemed to be a close second. She remembered Rosa's words, her despondent claim that Carlos and his wife wanted nothing to do with her. Elizabeth had seen for herself that Carlos had stayed in the yard instead of holding his sick nephew or comforting his sister. Perhaps Carlos, like Mrs. Jorgensen, feared contagion. If Lars's opinion that it was foolish to shun the Barclays was well known, that might account for the lack of friendliness between him and Carlos.

Lars waited with the horses while Elizabeth entered the hotel. She found Mrs. Diegel in the kitchen, which smelled of roasting chickens, cilantro, and orange. They expected a large crowd that evening, Mrs. Diegel said cheerfully, explaining her early start on preparing the meal. Both Mr. Milton and Mr. Donovan had parties of prospective homeowners spending the night at the hotel. Dinner promised to be lively, with both men and their clients gathered at the same table extolling the virtues of their own developments and pointing out the flaws in their competitor's.

"Will you stay for dinner?" Mrs. Diegel asked, wiping her hands on a dish towel. "I promise it will be entertaining."

"I wish I could, but I have to get back to work. I just came by to pick up our luggage."

"I suppose I don't have the space at the table tonight anyway."

Mrs. Diegel led Elizabeth to the storage room. "It's none of my business, but I'm curious where you're staying tonight."

Elizabeth had been prepared for this. She forced a smile and said, "Our original plans fell through, but Henry and I were fortunate to find work on the Jorgensen farm. We have a quaint little cabin all to ourselves on their property."

"Not that ramshackle old place," said Mrs. Diegel, aghast. "That's not fit for human habitation. Oscar should have torn it down long ago."

"It has seen better days," Elizabeth admitted, "but we'll fix it up nicely."

"With what? Did you pack tools? Supplies? How will you furnish it? You can't possibly have beds and tables and chairs packed away in these trunks."

"There was some furniture in the cabin already. Whatever else we need can wait until payday."

"Oh, my heavens." Mrs. Diegel clasped a hand to her brow and shook her head. "I admire your fortitude, but you need to pause a minute and think. How far do you think your paycheck will stretch if you have to furnish an entire cabin, even one that small? That place doesn't even have indoor plumbing. Where do you bathe? How will you cook for yourselves?"

"So far we've eaten all our meals with the Jorgensens," said Elizabeth. "If we want to dine alone sometime, we do have a cookstove."

"Yes, but do you have any coal? Any pots and pans?"

"No," said Elizabeth. Triumph Ranch was supposed to come furnished. She and Henry had assumed that included kitchen implements, and if not, they had planned to buy what they needed after taking inventory. Now their inventory included three old beds with worn and soiled mattresses, a chair and a stool, and two worn and faded quilts, and they had neither the money nor the credit to buy what they lacked.

Mrs. Diegel gestured to the Nelsons' luggage. "And all this? The wedding trousseau, I assume. Finery rather than the practical things you really need."

Elizabeth nodded, although that was only partially correct. She and Henry needed the quilts, bed linens, and dishes as much as they needed cooking pots and coal. But the wedding gifts were more meaningful to her than the sum of the practical roles they performed. They were the comforts of home, tangible reminders of loved ones so far away, relics of a time when they had been full of confidence and hope and promise. Elizabeth needed to surround herself with these souvenirs of a different age or she feared she might forget how she had felt on the train west as Henry's bride. Worse yet, Henry might forget.

But Mrs. Diegel was right. How long could they get by washing up at the kitchen sink? How would Elizabeth cook for them on Sundays, their day off?

"I suppose I could sell some of our things," she said reluctantly. She dragged one of the trunks into the open. There was a faint, musical chime of china delicately clinking.

"Is that china?" asked Mrs. Diegel.

Elizabeth nodded, unfastened the lock, and opened the trunk. She reached within the folds of the quilt and withdrew a cup and saucer. "It's our Blue Willow china," she said steadily. "Twelve five-piece place settings and several serving dishes. It was a gift from my grandparents."

"You certainly expected to entertain in high style, didn't you?" said Mrs. Diegel, admiring the china. "Well. I don't think you'll find much of a market for fine china in the Arboles Valley, but perhaps . . ." She glanced over her shoulder into the kitchen, and her gaze lingered on her own china closet before she turned back to Elizabeth. "I'd be willing to trade you some more practical necessities for the china service. You can try to sell them elsewhere first if you like; I'm in no hurry."

But Elizabeth was, and she would have no idea where to begin trying to sell her things. "What would you be willing to offer?"

Mrs. Diegel wanted to inspect the entire service first, so Elizabeth carefully unpacked the plates and cups and casseroles and placed them on the table. Not a single piece had broken, and as Mrs. Diegel held up a dinner plate to the light to admire the design, she proposed a trade: a mattress—rarely used, as it had been her grown daughter's before she moved to San Francisco and not for hotel guests—two feather pillows, a simple pewter table service for four, and three kerosene lamps for all of the china. Elizabeth pointed out that the china was new, whereas Mrs. Diegel's things were not. Mrs. Diegel added two scuttles of coal and a large copper stockpot to the deal, and since Elizabeth doubted she would go any higher, she agreed.

"What else do you have in there?" asked Mrs. Diegel, eying the remaining trunks eagerly.

With a twinge of regret, Elizabeth opened the rest of the trunks. She traded away the silver plate for a set of used flatware, a teakettle, and five pieces of cast-iron cookware. A pair of elegant candlesticks went for sacks of sugar, coffee, and flour. Mrs. Diegel tried to talk her into parting with all of the bedsheets, but Elizabeth insisted upon keeping one set for her and Henry. One by one she parted with her beautiful things, acquiring the practical necessities of everyday life in return.

When the last trunk had been emptied, Mrs. Diegel seemed sorry to end their bargaining, but Elizabeth felt drained, bereft. While she repacked the trunks with the secondhand goods, Mrs. Diegel instructed the porter to take the mattress from the spare bedroom in the family wing of the hotel and load it into Lars's wagon. Humming merrily, Mrs. Diegel carefully arranged the Blue Willow pieces in her china closet. "You brought this all the way from Pennsylvania bouncing and jolting in trains and wagons, and not one broken teacup, not one single chipped plate," she marveled.

And now it seemed all for nothing. "I suppose the quilts protected them."

"Quilts? What quilts?"

Elizabeth gestured. "In the first trunk. You saw them when I took out the china."

"I saw muslin sheets, not quilts." Mrs. Diegel put away the last saucer and hurried over. "Well, bring them out. Let's have a look at them."

"My aunts wrapped the quilts in muslin sheets to keep them clean," Elizabeth explained as she withdrew the bundles from the trunk. She unfolded the wedding quilt and spread it upon her lap, pride a warm glow in her chest as Mrs. Diegel exclaimed in awe and delight over the Bergstrom women's handiwork. Great-Aunt Lucinda's homespun scrap Chimneys and Cornerstones quilt evoked a more subdued reaction than the elegant Double Wedding Ring, but Elizabeth was pleased and comforted by Mrs. Diegel's declaration that they were the two most beautiful and well-made quilts she had ever seen.

"The women of your family clearly take pride in their work," she said. As Elizabeth thanked her and folded the quilts, Mrs. Diegel added, "What will you take for them?"

Elizabeth let out a small laugh of surprise. "Sorry, nothing. I couldn't part with them."

"Surely there's something else you need."

"Not more than I need these quilts."

"I have a copper bathtub left over from before we had indoor plumbing. It's been in storage in the carriage house for years. Polish it up a bit and it will be as good as new."

Elizabeth hesitated, but shook her head. "I'm sorry, but no."

"Oh, come now," said Mrs. Diegel. "A young girl like yourself, a new bride no less, and you're willing to go without a good soak in the tub at the end of a long day?"

Elizabeth closed her eyes, the quilts a soft, comforting weight in her arms. She could almost feel the steam rise from the hot bath, feel the water enveloping her, bubbles tickling her toes. Then she opened her eyes. "I'm sorry. It's not enough."

"We'll see how you feel after a month without a proper bath. We'll see how your husband feels."

Elizabeth felt a lump in her throat. She shook her head and returned the folded quilts to the trunk.

"What are these two quilts compared to a hot bath?" persisted Mrs. Diegel. "You've seen my needlework. I could never make anything so lovely, but you could always make others to replace these."

"Not like these, I couldn't. Not with only a needle and thread."

"I have a sewing machine."

"Our cabin doesn't have electricity."

"This runs by a treadle."

Elizabeth paused, her hand on the latch of the trunk.

Mrs. Diegel leaned forward conspiratorially. "The bathtub, the treadle sewing machine with enough thread and fabric to get you started, and I'll throw in ten dollars. There's bound to be something else you need, something you aren't thinking of at the moment. Or maybe you'll want to buy something nice for your husband. What do you say?"

Elizabeth knew what answer she wanted to give, and she knew what the only sensible reply could be. A bathtub was not only a luxury for soaking her cares away. Henry would want it, too, perhaps more than the beautiful quilts. And how long, indeed, would he continue to find her beautiful if she had to make do with the pump at the kitchen sink? Already her nails had become ragged, the skin of her hands red and rough. Already she was not the lovely young bride he had married.

"Someday," said Elizabeth. "Someday, when our circumstances have improved, will you allow me to buy the quilts back from you?"

Mrs. Diegel considered. "I suppose that's reasonable, but I can't guarantee their condition. I intend to use them in the hotel guest rooms."

Pained by the admission, Elizabeth said, "But you will allow me to buy them back, at a fair price, when I am able?"

"Very well." Mrs. Diegel extended a hand. "It's a deal."

Elizabeth shook on it, her heart aching. It was not much of a deal. They had not agreed on a price, and the quilts might be well worn by the time she had saved up enough money to buy them back. But without that agreement, without the glimmer of hope that she might one day have the quilts restored to her, she never could have parted with them.

Outside, Lars and the porter finished loading the wagon as Elizabeth climbed back onto the seat. She knew she had done the right thing, the only sensible thing, given their circumstances, but she felt hollow inside from longing. For months she had watched as her mother, aunts, and grandmother labored over her bridal quilt, each leaving her unique imprint upon the cloth. For months she had dreamed of sleeping beneath it in the arms of her adoring husband. In her mind's eye she could still see Great-Aunt Lucinda explaining the symbolism of the Chimneys and Cornerstones quilt to little cousin Sylvia, how the quilt carried with it the love and the stead-fastness of her family, a reminder that no matter how far she journeyed from them, she would always be welcomed home to a loving embrace. But now the beautiful quilts to which the Bergstrom women had contributed their finest handiwork would grace the beds of itinerant strangers, who might admire their beauty but would never suspect what they truly represented.

She blinked back tears and rested her hand upon the letters from home in her pocket. She could not cry over quilts and china when Henry had lost his life savings and his dream. The last thing he needed was the burden of his wife's childish grief. He would be proud of her when he discovered what she had acquired to make the cabin more comfortable. She would make it as cozy a home as the farmhouse of Triumph Ranch would have been.

Lars drove the wagon back to the Jorgensen farm in silence, sparing her questions about the unexpected change in their cargo. He bypassed the farmhouse and went straight to the cabin, where he helped her unload the wagon and carry things inside. They worked quickly, mindful of the chores awaiting them. Together they wrestled the old mattress out of the cabin and replaced it with the newer one. The trunks and smaller parcels they left in the middle of the front room for Elizabeth to sort out later. Lars set up the sewing machine inside in the front room between the window and the fireplace, but he hesitated at the sight of the old copper bathtub. "Where do you want this?" he asked.

"Let's put it in the second bedroom for now," said Elizabeth, pushing open the door. Her nose wrinkled at the stale, musty-sweet odor. She should have left the door open to allow the room to air out rather than vainly try to conceal the mess. "If we get that crate out of the way, we'll have enough space."

She crossed the room to the large wooden crate beneath the window, but Lars brushed past her and took hold of it first. "I can get it."

"It looks heavy," said Elizabeth, placing a hand on the lid. "Let me help."

"No need." Lars pushed himself between Elizabeth and the crate, jostling the lid aside a few inches, enough for Elizabeth to glimpse dozens and dozens of empty glass liquor bottles piled inside.

As the sticky-sweet odor wafted forth, Elizabeth stepped back, waving her hand in front of her face. "So that's what that smell was," she said. "It must be someone's pre-Prohibition stash."

"Some fool drank away a lot of years in this place," said Lars.

"It can't be anyone in your family, or you'd know," said Elizabeth. "Drinkers think they're keeping it a secret, they think they're fooling everyone just because they get up and go to work every day, but everybody knows. They're just afraid to say anything. As long as everyone pretends everything's fine, they can pretend he's different from that drunken bum on the street corner. The only real difference is that no one's afraid to tell the bum he's a drunk. As for the other kind—well, no one thanks the person who pops the bubble of the family's collective delusion, let me tell you."

Lars was staring at her.

"I'm not talking about Henry," she hastened to add. "My father. My father's the drinker of the family."

Lars regarded her with a mixture of curiosity and surprise. "Seems like every family's got one."

Elizabeth shrugged, feeling suddenly ashamed of her spiteful, disloyal words. "I suppose so. I—I don't want you to misunderstand. He's a good man. But—you just don't know what it's like, loving someone, wanting to believe in him, and knowing that sooner or later, he's going to let you down. That's one of the reasons I agreed to move so far from home. I just don't want to see him that way anymore."

"You didn't think you'd end up in a place like this or you wouldn't have come." Lars glanced around the room. "This cabin should be torn down, every last board and nail."

"Is that any way to talk about my lovely new home?" When Lars did not respond to her attempt at levity, she said, "You know our circumstances. You know we're lucky to have a roof over our heads."

"I know Mrs. Diegel is a shrewd businesswoman and you left that hotel a far cry more miserable than you walked in." Lars hefted the crate, ropes of muscles visible through his shirtsleeves. "You should have held out for more, both from her and my mother."

He hauled the crate from the room, glass clattering. Elizabeth sighed and rested a hand upon the copper bathtub, worn out from unloading the wagon, from disappointment and uncertainty. She had done the best she could. She did not know how to haggle over prices. At her father's hotel, he decided what to charge for a night's stay, for a meal, for any service a guest could imagine. He stuck a price tag on things and accepted that amount from the guest in cash or credit. Nothing in her life had prepared her for what she had faced today. Henry could do the work he had signed on for, but Elizabeth had no idea how to be a poor farmhand's wife.

She thought then of Mrs. Jorgensen, of the work Elizabeth needed to finish that day before she could return to the cabin and the tasks awaiting her there. She roused herself, left the letters from home on the chair in the front room, and joined Lars in the wagon, empty now except for the crate of bottles.

"I wonder what your brother will think when he sees those," said Elizabeth. "Will he suspect the farmhands?"

"By the look of them, those bottles have been empty for years," said Lars shortly. "I don't see what's to be gained by letting my brother know about them."

"Agreed," said Elizabeth. She saw no point in getting anyone in trouble. It was not as if she and Lars had discovered an illicit still, the farmhands gathered around filling flasks and hollow canes.

Mrs. Jorgensen put Elizabeth to work in the garden almost as soon as the wagon pulled up to the barn. Mary Katherine and her daughters were already there, and their cheerful company softened the ache in Elizabeth's heart. Before long they returned to the kitchen to help prepare supper. This time when the men came in, Henry took her aside, kissed her softly, and asked how her errand to the Grand Union Hotel had gone. She was torn between relief that he had not brushed her aside again and regret that he had chosen that particular question. "Mrs. Diegel was helpful," she began, but Oscar had sat down and was waiting to say grace, so she said in a quick whisper that she had much more to tell him when they had time.

She would rather show him, anyway. She hoped to leave as soon as she finished tidying the kitchen as she had the previous evening, but as if to make up for the time off she had been granted earlier that day, Mrs. Jorgensen kept her busy until dusk. When she was finally dismissed, she ran most of the way back to the cabin and raced to unpack the trunks before Henry arrived. She put their own fresh sheets on the almost-new mattress and tossed the larger of the two worn quilts over it, pausing for, a moment to take in the unusual star design. She had never seen the pattern before, nor that of the second quilt, which she folded and draped over the foot of the bed. In the front room, she lit one of the hurricane lamps, stacked the pewter dishes in the cupboard, and put the teakettle on the stove. Twenty minutes later, her bustle of cleaning came to an abrupt halt as Henry came home. From the doorway, he took in the sight of their own trunks, open in the center of the front room and spilling forth unfamiliar contents. "More castoffs from the Jorgensens?" he asked tiredly as he shut the cabin door behind him.

"No, these belong to us," said Elizabeth, and explained how she and Mrs. Diegel had traded goods.

Henry stood in the center of the room, fixed in place by shock and anger. "You gave away your family's wedding gifts?"

"I traded them for other things we needed more." Elizabeth searched his face for some clue to explain his reaction. She had expected him to be proud of her pragmatic sacrifice. "I didn't think you cared about china or silver plate. I thought we'd be better off able to cook for ourselves and bathe. Was I wrong?"

"No." He dropped wearily into a chair and tugged off his boots. "Of course not. You were right."

"Then why are you so angry?"

"I'm not angry with you." He rose, went to the kitchen, and pumped water into the sink. He scrubbed his face and hands, drying himself on one of their last clean rags. "I'm just sorry. Sorry that it has come to this. Remember what I said to you on the train? You should always be surrounded by beauty. Look what I've done to you. I've taken you from your family to live in a hovel and work at someone else's beck and call."

"It's not that bad," said Elizabeth. "I'm not waiting hand and foot on a spoiled lady of leisure. Mrs. Jorgensen doesn't ask me to work any harder than she does herself."

She did not expect that to satisfy Henry but it was the truth. He left her standing in the kitchen and disappeared into the bedroom, but he almost immediately emerged, his expression twisted and pained. "That old quilt is still on the bed."

"I know. It's fairly clean, and the pattern is nice. Once I can give it a proper washing, it will be lovely."

"The other one's even worse. It's full of holes and the stuffing's falling out."

"I can mend the holes. It will still keep us warm if the star quilt isn't enough."

"Where's our wedding quilt? That one your mother and all your aunts made, the one with the rings and the flowers?"

Elizabeth did not reply.

"All you've talked about for months was how much you wanted to see that wedding quilt on our bed." A muscle in Henry's jaw tightened and relaxed. "Tomorrow you'll go back to the Grand Union Hotel and give back whatever you traded for it."

"I can't," said Elizabeth sharply. "As much as I want my quilts back, we need the bathtub more. And she gave me ten dollars cash. We're going to need that, Henry. Until we get back on our feet and find our way clear of this, we're going to need it."

Henry sighed and rubbed hard at his jaw as if working the pain and disappointment out of it. "There's only one way out of this, Elizabeth, and that's for you to go home to your parents."

"I won't accept that. We'll find a way, Henry. This is not the way things are always going to be. In less than a year, we'll have enough money saved for the train fare home. What's one year? We'll go back to Pennsylvania and work Two Bears Farm with your family the way we always thought we would. They'll be so happy to have us back. And—and I'll be glad, too. California is lovely, but really, we will be much better off back home, with our families."

The bleakness in his eyes told her he did not believe it. Without another word, he disappeared into the bedroom again. She heard clothing drop to the floor and bedsprings creak. For a moment she hoped he would call out to her to come join him, playfully asking her to help him test out the almost new mattress and the clean linen sheets she had wisely held back from Mrs. Diegel. But he said nothing, and all the wistful hope and expectation drained from her like fragrance from a pressed flower.

She stood there listening until the steady rhythm of his breathing told her he slept. She ought to join him. She needed her rest, too; she ought to save the kerosene. But instead she picked up the letters from home and sank into the rocking chair to read. Her mother's letter, written two days after their departure, was full of wistful encouragement, fond recollections of the wedding celebration, and reminders to send out thank-you notes for the lovely gifts she and Henry had received. Tears sprang into Elizabeth's eyes, but she laughed softly, imagining how she would phrase those notes: "Dear Great-Aunt Lydia, thank you so much for the soup tureen. I'm sure the prospective buyers of Oakwood Glen will appreciate the beauty it adds to the table of the Grand Union Hotel."

The second letter was from little cousin Sylvia, whose accusatory tone had survived the filter of Aunt Eleanor's transcription: "Dear Elizabeth, I hope you had a good trip. I hope you like

California. I don't think you will like it as much as home, but I hope it is nice. I love you. I miss you. I hope you can come home soon to visit. Please bring me an orange from your tree when you come. Henry does not have to come. Love, Sylvia."

Aunt Eleanor had added a postscript: "Sylvia is happy for you in her own way. I'm sure you understand. We all miss you and hope it won't be long before you and Henry can visit. When you have a spare moment, Sylvia would love to hear from you. I hope ranch life isn't too busy to allow you time to write home, because we eagerly await news of your California adventure. I hope Triumph Ranch is everything you dreamed it would be. Love always, Aunt Eleanor."

Elizabeth returned the letters to their envelopes and closed her eyes. Aunt Eleanor had struck closer to the heart of the truth than she would ever know. Triumph Ranch was everything Elizabeth had dreamed, but it was no more than a dream, vanished now that she had awakened.

She did not have the heart to put that into a letter.

Soon Sylvia and the others would receive the letters Elizabeth had mailed the previous day, the last letters she had written in happy anticipation of reaching Triumph Ranch at last. Sylvia would expect more. Elizabeth's mother would expect more. Elizabeth could not put off responding forever. The family would worry and— she was struck by the sudden horror of realization—they might send someone to California to be sure she and Henry were safe. She could not lie to them—but how could she tell them the truth?

Her next letter home would have to wait until she knew how to write it.

When Elizabeth climbed into bed beside Henry, she tentatively snuggled into the crook of his arm. Instead of holding her close, he drew his arm free and rolled over onto his side, his back to her, never waking, or so she told herself. She lay on her back and looked up at the shadowed ceiling until she fell asleep.

❧

1904

As her children grew, Isabel resolved that they would have everything she had been denied as a young girl—an education, friends, a loving and happy home. Thanks to Miguel, they never lacked for the latter. He showered them with love and praise, and they returned his affection in equal measure. Their eyes shone when they knew they had pleased him; his pride in their achievements spurred them on to work hard at school and help their mother around the house, for which Isabel was grateful. Her children had what mattered most, she knew, but she also wanted them to have the same material things their friends had, and that cost money.

When the children were old enough, Isabel took a job as a housecleaner, starting with the few families who could afford one in the Arboles Valley and adding new clients as far away as Oxnard as one satisfied customer after another recommended her to friends. She arranged her schedule so she could see the children off to school before leaving for work and return home in time to greet them at the door after classes. In the summer, she worked mornings and traded babysitting with a friend from church who worked afternoons. The long, exhausting hours were worth it when she saw Carlos running across a grassy field in new, sturdy shoes, or Rosa laughing and playing in a new cotton dress and bright hair ribbons.

Isabel had no words to describe how she adored her children. Every night she prayed for God to watch over them; every week she lit a candle before a picture of the Blessed Mother, the Lady of Guadalupe, and prayed for her guidance and wisdom. She could not seek advice from her own mother, so she would turn to the Lord. It was all she could do. She had only a child's memory of how her mother had raised her, and her father's example was not one she wished to follow. Some days she did not know what to do or what to say so that her bright and lively children would grow into good and faithful adults. Some days she thought she ought to just stay out of the way rather than risk interfering with their intrinsic goodness. Some days she wanted to do nothing more than stand back and watch, basking in happiness as her children learned and grew.

But on other days, she longed to grasp hold of them and keep them close by her side, where she could keep a watchful eye over them. Rosa worried her more than Carlos—sweet, happy Carlos, so much like his father, forgiving and patient. Rosa was willful and intelligent, quick to anger, quick to laugh. She was also very beautiful, and becoming more so with each passing year. Her father joked that she would be a heartbreaker one day. Isabel did not doubt it. The question that troubled her most was whose heart would she shatter.

When Rosa was fourteen and Carlos twelve, they came home from school on a mid-February afternoon munching candy hearts and carrying paper sacks stuffed full of valentines. Rosa ran off straight to her room and shut her door. "Is she upset?" Isabel asked Carlos as he plunked his book bag on the kitchen table and reached for the plate of cookies.

"No," he said, disgusted. "She's just crazy."

"Carlos."

"It's true. She's acting like a dumb girl all because some boy gave her a flower."

"Don't call your sister dumb," Isabel said automatically, but her heart clenched. She left Carlos to his snack and rapped softly on her daughter's door. "Rosa?"

"What is it, Mami?" Rosa called from within.

Isabel opened the door. Rosa sat up in her bed and scrambled to hide something beneath her pillow. "Carlos said you were given a flower at school today."

Rosa shrugged dismissively. "Lots of girls got them. It's Valentine's Day."

Though she kept her eyes downcast, she could not hide her smile, or her glow.

"Let me see it," said Isabel sternly.

Frowning, Rosa reached beneath her pillow and handed her mother a long-stemmed pink carnation, identical to those she had seen for sale in the Arboles Grocery. Although slender pink-and-white ribbons were tied around the stem, no card or note was attached to reveal the identity of Rosa's admirer.

"Who gave this to you?"

"Someone left it in my valentine bag when I was away from my desk. There's no name."

"I can see there's no name. Who gave it to you?"

"I guess . . . it could have been any of the boys."

Isabel leveled a hard gaze at her daughter, recognizing the evasive words of a girl who did not want to confess the truth but was as yet unwilling to lie to her mother. Thank God she still had enough sense for that, enough respect. Isabel and Miguel could still nip this nonsense in the bud.

"I wonder what your father will think of your answer."

Rosa shrugged as if she were only mildly curious, but she bit her lower lip and glanced at the paper bag stuffed full of valentines. Isabel knew at once that the card for the flower was inside.

She resisted the urge to snatch up the bag and search through the valentines until she found the proof she needed. The Arboles School had only two classrooms, twenty-three students. It would not be difficult to figure out who had sent the flower. Carlos probably knew. Isabel knew and liked all the boys Rosa's age, but there were other children she did not know. It did not matter, however, whether she liked Rosa's unknown admirer. Rosa was too young to be accepting gifts and attention from boys.

She left Rosa alone to start her homework. Later, after the children had gone to bed, she told Miguel that she was astonished the teachers allowed tokens of affection to be exchanged in the classroom. "It's a valentine," said Miguel mildly. "At that age, a flower is a token of friendship, nothing more. It's no wonder the boys admire Rosa. She's a lovely girl, just like you were at her age."

"I was not as beautiful as Rosa," said Isabel, "but I was far more obedient. If I had come home with a flower from a boy, my parents would have been incensed."

"Maybe the boys knew this and that's why they didn't dare send you any flowers. Otherwise I'm sure they would have thrown bouquets at your feet, and not only on Valentine's Day."

Isabel was too troubled to be charmed by her husband's flattery. "We are talking about our daughter. Miguel, she's growing up too quickly. We've given her too much freedom." *I've given her too much freedom,* she thought. *I wanted her to have my share as well as her own.*

Miguel smiled and kissed her on the cheek. "You were just as beautiful as Rosa, but you're right, you were also more demure. Rosa is a good girl. Let her have her secret admirer. Nothing bad will come of it."

But Isabel brooded over this unknown boy who had turned her daughter secretive. As the days passed, Rosa had taken to smiling to herself at unexpected moments—while washing dishes, folding clothes. She gazed out windows dreamily when she was supposed to be studying.

Finally Isabel could bear it no longer. One evening as Rosa sat at the kitchen table with a half smile on her lips, staring at the fire instead of the schoolbook open before her, Isabel asked, "Did you ever find out who gave you the flower?"

Her question snatched Rosa from her reverie. "What, Mami?"

"The flower," said Isabel. "Who was it from?"

Rosa took a quick breath. "I don't know," she said. "Maybe it wasn't really for me. Whoever he is, maybe he put it in my bag by mistake. I sit next to Julia, you know. She's very pretty."

"I see," said Isabel. She gestured to Rosa's book. "Finish up. It's almost time for bed."

She knew Miguel would tell her not to worry, that Rosa was fourteen and a half now and many years away from wanting to carry on with boys. She was flattered by the admiration, nothing more. It was a harmless crush that would swiftly fade unless they made a fuss.

But Isabel knew differently. First her daughter had kept a secret from her, and then she had lied. Rosa knew who had given her the flower, but she did not want her mother to know.

Chapter Seven

1925

Elizabeth was grateful for the work that kept her too busy to write a letter home, work that filled up her hours and exhausted her so that she was too numb to feel fully the pain of her disappointment. For weeks she carried out the tasks Mrs. Jorgensen assigned her without complaint, as if she were watching someone else haul water and sweep floors and cook three meals a day for fourteen. As her hands grew calloused and shoulders strong, she observed the changes in herself with detached disbelief, as if a beloved character in a favorite book suddenly began saying and doing things that had never happened the other times she had read the story. This wasn't right, she thought as she went through her day, from the time she hurried to the yellow farmhouse before the sun had peeked over the eastern hills until she trudged back to the cabin as the last rays of light disappeared behind the Santa Monica Mountains to the west. Something had gone terribly wrong, but if she just went along and made do with her circumstances for a little while, eventually the error would be corrected and everything would return to its proper course.

After the shock wore off, she realized that she would have to make do for much longer than she had imagined when she had made Henry promise not to send her home without him. She found comfort in knowing that their exile couldn't last more than a year or two, and at the end of that time, Henry could resume his rightful place with his father and brothers at Two Bears Farm. From the Nelsons' house it was only a short, pleasant walk through the woods to Elm Creek Manor and all the familiar, beautiful places she had loved since childhood. Knowing what awaited her, Elizabeth resolved to endure any hardship, any humiliation, until their homecoming. She did not need Great-Aunt Lucinda's Chimneys and Cornerstones quilt to remind her of the welcoming fires on the hearth back home.

In the meantime, she resolved to make the best of things so that Henry would know she did not blame him for their circumstances. After all, she had wanted an adventure, and in the years to come, she would certainly be able to say she had found one.

As the weeks passed, the days took on a sameness, a pattern of daily chores and mealtimes that altered only in the work performed and the food prepared. Even that showed little variation. Sundays were not as restful as she had thought they would be when Mary Katherine had arranged for her to have the day off, for even though she could set aside the usual work of the week, she still had her own housekeeping to attend to, and Henry. On Sundays more than any other time of the week, she missed Elm Creek Manor, where all the women of the family pitched in and many hands made light work. Ruefully she told herself that she was fortunate that the cabin was so small, and that she had so little furniture to dust and linens to wash.

It was a small blessing, but fortunately not the only one Elizabeth was able to find. The Arboles Valley was truly as beautiful a place as she could have dreamed, with warm sunshine and balmy breezes that felt like a gentle benediction, a reassurance that all would be well in time. High, rolling foothills and low mountains sheltered the green and fertile land, in which it seemed any seed planted would flourish. The mornings were cool and misty, which Elizabeth supposed was a consequence of their nearness to the ocean. Sometimes she stood on the front porch of the cabin, looked toward the western mountains, and imagined waves crashing on the beach miles beyond them. Her heart stirred with the memory of happiness whenever she remembered how close the ocean was even though she could not see it, and how bracing the winds off the Pacific had been when she waded in the water for the first time. Sometimes she still felt the promise of prosperity in the air, although she did not speak of it to Henry, who seemed to have forgotten he had ever admired any part of the Arboles Valley.

Triumph Ranch was not quite as it had been described in the land agent's papers, and although this was the least of the deceptions played upon them, it still caught Elizabeth by surprise. The Jorgensen farm was not a cattle ranch at all, but a farm much like the Nelsons' back home, except that the Jorgensens grew barley and alfalfa instead of corn and wheat. Instead of herds of cattle, there were flocks of sheep, and a large, thriving apricot orchard on the southeastern portion of the property. Once Elizabeth remarked to Henry that she thought those particular crops and livestock suited his experience better than cattle would have done, but he merely returned a silent, bemused stare. She felt foolish and did not bother to explain that she had not meant to suggest that they were better off than if Triumph Ranch had been real. But perhaps, in the long run, they would be. They had been cheated and humiliated, but as a result, they would be going home to Pennsylvania. They were young enough to recover from a mistake even as great as this one, with the help of their families. In the years to come, they would look back with fond amusement upon their brief adventure in California and thank God they had returned to the people and land they so loved.

Elizabeth tried to say as much to Henry, but he cut her off abruptly whenever she said or did anything that smacked of optimism. Before long, she stopped trying, bewildered by his behavior. Would he prefer for her to mope and wail about how miserable she was, how homesick and lonely? She thought she was being a good wife by pointing out the bright side of things, especially the transitory nature of their predicament. He did not seem to hear her.

Elizabeth was grateful for Mary Katherine's company while she worked, even though she could never replace Henry as a confidant. Mary Katherine was friendly and kind, and if she complained too often about her mother-in-law, she did not seem to mind when Elizabeth did not join in. For her part, Mrs. Jorgensen remained as formidable a woman as she had first appeared, forthright and demanding, with no patience for jokes or teasing. Elizabeth quickly learned to treat her with respect and deference even if it meant biting her tongue rather than defend herself when Mrs. Jorgensen criticized the way she scalded a pan or ironed a shirt. Her patience for the sake of household harmony paid off, for the more Elizabeth proved herself to be a capable worker, the more Mrs. Jorgensen trusted her, rewarding her with more important, more interesting responsibilities.

Working so closely with the Jorgensen family, she learned a great deal about them in a short time. The farm had been in the family for three generations. Mrs. Jorgensen's grandfather, a Norwegian immigrant who had settled in Minnesota, bought the land after his physician diagnosed him with consumption and told him a milder climate would ease the suffering of his final years. The doctor's remedy succeeded so well that he lived another three decades in vigorous good health and might have continued to do so for many years to come if he had not been thrown from a horse and struck his head on a rock two weeks after his sixty-second birthday. But until his untimely death, he had lived so robustly and had touted the attributes of his new home so tirelessly that other Norwegian friends and relations had been encouraged to settle on nearby farms, creating a Norwegian colony within the Arboles Valley. United by kinship and a common language, they mostly kept to themselves. Only in the most recent generation had the old mistrust of strangers begun to fade.

Because the farm was so remote, the Nelsons had little opportunity to meet any of the neighbors, who often lived as much as a mile away. Elizabeth expected that would change in the years to come, but perhaps not before she and Henry returned to Pennsylvania. A frequent topic of dinner conversation was the sale—or rumors of upcoming sales—of nearby farmland to developers like Mr. Milton and Mr. Donovan. Oscar Jorgensen received a few offers from time to time, offers so good he wouldn't have believed them if he had not seen them in black and white with his own eyes. Developers encouraged him to sell the land, buy a cheaper farm in another part of southern California, and pocket a hefty profit, but Oscar refused. He would not sell the farm his father and grandfather had given their lives to cultivate so that their descendants would prosper. Sometimes over breakfast he eyed his two daughters as if wondering whether they would hold on, or if they would be the generation to sell out.

Strangely, or so Elizabeth thought, Lars never offered an opinion on whether the Jorgensen family should accept one of the offers for their farm. Elizabeth would have thought his opinion mattered, because surely the farm belonged to him as much as to Oscar, the younger of the two brothers. Mrs. Jorgensen, on the other hand, could not conceal her feelings on the subject, and it was readily apparent that she did not share Mrs. Diegel's opinion that these new housing developments would allow the valley to thrive and prosper. Elizabeth suspected she hated to see the farmland give way to streets and houses, because whenever someone mentioned

Oakwood Glen or Meadowbrook Hills, her mouth pinched in a tight line and she drew in a sharp breath as if she expected to smell something foul. It reminded Elizabeth of the expression Grandmother Bergstrom assumed when little cousin Sylvia and her sister Claudia argued at the supper table. Elizabeth understood Mrs. Jorgensen's feelings; the folks at Elm Creek Manor would not like it if the Nelson family sold off their land and forty families built houses there, all closely packed together. Their rural seclusion would be gone forever, and the advantage of many new potential friends close by could not begin to compensate for that.

Although Elizabeth saw the other hired hands only in passing, she learned enough about them to know that Henry worked twice as hard as anyone except Oscar and Lars. He plunged himself into his work with a ferocity that worried Elizabeth, as if the unfinished tasks were an enemy he meant to wrestle into submission. At the close of day he was so exhausted that he fell asleep almost as soon as he drew the quilt over himself, leaving Elizabeth disappointed and lonely beside him, hungry for a kind word, a gentle caress. She missed those nights on the train when he could not bear to let her go.

At those times, alone in the dark with her husband by her side, she missed her family and Elm Creek Manor so much she did not think she would be able to bear it. She even found herself longing for her parents' apartment at the hotel in Harrisburg and her own familiar room, which she had shared with her sister until she was sixteen, when her sister married. Their home had always seemed cramped and stuffily formal compared with the gracious country elegance of Elm Creek Manor, but it was a palace compared with the miserable cabin. She wished she had not taken for granted the comforts of home—or the presence of her family.

But as remote as home and family were, Henry seemed more distant still. Elizabeth told herself that their honeymoon had spoiled her, and that it was unreasonable to expect Henry to be her constant companion when there was so much work to be done. Even if he were the owner of Triumph Ranch, he would not have been able to grant her that. And yet, she had expected things to be different between them. Sometimes she wished they were still on the train heading west, with everything before them.

On nights when sleep eluded her, Elizabeth wrapped herself in the older quilt and settled in the front room with her scrap basket and needle and thread. The unexpected turn their journey had taken had not lessened Elizabeth's desire to sew a patchwork album of her memories. To the scraps Mrs. Diegel had given her, Elizabeth had added a few squares cut from an old bedsheet, worn so thin from use that it was almost translucent. Worn cotton from the cabin contrasted sharply with the silk scarf from Venice Beach and the elegant chintz floral from the Grand Union Hotel, but she was determined to include them in her quilt, determined to try to make something useful and even beautiful from them. The fabric was good, sturdy, printed muslin, and use had only made it softer. The pink rosebuds were faded, but the blue background was the lovely shade of the California sky on a sunny afternoon. Those patches would always remind Elizabeth of her first night on Triumph Ranch, and whatever else befell her until she returned safely home, she did not believe her quilt would be complete without them. In the months to come she would do her best to collect more appealing scraps—something newer, or prettier, or fancier—but faded cotton was what she had and it would do for now.

Just as the fabrics she gathered for her quilt had changed, so too had the pattern altered in her mind's eye. She felt herself drawn toward a Postage Stamp design, a straightforward arrangement of two-inch squares in horizontal rows, soothing in its simplicity. Artistic as well as pragmatic factors made a Postage Stamp quilt the appropriate choice. Her fabric scraps were too small for large star points or sweeping arcs or background panels for appliqué, and the use of so many different prints and colors almost required her to use a simple design or the quilt would be so dizzyingly busy no one could possibly sleep well beneath it. A Postage Stamp quilt required only simple squares and straight seams, making it the perfect sewing project for dim light and late nights when she wanted her thoughts to drift, when repetitive tasks would help ease her into sleep. She also found a certain ironic poetry in the name, considering that the troubles had begun with a visit to the Arboles Valley post office, and the only way Elizabeth could speak to the people she loved most in the world was through the mail. But most of all, she found comfort in reducing the troubles of her day to simple shapes, to cutting and shaping the upheaval in her life into simple two-inch squares.

Perhaps as autumn approached she could gather scraps of cloth made from the wool of the sheep Henry tended. Better things were coming. They had to be.

When the men finished sowing the barley fields, Oscar split the crew between tending the fields and caring for the sheep. Lars taught Henry how to tend the animals, what commands to call to the border collies to get them to round up the flock, how to spot potential hazards and avoid them. On those days Henry came home at night giving off the thick smell of sweat and sheep. When Elizabeth peeled off his clothes and ordered him into the hot bath she had waiting for him, he sank into the tub and closed his eyes without a word.

Elizabeth chewed the inside of her lip as she watched him from the doorway. She had hoped for at least a thank-you or a kiss on the cheek. Putting aside her hurt feelings, she rolled up her sleeves, knelt beside the tub, and picked up a washcloth and a bar of soap. "You're filthy," she told him as she washed his shoulders and neck, working the knots out of his muscles. "And you stink, too."

"Thanks," he said dryly, sinking deeper into the tub, eyes closed.

Encouraged by the brief glimpse of his old humor, she rinsed the washcloth, soaped it up again, and moved on to his chest. He rested his head against the rim of the tub and breathed out a barely audible moan. Emboldened, she worked her way lower, down the firm washboard of his waist to his hips, to his thighs—

Suddenly Henry shot upright, grasping the sides of the tub. "What are you doing?"

Startled, Elizabeth fell back onto her heels. "I'm sorry—I—I was only trying to help—"

He reached for a towel, bolted from the tub, and wrapped the towel around his waist, all without looking at her. "I'm going to bed."

Stung, Elizabeth watched him go. So this is it, she thought. This is married life. He had grown tired of her already.

They had spent their first few Sundays repairing the cabin and making it more comfortable. When there was nothing more toward that end they could do on their budget, Elizabeth resolved that they would enjoy their next day off. Whether they spent it relaxing on their own front porch or venturing out to explore the Arboles Valley, she didn't care as long as they passed the day together. If only they could spend some time enjoying each other's company instead of racing from one chore to the next, Henry would remember the hope and confidence that had brought them to California, and he would be affectionate again.

On Friday morning as they hurried to the Jorgensen home, Elizabeth proposed a picnic. "We could explore the Salto Canyon," she said. "I'll make us a lunch, and we can look for that waterfall Mary Katherine told us about."

"I can't," said Henry. "I have to work."

"But it's Sunday."

"The animals need to be tended on Sundays, too. Oscar offered to pay me extra if I'd take on the job, and you know I can't afford to turn away work." Henry spared her a glance. "But you should go. Ask Mary Katherine and the girls. They could show you the waterfall themselves and you wouldn't have to search for it."

"Maybe I'll do that." A spark of anger kindled within her. She didn't care about the waterfall. The search was part of the fun. She wanted to be with her husband. But if he didn't want her, she was not going to sit around the cabin every Sunday pining for him.

She gave him until lunchtime to reconsider, but when he seemed to have forgotten the invitation, she asked Mary Katherine if she and her daughters were free to go on a picnic Sunday afternoon. Mary Katherine suggested they go to Safari World instead. "It will be my treat," she added. "I haven't taken the girls in far too long."

Elizabeth agreed, curious to meet Charlie the movie-star lion, who woke her at least two mornings out of every seven with a threatening roar that made a shiver run down her spine each time it jolted her awake. When she announced her plans to Henry, it was with a hint of defiance. If he did not want her company, there were others who welcomed it. But without a hint of jealousy or regret, he told her to have a good time and that he would see her at home for supper.

On Sunday, long after Henry had left for work with nothing more for his bride than a quick kiss on the cheek, Elizabeth met Mary Katherine, Annalise, and Margaret at the Jorgensens' garage, where Mary Katherine was tolerantly accepting some last-minute instructions from Lars about how to handle the temperamental automobile. "I'm going to the post office tomorrow," he said to Elizabeth, "if you have any letters you'd like me to send."

Elizabeth thought of the letters to Sylvia and Aunt Eleanor she had struggled to write and could not bring herself to mail, full as they were of half-truths. "I have two I can finish tonight," she replied. "I'll bring them to breakfast tomorrow."

"You'll probably end up riding along to the post office," said Mary Katherine after she had turned east onto the main road. "Or running the errand on your own. Mother Jorgensen doesn't like Lars to go to the Barclays' alone. He and John don't get along. Do you know how to drive?"

"A little." Back in Harrisburg, Gerald had allowed her to take the wheel of his roadster, but only on a little-used stretch of road on the outskirts of town or on the broad, cobblestone circular drive in front of his parents' mansion. She had not thought of Gerald since Christmas, since Henry's proposal. She wondered how he had reacted to the news of her marriage. Gerald probably would not have tired of her so soon, judging by how often he encouraged her to drive that roadster into the seclusion of the countryside. How she had enjoyed teasing him by pretending not to know why he wanted to drive so far from prying eyes, and then turning around and driving them back to the city without setting the parking brake even once.

Gerald had probably moved on to another girl by now, one of the Dumb Doras in fringed dresses who clung to his arm at the speaks, a girl who wouldn't mind if he pulled over the roadster for a nip from a silver flask and a petting party.

"If you've driven only a little," said Mary Katherine as she pulled over to the side of the road, "you need the practice more than I do."

Elizabeth put up a show of protest but gladly took the wheel when Mary Katherine insisted they trade seats. Mary Katherine coached her through the unfamiliar controls, and soon they were jolting down the dirt road, Annalise and Margaret shrieking with delight in the backseat. They turned south where a road cut through the Jorgensen farm, passing newly sown fields and hills dotted with grazing sheep. Her attention on driving, Elizabeth caught only a glimpse of the high, rocky bluffs that marked the eastern edge of the valley and Jorgensen land. Before long, the southern road linked up with the road she and Henry had taken in Lars's wagon little more than a month before.

"Turn right here," Mary Katherine instructed, almost too late for Elizabeth to make the turn. They headed west, away from the Norwegian Grade and toward the Grand Union Hotel. Elizabeth had a sudden vision of Mrs. Diegel setting the long redwood dining table with her Blue Willow wedding china and had to quickly make herself think of something else.

"Turn left, turn left," Mary Katherine shrieked as they crossed through an intersection with a dirt road. Elizabeth yanked hard on the steering wheel and made the turn with a foot or two to spare. "Sorry," Mary Katherine gasped, clutching her seat with one hand and her hat with the other. "I forget you don't know the way. I didn't mean to take us on such a wild ride."

"What do you mean?" said Elizabeth innocently. "I always drive like this."

She caught Mary Katherine's eye and they laughed.

"We're almost to Uncle Lars's farm," Annalise sang out.

Elizabeth threw Mary Katherine a questioning glance. "It used to be his farm," Mary Katherine quickly explained. "He sold it long ago, years before I married Oscar. Now it's—well, you'll see in a moment."

The car climbed to the top of a low rise, and as it rumbled downhill, Elizabeth saw rows and rows of newly dug foundations and houses spread out before them, some only half complete, sprouting up like a strange experimental crop between furrows of freshly paved, blacktop roads.

"Welcome to Meadowbrook Hills," announced Mary Katherine as they approached.

Construction workers raised wooden frames for one-story dwellings as men in suits and ladies in smart dresses and heels wandered from one plot to another guided by real estate agents in loosened neckties. Bulldozers and hammers created such a din that Annalise and Margaret covered their ears, and the real estate agents were clearly shouting to be heard by the customers on the tour. The well-dressed couples carried themselves with so much carefree self-assurance that Elizabeth understood at once why Mrs. Jorgensen had suspected the Nelsons intended to be among them. No one would mistake them for prospective residents of a fashionable new neighborhood now.

"All this was Jorgensen land once," said Mary Katherine. "Everything from Moorpark Road to that hill. In his will, Oscar's father divided the farm and left one half to each of his sons."

"And Lars sold his half to developers?" It made no sense. Why would he sell his own land only to become foreman of his brother's farm?

"Oh, no. Mother Jorgensen wouldn't let him in the house if he had. He sold to the Fraisers, but they went broke in the drought a few years ago. They sold the land to the developers." Mary Katherine shook her head and sighed. "Lars tried to buy it back, but the developers beat his offer. When Mother Jorgensen found out what the new owners intended to do with those lovely, fertile fields, she vowed that she would never forgive them. Of course, I suppose the Fraisers don't know how much Mother Jorgensen despises them, and if they did, they wouldn't care. They moved out of the valley as soon as the sale was final."

"It's a shame Lars couldn't buy back the farm after he changed his mind." Elizabeth felt a deep pang of sympathy for Lars, who despite his taciturn reserve seemed to be a decent, respectable man. "I suppose the price had gone up since he sold to the Fraisers."

"Oh, that money was long gone. He invested it poorly." Inclining her head slightly toward the backseat with a look of warning, Mary Katherine extended her thumb and pinkie and made a tippling gesture her daughters could not see. "Prohibition was the best possible thing in the world for some people."

"I see." Elizabeth suddenly remembered the crate of empty liquor bottles she had discovered in the cabin and how disparagingly Lars had spoken of the man who drank away so many years there. She never would have guessed he was describing himself. She wanted to ask how Lars had come to such a bad pass, but she doubted Mary Katherine would reveal much in front of her daughters.

"All this happened long before I met Oscar," Mary Katherine said. "By the time I came to the Arboles Valley, all that land belonged to the Fraisers."

Surprised, Elizabeth said, "I assumed you were born and raised here, like the Jorgensens."

"Doesn't Mother Jorgensen *wish*," said Mary Katherine with a laugh. "I'm a Reilly, one of the Oxnard Reillys. My father made his fortune in sugar. Perhaps you've heard of the Reilly sugar beet? My father developed the variety himself. It has the highest yield of sugar of any sugar beet ever grown."

Mary Katherine regarded her so hopefully that Elizabeth hated to shake her head. "I'm sorry. I'm not familiar with the sugar industry."

Disappointed, Mary Katherine shrugged. "Well, you're new to this part of the country. Everyone from Oxnard to Los Angeles knows of the Reilly family, but of course that didn't matter to

Oscar's mother. She nearly wept when he told her he intended to marry me. She wanted so badly for him to marry a local girl who knew the local ways. She's never quite forgiven me for being an outsider and stealing her son's affections." She shifted to face the backseat. "I don't think I need to tell you girls not to repeat that to anyone."

"No, Mama," said Annalise indignantly. Margaret shook her head emphatically.

"I probably shouldn't speak so freely in front of them," Mary Katherine remarked, turning back around to face front. "It's just so difficult sometimes with so few other ladies around to chat with. My friends told me I was crazy to move out here to the country, but I was head over heels for Oscar and wouldn't listen to reason. I still am, and I still don't." She laughed. "That's one reason why I'm so glad you came to the valley. It puts my heart at ease to have a friend so near."

Elizabeth smiled, pleased that Mary Katherine claimed her as a friend, but she could not help thinking of someone else who might have been grateful for Mary Katherine's company. "Rosa Barclay isn't far away."

"I suppose not, but Rosa isn't exactly someone a girl can drop in on for coffee and a chat, is she?"

"What do you mean?"

Mary Katherine shrugged as if the answer was so obvious, the only mystery was why anyone would pose the question. "The Barclays keep to themselves."

"Is that their choice?"

Mary Katherine gave her a speculative look. "Well, I don't know exactly. Why do you ask?"

"It seems strange to me that John Barclay would run the post office out of his house if he craved solitude."

Mary Katherine hesitated. "I never thought of that. I suppose . . .

I suppose it's fair to say that their isolation isn't entirely of their own choosing. But don't judge us too harshly. We have good reason to leave them alone. John Barclay is so unpleasant even on his best days, and Rosa—well, it breaks your heart just to look in her eyes."

Elizabeth knew exactly what she meant.

"I don't think anyone means to be unkind, but it's hard not to be suspicious, and perhaps even fearful, when so much death and misfortune have beset that poor family." Mary Katherine clasped her hands together in her lap and gazed out the window at the construction site as they passed. "Some people say Rosa and John are doing something to bring on their children's illnesses—poison, or bad food, or even simple neglect. Others say it's God's will, and that He must be punishing Rosa or John for some terrible sin the rest of us can only imagine. I know that one of John's sisters died of a wasting illness as a young girl, so maybe it *is* a problem with their water, as some people think."

For someone who claimed to have few friends to chat with, Mary Katherine kept herself well informed regarding the opinions of her neighbors. "And what do you think?"

"I can't believe Rosa would ever harm her children," declared Mary Katherine. "She grieves every day for those lost babies. If anyone is to blame—and I'm not saying anyone is—I would look to John. If bitterness in a man's heart can poison a child, then he's the guilty party."

"Mr. Barclay poisoned his babies?" exclaimed Annalise in horror.

"Of course not! It's just an expression." Mary Katherine rolled her eyes at Elizabeth. "This is how rumors get started. Mark my words, the next time you go to the Arboles Grocery, someone will whisper in your ear that the sheriff found ten bottles of poison buried in the Barclays' barley field."

Elizabeth smiled and drove on.

Soon they left Meadowbrook Hills behind and reached the edge of the town, where Mary Katherine instructed Elizabeth to turn south. Accustomed to her guide's last-minute warnings, Elizabeth had slowed the car in anticipation as they approached the intersection and made the turn easily. In the backseat, the girls made noises of disappointment as they failed to be sent careening from one side of the leather seat to the other.

They drove south down Ventura Boulevard until they arrived at a long, low building with four-foot-tall letters spelling out HANNE-MAN'S SAFARI WORLD on the peak of the roof, which had been covered in thatch to give it a rustic appearance. Automobiles filled the parking lot, and a line of families with young children and couples holding hands snaked along the sidewalk to the front gate. They joined the end of the line, and when they reached the entrance, Mary Katherine paid their admission and thrust a souvenir map into Elizabeth's hand. "In case we get separated," she said, as Margaret seized her hand and pulled her through the open gate.

Elizabeth, who was expecting either a circus or a zoo, found that Safari World seemed to be a combination of both. As the girls darted from the monkey house to the camel rides to the elephant pens, Mary Katherine tried valiantly to keep up with them while giving Elizabeth a running commentary on the sights around them and the history of the place. George Hanneman, she explained as she pursued her daughters, had worked as an animal trainer and occasional movie extra for Galaxy Pictures. If an elephant went on a rampage in a film, it was almost certain George Hanneman was the rajah he seemed to trample underfoot. If a lion tried to bite off the head of a British explorer in the wilds of Africa, George Hanneman was the man Tarzan rescued in the nick of time. When Galaxy Pictures decided to close its studio zoo, George, who had become fond of the lions in particular, decided to open his own animal farm to supply movie studios with well-trained animal actors as needed.

Never one to overlook a business opportunity, after local boys began peering through knotholes in the fences to watch him train the lions, George decided to set up bleachers and charge admission. Within a year, he added monkeys, camels, panthers, tigers, and horses to the roster of performers and built a snack bar and gift shop on the compound. Circus troupes from all parts of the west came to Safari World for the winter, taking the train to Simi Valley and then parading over the grade and through the Arboles Valley, the smaller animals hauled along in cages on gaudily painted wagons, the elephants marching single file, each grasping the tail of the one before it with its trunk. The ground shook as they marched, frightening the residents of farms along the road with thoughts of earthquakes until they remembered it was circus season.

When a tall man in an elegant red coat and jodhpurs announced that the lion show was about to begin, Elizabeth and Mary Katherine grasped the hands of the younger girls and made their way through the crowd to the central stage. The bars separating the bleachers from the performance space seemed dangerously insubstantial to Elizabeth, especially when three lions suddenly bounded onstage guided by a slim, muscular man in a black shirt and slacks. At his command, the largest of the cats, an enormous male with a thick, shaggy mane, leapt onto a tall platform and let out a roar that made the crowd gasp. Margaret covered her ears and Elizabeth sank back into her seat, trembling.

"Charlie," said Mary Katherine breathlessly, her eyes on the lion. Elizabeth swallowed and nodded. She would have recognized that roar anywhere.

She watched, entranced, as George Hanneman put the lions through their paces. They jumped from platform to platform, awing the audience with their strength and agility. They reenacted scenes Elizabeth remembered from jungle movies she had seen years before. George Hanneman demonstrated how a lion attack would be staged and filmed, first explaining how he had trained Charlie to pounce upon him without hurting him, as he might in play. Even then, he warned, only a trainer who knew his cat exceptionally well should attempt such a stunt. In all the years he had known and cared for Charlie, he never allowed himself to forget that Charlie was not a pet, but a dangerous and potentially lethal wild carnivore.

The crowd shuddered and murmured in respectful fear, but Mary Katherine sighed and rested her chin on her palm. "The movies always lose a little magic once you know how it's done. I can't ever see an animal attack in a film now without seeing a trainer and a well-fed animal looking for the favorite toy hidden in his pocket."

Elizabeth did not agree. When George wrestled with Charlie, it looked every bit as dangerous as on film—and felt even more real with the musky animal scent and low snarls in the air, the scuffling of sharp claws in the dirt. She was so fearful for George's life that her stomach hurt.

When the lions' performance ended, she clapped until her palms stung. Some of the onlookers began to leave, but others remained in their seats to await the horse show. "May we stay?" asked Elizabeth when Annalise and Margaret took their mother's hands and began to drag her off to buy them peanuts and lemonade.

Mary Katherine hesitated, clearly surprised that Elizabeth wanted to stay. Like the Jorgensens, she should have had her fill of horses every day on the farm. But those were work horses, not show horses, and certainly not trained, performing horses. For Elizabeth, they called to mind Bergstrom Thoroughbreds and Elm Creek Manor, and even though she knew it was unlikely any of Safari World's horses had come from Uncle Fred and Aunt Eleanor's farm, she felt a sharp stab of longing to see them, just in case.

Mary Katherine must have read the longing on her face, for she suggested that she take the girls for their treats and meet up with Elizabeth after the show. After they left, Elizabeth waited for another ten minutes for the show to begin. When a woman in her midthirties rode into the ring on the back of the most beautiful horse Elizabeth had seen since leaving Pennsylvania, a shock of familiarity rippled through her. The gait, the coat, the speed—every feature identified the proud horse as a Bergstrom Thoroughbred.

Elizabeth could hardly tear her eyes from the horse throughout the twenty-minute performance, hungrily taking in the unexpected glimpse of home. An older gentleman who had taken Mary Katherine's seat misinterpreted her rapt attention. "She's quite a horsewoman, isn't she?" he remarked. "That's Caroline Hanneman. To look at her, you'd never suspect she didn't know anything about show biz until she married George."

Elizabeth looked away from the Bergstrom Thoroughbred long enough to reply. "She's not from Hollywood, like her husband?"

"Not at all. She was born and raised in the valley, on a farm right next to this one." He chuckled. "She tells a story about how she and George met. It so happened that George fed his lions at the same time every morning when it was milking time on her parents' farm. The lions' roars scared her cows so much that they kicked over their buckets of milk. One morning she got so fed up, she marched over here to give George Hanneman a piece of her mind. Two years later, they were married."

Elizabeth smiled. "I suppose there's a lesson there for all of us."

"That's for sure. The way George tells it, he had to marry her to get her to stop complaining."

Elizabeth managed to keep her smile in place as she returned her attention to the show. She would have preferred a lesson about how love could blossom from enmity, how affection could overcome anger. The last moral she wanted to hear was that marriage meant the end of a woman's right to speak her mind. She could not imagine any Bergstrom woman standing for that, or any Jorgensen woman, either. As for Caroline Hanneman, any woman who could handle a Bergstrom Thoroughbred with such confidence wouldn't back down to a mere husband.

Midway through the show, two men in denim and cowboy hats took over while Caroline disappeared backstage and emerged moments later in similar western attire. For the rest of the performance, the three demonstrated how horses were trained to fall down on command without injuring themselves, how to lie down as if wounded, how to rear back threateningly. "None of these learned behaviors hurt the horses," Caroline assured her listeners. "We would never allow our animals to appear on any set where they are not respected and properly cared for. That's the first thing we tell any producer who sets foot on this property."

Elizabeth instinctively sat up straighter and, with a glance around for anyone who looked out of place, fluffed the curls of her blond bob. A movie producer, here? It made sense, of course; it was far easier for producers to come to Safari World than for George Hanneman and his trainers to parade wild animals through the streets of Hollywood.

Perhaps Henry was wrong, and Elizabeth didn't live too far from Los Angeles for a career in the movies. He couldn't object if she would not have to travel far for a film role, especially if the job paid well.

The show ended and Elizabeth climbed down from the bleachers to join the flow of people leaving the arena. She consulted the map Mary Katherine had given her and made her way to the animal pens, where they had arranged to meet. On the way she passed a corral and a stable, where the two men from the show had removed their costumes—which meant that they had removed the cowboy trappings from their usual work clothes—and were tending to the horses. She paused to watch, wondering how on earth a Bergstrom-bred horse had ended up in Safari World, and with a Hollywood résumé that would make any would-be starlet envious.

As she lingered, she overheard the wranglers discussing a recent failed attempt to buy a horse. The prices local farmers charged amounted to robbery, the men griped, and that's if they had anything to sell. Safari World's wranglers did not have time to scout around the whole valley and beyond to find the animals they needed. Times were better, the taller of the two men said, when farmers brought the animals to them.

"I can find horses for you," said Elizabeth.

The two men looked up. The smaller man eyed her with a smirk. "What'd you say, girlie?"

"I can find the horses you need."

The taller man scratched at his beard. "Why would you want to do that?"

Why not? If Henry could take on extra work, so could she. "Because I know horses and I know where to find them, and you don't have the time to look. And because of the finder's fee you'll pay me in return."

The men exchanged a grin, amused. The shorter man said, "Listen, doll, why don't you send your husband over and we'll talk business with him?"

"Because my husband isn't here and your business is with me. I know horses better than he does, anyway. I was practically born and raised on a horse farm." That last bit was an exaggeration, but these men couldn't possibly know that. She indicated the horse the taller man was grooming. "I'll prove it. That impressive stallion is a Bergstrom Thoroughbred, bred at Elm Creek Manor in Pennsylvania. That brown horse with the black mane and the star on his forehead is a little more difficult to place, but I would guess that it was bred on the Compson farm in Maryland. Am I right?"

She held her breath while the men took this in. She knew of no other breeders by name besides her uncle and his strongest rival, but that might be enough to convince these two.

"Is she right?" the shorter man asked the other in an undertone, his smirk vanishing.

The taller man shrugged. "Beats me."

Elizabeth hid her relief with a smile. "Well, gentlemen?"

"All right," the taller man said grudgingly. "You find us horses, and we'll pay you ten cents for each one we buy."

"Twenty-five."

"Ten," the shorter man shot back. "And we ain't payin' an arm and a leg for the horses, neither, so talk the price down before dragging us out somewhere to buy a horse we haven't seen."

"You won't have to go anywhere," Elizabeth assured them. "I know a place that will send the horses to you—Bergstrom Thoroughbreds."

The taller man looked perplexed. "Didn't you just say they were in Pennsylvania?"

"We can't wait for horses to come all that way," the shorter man said irritably. "What do you think this is? We need them now."

"All right," said Elizabeth, taken aback. "I'll find some horses a little closer to home, but I can tell you right now they won't be as good as Bergstrom Thoroughbreds."

"They'll be good enough," the taller man said.

Elizabeth promised to bring them a list of horses and prices within the week. They responded by frowning and shaking their heads as they returned to their work, as if they did not expect to see her again and would forget their arrangement as soon as she left their sight.

She hurried off to meet Mary Katherine and the girls, her thoughts racing. When she had asked for the job, she assumed she would simply be the middleman between her uncle and Safari World. Now she would have to scout throughout the Arboles Valley and perhaps beyond, finding suitable horses where those two had already failed. She would need a car, and time to search. From the looks the men gave her, they expected her to fail—but that just made her more determined to succeed. All she had to do was find a horse or two that met their expectations, and perhaps then they would trust her judgment enough to consider Bergstrom Thoroughbreds for future purchases. The movie producers would surely recognize quality when they saw it, and perhaps one day, movie studios throughout Hollywood would insist upon Bergstrom Thoroughbreds for their pictures. It would benefit them, it would benefit Uncle Fred—and it would put some money in Elizabeth's pocket. If she happened to catch the eye of a movie producer at the same time, so much the better.

She must put the wages she earned from the Jorgensens toward Henry's lost savings and their train fare back to Pennsylvania. Anything she earned from additional work accomplished on her days off—time she would much rather spend enjoying Henry's company—was hers to do with as she pleased. It would please her very much to buy back her quilts from Mrs. Diegel.

She found Mary Katherine and her daughters by the monkey cages. The girls had saved some peanuts for Elizabeth, and Mary Katherine insisted upon treating her to a glass of lemonade as they strolled through the park. Trailing after the girls as they bounded from one spectacle to another, Elizabeth asked Mary Katherine if it was true that movie producers occasionally came to Safari World.

"Not only to Safari World, but all over the Arboles Valley," Mary Katherine replied. "Think of any Western you've ever seen, and chances are it was filmed beneath the bluffs west of our farm."

"Is that so?"

"When Annalise was a baby, our pasture and sheep appeared in a movie about Nebraskan pioneers." Mary Katherine frowned comically. "You'd think that we could have asked for more for their wool after that, but you'd be wrong."

Elizabeth laughed, spirits rising. "It must have been exciting to watch a Western being filmed."

"It was a lot of standing around, mostly, or so it seemed to me. I couldn't see much of the action from the garden and the house. A movie called *Trouble at Rocky Ranch* was filmed out here more recently, but I saw even less of that."

"I saw that movie," said Elizabeth, as the familiarity of the bluffs east of the Jorgensen farm suddenly made perfect sense. "At the Egyptian Theater in Hollywood, the night before we came to the Arboles Valley."

"I bet you've seen the Arboles Valley in more movies than that. It's been the setting for more than just Westerns. How do you think Lake Sherwood got its name?"

Elizabeth had not known of any Lake Sherwood in the Arboles Valley, but she guessed. "Not *Robin Hood,* with Douglas Fairbanks?"

"The one and only. Once I saw him and Mary Pickford having lunch at the Grand Union Hotel. She was even more beautiful in person, and he was so handsome." Mary Katherine looked wistful. "Can you imagine such a glamorous life? Fame and fortune, the prettiest clothes, people to do all the cooking and cleaning and laundry for you, the chance to travel and see the world—and all because you know how to pose and recite some lines. It must be heavenly."

Privately, Elizabeth agreed, but she knew that for every Mary Pickford there were probably hundreds of chorus girls and thousands of aspirants whose faces never made it to the silver screen. But one producer had already told her she had star quality, so perhaps her chances were not so remote. If the Jorgensen sheep could land movie roles, surely she could.

When the girls grew tired, they drove home, Mary Katherine at the wheel so that Lars would not become incensed when he saw Elizabeth in the driver's seat. "Not that I've ever seen him terribly angry," said Mary Katherine with a grin. "He's as mild as an afternoon in May. He wasn't always like that, or so I've heard. He had a temper back in the day when he was drinking."

She spared a quick glance for the backseat, and was visibly relieved to find that the girls had fallen asleep. Since Mary Katherine was apparently the only Jorgensen who willingly divulged information about the family, Elizabeth decided to risk pressing her for more details. "I understand why Lars couldn't buy back the old farm," she said as they drove past Meadowbrook Hills, where construction continued at the same industrious pace, although the real estate agents and flocks of prospective residents had departed. "But why did he sell it in the first place?"

"Why does anyone sell a family farm?" Mary Katherine replied. "Maybe he was tired of the hardships and uncertainties of farming. We all know we could be only one drought away from going belly-up. Maybe he wanted to leave the Arboles Valley, strike out on his own, go into business in a larger city. Or put his earnings into the stock market and get rich without having to drag himself out of bed before dawn every day. Maybe the money sounded too good to pass up. How was he to know how much more the land would be worth in just a few short years?"

Elizabeth knew there had to be more. "But to do nothing with the money once he had it in hand, to just drink it all away, and then to return to farming anyway—"

"Once the money was gone, he probably had no other choice. And of course my Oscar would never turn his brother away. Lars was the true Prodigal Son."

Silently Elizabeth disagreed. The biblical father had welcomed back his wayward son with great joy and celebration and restored him fully to his birthright. He had not, as far as Elizabeth could recall, allowed him to come home only to serve his more dutiful brother.

When Henry returned to Two Bears Farm, his family would celebrate his homecoming even more than the Prodigal's so long ago, for Henry had never sold his birthright, nor squandered his inheritance. He had been deceived through no fault of his own, but he would earn back what he had lost. Although they might not return to Two Bears Farm for years, it was a great comfort to know that someday they would.

"It seems like such a waste," said Elizabeth. She was not sure if she meant Lars's rash behavior as a young man, or all the years since then he had spent atoning for his youthful mistakes.

Mary Katherine sighed. "I'm not sure what sorrows Lars was trying to drown back then, but in all the time I've known him, he's never shirked his duties and he's never fallen off the wagon—and we all know liquor isn't that hard to come by, Prohibition or no Prohibition. I think everyone would just as soon forget that he was ever anyone but the man he is today."

Elizabeth understood this as a gentle admonition to stop probing into Lars's past, and she reluctantly complied.

Back home in the cabin, she made supper and had it waiting on the table when Henry came in, smelling of sheep. She tried to amuse him by revealing that the sheep he tended were no ordinary barnyard animals but a flock of woolly movie stars. Henry seemed not to hear her as he hungrily cleaned his plate of fried potatoes, dried apples, and onions seasoned with the black pepper and caraway seed Mary Katherine had generously offered from her own pantry. Elizabeth kept up her cheerful patter even though inside she was seething with annoyance. If he were determined to avoid her on their one day off and then not even listen to how she had spent her afternoon away from him, she would not bother sharing her good news about her prospective business deal with the wranglers of Safari World. She would wait until she could fan a handful of greenbacks in Henry's face. That would make him pay attention.

After supper, he built a fire on the hearth to ward off the chill brought on by the ocean mists that cooled the late spring nights. She cleared the table and heated bathwater for him. While he bathed—alone, with the door closed—she searched her pocketbook and retrieved the business card that Grover Higgins of Golden Reel Productions had given her at the dance marathon in Venice Beach. If a movie producer didn't come to the Arboles Valley, she did have other options.

If only the cabin had a telephone. She could imagine Mrs. Jorgensen's response if Elizabeth asked to borrow hers to make a long-distance call to a movie producer.

She sat down on the bed, working out a plan. Mrs. Diegel had a phone. Lars seemed protective of the car, but twice already she had seen him reach out a hand to someone in need. If she explained why she needed the car, he might let her borrow it. As she drove around the valley in search of horses, she could stop by the Grand Union Hotel and call Grover Higgins. What Mrs. Diegel would expect in trade, Elizabeth could only guess. Perhaps a lien on any future quilts Elizabeth pieced on the treadle sewing machine.

Her gaze fell upon the worn scrap quilt she had found in the cabin. It had held up well to washing, but she had paid little attention to it since then except to feel grateful each night for the warmth it provided. It was wrinkled and faded, especially compared with the quilts she had given up, but now that she studied it more carefully, she could not help admiring the ingenious design. She had never seen a star pattern quite like it before, despite the hundreds of quilts she had witnessed the Bergstrom women make through the years. At first glance she had mistaken it for a traditional Blazing Star quilt, the blocks arranged in seven rows of five blocks each, but on closer inspection, she saw that smaller diamonds fanned out in a half star in the four corner squares of each block, giving the quilt the illusion of brilliance and fire. Such care must have gone into the making of each block for each divided star to fit the corner exactly so.

Elizabeth wondered who had made it. Mrs. Jorgensen's grandmother, perhaps, or could the quilt be even older than that? It seemed to be pieced of scraps of clothing, which always made it more difficult to date. Had the fading and wear to the fabric occurred before or after the pieces were sewn into a quilt? Perhaps the quilt had been made far away and brought to the Arboles Valley by a young bride trusting in her husband's decision to bring her out West, far from home and family, trusting that he would always cherish her and never give her reason to regret her decision.

Elizabeth rose and reached for the second quilt, neatly folded at the foot of the bed. She spread it out on top of the star quilt, marveling at how much her first dismissive glances had missed. Pieced of homespuns and wools, it was sturdy and warm, obviously intended for daily use rather than a best quilt brought out only on special occasions or for visitors, but for all that, it was as complex and well fashioned as any quilt to grace a bed at Elm Creek Manor. It was composed not of square blocks but of hexagons, each formed from twelve triangular wedges with a smaller hexagon appliquéd in the center where the points met. Elizabeth smiled, recognizing the familiar quilter's trick of covering a bulky seam or hiding a place where points did not match up as precisely as they should. Sewing the pieced hexagons together was much more challenging than simply stitching together rows of square blocks, but this unknown quilter had managed admirably. Even now, with some of the binding hanging from the edge and the cotton batting thin in patches, the quilt lay perfectly flat, with no puckering or bulging seams except for an overall patina of wrinkles created by the slight shrinkage of the wool in the wash.

Had the same unknown woman made both quilts? Though both were the work of accomplished quilters, the fabrics used and patterns chosen suggested they were not of the same era. And yet Elizabeth had found them folded together. Surely they had both belonged to the Jorgensen family. But why had they been left in the cabin? Why had such painstaking needlework not earned these quilts a place in the yellow farmhouse? They certainly would have endured better had they been sheltered behind sturdy walls rather than left to the drafts and damp of the cabin and the nibbles of inquisitive mice.

Her thoughts flew to the scraps she had brought from home and the pieces of fabric Mrs. Diegel had included in the sewing machine trade. While none of the fabrics was identical to those in the two quilts, some were a fairly close match. She ought to have enough to repair them.

Henry refused to return to Pennsylvania until he had earned back all he had lost. Well, Elizabeth had lost things, too, and she was just as determined to recover them. When they finally did go home to the Elm Creek Valley, it would be with her bridal quilt and the Chimneys and Cornerstones quilt tucked safely in their trunk with two newly restored antique quilts beside them. The Bergstrom women would marvel at her fortunate discovery and praise her for her skill when she described how she had restored the worn pieces and replaced the broken threads. Elizabeth's heart sank a little when she realized that she could never tell her mother and aunts the whole truth of how the quilts had come to her, not if she meant to spare Henry from shame.

She would tell them as much as she could. She had already written about the Jorgensens, so she would not be divulging too much to say that she believed the quilts had been made by one of the first women of their family to come to the Arboles Valley. She could say that she had stumbled over the quilts in an old, abandoned cabin on the ranch property without adding that she and Henry had made the ramshackle place their home. The Bergstrom women would be more interested in the quilts themselves, anyway—the remarkable patterns, the exceptional handiwork, the charming fabrics. They would not think to ask the questions she least wanted to answer.

The Bergstrom women need never know how she and Henry had lived while they were far from home, nor that Elizabeth had ever parted with the precious quilts they had so lovingly sewn for her.

✒

1910

Isabel had dreamed of Rosa finishing school and going off to college to become something important, perhaps a teacher like her aunt, but when the time came, Rosa did not want to go. She loved the Arboles Valley, she told her parents passionately, and her soul would wither away to dust if she had to leave it.

Miguel accepted her dramatic declaration, but Isabel grieved, not only to watch her daughter throw away an opportunity her parents had never had, but to hear another lie pass her lips. It was indeed love that kept her in the Arboles Valley, but not love for the land.

Rosa, who had always excelled at math, obtained a job as a clerk and bookkeeper at the Grand Union Hotel. For two years she balanced accounts and paid bills for Mrs. Diegel, the young widow who had returned to the Arboles Valley from Los Angeles to assume responsibility for the hotel when her father's health failed. For two years Rosa was, by all appearances, a good and obedient daughter. After working all day at the hotel, she returned home and helped her mother with the housework. She gave half of her earnings to her parents for household necessities and saved the rest, except for the little she spent on sensible clothes suitable for work. She went to Mass with her family every Sunday morning, helped her brother with his homework, and spent Saturday afternoons in the company of friends, young women from good families with whom Isabel could find no fault.

But there were also mornings when Isabel went to the kitchen to find Rosa already awake, breathless and bright-eyed, preparing breakfast for the family, overly solicitous of her mother—squeezing her a glass of orange juice, asking if she had slept well. There were afternoons when Isabel passed through the Arboles Valley on her housecleaning route and crossed paths with the friend Rosa had said she planned to spend the day with—but Rosa was nowhere in sight. There were rumors passed along to Isabel by observant friends claiming that a young man stopped by the hotel on Rosa's lunch hour nearly every day, and that he and Rosa had been spotted in the citrus grove holding hands or in the Arboles Grocery buying food for a picnic. Isabel did not trust the rumors entirely because some described the young man as black-haired and others as blond, but she knew the tales must have sprouted from some seed of truth.

When Isabel shared her worries with her husband, Miguel spread his hands helplessly and said there was little they could do. It was disappointing to think that their daughter might be keeping a secret romance from them, but she was twenty years old, a woman grown, and it was hardly surprising that she had fallen in love. They had done their best to raise her properly, and they had to trust that she would use good judgment and not stray into anything that might ruin her reputation.

"With all the rumors flying about, she may have already ruined her reputation," retorted Isabel. "If she has such good judgment, why keep this romance secret? If she's in love with a decent young man, why hasn't she told us about him? If his intentions are good, why hasn't he asked to meet us?"

Miguel had no answer for her except to say that perhaps an introduction would come in time. He did not like to argue, and he could not believe that his beautiful daughter could do any wrong. Isabel reluctantly dropped the subject. Without Miguel's support, she could not bear to confront the daughter she adored with accusations that might have no merit. Perhaps Miguel was right. Perhaps Rosa was not sure how she felt about her admirer, and she was waiting until she knew her own heart before bringing the young man home.

Then one afternoon Miguel came home from work, beaming. He took Isabel aside and quietly told her that he believed he had discovered the identity of Rosa's young man. Earlier that day he had stopped by the feed store on an errand for his employer, and while he was making his purchases, a young man struck up a conversation with him. "He knew a lot about Rosa," Miguel said. "Things only someone who spoke with her often would know. Who her best friends are, what she thinks of her job, that your father's tamales were the best in the valley—"

"Everyone knows that," Isabel broke in. Her father's cooking had become the stuff of local legend. She always regretted not forcing him into the kitchen sooner.

"The point is," said Miguel, amused, "that since he felt confident enough to approach me in the feed store instead of ducking into another aisle, Rosa might intend to tell us about him soon. I almost invited him over for dinner, but I thought Rosa would never forgive me."

"But who is he?" demanded Isabel in a whisper, peering over her shoulder to be sure Rosa was not within earshot.

"John Barclay. You remember. Donald and Evelyn's son."

"But he's four years older than Rosa."

"And maybe that's why she hasn't told us about him."

Suddenly Rosa's secrecy made perfect sense. Isabel and Miguel certainly would not have approved of an eighteen-year-old man giving their fourteen-year-old daughter a Valentine's Day carnation so many years ago. But Rosa was twenty now, and no longer had any excuse not to reveal the truth to her parents. If John Barclay truly loved their daughter, why did he not insist upon it? Unless he wanted to, but had promised to abide by Rosa's wishes. Perhaps her secrecy had become a habit she had forgotten to break, even after the need for it had passed.

Isabel sighed. Apparently they would still have to wait and see. When Rosa was ready, she would tell them everything. In the meantime, Rosa's circumstances were not as bad as Isabel had feared. While her prolonged secrecy was insufferable, at least she had chosen well. John Barclay was Catholic, thank goodness, although he did not attend Mass as regularly as Isabel would have liked. He owned his own land, a small farm near the Salto Canyon that he had inherited upon his father's death and had run almost single-handedly ever since his mother moved to Oxnard to live with John's only living sibling, an elder sister. If John could at twenty-four run his own thriving farm, he surely was hardworking and industrious and would be a good provider. If Rosa married him, she would have land of her own, very near the old Rancho Triunfo, the land that should have been her inheritance.

Isabel waited for Rosa to confide in her, but the days passed as they always had, with the customary routine occasionally broken by those strange early mornings when Rosa was up before the sun rose, bustling about the kitchen with bright eyes and flushed cheeks. Then one night Isabel started from an unpleasant dream and went to the kitchen for a glass of water. On a sudden impulse, she quietly peeked into Rosa's bedroom and found the quilt turned back and the curtains swaying in the open window. Rosa was nowhere to be seen.

Her heart sinking, Isabel returned to bed and lay awake until morning. She left her room only after she heard someone opening cupboards and turning on a tap in the kitchen. There she found Rosa preparing breakfast, smiling to herself and humming. She looked up in surprise when her mother entered. "You're up early," she said, offering Isabel a cup of coffee.

Isabel took it with a murmur of thanks. She did not point out the obvious, that Rosa had risen even earlier, if she had slept at all.

Isabel brooded throughout the morning as she worked, scrubbing bathtubs with angry vigor. By midday she had resolved to confront Rosa with the truth. If she and John were in love and his intentions honorable, they had nothing to hide. If not, Isabel had a mother's duty to demand they break off their relationship without delay.

Between stops on her housecleaning route, Isabel went to the Grand Union Hotel, unwilling to wait until after supper to speak to her daughter, when her resolve might weaken beneath Miguel's constant reassurances and calls for patience. As she crossed the front porch, she passed one of the Jorgensen boys on his way out. He greeted her politely, but she pretended not to see him. If she had her way, she would never lay eyes on any Jorgensen. She caught a whiff of alcohol on his breath and she recoiled in disdain and disgust. Drinking at one o'clock in the afternoon on a weekday, when he ought to be working! He had inherited one-half of what had once been the Rancho Triunfo upon his father's death, and this was how he respected that legacy. She should have expected as much from that family, but the unfairness of fate wrenched at her. It was a disgrace, and she would not be surprised if that Jorgensen boy drank those precious acres away.

It was a pity the hotel had a bar. Isabel did not care for the sort of person it brought into her daughter's workplace.

Inside, she found Rosa at her desk in the small office off the lobby. She was just sitting down after finishing her lunch, but she jumped to her feet at the sight of Isabel. "Mother," she exclaimed, coming around the desk to kiss her on the cheek. Her hand upon Isabel's shoulder trembled. "What a surprise! Is everything all right?"

"No, in fact, something is very wrong." Isabel regarded her sternly, but her resolve melted when Rosa sank into her chair, blanching from alarm. "I didn't mean to worry you, but *mija,* I am very troubled by your secrecy. I know—your father and I know—that you are in love. We think we know why you've been hiding this from us, but the time has come for you to tell the truth."

Rosa clenched her hands in her lap, her dark, lovely eyes wide and apprehensive. "How long have you known?"

Since Rosa was fourteen. "We waited as long as we could, hoping you would tell us on your own."

"You aren't angry?"

"Because you have deceived us, yes, very. Because you have fallen in love, no. Never." Isabel managed a small smile. "You're a beautiful, loving young woman, Rosa. If you've found the love of a good man, we're happy for you. We want to share in your happiness."

"I—" Rosa hesitated. "I didn't think you would approve. And I love him, but—I'm still not sure. He's a good man, but—it's just so hard to know what to do. There are things about him I wish he would change. I pray for him to change. Can I really love him if I want him to be different?"

"Oh, Rosa." Isabel embraced her. "Why did you keep your troubles to yourself for so long? I'm your mother. You can always talk to me about anything. You know I will always love you."

"And I will always love you." Tears welled up in Rosa's eyes. "And I will always love him. I know I will. But that doesn't mean I should marry him."

Isabel was surprised—and proud—to hear Rosa express such wisdom in the midst of her uncertainty. Most young women her age would think only of the passion of first love and not of the hard, practical realities of building a strong, enduring marriage. "Has he asked you to marry him?"

Rosa nodded.

"He should not have done that without speaking to your father."

"You're right. I know that. But it's—well, you know how things are." Tentatively, Rosa added, "I'm surprised you're taking it so well yourself."

"It's your deception that troubles me, not your feelings for this man, or his for you."

Rosa's cheeks flushed. "It seemed best to keep it to ourselves."

"There's no need for secrecy any longer," Isabel assured her. "Invite John to join us for Sunday dinner. We need to get to know the man who wants to marry our daughter."

Rosa stared at her. "Invite . . . John?"

"Yes, and without delay. We must have this out in the open. I don't approve of how he has handled things so far, but your father and I are willing to give him a chance to redeem himself. This will help you, too. Concealing the truth from us has distracted you from deciding how you really feel about him."

When Rosa did not reply, Isabel said, "Either invite him to meet the family or promise never to see him again. Your father and I are willing to overlook how this matter began so we can see that it has a proper resolution. We will allow him to court you in a respectable manner, but this sneaking around and staying out all night must end."

Still Rosa stared at her. Finally she said, "I'll speak to John today."

"Good." Isabel embraced her daughter, but Rosa seemed dazed and shaken in her arms. "It will be all right in the end, whether you accept John's proposal or marry someone else. Take all the time you need. Don't let him rush you. If he truly loves you, he'll wait until you're ready to answer." She thought of the three years she had made Miguel wait, three years that seemed like only moments now. Their marriage had been blessed, and well worth the wait. She wished someday for her children to know such a rich blessing.

Wordlessly Rosa clung to her, tears in her eyes.

Chapter Eight

1925

After Henry went off to bed, Elizabeth tore up her unfinished letters home and started over, writing cheerful, breezy accounts of their arrival at Triumph Ranch, the Jorgensen family, and the work of the farm. "Although the ranch is not precisely as it was described to us," she wrote to Aunt Eleanor, "it is a lovely, thriving place, and I hope we will do well here." She described their discovery of sheep where they had expected cattle as a comical misunderstanding, and wrote in lavish detail of the beauty of the landscape. To Sylvia she wrote of befriending Mary Katherine and her daughters, and of their visit to Safari World, where she met Charlie the lion and discovered a Bergstrom Thoroughbred among the performing horses.

Then she sat awake in the front room with the homespuns-and-wool hexagon quilt spread upon her lap, unable to silence her nagging conscience long enough to drift off to sleep. Sylvia admired her, and Elizabeth had always tried to be worthy of her young cousin's trust. Nothing in her letter was, strictly speaking, a lie; she had written that she liked to walk among *the* apricot trees, not *her* apricot trees, and it was fair to call the sheep Henry's flock because he tended them. While Elizabeth's mother might chide her for lies of omission, no one could say that she had betrayed Sylvia's trust by lying outright—except when she referred to Triumph Ranch. No such place existed anymore, and to pretend she lived there crossed the line from evasiveness into outright dishonesty.

Elizabeth worked her needle in tiny stitches through a wool patch she was appliquéing over a small hole in the quilt top. The quilt's hexagonal pattern made her think of wagon wheels rambling over the Norwegian Grade into the Arboles Valley, or the sun rising over the bluffs east of the ranch. When she looked upon the quilt, she wondered about the woman who had made it, whether she pieced these unusual hexagons here or in a city back east, and whether she found happiness in the Arboles Valley or disappointment. What had she written to loved ones far away?

Exasperated with herself, Elizabeth set the quilt aside. She could not tell the truth for Henry's sake, and yet she could not bear to lie. She had to write something, or the folks back in Pennsylvania would fear the worst.

Her gaze fell upon the smoldering embers in the fireplace. Suddenly a way out of her predicament occurred to her, and although it did not completely silence her nagging conscience, it would have to do until she thought of something better or Henry changed his mind about divulging the truth. She drew her dressing gown tightly around herself and hurried outside into the starlit night, trying not to think about coyotes and rattlesnakes and the other nocturnal creatures Annalise had enthusiastically assured her lurked in the valley. She dug into a stack of discarded wood behind the cabin until she found a flat board about two feet long and a foot wide. She brushed off the dirt and took it inside.

Kneeling beside the fireplace, she searched the embers until she found a thick splinter of wood that was charred on one end but unburned and cool on the other. Using the blackened tip as a pencil, she wrote upon the board in clear, bold letters: TRIUMPH RANCH.

She took her hand-lettered sign outside and propped it against the cabin wall on the porch near the front door.

"I hereby christen thee Triumph Ranch," she said softly, a lonely soloist backed by a choir of chirping insects. If she had a bottle of champagne, she would smash it against the porch steps. Better yet, she would trade it to Mrs. Diegel for eggs, coffee, and bacon for Henry's Sunday breakfast.

They were no better off, but at least a place named Triumph Ranch existed now. It was not only a dream, and when she wrote to her family of her new home, she would not be a liar.

She returned to bed and was at last able to sleep.

In the morning, when Henry returned from the outhouse, his face was grim. "Is that your idea of a joke?"

For a moment Elizabeth had no idea what he was talking about, and then she remembered the sign. "It's not a joke. When I write home, my family will expect me to talk about Triumph Ranch, my new home. I don't want to lie to them, and now I won't have to."

"You don't consider this a lie?"

The bitterness in his voice shook her. "It's the best I can do under the circumstances. Would you prefer that I tell them the whole story? Should I borrow a camera and send some snapshots?"

Henry muttered something she couldn't make out, but his meaning was perfectly clear. He strode off to the farmhouse so quickly that she could barely keep up with him. He did not kiss her good-bye at the back door or tell her he would see her at breakfast, as he had done every other morning since they had come to work for the Jorgensens.

She was upset and worried and angry, and she regretted ever trying to ease her conscience with a silly sign that she should have known would insult him. Mrs. Jorgensen looked at her sharply when she came into the kitchen, red-faced and breathless, but Elizabeth composed herself as best she could and got to work. She knew Mrs. Jorgensen wasn't fooled, but she was not the sort of woman to pry into someone else's business. When Henry came in for breakfast with the other men, he no longer seemed angry, but the kiss he gave her every morning on his way to the table, the kiss the others would have noted for its absence, was so swift she barely felt his lips brush her cheek.

After breakfast, Lars reminded Elizabeth of his intention to stop by the post office that afternoon and asked if she had any letters for him to send. As she took them from her pocket, Mrs. Jorgensen said, "Why don't you go with him? Mary Katherine tells me you can drive, so if you learn the way, on days when Lars is too busy you can run the errands for him."

Mary Katherine gave Elizabeth a meaningful look over her mother-in-law's shoulder while Elizabeth arranged to meet Lars in the garage after cleaning up the kitchen after lunch. She had not expected Mary Katherine's prediction that Mrs. Jorgensen would not allow Lars to go to the Barclay farm alone to come true. Did Lars really need a watchful eye more than Mary Katherine needed Elizabeth's help in the garden? If Lars's old temper really could resurface after years of dormancy, Elizabeth doubted her presence would do anything to prevent it.

She spent the morning doing the laundry, load after load of men's work shirts and denim overalls so filthy that she expected to look out at the barley field and discover that an entire layer of top-soil was missing. She much preferred to wash the ladies' cotton dresses and the girls' sweet pinafores, admiring them as she hung them on the line to dry in the fresh air that blew down from the Santa Monica Mountains from the west, but she would have gladly given up that pleasure if it meant never again having to wash a stranger's undergarments. She knew her distaste was prim and patrician, but she could not help it. As much as she liked the other hired hands, as much as she was learning to respect Oscar and his mother, handling their undergarments was too intimate, and in the case of some of the hired hands, too overpowering. On laundry day, she could always tell who had spent most of the week in the orchard and who had been herding sheep.

For hours, she and Mary Katherine and the girls went from washhouse to clothesline hauling water and heavy baskets of damp clothes. After several weeks of working for the Jorgensens, Elizabeth had grown accustomed to the labor, but even so, the muscles in her neck and shoulders ached long before Mrs. Jorgensen called her to the kitchen to help prepare lunch. Still, it could be worse and she counted her blessings, especially the Aerobell washing machine Oscar had purchased for Mary Katherine on their eighth anniversary. ("Mother Jorgensen called it a waste of money," marveled Mary Katherine as they filled the round copper tub with soiled clothes. "She wouldn't think so if *she* had to do the laundry for the family and eight farmhands.") Since the washhouse was not wired for electricity, Oscar had hooked up the machine to a kerosene generator, which gave off a deafening roar and made conversation in the washhouse difficult.

On that day, Elizabeth preferred not to chat, because for all her aspirations of stardom, she doubted she could act well enough to conceal her dismal mood. Also, Mary Katherine was still smarting from some disagreement with Mrs. Jorgensen the previous evening and was determined to draw Elizabeth into finding fault with her. While Elizabeth liked Mary Katherine and preferred her company to that of her demanding mother-in-law, she was far too clever to be caught saying anything against Mrs. Jorgensen that might be used against her later. Back in Harrisburg, her taste for gossip had been nearly unrivaled among her friends and she had never shied away from speaking her mind, but now she was a different person in a different world. Her position on the farm was far too uncertain to risk, no matter how good it might make her feel at that moment to top

Mary Katherine's complaints with the mental list she had been keeping since her first day with the Jorgensens. How Mrs. Jorgensen swore there was only one proper way to slice a potato, for example, or how she made Elizabeth clean every last speck of dirt from the corners of a room by digging the sharpened end of a clothespin into the crevices where the baseboards met.

After washing the lunch dishes, Elizabeth hurried to the garage to meet Lars, grateful for the reprieve and worried that he might leave without her if she was late. Instead, she was the first to the car, and it was Lars who arrived a few moments after, coming not from the fields but from the house, his face and hands washed, his thinning blond hair neatly parted and combed. He crossed in front of the car and opened the driver's side door for her. "I best see how you can drive before I let you take her out on your own," he said.

She gladly climbed into the driver's seat, and before long they were on their way. As they rode along, Lars provided directions, which were helpful, and driving advice, which was not. When they reached the Barclay farm, Elizabeth set the parking brake and gave Lars a bright, inquisitive smile. "Well, what do you know?" she said. "We made it in one piece."

"I guess you can handle an automobile all right," he said reluctantly. "But maybe you should get more practice."

"I'm glad I've earned your trust," she said, smothering a laugh. He was not the first man to contrive some excuse to be in her company, and although Lars was at least fifteen years her senior, his interest was flattering. Henry had scarcely touched her since they had made the cabin their home. She had begun to believe that she was no longer pretty, that worry and hard work had robbed her of her beauty. She did not know whether to be relieved or upset by this sign that men still found her attractive. If Henry did not, it mattered very little what other men thought.

She decided to press her advantage. "Do we have time to swing by the Grand Union Hotel on our way home?"

"It's not on our way," he pointed out, "but we have time."

She smiled at him, but he looked away as Marta and Lupita came running up. "Hello, Mr. Jorgensen," Marta said shyly.

"Hello, Marta," Lars said gently, although he looked pained. "Where are your parents?"

"Papi's working and Mami's inside with Miguel and Ana."

"How are they?" asked Elizabeth.

Marta bit her lip and glanced at the house. "Miguel cried and cried and cried, but now he doesn't cry anymore. Ana didn't get out of bed today. Mami stays inside all the time."

"All the time?" echoed Lars.

Marta nodded. Grim, Lars drew in a deep breath, and Elizabeth followed his gaze as it traveled around the yard. The neatly planted flowers had turned dry and brown; a layer of windblown dirt covered the stone walkway that had been so carefully swept on Elizabeth's last visit.

Lars pulled a brown paper sack from his pocket and handed it to Lupita. "Share the candy with your big sister," he instructed. The girls beamed, thanked him, and ran off to enjoy the treat in the shade of the orange tree.

"Should we fetch the doctor?" asked Elizabeth as she trailed after Lars to the small, silent adobe house.

"No doctor around here can help them," Lars said, with a trace of anger, as if he was certain that other, more capable doctors elsewhere could, if only the children could get to them. He knocked on the door, and after a long moment, Rosa opened the door a crack and gazed out at him without speaking.

"How long has it been since you've been outside?" he asked gruffly.

"I don't know," she replied softly. "Days, perhaps."

"You're killing yourself, you know."

She blinked, surprised, as if that had not occurred to her. "Do you think I care?"

"Marta and Lupita will still need you after—after—"

"After my other two children die?"

"Come out into the sunshine," said Lars. "It's a beautiful day. Fresh air will do you good."

Rosa glanced over her shoulder into the darkened room. "And leave my babies alone in this house?"

"I'll stay with them," said Elizabeth quickly. "I love children. I've cared for my nieces and nephews from the time they were born. They'll be fine."

"They will not be fine," said Rosa without emotion.

Lars gently pushed the door open wider, and Rosa did not prevent it. "Come on outside. You don't have to go far. If anything happens, Elizabeth can yell for us and we'll come running."

Lars held out his hand. Rosa looked at it, then took a deep breath and nodded. She did not take his hand, but she did step through the doorway and tell Elizabeth where she could find the children.

Though the house was larger than the cabin, it was small enough that Elizabeth would have found them just as quickly on her own. Miguel slept in a cradle next to his parents' bed, while Ana tossed fitfully in a bed in the smallest of the bedrooms, which she likely shared with her sisters. Assured that they were fine for the moment, Elizabeth explored the house, listening for Rosa's return. From the bright quilts on the children's beds to the tidy kitchen and the front room decorated with religious illustrations, nothing hinted at the misery that had occurred—that *was* occurring—within those walls. It could have been any small adobe farmhouse in southern California.

Little more than ten minutes passed before Rosa and Lars

returned. "The children?" Rosa asked breathlessly as she closed the door behind her.

"Sleeping," Elizabeth assured her. Rosa managed a small smile of thanks. It did seem to Elizabeth that the bleak worry in her eyes had eased somewhat. Elizabeth found herself wishing she could come every day to offer the overwhelmed mother a brief respite, a few minutes to catch her breath, to play in the sun with Marta and Lupita.

"We'll come back next week," Lars promised, as if he had been reading her thoughts.

For an instant Rosa looked pleased, but then her mouth creased in worry. "John won't like it."

"Then he shouldn't be postmaster," said Elizabeth, feigning ignorance. "I can't help it that my family expects me to write to them."

"Oh, your letters," said Rosa with a start. "I forgot. Several have come for you."

"We have an errand at the Grand Union Hotel," said Elizabeth, thinking of Rosa's brother, "if you have any messages you'd like us to deliver."

"No messages," said Rosa. "But perhaps you would take them their mail."

She disappeared into the kitchen and returned with two envelopes, which Elizabeth traded for the two she had brought along. Rosa also gave Lars several envelopes and a Sears Roebuck catalog tied into a bundle with twine for the Jorgensens, and a smaller bundle of letters for the hotel. They thanked her and left the house.

Outside, they spotted John Barclay approaching almost in a run. "What are you doing in my house?" he demanded, glaring at Lars.

"Picking up the mail," he replied.

"You don't need to go inside for that."

"I invited them in," said Rosa. "I needed time to sort the Jorgensens' mail and I saw no reason to keep them waiting on the doorstep."

John turned his glare upon Elizabeth. "Weren't you afraid you might catch something?" His eyes shifted to his wife. "But why should she? I haven't gotten sick, you haven't gotten sick, Marta and Lupita haven't. Why do you figure that is? Why the others, but not Marta and Lupita?"

"Some men would consider that a blessing," said Lars.

"Maybe, maybe not. Maybe he'd start to wonder how this 'blessing' came to be. Maybe I'm getting wiser every day." John strode toward his wife, who instinctively took a step back, her grip on the door tightening. "Maybe Rosa knows. Want to explain why Lupita hasn't taken sick?"

"Have a care, John," warned Lars.

"Don't tell me how to speak to my wife," John shot back. "This is my family, my house, and don't you ever set foot inside it again."

Rosa said, "John, please—"

"You shut your mouth." John pushed Rosa ahead of him into the house and slammed the door. Lars hesitated for a moment as if considering whether to follow, but he turned away. After a moment, Elizabeth followed, and her gaze fell upon Marta and Lupita, who had watched the whole scene unfold from the shade of the orange tree.

"Take care of yourselves, girls," Lars said to them as he helped Elizabeth into the passenger side of the car. Marta nodded, but Lupita just watched them go, wide-eyed.

"What a cruel, spiteful man," Elizabeth said as Lars turned the car around and drove back to the main road. "As if Rosa isn't suffering enough. Why does he add to her burden with his ridiculous questions? It's almost as if he believes she's responsible for her children's illness."

"He wouldn't be the only one," said Lars.

"That's just the speculation of gossipy, small-minded people who ought to put their idle time to better use. You can't listen to that."

"I don't."

"There must be a doctor somewhere who can help the children."

"Not one around here, not one they can afford."

Elizabeth fell silent as they drove on to the Grand Union Hotel, wishing she could do something to help Rosa. She thought of her own family's doctor back in Harrisburg and Dr. August Granger in the Elm Creek Valley, who was reputed to be a brilliant physician. His care had seen Aunt Eleanor through many struggles with her weak heart, and by all accounts he had seen the entire valley through the influenza pandemic of 1918 almost single-handedly, assisted only by volunteers and his aged father, a retired doctor.

She would write to Dr. Granger and seek his advice. Perhaps he could recommend a treatment or knew of a skilled doctor in southern California who would waive his fees for a family in need.

When they pulled up to the hotel, Carlos stepped out from the garage to see who had arrived. At the sight of Lars, his face turned to stone. He greeted Elizabeth stiffly, his watchful gaze fixed on Lars until he turned and disappeared back into the garage. Elizabeth glanced questioningly at Lars, but he ignored her curiosity and told her he would wait outside.

She found Mrs. Diegel behind the front desk in the lobby, writing in a ledger. "Well, hello there, Elizabeth," she said. "What can I do for you? Have you come to trade?"

"You know I don't have anything left to trade," said Elizabeth, without acrimony. She placed the bundle of letters on the desk. "Lars and I stopped by the post office and brought you your mail. I've also come to ask a favor."

Mrs. Diegel peered across the room and out the window, where

Lars stood by the automobile. "The post office and then here," she remarked offhandedly. "One might almost think he was on the sauce again, the way he insists upon putting himself in the way of the two men in the valley who most despise him."

"You knew about his drinking?" said Elizabeth.

Mrs. Diegel paged through the envelopes. "Everyone knew about his drinking. It was hard to miss."

"Why would Carlos and John despise Lars?"

Mrs. Diegel looked up sharply. "You caught me gossiping. You should know better than to listen to an old woman rambling on wherever her mind wanders."

"Please tell me. Why would they hate him? He seems like a good man."

"He is, now. Perhaps he was then, too, in his way, despite the drinking, or Rosa never would have loved him."

"Rosa loved Lars?" exclaimed Elizabeth.

Exasperated, Mrs. Diegel held up her hands to quiet her. "Must you shout?"

"I'm sorry. I'm—just surprised." Astounded was more like it. "How do you know?"

"Rosa worked for me for a few years after high school, until she married. Lars and John both used to call on her here, to bring her flowers, take her to lunch, pass the time—you know how young men carry on. Rosa preferred Lars, or so it seemed to me, but she was fond of John, too, or she would have told him to leave her alone. She was straightforward like that back then."

"If Rosa loved Lars, then why did she marry a man like John Barclay?"

"I've often wondered that myself." Mrs. Diegel sighed, thoughtful. "I suppose because she couldn't marry Lars and she had to marry someone, or she thought she did. I've done just fine many years without a husband, but not all women believe it's possible."

"Why couldn't she marry Lars? Because of his drinking?"

"That was part of it. She hated his drinking and begged him to quit. If he showed up here drunk she sent him right back out that door. But more important, her parents wouldn't allow her to marry a Jorgensen. You're a newcomer, so you wouldn't know anything about their feud. The Jorgensen farm used to belong to the Rodriguez family. A distant ancestor was awarded the land grant back when the Spanish still owned most of California. When Rosa and Carlos's great-grandparents went bankrupt after a two-year drought, they sold the farm to Hannah Jorgensen's grandfather for pennies on the dollar. The Rodriguez family has never forgiven the Jorgensens for taking advantage of them when they were in desperate need, for profiting from their misfortune." Mrs. Diegel shrugged. "It happens all the time. It's just sensible business to buy as cheaply as you can."

"Not if it's unfair," said Elizabeth. "It's unethical to offer less than the land is worth if the person has no choice but to accept or starve."

Mrs. Diegel smiled at her fondly. "And that, my dear, is why you will never be a businesswoman. But the Rodriguezes agree with you, not me. Allow a Rodriguez girl to marry a Jorgensen boy? Absolutely unthinkable."

"Even after so many years?"

"Resentment has a long memory."

"That explains why Rosa couldn't marry Lars, but not why she settled for John."

"It probably didn't seem like settling at the time. He might not look like much to a girl your age today, but back then, he was considered one of the more handsome young men in the valley—and he owned his own farm. He was someone Rosa's family accepted, and he had always admired Rosa. John and Lars had vied for her affection since they were boys in school." A troubled frown briefly clouded Mrs. Diegel's expression. "Although Lars was the one

Rosa truly loved, I believe she was still fond of John. They might have had a happy life, had tragedy not turned John so bitter."

Perhaps, but Rosa never could have imagined what would befall her in the years to come. She had chosen a path when she chose her husband, as all brides did. It had probably seemed as smooth and as sunny as any she could have walked along. But no young wife knows what sort of man her husband will become. She only knows what he is at the moment she marries him and trusts that he will not fail her, that his love will always be true, no matter what hardships they encounter.

"That's all in the past," said Mrs. Diegel. "Rosa married John and that was the end of it. You said you had a favor to ask me?"

Her question brought an abrupt end to Elizabeth's reverie. "Yes. I wanted to know if I could use your phone. I'll pay the charges, of course."

Mrs. Diegel's eyebrows rose. "Is the Jorgensens' phone out?"

"No, but I wanted some privacy."

"And you didn't want to ask Hannah's permission." Mrs. Diegel gestured toward her office, through an open doorway behind the desk. "Help yourself. Don't worry about the charges. You brought me my mail and spared Carlos a drive today. I suppose I owe you a favor in return."

Elizabeth thanked her, with misgivings. It had not occurred to her that by bringing Mrs. Diegel her mail, she would cost the isolated Rosa a visit from her brother. Even though the siblings were apparently estranged, Rosa probably would have been glad to see him, and perhaps the sight of his nieces and nephew would eventually soften his heart.

Suddenly Elizabeth was struck by a puzzling question: Why should Rosa and Carlos be estranged? Hadn't Rosa followed her family's wishes and married the man they approved of, even though she loved his rival more?

Elizabeth pondered this as she dialed the operator and read Grover Higgins's number off the business card, but she quickly set her curiosity aside when the operator connected her with the office of Golden Reel Productions. "Go ahead," a man barked into the phone before she had prepared herself.

"Mr. Higgins? Grover Higgins?"

"Speaking. Who's this?"

"I'm Elizabeth Nelson. We met at Venice Beach a couple of months ago. You gave me your card and encouraged me to call you if I was interested in appearing in one of your films."

"I did, did I? Venice Beach . . . Hold on, I think I remember. Are you that redhead?"

"No, I'm a blonde." Confidence wavering, Elizabeth added, "You said that girls only half as pretty as I am become stars in Hollywood every day."

He chuckled. "I say that to a lot of dolls. You're going to have to remind me."

"We met at a dance marathon," said Elizabeth. "At first you mistook me for the actress from *Thief of Baghdad.* You said you had several scripts on your desk that I would be ideal for."

"Say, I remember you now. You're that wholesome-looking girl from Ohio, the one with the pushy husband."

"Pennsylvania," said Elizabeth. "But otherwise, that's me."

"And now you've decided you want to be a star after all."

"Yes, please. I would. Is the offer still open?"

"Maybe it is and maybe it isn't. How's your husband feel about this?"

Elizabeth took a quick breath and instinctively glanced over her shoulder as if she expected to find Henry there, arms folded over his chest, glaring at her. "Like you said that day, I'm a girl who makes her own decisions."

"I'm glad to hear it. Well, when are you coming to Hollywood? I could set up a screen test. Not this week, maybe next week." She heard his chair creak and papers rustle. "We could have dinner, maybe go dancing. I can get us into the most exclusive speakeasies in Los Angeles. A looker like you would fit right in. Are you a drinking girl?"

"Not really. Actually, I was rather hoping that you might be coming my way. I live in the Arboles Valley now and I understand that—"

"You live where?"

"The Arboles Valley."

"Where the hell is that?"

"It's about forty-five miles north of Los Angeles. It's where Safari World—"

"Oh, right, right. George Hanneman's wild animal farm. Great fellow. You're really out in the sticks, aren't you?"

Elizabeth ignored that. "I thought that perhaps if you came out to Safari World, we could arrange to meet—"

"Hold on, sister. As much as I hate to turn down a meeting with a pretty blonde, I'm not producing anything that would take me out to Safari World any time soon. Besides, we always do our casting here in the office, not on location."

"I see, but if you—"

"If you want to be a star, you have to go where the action is. Why don't you ditch the stiff and come out to Hollywood?"

"Ditch the—"

"The husband. Lose the husband. He's holding you back, doll."

"I couldn't leave my husband," said Elizabeth. "I love him."

"That's too bad. If you ever change your mind—"

"It's not something I can change my mind about. You either love someone or you don't, and I do."

"If you say so, sister. You don't need to bite my head off. I'm not the one calling on the sly."

"Thanks anyway, Mr. Higgins. Good afternoon." Elizabeth hung up the phone. How dare he suggest she leave her husband? How dare he imply that she was so fickle that she would cast Henry aside and dash off to Hollywood on his word alone? Not that she would leave Henry even for an iron-clad contract and a guaranteed starring role as Rudolph Valentino's leading lady, but still. What did he take her for?

She could never work for Mr. Higgins, that much was obvious. Her only hope now was to meet a director through Safari World. Perhaps if she pleased Caroline Hanneman and the wranglers by finding them the perfect horses for their show, they would introduce her to some of their Hollywood friends. She would not count herself out yet.

Mrs. Diegel peered at her inquiringly as she stormed out of the office. "Bad news?"

"Not bad, exactly, just disappointing. It wasn't even worth the price of the call."

"Good thing you're not paying for it, then." Mrs. Diegel glanced toward the bar as a burst of laughter floated through the open doorway. "Such carrying on in the middle of the day when honest folk are working. Still, can't complain, as long as they keep buying her ginger ales. Goodness knows how she's doctoring it up. No one likes ginger ale that much."

Elizabeth was lost. "Who are you talking about?"

"A woman from back east who came up from Los Angeles last night." Mrs. Diegel shook her head in amused disapproval. "I didn't like the look of her at first. She's not the sort of young lady I usually welcome into my hotel. I thought she was searching for gentlemen callers of the paying kind, if you get my meaning. But she hasn't gone upstairs with a man on her arm, so I suppose she's harmless. It would be bad for business, you know. These days most of my guests are married men looking for lots in the new developments.

Their wives would put a stop to any deal if they thought we encouraged licentious behavior in the Arboles Valley, and that's money out of my pocket."

"You mean you get a cut from the real estate agents?"

Mrs. Diegel winced as if she had said too much. "To steer customers their way, yes. Don't say anything. They each think I'm working for them alone, to praise their development and criticize their competitors.' I'm not doing any harm. All I do is figure out which way the customer is leaning and then prod them along in that direction."

"It's just business," Elizabeth finished for her, although something about it seemed vaguely improper.

"You're catching on." Mrs. Diegel shook her head at another roar of laughter. "Funny, she didn't seem especially witty to me, especially the way she kept going on about that Triumph Ranch, but she sure knows how to entertain."

Elizabeth's heart thumped. "What?"

"She didn't strike me as very witty. You know the type—scandalously short skirt, cigarette holder, bobbed hair—no offense to you, of course—but maybe not a lot going on upstairs."

"No, I mean—you said she was talking about a place called Triumph Ranch?"

"Oh, yes. She insists it's a prosperous cattle ranch here in the Arboles Valley. When I told her I had never heard of it, she looked at me as if I must not be very bright or I don't get out much. She has some nerve. I know the name of every ranch in this valley, and if I haven't heard of it, it isn't here." Mrs. Diegel frowned thoughtfully. "Carlos and Rosa's great-grandparents called their land El Rancho Triunfo before they sold to the Jorgensen family, but it hasn't been known by that name for decades. If that's what this girl is looking for, why didn't she simply ask for the Jorgensen farm?"

"Oh, no." Even through her surprise Elizabeth felt the prickling of conscience. She and Henry had only thought of themselves when they decided not to go to the authorities to report how they had been swindled. Why had it not occurred to them that the con man who had sold Triumph Ranch to the Nelsons and two others before them would stop there?

"What's wrong?" Mrs. Diegel asked.

"I think your new guest has been deceived by a con man," said Elizabeth, steeling herself. Someone had to tell this unfortunate woman the truth, and it would be better to hear it from a sympathetic fellow victim than John Barclay, who had been more concerned with the inconvenience to himself than the Nelsons' misfortune when they tried to pick up the deed of trust at the land office.

Before Mrs. Diegel could press her for more details, Elizabeth entered the barroom.

There, sitting at the bar, surrounded by a cluster of admiring men, was a slender, fashionably dressed young woman wearing dark red lipstick and a cloche hat on her sleek black bob. She glanced toward the doorway and her face lit up in recognition.

"Hiya, kid," Mae called to her. "How's tricks?"

"Mae," Elizabeth managed to say. "What—you're—"

"Yeah, I'm happy to see you, too." Mae slipped gracefully from her bar stool and crossed the room. The men's eyes followed her swaying hips appreciatively. Elizabeth stood frozen just inside the doorway as Mae gave her air kisses on both cheeks. "Where have you been hiding? Not even the hotel keeper knows about this ranch of yours, and there can't be *that* many ranches for her to keep straight."

Elizabeth forced a shaky smile. "Things didn't turn out as we had planned. What—what are you doing here?"

"I came to visit you and that handsome husband of yours, of course." Mae linked her arm through Elizabeth's and steered her from the barroom. "I've been cooped up in this hotel long enough. Let's go to your place."

Mrs. Diegel watched them cross the lobby together, but with an innkeeper's practiced discretion, she pretended to find nothing unusual in the sight of a stylish flapper carrying on as if she were the stunned farm wife's dearest friend. Outside, at the sight of Mae, Lars's stoic mask slipped and he shot Elizabeth a look of astonishment.

"Why, Henry," Mae said with mock sternness when Elizabeth failed to introduce them. "Ranch life has not been kind to you."

"Mae, this is Lars Jorgensen," Elizabeth quickly said. "Lars, this is Mae. We met on the train coming west."

"Charmed, I'm sure." Mae gave Lars a winning smile and gracefully extended a hand.

Lars shook it somewhat awkwardly and helped her into the front seat of the car while Elizabeth climbed into the back. As they drove away from the hotel, Mae held up the burden of conversation, asking questions about the town with a curiosity that would have been charming in other circumstances, admiring the scenic beauty of the landscape, marveling at the loveliness of the weather. Elizabeth responded as well as she could, but all the while her thoughts were racing. This could not possibly be a simple social call. When they had parted with Mae in St. Louis, she had said she would return to New York. What was she doing in California, and in a place as remote as the Arboles Valley?

What would Henry say?

All too soon and not soon enough, the yellow farmhouse came into view. "This is quite a place you have here," said Mae admiringly.

"Thank you," said Lars, although Elizabeth knew the remark had been directed at her. Mae glanced at Lars, eyebrows arched in mild surprise, but she said nothing.

"Henry and I have our own place about a half mile south," said Elizabeth quickly. "Lars, I don't think Mae can make that walk in those shoes. Would you mind dropping us off there?"

Lars shrugged and agreed. When the cabin came into sight, Mae said nothing until the car came to a stop a few yards away. Then she laughed in astonishment. "This is the place?"

Elizabeth nodded. "This is home."

"And the cattle?" Mae asked. "They're hiding out back, I guess?"

"There are no cattle." Elizabeth could not bear to look Lars's way as she climbed out of the car, clutching the mail. "Come on. I'll take you inside."

"It's . . . cozy. A little rustic, but nice," said Mae consolingly as she picked her way across the dusty yard and up the front stairs. "I think I'll be staying at the hotel tonight, though."

Elizabeth showed Mae inside, leaving the letters on the mantel. "Please make yourself at home. There's bread in the pantry and you can get fresh water from the pump at the kitchen sink. I'm sorry I can't stay. I have to get back to work."

"Don't worry about me." Mae settled herself into the best of the chairs. "I'll just put my feet up and relax, you know, take in the fresh country air."

"I'll be back by seven," Elizabeth promised. "I'm sorry to be such a poor hostess. I'll bring you supper."

When Mae cheerfully waved off her apologies, Elizabeth gave her a quick smile and hurried outside to the car. "Don't ask," she told Lars as she climbed in and slammed the door.

"I wasn't going to," he replied.

They drove the short distance back to the garage in silence. Once there, Elizabeth said, "Mae will need a ride back to the hotel this evening. May I borrow the car?"

"That's all right. I'll take her."

"That's kind of you, but I don't want to impose."

"It's no trouble."

Grateful, Elizabeth thanked him and hurried into the kitchen. Later, when Henry and the other men came inside for supper, Elizabeth took him aside for a moment. "We have company back at the cabin."

Henry blanched. "Who?"

"Mae. From the train."

Relief mingled with surprise in Henry's expression. "I thought you were going to say it was someone from home." Then surprise won out. "Mae? Here? What does she want?"

"I don't know."

"Is Peter with her?"

Elizabeth shook her head. "She hasn't spoken a word about him. I assume he's in prison."

"She's not coming up to the house for supper, is she?"

"I hadn't thought to invite her." How could she extend an invitation without seeking Mrs. Jorgensen's permission first? "I promised to bring her something to eat."

"Get back to the cabin as soon as you can and keep an eye on her. I'll try to find some excuse to come home early. The last thing we need is for her to rob us blind."

Elizabeth knew he was thinking of their carefully saved wages, hidden in a coffee can in the chimney. "If she wanted to rob someone, I think she would have chosen a more affluent victim."

"She and Peter aren't exactly pillars of the community. I don't think she'd pass up an opportunity to make a fast buck."

Elizabeth could not defend Mae, so she merely nodded and hurried to the kitchen to begin serving dinner. Mae had been kind to her on the train, but obviously she wanted something from the Nelsons or she would not have come. If she *had* intended to rob them, she had surely changed her mind when she discovered that they were not wealthy ranch owners after all.

Throughout the meal, Elizabeth waited for Lars to mention the unexpected guest he had escorted back from the Grand Union Hotel, but he said nothing. The longer she knew him, the more she realized that he knew how to keep a secret. Afterward, as she cleared the table, she wrapped two pieces of fried chicken and several biscuits in a clean cloth and hid them in the pantry. When Mrs. Jorgensen dismissed her for the evening, she quickly retrieved the bundle and raced back to the cabin.

There she discovered Mae had built a fire on the hearth and was sitting beside it in a rocking chair reading Elizabeth's mail. Not only the new letters she had left on the mantel, but all of the letters from home she kept tied with a ribbon in her trunk.

"What do you think you're doing?" Elizabeth exclaimed, crossing the room and snatching up the letters.

"Don't be sore," said Mae. "I got bored. There's not a lot of entertainment around here. Say, what kind of scam are you running on the folks back home?"

"It's not a scam." Elizabeth returned the letters to the trunk and fastened the latch firmly.

"They seem to believe you and Henry are big-time cattle ranchers. Come to think of it, that's what you told Peter and me. What happened?"

Elizabeth hated to admit the truth, but that was preferable to being thought of as a con artist. "We aren't scamming anyone. We're the ones who were cheated. It was all a lie. Henry gave his life savings for a handful of worthless papers. Now we work for the real owners of the property—but they don't know the truth about us, so please don't tell them."

"My lips are sealed." Mae shook her head in sympathy. "That's a tough break, honey. Any chance you'll find the guy and get your money back?"

"I doubt it." Elizabeth looked up as the door swung open and

Henry entered, grim-faced. "Hi, sweetheart. You remember Mae."

"Of course." Henry went to the kitchen, pumped water into the sink, and briskly washed his face and hands. Elizabeth quickly offered him a towel. "What brings you to the Arboles Valley? I have to admit, you're the last person I expected to see here."

"You get right down to business. I like that." Mae crossed her ankles and folded her hands in her lap. "Why don't you pull up a chair and we'll talk?"

Henry left the damp towel on the kitchen counter and took a seat on Elizabeth's steamer trunk across from Mae. Elizabeth hesitated before following. When all were seated, Mae gave them a dim smile. "I think you know that Peter works for some tough characters."

"He's in prison now, though, isn't he?" Elizabeth asked. Somehow that seemed to offer some protection against whatever it was that Mae had come to tell them.

"Yes, but that doesn't let him off the hook," said Mae. "His bosses sent him to Los Angeles to solve a transportation problem bringing certain goods from the city to their clients in Oxnard and other places further north. If they manage to avoid getting hijacked or having their drivers run off with the merchandise, they have to dump the cargo when the Feds set up a roadblock. It's always one thing or another, and it's ruining business."

"Peter mentioned that," said Henry. "He asked for my help and I refused. I haven't changed my mind."

Mae held up a hand, a request for patience so she could continue. "Peter was also supposed to deliver a payment—a huge chunk of change—to the Los Angeles bosses. When the cops took Peter in St. Louis, they also took the money." Mae took a deep breath and clasped her hands tightly in her lap. "They expect me to pay them back, or work off Peter's debt."

"Why you?" exclaimed Elizabeth. "None of this is your fault."

"That's not how they look at it. They don't like losing money. They think—or at least they *say*—that Peter's too smart to allow himself to be taken in with that kind of cash on him. They think he must have left it on the train, and that I picked it up."

"Is that true?" asked Henry.

"No," retorted Mae. "What do you take me for, some Dumb Dora who'd steal from the Mob? If I did have the money, you'd better believe I'd hand it over rather than be in the spot I'm in now."

"What spot is that, exactly?" asked Elizabeth.

"Like I said, I have to pay them back. Either I give them the cash or I work it off by setting up the deal Peter wasn't able to arrange."

Henry's expression was stony. "And if you don't?"

Mae took in a shaky breath, but she met Henry's gaze steadily. "They'll kill me. Not only because I'll have proven that I'm not useful, but to get back at Peter for letting himself get caught with their cash on him."

"You should go to the police at once," said Elizabeth.

Mae made a strangling noise, incredulous. "You're a regular laugh riot, Liz. You should be on the radio. Me, go to the police with this story? I don't think it would wash."

"We can't help you," said Henry, rising abruptly from his chair. "I'm not about to get mixed up in criminal activities. Even if I were, take a look around. This is all we have now, and it's not even really ours. Peter would be the first to tell you to look somewhere else."

"No, he wouldn't. Are you kidding?" Mae rose and turned around in the center of the room, taking in the cabin. "This is even better than Triumph Ranch. This is perfect. What cop is going to suspect a farmhand and his wife living in a dilapidated old cabin in the middle of nowhere? Let me tell you, the people who work for Peter's bosses live it up. They don't rough it. No one would ever think to look here."

"And we're going to keep it that way." Henry strode across the room and opened the door. "I'm sorry you're in trouble, Mae, but I have to ask you to leave."

"But her life is in danger." Elizabeth rose and put her arm around Mae's shoulders. "They've threatened to kill her. We can't just send her away."

Henry hesitated before closing the door. "Can't you just disappear, Mae? Can't you change your name, start over in San Francisco or Seattle, someplace as far from New York as you can get?"

"You don't know these people. They'll look for me no matter where I go." Mae chewed on her lip then shrugged "If I lie low for a few years, dye my hair, keep my nose clean—I don't know. It might work. Except that I'm broke. Peter's bosses took every cent I had. I can't even pay for that tiny room in that hotel where Liz found me. If I get caught stowing away on a train to San Francisco, Peter's bosses will send someone to finish me off."

"You won't have to stow away." Henry went to the fireplace, reached up into the flue, and pulled out the coffee can, covered in soot. He lifted the lid and took out three rolls of bills bound with rubber bands. It was every dollar they had saved since coming to work for the Jorgensens.

Henry weighed the rolls in his palm for a moment, and then pressed them into Mae's hands. "Here. Take them." He let the coffee can fall to the floor with a thin clank. "Make a better life for yourself somewhere, and don't come back."

Mae fingered one of the rolls, and Elizabeth could tell she was rapidly calculating her windfall. "Are you sure you can spare it?"

Henry dropped tiredly into a chair. "Just take it and go before I change my mind."

Elizabeth quickly guided Mae to the door. "Come on." Without a word, Mae hurried along beside her across the sagging porch and down the steps. "Lars Jorgensen offered to drive you back to the hotel. Wait in the garage while I get him." How she would do that without provoking curiosity from the other Jorgensens, she had no idea.

When they were halfway to the yellow farmhouse, Mae said, "Thank you for this."

"You're welcome," said Elizabeth, because she could think of nothing else to say. She was proud of Henry for the sacrifice he had made to save Mae's life, and yet—all of their wages, gone. They were as poor as they had been on their first day in the Arboles Valley.

"I'll repay you someday."

"When you can," agreed Elizabeth, although she did not expect to hear from Mae ever again.

"Wait, Liz." Mae stopped short. "Even if I disappear, Peter's bosses are still going to want a place to stash their merchandise. If not Triumph Ranch, then somewhere else in the valley. Someone's going to get paid to help them. It might as well be you."

"You heard Henry. It won't be us. We can't help it if someone else goes into business with Peter's bosses, but we won't. How could you suggest we get tangled up with those people after what they've done to you?"

Mae shrugged, acknowledging her point. "Maybe there's another way. What's the name of the fellow who conned you?"

"J. T. Simmons, or at least that's what he called himself. But he's long gone. As far as we know, he's back east looking for his next victim."

"Peter has connections all along the East Coast. Maybe they can track this fellow down and get your money back."

"If he hasn't spent it already."

"It's worth a try." Mae grinned. "At least we can make him sorry he picked Henry for his mark."

"No, Mae." A vision of how Peter's friends might punish the con artist came unbidden to her mind. Sickened, she forced the thoughts away. "Please don't do anything rash. If Peter's contacts do find this Mr. Simmons, turn him in to the police."

"Liz, don't you know me by now?" Mae gave her a smile that was almost wistful. "Peter and me and his friends, we don't go to the cops. Cops aren't for people like us. They're for people like you."

Elizabeth muffled a sigh. Mae did not sound like a woman who intended to break all ties with her past and start a new life as a law-abiding citizen. "I don't want any man, however despicable, to be killed for any wrong done to me. Besides, you can't contact any of Peter's old friends. Someone will talk, and then Peter's bosses will know where to start searching for you."

Mae nodded, and Elizabeth could read in her expression her dawning awareness of all that her self-imposed exile would require to succeed.

They walked the rest of the way in silence. To Elizabeth's relief, Lars had anticipated their arrival and was waiting for them in the garage, sparing her a trip into the farmhouse, where Mrs. Jorgensen and Mary Katherine were sure to wonder why she had come. Mae squeezed her hand in farewell and gave a jaunty wave as the car pulled away. Then she was gone.

Elizabeth made her way carefully along the moonlit path back to the cabin, where she found Henry slumped wearily in his chair, staring at the dying embers in the fireplace. "I'll get more wood," she said, turning to go back outside.

Henry jumped up from his chair. "No, I'll do it." He paused as he passed her in the doorway, then reached out to brush a loose curl off her cheek. "Your hair is growing out."

She nodded, knowing what that meant.

"You would have been able to go home soon." His hand fell to his side. "Now it will be months."

"You did what you had to do," said Elizabeth firmly. "We couldn't send Mae back to those vicious men."

"How do we know she isn't on her way to them right now?" he countered. "She could use our money to pay off part of Peter's debt, then turn around and find someone else to help stash his bosses' contraband. Next thing you know, she'll be up to her neck in a sea of other problems."

"When someone desperately needs your help, you don't stand around and ponder what they'll do once you help them, or philosophize about whether they deserve your help. You simply help them."

Henry stared at her for a moment before choking out a bleak laugh. "You sound exactly like your aunt Eleanor. Without a doubt, you belong back in Pennsylvania with your family."

"*You* are my family," said Elizabeth. "I'm getting tired of repeating myself. I'm not going home without you."

Without a word, Henry touched her cheek gently with the back of his fingers, but his eyes told her he was resolute. Before she could seize hold of his hand, he stepped outside into the night. For one fearful moment, she forgot he was only going out back for more wood for the fire. For a moment, she forgot that he would return to her.

1912

John Barclay courted Rosa for two years. Once a month he came to Sunday dinner at the Diazes' home, and every other Saturday he took Rosa out on a date—a picnic, a dance at the church social hall, a day at Lake Sherwood with friends. John was courteous, polite, with a smoldering reserve that lingered long after the couples' secret was exposed. Isabel was glad that Rosa seemed to be taking her time to make up her mind about him, because she wasn't sure how she felt about him herself. John had a steeliness about him that made Isabel uncomfortable. He was so unlike her Miguel, warm and affectionate, that she wondered how Rosa had ever become fond of him. Perhaps he had hidden qualities, rich strains deep within, that only Rosa had discovered. In time, perhaps Isabel and Miguel would find them, too.

Isabel had hoped that allowing Rosa to see John openly would bring an end to her late-night disappearances, but in this, Rosa bitterly, bewilderingly failed her. Isabel begged her to stop running off at night, wept over her, threatened to tell her father, but it was little use. Rosa would mend her ways for a little while to appease her mother, but within a month or two, Isabel would wake in the night to find her daughter's bed empty.

"Why don't you just marry him?" she begged, meeting her daughter at the door one morning before dawn. Rosa was pale and frightened to have been caught in the act of returning home after staying out all night, but she was also resolute. Although she apologized for upsetting her mother, she would not promise to put an end to her illicit disappearances. Isabel knew then that nothing she said or did would prevent her daughter from following the path she had chosen, even if it led to her ruin.

She was at a loss to explain Rosa's behavior. She was twenty-two, old enough to be married with a home of her own. Why sneak off at night to be with the man she loved when she could become his wife and be by his side for the rest of her life? Nothing impeded Rosa except her inexplicable reluctance to give her consent. Isabel marked John's growing impatience and feared that he would tire of waiting, tire of Rosa herself. What would Rosa do if John decided not to wait anymore and found someone else, someone more willing to become his bride?

After so many years, if Rosa could not decide whether to marry John, perhaps that was a sign he was wrong for her. But there was nothing Isabel could do but hold her breath, pray for God's protection, and wait for Rosa to reach her own conclusions.

Carlos had finished school and, with a recommendation from his sister, had obtained a job as a handyman at the Grand Union Hotel. He had his father's friendly, cheerful disposition and had become an entertaining storyteller as well. As Isabel cooked in the kitchen or sewed in the evenings in her rocking chair, Carlos would have her alternately laughing and marveling over his tales of the people who came and went at the hotel. She hoped he embellished his stories liberally, because otherwise she was not sure she should allow her children to work there. A married, churchgoing businessman who met his sister-in-law in a private room every Monday at ten in the morning and checked out by noon. The card shark who passed through town in a whirlwind and left the wallets of some of the Arboles Valley's most prominent citizens lighter when the dust settled. Strange phone calls Mrs. Diegel received on the last Friday of every month, sending Rosa out of the office as soon as the operator rang so not a word would be overheard by anyone.

Most of his tales were so shocking or amusing or both that it passed unnoticed when Lars Jorgensen, the eldest of the two sons, began appearing more frequently in them. Lars frequently came to the hotel to drink at the bar; Isabel already knew this disgraceful fact about him and dismissed his presence at the hotel as she dismissed the whole Jorgensen family. Then Carlos mentioned that he had heard raised voices in the citrus garden once, and when he had gone to see what was wrong, he found Lars and John Barclay in a shoving match. Then one afternoon in July he came home from work remarking that the Jorgensens' apricot harvest must have gone well, because he had seen Lars carrying a basket of the fresh, ripe fruit into the hotel office. "Probably gave it to Mrs. Diegel to pay off his bar tab," he joked.

Not ten minutes later, Rosa walked in smiling and carrying a basket of apricots.

Isabel went cold, but she forced herself to remain calm. "Where did you get those?"

Rosa glanced at the basket in her hands. "Mrs. Diegel gave them to me." She set the basket down on the counter, too quickly. "She didn't want them, so she gave them to me."

It was a lie. Mrs. Diegel never gave away anything unless she received something in return. And she would never give an employee an entire basket of fruit that could be put to better use as dessert for the guests of the hotel.

Suddenly all the lies and deception since Rosa was a girl of fourteen made perfect sense.

It was that Jorgensen boy Rosa loved, not John Barclay. Lars Jorgensen, who stank of alcohol and whose grandfather had stolen the Rancho Triunfo from her own dear *abuelo* and *abuelita*.

"You will never see him again," she said quietly.

Rosa looked back at her, eyes wide and startled. "Mami?"

"Marry John or don't marry him, but you will never see Lars Jorgensen again. If you promise me this, I will not tell your father. I am thinking of him as much as you. You would break his heart if he knew."

"He wouldn't care," Rosa choked out through her tears. "*You're* the only one who cares. Papi doesn't hate the Jorgensens; you do."

"They have destroyed our family!"

"They haven't! We're here, aren't we?"

"They stole our land. They killed my mother."

"They *bought* our land. Cancer killed your mother. If you were not such a bitter old woman with nothing but hatred in your soul, you would see that. Then Lars and I could be happy."

"Happy? With that drunk? If you think he would make you so happy, then why don't you tell your father about him? He'll be home soon. You tell him how you've been running out at night to meet with that Jorgensen boy and see how happy he is to hear the news. We'll see whose side he takes—the deceitful daughter's or the bitter old woman's. We'll see."

Sobbing, Rosa fled to her room, overturning the basket of apricots. The fruit tumbled to the floor. Isabel scrambled after it, but it was too late; the fruit was bruised and soiled.

She did not care, except for the mess. She would never feed her family anything that grew in Jorgensen soil. It was poison to her, just as she had told Miguel so many years before. Everything that grew on Jorgensen land was poison to her, to her family, to her children.

Chapter Nine

1925

With their savings exhausted, Elizabeth resolved to allow nothing to prevent her from searching for horses for Safari World on her next day off—assuming Lars would let her borrow his car. When Mary Katherine invited her to spend the next Sunday afternoon at Lake Sherwood with her and the girls, Elizabeth reluctantly made the excuse that she had letters to write and work to catch up on at home.

"You and that husband of yours," exclaimed Mary Katherine. "Honestly. You two are a perfect pair. All you enjoy is work, work, work."

"I didn't say I enjoyed it," Elizabeth said, smiling. But her amusement swiftly faded. Once, not very long ago, she had considered herself and Henry to be a perfect pair, too, if not for the reasons Mary Katherine stated. She was surprised anyone found them a perfect pair anymore. Elizabeth felt as if a chasm stretched between them, so wide and deep that it could not have existed without years of erosion and toil. But it was newly sprung up between them, and for that reason alone, Elizabeth clung to the hope that the distance was not unbridgeable.

If only she could figure out why Henry insisted upon standing alone on his side of the gulf, when all she wanted to do was stand beside him.

All week she tried to think of an excuse to borrow the car, but she could not. Finally, on Friday afternoon, she went to Lars and told him straight out that she had errands to run the next day. "Barclay doesn't open the post office on Saturdays," he told her.

"I'm not going to the post office."

He regarded her with barely concealed amusement. "Before I let you drive off in my car, I'd like to know where you might be taking it."

"Very well, if you insist, I have a business arrangement with Safari World and I need transportation to carry it out."

"Becoming a lion tamer, are you?"

"And give up my glamorous life here? Not likely. May I borrow the car? Yes or no?"

"No." Before she could protest, he added, "Oscar and my mother need it on Saturday, but I'll hitch up Bonnie to the wagon for you if that will do."

"In that case, I'd prefer to go on horseback."

Lars seemed surprised that she knew how to ride, but he agreed. On Saturday, when Mrs. Jorgensen allowed her a few hours off after lunch, he saddled up a horse for her, although she had assured him she could do it herself. She rode off along country roads, exploring the southern half of the valley and taking note of the horses she spotted in corrals and pastures along the way. She found many suitable animals, but none as swift or as beautiful as Bergstrom Thoroughbreds. When she came across an especially fine animal, she would stop and inquire at the farmhouse to see if it was for sale. Most often the owners were not interested in parting with their horses; other times they were, but set a price far higher than she suspected the wranglers would be willing to pay. Still, she wrote down the relevant information for the most likely purchases and by the time she had to return to the farmhouse to help prepare supper, she had a modest list of horses comparable to those she had seen performing at Safari World.

On Sunday, she did not bother to ask Henry if he wanted to spend the day together. She could not bear for him to refuse her again, and for a change, she actually preferred to be on her own. Lars had a horse saddled and ready for her, so she set out for the northern half of the valley. Since fewer farms were scattered over a wider area, and the Salto Canyon took up much of the land, she hoped to finish searching the valley by late afternoon, allowing her just enough time to ride out to Safari World and report her findings to the wranglers before the end of the day.

She added two prospective horses from the northeastern part of the valley to her list, wondering how the wranglers had missed them, since they were fine animals and the owner eager to sell. Then she headed west, where the road passed by a mesa that stretched as flat as a tabletop for acres before dropping abruptly at the canyon's edge.

In the distance, not far from a sudden descent so sharp that it looked as if a blade had cut into the earth, Elizabeth spotted a wagon and, nearby, two horses grazing. The wagon appeared empty, but in the golden-brown grasses between it and the canyon, several smaller figures moved. Curious, thinking that perhaps the wagon had thrown an axle and its passengers might be waiting for help, Elizabeth directed her horse off the road and across the mesa toward them. When she had closed the distance to a quarter mile, she recognized Rosa Barclay and her children.

Seated on the grass, Rosa looked up quickly when Elizabeth's horse whinnied a greeting. Just as quickly, Rosa turned her head away and tugged on the wide brim of her hat to partially conceal her face. Pretending she had not noticed the snub, Elizabeth called out, "Hello, Rosa. What brings you out this way?"

"I promised the children a picnic," said Rosa, stroking Miguel's dark, curly locks as he rested on her lap. Her voice was hesitant, but not chilly.

Encouraged, Elizabeth dismounted from her horse, who promptly lowered his neck and began grazing. "I think you found the perfect place for it." She smiled as she went to join Rosa, watching Marta and Lupita play. Ana sat just outside the circle of her sisters' play, laughing at their antics. She looked as if she had long ago accepted that she could not join in.

"The mesa offers the most beautiful view of the canyon and it is not too far from home." Softly, Rosa added, "It is just far enough away for me to feel as if I am somewhere else." Suddenly she smiled as if they shared a secret. "My husband believes my mother's spirit haunts the mesa. He does not wish to see her, so he avoids it."

Elizabeth tucked her skirt around her legs and sat down beside her. "Ana seems better today."

"Yes, she is out of bed for now," said Rosa. She hesitated before adding, "That is how the illness runs its course. They fall ill, then recover, then fall ill again, and recover, until one time they fall ill and do not recover."

"Perhaps . . . perhaps Ana and Miguel are not doomed to that fate. Don't lose hope."

"They're my children. I'll never stop praying for a miracle. Not while there is breath in my body."

Tentatively, Elizabeth said, "Forgive me for prying, but have you considered a doctor in a larger city, Los Angeles or San Francisco, perhaps?"

Rosa gazed down at her sleeping son. "We don't have the money to travel so far, or the money to pay for such a skilled doctor."

"Some doctors are willing to waive their fees in certain circumstances."

Rosa shook her heard. "Even so, I doubt my husband would be willing to travel so far. He will not leave the farm. He has no hired hands to look after our place."

How could any father, even John Barclay, not pursue any course that might save the lives of his children? "Why don't you at least write to some other doctors and tell them about your children's affliction? Maybe they've seen cases like this before. What if they could recommend a new treatment the doctors around here haven't considered? If a doctor could figure out why some of your children fall ill and some do not—"

Sharply, Rosa turned to look at her—and that was when Elizabeth saw her bruised face, her swollen, cut lip, which she had tried to conceal with the wide-brimmed hat. "Rosa," she gasped. "What happened to you?"

Rosa looked away and with her fingers tried to comb her dark brown hair over her bruised cheek. "It's nothing. I tripped on a stone and fell against the wagon."

"How many times?"

Rosa held perfectly still for a moment, but then her hand came to rest lightly upon Miguel's head. "I told you, it's nothing."

"It never ceases to amaze me how the wives of cruel men are always so clumsy."

"I know you're trying to be kind, but this is not your concern. You don't know how I have provoked him."

Elizabeth began to rise. "If you aren't going to defend yourself, perhaps your brother will."

"Elizabeth, no." Rosa seized her hand and pulled until Elizabeth had to sit back down or fall. "Don't get Carlos involved in this. He would do nothing to help me even if he knew."

Elizabeth immediately thought of Lars, but said nothing, suspecting that would only upset Rosa more. "Rosa, please. You can't stay with a man who beats you."

"He's my husband and the father of my children. Where else would I go?"

"You and the children can stay with me and my husband."

At that, Rosa smiled. "You're very gracious, but I don't think your husband would like to share that little cabin with five strangers."

"Henry would be the first to insist you stay as long as you like. We have plenty of room. Our cabin is more spacious than it seems from the outside."

Rosa shook her head, but she regarded Elizabeth kindly. "I have seen the inside of the cabin as well as the outside, and I know there isn't room for seven."

Surprised, Elizabeth said, "When did you ever visit the cabin?"

"Long ago. My great-grandparents built it. My mother was born there."

"I had no idea."

Rosa watched her daughters for a moment, and when she spoke again, her voice was far away. "It was a good home, once, before it fell into ruin. My mother lived there as a very young child with her parents and grandparents, after they sold the ranch and stayed on as hired hands. Her stories of her childhood there were full of happiness and longing, even though her family left when she was very young, even though our own home was just as happy and full of love as the cabin of her memories."

"If you grew up surrounded by love," said Elizabeth, "I don't know how you can settle for anything less now."

"I brought this fate upon myself," replied Rosa. "Every choice I ever made led me to this place. Please don't feel sorry for me. I have my children. I am not without love."

Elizabeth did not know what to say. Rosa had her children, but for how long, unless she could get them the medical care they so urgently needed? And why on earth would John Barclay stand in the way? She would not expect compassion from any man who beat his wife, but even so, how could anyone be so coldhearted toward his own children?

. "If there is anything I can do for you," said Elizabeth, "if you ever need help or a place to go, my house is small, but the door is always open to you and your children."

Rosa smiled and reached out for her hand. "Thank you. You are very kind, kinder than I deserve, considering how my husband treated you in your misfortune. I can see why Lars thinks so highly of you."

"I don't consider any woman responsible for her husband's behavior." Elizabeth stood and brushed off her skirt, surprised to find herself warmed by Lars's approval. Suddenly she wondered how Rosa would know how Lars felt about her. When would he have told her? Elizabeth had accompanied him on every trip to the post office since she came to the Arboles Valley, and they had only left her sight that one time she had stayed in the adobe with Ana and Miguel. That must have been it, she supposed. She wondered what Lars would do if he could see Rosa now. He had loved her once, and he had treated her with compassion when no one else would. He would not stand by and let John hurt Rosa—but if Lars interfered, John might lash out at Rosa in revenge. If Rosa would not help herself, anyone else's actions might only make matters worse.

Reluctant to leave Rosa before convincing her to seek help, Elizabeth nonetheless mounted her horse and rode off, wishing she could do more for her. Rosa was in her thoughts as she rode through the rest of the valley, skipping only the Barclay farm in her search for suitable horses. By midafternoon she had compiled a list of more than a dozen possibilities, none new to the valley, which convinced her that the wranglers must have been lazy, disinterested, or tightfisted in their own efforts or they would have found the same horses she had.

On her way south toward Safari World, she decided to stop by the Grand Union Hotel to see if Mrs. Diegel knew of any farmers with horses to sell that she had overlooked. She found the innkeeper in the kitchen, discussing the supper menu with the cook. "You're too late to bid your friend good-bye," said Mrs. Diegel. "She checked out this morning."

Elizabeth waited for Mrs. Diegel to add that Mae had skipped out without paying her bill, and breathed a sigh of relief when she did not. "She's not really a friend," she felt compelled to explain. "I met her on the train and we parted ways in St. Louis. Her visit was . . . a surprise."

"She left a far sight happier than when she arrived, I'll say that much for her." Mrs. Diegel broke off to correct the kitchen maid's choice of serving platters, then took Elizabeth by the arm and led her to the parlor. Elizabeth had not intended to make a lengthy visit, so she explained her errand as they walked. Mrs. Diegel seemed surprised that Safari World had assigned her the task of finding performing horses, since usually Caroline Hanneman preferred to select them herself from a favorite horse breeder just north of Los Angeles. She scanned Elizabeth's list, said that she couldn't think of any other possibilities Elizabeth had missed, and commended her for striking out on her own in business.

"I'm just doing what's necessary," Elizabeth replied. "The sooner I earn enough money, the sooner I can buy back my quilts from you."

Mrs. Diegel's approving smile faded. "Well. As to that . . ." She gestured to an overstuffed armchair, but something in her tone fixed Elizabeth in place. "I'm still happy to sell you the Chimneys and Cornerstones quilt, but you'll have to contact the new owner if you wish to purchase the Double Wedding Ring."

Elizabeth felt faint. "New owner?"

"One of my guests fell in love with it and insisted upon buying it.

She made such a generous offer I couldn't reasonably turn her down."

"Of course you could have," said Elizabeth. "We had an agreement. You said I could buy it back from you when I had saved enough money."

"I didn't promise to wait forever," said Mrs. Diegel. "If you recall, I told you I couldn't promise what condition the quilt would be in by the time you could afford it."

"Yes, but I expected it to be here. Worn or faded, perhaps, but still here. I never dreamed you'd sell my quilt to anyone else."

"Elizabeth, dear, you know I'm a businesswoman. My guest made an offer you couldn't possibly match, not without years of saving."

Elizabeth had intended to do exactly that, if necessary. "I didn't know our understanding had a time limit." She took a deep breath to calm the swirl of her emotions. "Would you at least be willing to give me the new owner's name, so I can look into buying it back from her?"

For the first time, Mrs. Diegel looked as if she regretted what she had done. "Certainly, but I doubt she'll sell. It may not be easy to reach her. She and her husband came to view lots in Meadow-brook Hills, but I overheard her tell her husband several times that she's reluctant to live so far from Los Angeles." Shaking her head, Mrs. Diegel led Elizabeth to the lobby, where she looked up the woman's name and address in the guest registry and wrote them down in a quick scrawl. Handing the slip of paper to Elizabeth, she added, "I sold her the quilt as one last goodwill gesture to entice her to buy, but she was adamant, and her husband seemed eager to please her. I doubt she'll return."

Elizabeth's heart sank as she imagined the precious quilt that the women of her family had sewn with such care and affection lost in the city far to the south. She never should have agreed to part with it, not for the world.

She was too upset to do more than close her hand around the paper and leave without another word for Mrs. Diegel. If she could have taken the Chimneys and Cornerstones quilt with her, she would have. She stormed into the stable, where Carlos had offered to care for her horse. "Are you all right?" he asked as she brushed past him and began to saddle the horse.

It galled her that he showed concern for her while ignoring his own sister, who was in much greater need. "If you want to help someone, help Rosa," she said shortly, tightening the girths.

She had caught him off guard, but he quickly recovered. "She made her bed, and now she has to lie in it."

"With a husband who beats her?"

He hesitated. "John Barclay is not a kind man, but he loves my sister. He would never lay a hand on her."

"Oh, really?" Elizabeth tugged on the horse's reins and led him from the stable. "Then I wonder who gave her that black eye and split her lip."

Carlos stopped her with a touch on her arm. "What do you mean?"

"I saw her myself, on the mesa, right before I came here." It occurred to her then that the children had not seemed disturbed by their mother's appearance, which implied that they had grown accustomed to seeing her in that condition. "At first she claimed that she had tripped and hit her head on the wagon. I told her to seek help, but she seemed to think she would search in vain. Now I'm inclined to believe her."

"You saw her on the mesa? Near the Salto Canyon?"

"Is there any other mesa in the Arboles Valley?" Elizabeth swung herself up into the saddle and touched the horse with her heels. As she left, she called over her shoulder, "My brother would never allow any man to hit me."

She rode off, but she had not gone far before she began to

regret her words. She had not meant to goad Carlos into retaliating against John, which could make matters much worse for Rosa and the children. Rosa had refused Elizabeth's offers of help and would not thank her for her interference.

But she could not bear to stand aside and do nothing while the people of the Arboles Valley continued to ignore Rosa's suffering. Still, what could she do, especially if Rosa refused to leave her husband?

Deeply troubled, she continued south to Safari World, eager to complete her task and return home. Henry had grown so distant since they had come to this place. He had not kissed her or held her in his arms at night, and although her aunts had warned her that sometimes a husband's ardor faded, she had not expected that of Henry, and never so suddenly or so soon. She ached for him to love her as he had in the first days of their marriage, but if she could not have that, at least, perhaps, they could return to the friendship they had shared in the years before they married. She had been able to tell him anything then, and he had listened and offered his opinion—even when it starkly contradicted her own. If she could unburden herself to him now, perhaps he would help her figure out what to do. He had helped Mae, a woman he disapproved of and did not trust. Surely he would do even more for Rosa.

When she arrived at Safari World, she tied up the horse at the hitching post near the parking lot, more than three-quarters full. Over the roars of Charlie and his pride, she explained her errand to the woman at the ticket booth, who eyed her curiously for a moment before allowing her through the gate without paying admission. Elizabeth waited at the corral for the trainers to finish a performance, and waited some more rather than interrupt them as they cared for the horses afterward. Only then did she approach, striding confidently into the stable yard rather than calling out to the men over the fence as she had done before. If she expected them to see her as a woman of business, she had to play the part.

The men looked up as she approached. "Miss, all visitors have to stay on the other side of the fence," the taller man called out.

"I'm not a tourist. I'm here on business." She patted the flank of the horse whose reins the man held. "I'm sure you remember me. We spoke a week ago after the three o'clock performance."

The shorter man looked her over. "Yeah, I remember you. You don't forget a blonde with gams like yours. You ought to be in the movies."

Despite the rather crude appraisal of her figure, Elizabeth fervently hoped he would pass along his opinion to the very next movie producer to come to Safari World. "Then I'm sure you also remember our arrangement. You needed horses, and I agreed to find them for you."

"That's right," said the shorter man. "We said we'd pay you five cents each."

"Ten cents, and a bargain at that rate," replied Elizabeth, giving both men a winning smile and taking the list from her skirt pocket. "I've found fourteen horses whose owners are willing to part with them for a reasonable price, and although none of them are as fine as this Bergstrom Thoroughbred here, I'm sure you'll find them suitable."

The men exchanged a look of surprise as the taller reached for the list. "Fourteen?" he asked his companion. "How could we have missed fourteen? The valley's not that big."

Elizabeth shrugged modestly, but the men were busy scanning the list. "What happened to Cormier's mare?" the shorter man asked. "That there's a fine horse. Did she come up lame?"

"No, she's perfectly sound," said Elizabeth. "All of these horses are, or I wouldn't have put them on the list."

The shorter man glanced up at her, perplexed, but the taller shook his head and smacked the paper with the back of his hand. "Look at these prices. They're outrageous! We could almost buy two-year-old show horses for what they want to charge us."

"Well, of course." Elizabeth looked from one man to the other, uncertain. "Isn't that the idea?"

"You got it all wrong, girlie," the shorter man said. "We don't need performers. We need meat."

"Meat?"

"For the lions," the taller man said. "So unless you have a list of lame old nags we can get for a song, you're wasting our time."

Elizabeth pressed a hand to her throat. "You feed the horses to the lions?"

"Well, what do you think we feed them?" the shorter man retorted. "Apricots? Barley? Let them graze in the pasture?"

With a heavy sigh, the taller man removed his hat and scratched his head wearily. "Did you find the horses we need or not?"

"I'm afraid not."

He jerked his thumb toward the fence. "Then you need to get out of my corral."

Elizabeth nodded and hurried through the gate, pausing only long enough to latch it behind her. She had never felt more humiliated—or rather she had, but only once, when she and Henry tried to pick up the deed to Triumph Ranch. Two whole days of searching, wasted. Her chance to earn her own money, ruined. An opportunity to impress people who might introduce her to a movie producer, lost.

Henry had abandoned her, Mrs. Diegel had betrayed her, and her own ignorance had undone her. If she had any sense, she would give up hoping for a better life in this place, as Henry and Rosa had done.

❧

In her only stroke of good luck that day, no one was in the stable when Elizabeth returned to the Jorgensen farm. She tended to the mare and the tack, and gave the mare extra feed to thank her for carrying her on such a long journey. She managed to avoid any of the family or their hired hands as she hurried home to the cabin. She quickly prepared a simple supper, which was on the table just as Henry came through the door. He washed, ate, and then stumbled wearily off to bed with barely a word.

Her thoughts were too troubled for sleep. Slipping quietly into the bedroom, she took the hexagonal quilt from the trunk at the foot of the bed and carried it to the fireside, where she had left her sewing basket. The summer nights were mild enough for only one quilt. Henry seemed to favor the one she called the Arboles Valley Star, although sometimes he kicked it off, restless in his sleep.

By Elizabeth's best guess, the Arboles Valley Star quilt was at least fifty years newer than the wool-and-homespun quilt she had named the Road to Triumph Ranch. The twelve wedges making up each large hexagon reminded her of the spokes of a wagon wheel, with the small solid hexagon appliquéd in the center as the hub. As she patched the holes and mended ripped seams, she thought of all the pioneer women who had come to the valley in wagons whose wheels rumbled over the rocky grade, women who had dreamed of the prosperity and happiness they were certain to find on those sun-drenched hills. Now trains sped the overland journey, machines made the work of farming easier, but the promise of prosperity remained as elusive as it had been in those bygone days.

If not for her quilts to work on in the evenings, she might not have endured her longing for Henry's company. She had never imagined married life would be so lonely. If she had known— She could not bring herself to say that she would not have married Henry if she had known, because she loved him despite everything, but she would have insisted they remain in Pennsylvania, among the women of her family. Often she recalled her father's pronouncement that there was no money in farming anymore, and that business was the place for a young man with ambition. At the time she had dismissed the notion, believing that her father was only trying to keep them close, and perhaps to justify his own decision to sacrifice his birthright to marry her mother. Now his words rang with truth. All around them, people were enjoying their newfound wealth; she saw it in the expensive automobiles and fashionable clothes of the men and women who toured the Arboles Valley on their way to view lots in Oakwood Glen and Meadowbrook Hills. Fortunes were won every day in business, as her father had said, but the boom times had not reached the farms.

Taking up her scissors, Elizabeth trimmed a small octagon from a scrap of blue-and-brown wool she had found among the fabrics Mrs. Diegel had traded to her. With careful stitches that would have made Aunt Eleanor proud, she appliquéd the shape to the center of one of the larger hexagons where the original patch had worn away to a frame a few threads wide. When she had first begun restoring the quilt, she had assumed the long-ago quiltmaker had used the appliqués to disguise a bulge in the seams where the six wedges met in the center, but while replacing some of the worn pieces, she discovered that the center points of the wedges met perfectly, with the bulk of the seams neatly trimmed away so the quilt top would lie flat. Why would any quilter disguise such an impressive display of her skills? Had she valued the artistry of her design more than the opportunity to show off her mastery of precise piecing? Perhaps she had taken such pride in her painstaking handiwork that it did not matter if anyone else knew it was there. Some of Elizabeth's aunts were like that. As for Elizabeth, she preferred to showcase her quilts' best features in hopes of distracting the viewer's eye away from the flaws that inevitably appeared despite her best efforts, scattered throughout her quilts like dandelions in a field.

Elizabeth sewed as thoughts of Henry, of Rosa, and of her failures that day tumbled through her mind. She worked her needle through scraps of wool until the windstorm of thoughts subsided. Only then did she put away her needle and thread, fold the quilt carefully, and tuck it away in the trunk they used as a table. Sleep eluded her so many nights that she knew it would not be long until she worked on the quilt again.

Back in Pennsylvania, a good night's sleep could cure her of most worries, but not so in the Arboles Valley, where her secrets were many and confidants few—and where a captive lion roaring with indignation woke her before daybreak. There was no time before hurrying off to the Jorgensen farmhouse in the morning to speak with Henry about Rosa, so Elizabeth's worries steadily grew as she helped Mrs. Jorgensen and Mary Katherine prepare breakfast. Elizabeth did not want to goad John Barclay into lashing out at Rosa again, but if she did nothing, she would become his silent accomplice, and she could not bear that.

Finally she decided not to wait until Henry found time for her but to speak to Mrs. Jorgensen instead. Despite her stern demeanor and strict management of the household—which Elizabeth would gladly have done without—she was a woman of great common sense, and even kindness. In the months they had worked side by side, Elizabeth had grown to respect her, though she doubted they would ever become close friends. Mrs. Jorgensen might keep her granddaughters away from the Barclay children out of fear of disease, but in this she was not unlike the others in the valley, and Elizabeth could forgive her that. Mrs. Jorgensen had agreed to take on the Nelsons as nothing more than would-be homeowners down on their luck. Elizabeth could not believe she would close her heart to Rosa if she knew what John had done.

The story spilled from her as they set the table for breakfast. Mrs. Jorgensen drew herself up, her mouth in a hard line, as Elizabeth described Rosa's bruises, her split lip, and how the children had played on as if nothing out of the ordinary had befallen their mother. At Elizabeth's mention of Carlos, Mrs. Jorgensen pressed, "What did he say when you told him you had found his sister on the mesa?"

"You found Rosa where?"

Elizabeth spun around to discover Lars standing behind her in the kitchen doorway, his face a thundercloud. For a moment she glimpsed the man he might have been in his younger years, the man who drank, the man who had frightened the love of his life into marriage with a man she thought safer.

"At the Salto Canyon," said Mrs. Jorgensen when Elizabeth did not speak. "On the mesa. You know the place."

Without a word, Lars stormed back outside. "Go with him," barked Mrs. Jorgensen, pushing Elizabeth toward the door.

Elizabeth snatched off her apron and pursued him, bumping into Oscar Jorgensen on the way out the door, brushing past Henry as she ran. She reached the garage only moments after Lars, but he ignored her pleas to wait and drove off in a cloud of gravel and dust.

Naturally Oscar and the other men couldn't help speculating over the source of Lars's fury. As she set platters of food on the table, Elizabeth overheard Mrs. Jorgensen briefly inform Oscar. Even her discreet words set in motion rounds of conjecture about what Lars intended to do to John Barclay, until Mrs. Jorgensen finally insisted that they not speak of the matter at the table, in a voice that strongly encouraged them not to speak of it elsewhere, either. The men fell into a subdued silence, and for the rest of the meal, Mrs. Jorgensen kept a watchful eye on the window.

The men returned to their work, with still no sign of Lars. As they cleared away the dishes and cleaned the kitchen, Mary Katherine questioned Elizabeth so precisely on her encounter with Rosa that revealing each new detail made Elizabeth feel as if she were gossiping rather than seeking help for a woman in trouble. "Why does everyone seem more concerned with where I found Rosa than with what John did to her?" Elizabeth exclaimed.

"The Salto Canyon takes its name from a Spanish word meaning 'the jumping-off place,' " said Mary Katherine. "It was called that because of the many people who fell to their deaths there, often by accident while crossing the mesa in darkness or heavy fog, but sometimes not. Rosa's mother took her own life in the exact spot where you say you found Rosa with the children."

Elizabeth felt a sudden swell of fear. "Do you think Rosa intends—"

"I don't know, but Lars—" Mary Katherine shook her head, pressing her lips together tightly. "I'm sure that's what he fears."

Filled with a sickening dread, Elizabeth imagined Rosa poised on the edge of the canyon, frozen in space for one dreadful moment before leaning forward to embrace the air and plunging to the rocks below. She pressed a trembling hand to her mouth and grasped the counter behind her for support. She never should have left Rosa alone on the mesa.

She worked through the morning anxiously awaiting Lars's return. It was nearly lunchtime when at last she heard the sound of the car pulling up to the garage. At once, she and Mary Katherine dropped their gardening tools and ran to meet him, passing Mrs. Jorgensen on the way. Lars took one look at their worried faces and answered their unspoken question. "She's all right," he said, dropping his gaze and heading out to meet the other men in the orchard.

"Lars." Mrs. Jorgensen caught him by the arm in passing. "What happened?"

"I found her at the house. She didn't want me to see her, but when I told her I wouldn't leave without making sure she was safe, she let me in. Barclay won't hurt her again, not if he values his life."

"Lars," Mrs. Jorgensen said, a faint tremor in her voice. "What did you do?"

Without a word, Lars patted his mother's hand before freeing himself from her grasp and continuing on his way.

"He didn't hurt John," said Mary Katherine, as if thinking aloud, as if trying to persuade herself. "John would have put up a fight, and Lars doesn't have a mark on him."

"Mrs. Jorgensen, I'm so sorry I brought this trouble on your family," said Elizabeth. "I came to you because I didn't know what else to do. I never meant for Lars to threaten John Barclay."

"We don't know if that's what he did," said Mrs. Jorgensen, resigned. "You did the right thing, Elizabeth. Rosa needed help, and you may be the only person in the Arboles Valley who is not too busy avoiding her to notice."

"Lars doesn't avoid her," corrected Mary Katherine, her eyes fixed on him as he strode off into the distance.

Mrs. Jorgensen gave her a quick, inscrutable glance before returning her gaze to her elder son. "It's tempting to turn away when a woman is mistreated by her husband, to call it a private family matter and hope it cures itself. That's the last thing we should do. If we don't stand together as women against such behavior, it will worsen and spread. If one man hits his wife and gets away with it, it will become more tolerable for other men to do the same. If one woman accepts a beating, other women will believe they should bear it as well."

"Rosa never should have married John," said Mary Katherine.

"Well, she did, and that's that," said Mrs. Jorgensen sharply. "We have work to do, so get back to it. That garden won't weed itself."

She strode off briskly to the house, the screen door slamming shut behind her. Elizabeth trailed after Mary Katherine back to the garden, wondering what Lars had done at the Barclay farm. How could he be so sure that John would not harm Rosa again? How could any of them be sure she was safe?

"You said that Rosa's mother took her own life," said Elizabeth after she and Mary Katherine had pulled weeds in silence for several minutes. "Do you know why?"

Mary Katherine stuck her trowel into the earth and sat back on her heels. "Why does anyone do such a dreadful thing? No one knows for certain—or if they do, they aren't telling. I suppose Rosa or Carlos might know, but who can ask them?" She shook her head and nimbly plucked a few spindly weeds from between the lush carrot tops. "Some people say Mrs. Diaz was never right in the mind after her first grandchild took sick and died, but I think it goes back even further than that, to the time when her parents sold the farm to Mother Jorgensen's grandparents. To go from owning the land to working it as hired hands for another family must have turned them bitter. I often wonder why they stayed instead of moving on, starting new somewhere else."

"Perhaps they loved the land too much to leave it," said Elizabeth. "Perhaps they thought one day they could earn back the farm they had lost, or if they couldn't do that, perhaps their children might."

"It could be something like that, I suppose. At any rate, when Rosa and Lars fell in love, Mother Jorgensen and Lars's father didn't object. Lars was still drinking then and I think they thought marriage would settle him down. It was Rosa's parents who were absolutely dead set against it. Rosa might have disobeyed them if not for Lars's drinking. Oscar told me once that she had agreed to marry Lars on the condition that he get sober, and that he tried, and had nearly succeeded even before Prohibition."

"Then why on earth did she marry John?" asked Elizabeth.

"I don't know. Maybe Lars's sobriety didn't come soon enough, or maybe she didn't believe it would take. He sure fell off the wagon hard when Rosa married John. No one had seen that coming. When he finally learned of it, two days after the wedding, Lars got as drunk as a lord and nearly killed himself driving over to the Barclay farm to beg her to run off with him. She wouldn't even open the door, not that any sensible woman would have to a man in that condition. Oscar had to drag him away before John turned the shotgun on him. Lars was sick for weeks, but after that he never touched another drop of liquor. It was too late, though. He had already lost her."

When Mary Katherine's voice trailed off, Elizabeth could not bear to prompt her to continue. It was so unbearably sad for everyone involved, but why had Rosa married John instead of waiting for Lars, as she had promised? As for the tragic fate of Rosa's mother, surely she must have blamed herself for her daughter's grief, for the burdens of sorrow she was forced to bear. If she and her husband had not objected to Rosa's marriage to Lars, they could have lived out their lives in happiness, and the old resentments between the two families might have been forgiven.

A few days later, when Lars announced that he would be going for the mail after lunch, his mother said sharply, "You were up at the Barclay farm for hours on Monday and you forgot to fetch the mail?"

"I guess it slipped my mind."

She turned to her younger son. "Don't you need him in the orchards today, so close to picking time?"

Oscar held his brother's gaze for a moment. "I've put Henry in charge of the orchards," he said shortly. "He can manage without Lars for a while."

Surprise lit Henry's expression, and Elizabeth immediately knew that this was the first he had heard of his promotion. Mrs. Jorgensen was clearly displeased, but she never undermined her son's authority in front of the hired hands, so she merely nodded. As soon as she could get Elizabeth alone, however, she instructed her to accompany Lars to the post office.

"Last time he drove off without me," Elizabeth pointed out, although she was more than willing to accept the errand. She was eager to see Rosa again, to see with her own eyes that she was all right.

"Be sure that he doesn't this time," said Mrs. Jorgensen. "Under no circumstances is my son to go to the Barclay farm alone."

This time, when Lars went to the garage after lunch, he discovered Elizabeth waiting for him in the car. He did not seem surprised to see her. "Don't you have work to do?"

She gave him her most disarming smile. "You know me. Always ready to shirk my duties."

He snorted, but took the driver's seat and started the car. If he did not openly object to her presence, he did not seem to welcome it, either. He drove along in studied silence, ignoring her, until they reached the end of the Barclays' driveway. "Thanks for speaking up for Rosa."

"Of course," said Elizabeth. "Anyone would have, if they had seen her."

"That's where you're wrong."

Elizabeth did not know what to say. The car rumbled to a stop just before the house. Marta and Lupita came running, their feet bare, their long, dark hair hanging loose and streaked with bronze from the sun. "Hi, Mr. Jorgensen," said Marta, reaching shyly for his hand.

"Hi, girls." He knelt down to hug them. "Where's your mother?"

"Inside," said Marta.

"Don't go in." Lupita took his other hand and tugged him toward the grass beneath the orange tree. "Play with us."

When he hesitated, Elizabeth smiled and waved him on. "Go ahead. I can get the mail."

With an uncertain smile, he let the girls lead him off to play. When Elizabeth knocked on the door, Rosa opened it quickly, as if she had been waiting. "I have some letters to mail," said Elizabeth, including hers in the pile from the Jorgensen family. "How are you?"

Rosa took the bundle. "Better, thank you." The bruises on her face had taken on a yellowish hue and a scab had formed on her split lip. As far as Elizabeth could tell, John had not added to her injuries. Whatever Lars had said or done, apparently it had stayed John's hand, for now.

Rosa disappeared into the kitchen and soon returned with a small bundle of mail for the Jorgensens and three letters for the Nelsons. "Thank you," said Elizabeth, tucking the Jorgensens' mail under her arm and leafing through her letters to read the return addresses—Aunt Eleanor, Elizabeth's parents, Henry's mother.

"I think you should know," said Rosa, "while I appreciate your concern, I would never take my own life, not while my children live and need me."

Startled by Rosa's directness, Elizabeth looked up from her letters and was even more surprised to discover Rosa smiling at her with something close to amusement. "And after that?" said Elizabeth, deciding to be equally direct. "What then?"

Rosa was silent for a moment. "I no longer believe all of my children are fated to die from this cursed illness. Some of them will be spared, and they will need me."

She spoke with so much certainty that Elizabeth believed her. "Children always need their mothers in some way, even after they are grown. I know I still depend upon my mother's advice—and my aunt's. That's why I write so many letters home."

Rosa's smile deepened, became more knowing. "You tell me this because you hope to convince me to wait until I am an old woman before I take my own life. I assure you, you—and Lars as well—you need not trouble yourselves."

"Then why were you there, in that place?"

"You mean where my mother died?"

Elizabeth nodded.

"Because I loved my mother deeply and I feel her presence most strongly there." Rosa glanced over her shoulder at the sound of Miguel murmuring in his sleep. "My mother often told me she considered the view of the canyon from the mesa to be the most beautiful place in the valley. She never would have despoiled it by committing such a terrible act there. I miss my mother very much, but I find consolation in knowing what happened to her must have been a terrible accident. She never would have taken her own life, I am sure of it."

Unwilling to dispel a belief that seemed to bring Rosa comfort, Elizabeth merely nodded.

"Would you like to see her photograph?" asked Rosa. "It was taken on her wedding day."

When Elizabeth agreed, Rosa took a brown leather album from a shelf beside the fireplace and turned to a page about halfway through the book. A young dark-haired woman, lovely but wearing only a hint of a smile, sat tall in a straight-backed wooden chair, her eyes fixed on the camera and bright with happiness. She wore a dark dress with a satin ribbon around the waist and a cascade of white lace around her neck and shoulders. Behind her stood a solemn, handsome man with a neatly trimmed mustache, broad-shouldered but only of medium height. His hand rested upon his bride's shoulder.

"You would not know it from this picture, but my father was a very cheerful man. He was almost always smiling." Rosa smiled herself, wistful, and turned a few more pages, flipping past newspaper articles, letters, and sketches pasted into the album. "Here is a picture you may enjoy more."

She held out the album, and Elizabeth gasped in recognition at a newer, sounder version of the cabin where she and Henry now lived. A little girl about four years old sat on the front porch steps wearing a lacy white dress, ankles together, hands clasped in her lap. On the grass to her left stood a couple in their midtwenties, but they were not the same couple from the wedding portrait. The man grasped the railing and had planted one foot on the bottom step; the woman stood with her hands straight at her sides. Behind them on the porch, an elderly man and woman sat on rocking chairs. The woman held a baby on her lap bundled in the quilt Elizabeth called the Road to Triumph Ranch.

"My grandparents, and my grandfather's parents," said Rosa, indicating the younger and older couples in turn. She pointed to the young girl on the porch steps. "My mother. She could not have been more than four years old when this portrait was made."

"Did your grandmother or great-grandmother make this quilt?" asked Elizabeth.

Shouts from outside interrupted Rosa's reply. She hurriedly set the album aside and ran for the door, Elizabeth close behind. In the shade of the orange trees, John had seized his daughters by the arms and was dragging them away from Lars, his face red with rage. "I told you to stay away from my family!"

"Settle down." Lars raised his palms in a gesture of calm, keeping pace with John as he wrestled the stumbling girls toward the house. "You're hurting the girls."

Rosa darted past Elizabeth and flung herself at her husband, fighting to tear his hands from her daughters. John shoved her hard with his shoulder and she fell to the ground. In an instant, Lars was beside her, helping her to her feet. Cursing, John shoved the girls ahead of him into the house and slammed the door.

When Lars began pursuit, Rosa seized him by the arm. "Don't," she begged. She placed her hands on his chest and refused to let him pass. "Stay away from him. He'll kill you."

Lars did not look as if he cared. "I won't let him hurt them."

"It's you he wants to hurt, not the girls. If you leave now—"

"Rosa, I've done everything you've ever asked of me but I won't—"

"Please, just go." Desperate, Rosa pushed him toward the car. "Go!"

She whirled around and ran back toward the adobe, but before she reached it, John tore open the door and stormed out, something hard and glinting in his grasp. Elizabeth cried out in alarm as he raised his hand to Lars, but suddenly he drew back his arm and flung the object at Lars's chest. Instinctively, Lars caught it. Clear liquid sloshed inside the glass bottle.

"I remember what you are even if she doesn't," John snarled. "Crawl back inside your bottle and leave us alone."

Rosa threw Lars one last, beseeching look as John clamped his hand around her arm and shoved her inside. Lars stood frozen in place, clutching the bottle in stunned disbelief. Elizabeth expected him to cast the liquor aside, but he turned the bottle over in his hands in a trembling caress, his eyes fixed on the closed door of Rosa's home.

"Lars, leave it." When he did not seem to hear her, Elizabeth hurried over and reached for the bottle. "Just leave it and let's go."

But Lars's grasp tightened on the bottle. "I can't just leave them. Not again."

"There's nothing you can do today." Elizabeth tried again to take the liquor from him. "We'll think of something. We'll come back. Leave the bottle and let's go."

Slowly Lars's gaze traveled from the adobe to the bottle. He stared hard at the label and took a step back, then tucked the bottle into his pocket.

Elizabeth wanted to snatch it from him and pour it out on the dusty ground, but Lars returned to the car so quickly she had to run to catch up with him. He started the engine barely before she had shut her door and drove off as if determined to put distance between himself and John before his anger overcame his better judgment. Suddenly he shifted in his seat, winced, then pulled the liquor bottle from his pocket and tossed it into the backseat.

"You should have thrown it from the car," said Elizabeth. "What good is that going to do you?"

Lars ignored her. When they reached the Jorgensen farm, she scrambled over the backseat for the bottle, but he grabbed it from her fingertips. He slipped it into his pocket as he strode off to the house.

She watched him go for a moment before collecting the mail she had scattered over the front seat, disappointed and afraid. It chilled her to think how precisely John Barclay had aimed his attack, stabbing at Lars's old wound, handing him the means with which he could destroy himself. Should Elizabeth tell Oscar his brother had a bottle on him? Should she warn Mrs. Jorgensen?

Mary Katherine had declared that her brother-in-law had lost so much because of his drinking that liquor had lost the power to tempt him anymore. How could she be so sure? Why keep the liquor if not to drink it?

How could Lars risk falling back into his old ways when Rosa needed him so desperately?

Henry surprised Elizabeth by returning to the cabin early, before she had a chance to read the letters from home. "What's going on with Lars and the postmaster?" he asked, tugging off his boots.

She bent her head over the envelopes to conceal her disappointment. When the door had swung open, her first, foolish instinct was to think he had hurried home to see her, the way he had once hurried over to Elm Creek Manor as soon as his chores were done. Now he came home in a rush only to satisfy his curiosity, not because he couldn't bear another moment apart.

As she fixed him a cup of tea, she told him what she knew about Lars, John, and Rosa. Henry listened intently, prompting her with questions until the entire story had drained from her. Or at least, most of the story.

When she had finished, Henry disappeared outside and returned with firewood. With nightfall, the cool ocean mists had rolled in to blanket the valley. As Henry lit the fire, he said, "Why were you out riding that Sunday when you found Rosa on the mesa?"

After all that had happened, she had almost forgotten what had taken her past the mesa that day. "After everything I've told you, that's what you find most curious?"

"Don't evade the question. Why were you going for a ride by yourself?"

She leveled her gaze at him. "I've asked you many times to spend Sundays with me. I would have preferred to have your company that day, but as you've often said, you have to work."

"So why go alone?"

"It's better than staying here," she snapped, "shut inside the four walls of this cabin wondering what I did to displease my husband so much that he can't bear to spend a Sunday alone with me."

"That's not why I took on the extra work and you know it."

"Oh, yes, I know." She flung back the lid of the blue trunk, snatched up the Road to Triumph Ranch quilt, and sat down with her back to him. "You can't wait to earn enough money to put me on the fastest train east."

"What were you up to, Elizabeth?" He came around to face her and planted his hands on the arms of her chair, but she ignored him and threaded her needle with trembling fingers. "I know you weren't out sightseeing. What were you looking for—or whom?"

"Oh, for pity's sakes! Horses! I was looking for horses! Do you honestly believe I was riding around looking for some handsome farmer to cure me of my loneliness?"

He drew back as if she had struck him. "No. I thought you might be looking for Mae."

"Mae?" she echoed, incredulous. "Mae's long gone. Honestly, Henry."

He scrubbed a hand through his hair distractedly until it tumbled into his face. He looked suddenly like a hurt little boy. "Is it true that you're lonely?"

"Of course I am. How could I not be?"

"But we're together every day."

"You hardly speak to me. You never touch me. I feel farther apart from you than when I lived in Harrisburg and you lived at Elm Creek Manor."

"I never lived at Elm Creek Manor."

"You know what I mean. When I stayed at Elm Creek Manor, and you came to see me there."

"I know exactly what you mean." He lowered himself wearily into the other chair. "Why were you looking for horses?"

For a moment she considered refusing to tell him, to punish his silence with her own. Instead she told him about the deal she had struck at Safari World, her misguided search of the valley, her inevitable failure. She did not tell him that she had meant to put her earnings toward buying back her quilts from Mrs. Diegel, or that she had hoped to win over the wranglers so they might introduce her to their colleagues in the movie business. Henry would not approve of either venture.

"I should have known they didn't want prize horses when they dismissed my suggestion to buy Bergstrom Thoroughbreds," said Elizabeth. "That Bergstrom is the most beautiful horse in their stables. Why wouldn't they want another?"

"It's a good thing they didn't."

"Why not? Everyone stood to gain. My uncle would have made a good sale, Safari World would have acquired more of the finest horses anywhere, and I would have made a commission."

"I guess you didn't consider how those horses would have been delivered to their new owners."

Elizabeth did not understand his concern. "By train, of course."

"Yes, and your uncle Fred likely would have come with them. He never sells to any man he hasn't shaken hands with, and he never delivers horses to a new home sight unseen. Can you really imagine him putting his horses on a train in Pennsylvania and taking a chance they'll be well cared for on the trip west and that the new owners will be there to meet them in Los Angeles? Of course not. He'd accompany them every step of the way. And do you really think that after traveling all the way to Safari World, he wouldn't go the extra few miles to visit his niece?"

"I certainly hope he would."

"Do you? Do you really? Do you really want the folks back home to see how we live here?"

"I'm not ashamed of where we live," she retorted. "We've fixed up the cabin nicely considering our circumstances, and anyway, it's not forever. It's just until we can go home."

"We can't go home."

"Of course we can. We've had a setback, but we'll save up the money again, and then we'll go—but not until we can go together."

"You don't understand," said Henry, agitated. "We can't go home. There's nothing waiting for us back in Pennsylvania. Nothing."

Elizabeth stared as he bolted from his chair and began to pace the floor. "You're not making any sense. How can you say nothing's waiting for us? What about our families? What about Two Bears Farm? Your family will be overjoyed to have you back. You're the oldest son. Two Bears Farm is your rightful place."

"Not anymore it isn't." Henry halted and covered his eyes with his hand. "Elizabeth. How do you think I got the money to pay for Triumph Ranch?"

"You said . . ." She tried to remember exactly what he had told her. "You said it was your life savings."

"What is the life savings of a man who works the family farm?"

Then she understood.

At first she said nothing. Until she said the words aloud, she could pretend nothing had changed, that the haven of Two Bears Farm still awaited their homecoming. When the silence stretched on unbearably long, she murmured, "Your inheritance."

Henry nodded bleakly. "When I told my father I wanted to strike out on my own, he gave me my inheritance in cash. No part of Two Bears Farm belongs to me anymore. If I go back, it will be as Lars returned to the Jorgensen farm, as a hired hand working for my brothers."

"But—" Elizabeth's thoughts churned. "But when we told your parents about our plans to go to California, your father seemed as surprised as anyone."

"That was a show for my mother. I knew she would object to my leaving and I didn't want her to blame my father."

Elizabeth remembered how Mr. Nelson had studied the photographs of Triumph Ranch, how he had nodded approvingly and passed them on to his wife, how he had not voiced a single concern about his son's sudden announcement. At the time, she had assumed he trusted his son's judgment so implicitly that he had simply had no reason to believe Henry had not made a sound decision. Now she imagined the weeks of debate and argument and persuasion that must have preceded the purchase of the land. Henry would have worn his father down with the facts, with the logic of his plan, and his father would have given in out of love, because he could not bear to stand in the way of his son's dream.

"You see now why I can't go back," said Henry. "I can't face my father. I can't look him in the eye and tell him I lost everything he had given me. It wasn't my life savings I lost, but his."

Elizabeth could hardly bear to look at him, but she could not tear her gaze away. Before her eyes he had transformed into a man she did not know. "Why didn't you tell me?" In all the years she had known him, he had never lied to her. His integrity and truthfulness were the bedrock of her world. "You never intended to return to Pennsylvania, did you?"

"I can't. But you still can."

"How can you say that?" she cried. "How can I go without you? I love you."

"It's Elm Creek Manor you love," he shot back. "My family's farm was right next door, the closest you could come to owning the land you loved. Out of all the men who wanted to marry you, only I could offer you that."

Her heart cinched. At last she understood why he had bought Triumph Ranch, why he had not included her in his plans but made his decision before asking her to marry him. Unless he gave up Two Bears Farm, he would never know if she had married him for love or to be close to the land she longed for, the land that could never be hers. It had been a test, and she had passed, and yet he still doubted her.

She felt the blood rush into her head until it spun. He had lied to her. Like every other man she had known, he had created a world of lies and expected her to live in it without questioning the fragile threads of deception that bound it together. He was no different from her father. He had sold his birthright and would regret it for the rest of his days. He expected her to believe his words and not the evidence of her own senses. He desperately wanted her to pretend that the ground was not constantly shifting beneath their feet, because only then could he keep walking.

She sat with her fists knotted in the patched and faded quilt, angry, helpless, lost.

Then the truth whispered, gently but urgently. That was her father, not Henry. Henry had never pretended that what had befallen them was anything but the most brutal of disappointments. He had never blamed anyone but himself for the choices that had led them there. He had never asked her to pretend that everything was fine when their world was crumbling apart all around them.

As for his test of her love, she could not bring herself to fault him for that. If not for her flirting, her capricious teasing, her foolish attempts to make him jealous, he would never have questioned whether she loved him or only his land.

Henry broke the silence with words that threatened to strangle him. "You never should have married me. I thought if you went back, alone, you could start over. . . ."

His voice faltered and failed. Elizabeth set the Road to Triumph Ranch quilt aside and went to him.

"Henry." She touched his shoulder gently.

He trembled but did not pull away as she kissed his cheek, tracing the rough stubble of his beard with her lips. "I lied to you. I deceived you."

"I know. But it's going to be all right."

"All these weeks I've wanted to tell you the truth. I've taken you away from the home you love and given you nothing in return."

"That's not so." She pressed herself against him until Henry put his arms around her. "All I've ever wanted since I was fourteen was for you to love me. It wasn't Elm Creek Manor I wanted. It was you. It was always you. *You're* the home I love."

"Elizabeth—" Then he said nothing more, because he was kissing her. She tangled her fingers in his hair and returned his kisses fiercely, to make up for the long weeks when shame and secrets had kept them apart.

❧

1913

Isabel wrapped the warm tortillas in a towel and placed them in the basket on top of the layered tamales, still hot within their corn-husks. She smiled as she drew on her shawl, remembering her own pregnancies. After the queasiness of the first three months had passed, she had craved tortillas and tamales at all hours of the day and night. Isabel had never been able to equal her father's skill at making perfect tamales, but hers were still tasty and nourishing, just the thing to satisfy an expectant mother's appetite.

She did not know for certain whether Rosa's cravings mirrored her own, but they were alike in other ways, so Isabel took a chance that their tastes would be similar. If only she saw her daughter more frequently, she would know what aromas tempted her to eat her fill so her baby would grow strong, but Isabel had seen her daughter only infrequently since her marriage seven months before. The five miles separating the Barclay farm and Rosa's child-hood home might as well have been one hundred. Isabel supposed Rosa's unexpected withdrawal from her mother was only natural. If it was not, Isabel would not know it. Her mother had died before she had even met Miguel. She had never been in Rosa's place, leav-ing behind a mother who missed her as she embarked on a new life as a married woman. With no similar experience of her own to con-sult, Isabel told herself Rosa was a young bride and wanted to devote herself to her new husband, rather than come to her mother's kitchen for a home-cooked meal and unsolicited advice. Once Rosa was settled and more confident about running her own household, she would visit more often, especially when she wanted help with the baby.

But what expectant mother, fiercely independent or not, would turn down tortillas and tamales, a Christmas delicacy in June? Isabel smiled to herself as she placed one last gift into her basket— a cradle quilt, pieced of the softest cottons she could find. As Isabel had sewn the Four-Patch blocks, she had imagined snuggling her tiny grandchild within its soft folds. In less than two months, God willing, she would. She prayed that Rosa would have an easy labor and a strong, healthy baby blessed with his mother's beauty and his grandfather's kindness and—Isabel searched for something of John's she hoped the child would inherit. His diligence. His cleverness. They had served John well and perhaps would do the same for her grandchild one day.

Isabel walked to the Barclay farm, enjoying the brilliant sunshine and clear skies of late June. The farmers were hard at work in their fields. Oranges, lemons, and apricots thrived in the orchards. Late summer and autumn would bring a bountiful harvest to the farmers of the Arboles Valley. Isabel, who would soon receive the richest blessing of all, did not envy any of them. She could almost wish even the Jorgensens well. By the end of summer, Rosa would surely be ready for an excursion. They could take the baby to the mesa and play with him on a blanket as they enjoyed the view of the canyon and marveled at his darling little feet, his sweet toothless smile, his strong and insistent grip when he curled his fist around their fingertips. Or perhaps the baby would be a little girl, with a tumble of dark curls and a sweet rosebud mouth. Isabel would tell her stories and when she was old enough, teach her to quilt and make tortillas and tamales the way her mother and grandmother had taught her.

At last her daughter's new home came into view, a snug adobe house on a hill with orange trees in the front yard. Acres of rye stretched to the hills lining the western edge of the Salto Canyon; John walked among the rows, inspecting the slender shafts that swayed in unison as the wind moved over them. Isabel broke into a smile, called out a greeting, and quickened her pace, careful not to jostle the basket.

John looked up and crossed the fields to the dirt road leading up to the house. He stood there and waited for her to come to him.

"How's Rosa?" Isabel asked, breathless from her five-mile walk.

He shrugged, removed his hat, and mopped his brow with his shirtsleeve. "Fine, I guess."

"Well, it won't be much longer now. I imagine you must be getting excited." Isabel was determined to be cheerful and pleasant to her son-in-law, although he did not make it easy. "Does Rosa say if she has a feeling whether the baby is a boy or a girl? Sometimes a mother knows."

John flicked his unsmiling gaze over her. "It's a girl."

Isabel had to laugh. "You sound very certain, but for the next two months, we can only guess." She indicated the basket. "I brought Rosa some things, some food and a gift for the baby. Is she resting?" As much as she longed to see her daughter and chat about their plans for the baby, if she had to, she would leave the basket in the kitchen rather than disturb Rosa's sleep.

John took the basket from her so unexpectedly that Isabel had no time to protest. "I'll see that she gets it."

"I don't want to interrupt your work." She reached for the basket, but to her astonishment, John held it out of reach. "Honestly, John, I'm happy to take it to her myself."

"She doesn't want any visitors."

"I'm not a visitor; I'm her mother."

"She doesn't want to see you."

Bewildered, at first Isabel could only stare at him. "I don't believe that," she said. "I came to help. I'll cook supper for the three of us and do some housekeeping so my daughter can rest. I know Rosa, and I know she'll try to keep the house in perfect order even though she should stay off her feet as much as she can in her condition."

"We don't need your help. My mother and sister came down from Oxnard to help out when the baby was born."

His flat statement staggered her. "What? The baby—"

"A girl. Born three weeks ago. Isabel calls her Marta."

"Three weeks ago! But—that's much too early. And you sent no word to us. Is she—is my granddaughter—"

"She's healthy. She's fine."

"And Rosa?"

His expression hardened. "She's fine, too. But she doesn't want to see you. If you come, I'm supposed to send you away."

Isabel felt tears gathering. "But why?"

"You know you two haven't always gotten along. Rosa needs peace and quiet. She doesn't need someone around always criticizing, always questioning what she does, who she marries."

Stung, Isabel said, "We didn't object to you. It was just so sudden. We didn't understand the reason for such haste."

"Haste? I courted Rosa for years. We were practically engaged for most of that time."

As his voice rose, Isabel suddenly wanted nothing more than to put the past behind them. "I've made many mistakes as a mother. I've done things I regret. But I have always loved my children and cared for them as best I knew how. Please don't keep me from seeing her. Please let me see my granddaughter."

"It's Rosa's choice, not mine," he said. "I'll tell her you came by."

Isabel walked home in a daze.

At home that night, Isabel wept in her husband's arms. "What did I do?" she asked over and over. "Why would Rosa turn me away?"

Miguel tried his best to console her, but Rosa's thoughtless cruelty distressed and bewildered him. "She'll change her mind," he said, patting Isabel on the shoulder. "It's new-mother nerves, that's all. When things settle down, she'll let us see the baby. You'll see."

Isabel desperately wanted to believe him.

She waited. Two months passed. She was in the Arboles Grocery picking out a chicken for Sunday dinner when from behind her, a voice she had ached to hear said, "Mami?"

She whirled around. "Rosa."

Rosa smiled at her, soft and wistful, yet guarded. Isabel rushed forward to embrace her and stopped short at the sight of the baby in her arms, nestled in a familiar quilt, the one she had made, the one she had left in the basket John had taken. "Oh, my darling." She began to weep for joy. "Oh, what a perfect angel."

Rosa beamed and passed baby Marta to Isabel. Isabel held her gently, soaking in every detail—her sweet baby scent, her long eyelashes, her tiny nails on tiny fingers. She was precious, and yet she was larger and more robust than Isabel had expected of a child born nearly two months early.

She closed her eyes and tried to shut out the sudden thoughts that crowded in. It did not matter. Nothing mattered except that she held her grandchild at last.

"Thank you for the quilt," said Rosa hesitantly. "And the tortillas and tamales. They were delicious."

Isabel held the baby close as if some small part of her feared Rosa would snatch her away. "I wanted to do so much more."

"I've missed you. I—I understand why you stayed away."

Did Rosa have any idea how Isabel had longed, every day, to rush to her door and pound upon it until someone let her in? "I stayed away because you asked me to. Otherwise I would have been there, every moment."

Rosa shook her head, bewildered. "I never asked you to stay away."

Isabel did not want to argue. All she wanted was to savor that moment, to rain kisses upon her granddaughter and be thankful that her daughter had apparently forgiven her for whatever offense

Isabel had inadvertently committed. "Your husband passed along your message."

Rosa shook her head. "No. You must have misunderstood him. He wanted you to reconsider. He told me that you and Papi had disowned me when you heard about Marta, about when she was born. . . ."

Isabel stared at her daughter, at her perfectly healthy grandchild, and suddenly could no longer ignore the truth. "Marta was not born early."

Rosa flinched, and Isabel knew she had only at that moment realized her parents had not known her secret shame. She dropped her shopping basket and quickly took Marta back. "I have to go."

"Rosa—"

"Tell Papi I'm sorry."

Before Isabel could beg her to stay, Rosa fled from the store.

Sick at heart, Isabel went home and told Miguel what she had learned, that it was John Barclay who was keeping them apart. But that disturbing revelation was lost on Miguel, who heard only that his beloved, precious only daughter had been two months pregnant when she married. The daughter he had cherished had lied to them. She had disgraced herself and betrayed them all.

"What does it matter?" Isabel pleaded with him when he insisted that Rosa was dead to him, that Isabel must disown her as well. "They're married now. They have a beautiful child. Their sins are between them and God. If Rosa confesses to Him and atones for her sin, God will forgive her, and we must forgive her, too."

She said this for Miguel's sake. She wanted Rosa and Marta in her life. She would have forgiven her daughter even if God could not. But Miguel had believed in Rosa's perfection too long to recognize this flawed woman as the daughter he loved.

His heart had been shattered, and he could not endure a second betrayal. His wife and son must stand with him or he could not bear it. But even as Isabel promised to abandon her daughter to the fate she had willfully chosen, she resolved to break her promise as soon as she could. She could not forget John's sullen dishonesty that June afternoon when he turned her away.

She feared for her daughter.

Chapter Ten

1925

With freedom from upholding the pretense that they could return to Two Bears Farm came Henry's determination to make the cabin a suitable permanent home. He told Oscar he could work only half days on Sundays and instead spent his Sunday afternoons sealing cracks in the walls, repairing the sagging porch, and making the outhouse more tolerable. He spent his evenings in Elizabeth's company and his nights in her arms. It was in this way that Henry told her he would never again think of sending her back to Pennsylvania alone.

Elizabeth was so grateful to have her husband restored to her that the thought of Rosa's unhappiness became increasingly unbearable. She readily assented when Mrs. Jorgensen assigned her sole responsibility for the weekly mail run and other errands, thinking that this would allow her more opportunities to look in on the Barclay family. Yet Lars squandered no opportunity to express his feelings of betrayal. For a time he hardly spoke to her, although he always happened to be in the garage when she returned from the post office, and pressed her to report on what she had seen at the Barclay farm. John glared at her ever more mistrustfully, but he did not try to prevent her from seeing Rosa. Ana and Miguel continued their slow and inexorable decline into sickness. Marta and Lupita played together beneath the orange trees as they had always done, so that Elizabeth thought they were unaware of the turmoil in the family until she saw how they darted away at their father's approach. Once, when Elizabeth did not see John in the fields and knew he was not in the adobe, Marta confided that her parents had fought a few days before, after her father went to Oxnard one morning and came home with a new car.

Appalled that John could find money for a car when he had none to spare for a doctor for his children, Elizabeth concluded that his cruelty knew no limits. She kept a watchful eye out for any sign that he had resumed his violence toward his wife, but whenever she asked Rosa how she fared, Rosa forced a tight smile and said that every day with her children was a blessing. And yet she could not disguise her anger about the car. Whenever John left the fields early to go for a drive or raced up the gravel road to the house after an invented errand into town, her eyes narrowed and her mouth turned in disgust until Elizabeth thought she would rather endure another beating than the sight of that gleaming, elegant Chrysler roadster.

It seemed the entire Arboles Valley had an opinion about John Barclay's new car. Some of the men acknowledged that he was entitled to spend his money as he saw fit, but they were surprised he would put his money into something so impractical when his tractor and tiller were falling apart. A handful of foolish, ignorant women envied Rosa and considered befriending her so she might invite them for a ride, unaware that Rosa refused to set foot in the car. Most of the other women shared Mrs. Jorgensen's opinion that the roadster was a wasteful extravagance for a family with little money to spare.

Elizabeth agreed. "The only benefit of that car is that it takes John away from the farm for hours at a time," she declared upon returning from one trip to the post office to find Lars waiting for news. "These days he's more likely to be out tearing around the Arboles Valley than working in his fields."

Lars helped her gather up the mail from the passenger seat. "Is that so?"

"Even I can see that he's neglecting his crops. He'd much rather play with his new toy. I don't know how he expects to feed his family if he doesn't tend his farm. The post office can't possibly pay that much."

"Rosa will contrive something," said Lars, more confidently than Elizabeth thought the circumstances warranted. She was not surprised when later that evening, Henry told her that Lars had left the orchards early, telling no one where he was going and returning just in time for supper as tired and dirty as if he had worked the barley fields all day. Elizabeth assumed he had gone to help Rosa, but she worried about what John might do if he found Lars working his fields, caring for his family in his absence.

Henry told her not to worry. As the summer waned, he had worked every day side by side with Lars—except for those few hours Lars stole off alone—and Henry had seen nothing to suggest that Lars was doing anything more than helping a neighbor in need, or that he had resumed drinking. Elizabeth considered herself a reluctant expert on that subject and after watching Lars carefully for several weeks, she was forced to admit that her observations contradicted her instincts. She could not believe a drinking man would tuck a bottle into his pocket unless he intended to empty it later, but Lars had never once smelled of alcohol, nor did his hands shake, his words slur, or his eyes grow bloodshot. He had become neither more violent nor more charming. Without a doubt, he had become more secretive about his comings and goings, but she knew he had other reasons for that. Perhaps, contrary to all the wisdom on the subject she had gathered since childhood, he had been able to quit after that one bottle, after that first drink. Perhaps he was made of stronger stuff than her father and had thrown away the bottle untasted.

By mid-July, the apricot trees were heavy with fruit. Elizabeth admired the flourishing orchard with some alarm until Mary Katherine explained that Oscar always hired high school and college students on summer break to pick the fruit. Helping with the apricot harvest had become a summertime tradition for young people from miles around, who came to the Jorgensen farm to work, earn money for school, and socialize with friends.

On the first morning of the harvest, young men and women from throughout the Arboles Valley and from as far away as Oxnard descended upon the Jorgensen farm in droves. Elizabeth reveled in the festive atmosphere, looking on with pride as Henry organized the most recent arrivals into work teams. Even though he had never worked an apricot harvest before, Oscar trusted his judgment so much that he had placed Henry in charge of the seasonal workers. When Elizabeth reflected upon how well Henry had proven himself, and how he had come to be second only to Lars in authority on the farm, she could not help thinking of how he would have thrived as the owner of Triumph Ranch. As she watched her husband issuing instructions to the new employees, she allowed herself a moment of regret that they had not taken Mae up on her offer to use Peter's underworld contacts to track down the man who had swindled them. She quickly dismissed the notion. Justice would have to catch up with J. T. Simmons on its own. The Nelsons could not allow themselves to be drawn into any dealings with the sort of men Mae and Peter called friends.

Mary Katherine called Elizabeth over to help distribute buckets, hooks, and punch cards to the pickers while Oscar and Lars set up the cutting shed. Earlier, several yards from the first row of apricot trees, the hired hands had set tall, sturdy posts into holes that looked as if they had been dug years ago. The Jorgensen brothers made a roof by tying wooden trays about eight feet long and three feet wide to the top of the frame, then, in a similar fashion, they added a wall of trays along the southern side. By the look of it, Elizabeth guessed that the structure was meant only to provide shade, which was surely all the protection from the elements they needed. The clear, blue skies promised sunshine and warm breezes.

While the women worked in teams to arrange sawhorses in the cutting shed and place more of the long trays on top of them to make tables, the men dispersed into the orchard. They chose trees and set up their ladders, ten feet tall and broader at the base than the top. Using the hooks Mary Katherine and Elizabeth had given them, each picker attached a bucket to the top of his ladder and plucked all the ripe, sun-warmed fruit within reach. When a bucket was full, the picker climbed down the ladder and emptied it into a wooden box that Mary Katherine said could hold about forty pounds of plump apricots. When a box could hold no more, an empty box was stacked on top of it and filled in its turn. Up and down the ladders the pickers went, filling buckets and boxes, moving their ladders to find boughs still laden with fruit. They called out to one another as they worked, laughing and joking and grinning at the young women who watched.

The women did not have much time to stand idle and observe them. Not long after they finished setting up the makeshift tables in the cutting shed, Lars drove a flatbed wagon pulled by a team of horses through the rows of trees. Every few yards, the wagon halted and Henry and another regular hired hand jumped off to load the boxes into the back and to punch the pickers' cards to indicate how many boxes each had filled.

When Lars turned the wagon around, the women hurried back to their places in the cutting shed, four to a table. Mary Katherine waved Elizabeth over to her side, so Elizabeth joined her, unaware that she had committed a serious breach of etiquette. "What did I do?" she asked Mary Katherine as a few of the younger women let out cries of disappointment.

"You took the best place," remarked another woman at their table, who appeared to be in her early forties. "Newcomers are supposed to start out at the tables in the back and work their way closer to the orchard as they become more experienced."

"I'd be happy to move," said Elizabeth, reluctant to offend anyone who deserved the coveted spot.

"Don't be ridiculous," said Mary Katherine. "If I have to be on my feet all day, I ought to get a say in who stands next to me. Those girls pretend they want these places so they're closer to the truck, but the men unload the boxes and bring them to each table anyway, so what's the difference? They just want to have a better view of the pickers."

The last woman at their table, slightly younger than the first, shook her head. "Work slows down terribly when they do that. Me, I can cut apricots and admire a handsome young man without missing a beat."

The first woman grinned. "I'm going to tell your husband you said that."

"You go right ahead."

Henry interrupted the teasing by emptying a box of apricots onto their table. Working swiftly, the other three women took up their knives and began slicing fruit even as the apricots were still rolling down the tray. Elizabeth scrambled for an apricot, but the other women worked so rapidly that they had already finished stoning their second and third fruits while she fumbled with her knife for a secure grip.

"Here. Watch me," said Mary Katherine when she saw how Elizabeth struggled to slice the fruit cleanly with one swift stroke as the others did. She held the knife firmly in one hand and ran it around the fruit, separating the halves and removing the stone, which she tossed into a basket on the side of the table. Then she lay the halves split up in the center of the tray. "That's all there is to it."

Elizabeth nodded and tried again, and before long, the motions became more confident, smoother, though her pace still lagged well behind that of her companions. When they had cut all the apricots on their table, a hired hand named Marco brought them another box, which he stacked upon the empty box Henry had left beside their table. Elizabeth noticed that whenever the stack beside a table reached four empty boxes high, Marco collected the cutters' punch cards and added one mark to each. They were given credit for finishing the four boxes as a team, Elizabeth understood, since it was impossible for Marco to tell who at the table had cut which apricots.

Elizabeth realized that the complaints over her joining Mary Katherine's group had a second, more pragmatic bent. She quickened her pace, determined not to drag down her team and make Mary Katherine regret her decision.

When her table finished their first stack of four boxes, Marco put two punches each in the cards of the other two women. "What about Elizabeth?" asked Mary Katherine.

"I don't have a punch card," said Elizabeth. Since Henry and the other regular hired hands were receiving their usual pay for working on the farm, she had thought nothing of it. "Oscar didn't give me one."

"It must have been an oversight." Mary Katherine beckoned to Marco. "Give Elizabeth a punch card, please."

"I can't do that, ma'am," said Marco. "Your husband said only the harvest workers."

"That's nonsense. This is extra work on top of her regular duties, and she should receive extra pay."

Marco grimaced as if he wished he were somewhere else. "I guess you'll have to take it up with your husband, ma'am."

"I'll talk to him, all right," said Mary Katherine indignantly as Marco walked away.

"That's not necessary," said Elizabeth quickly. "It's not really extra work. I'd be working in the garden or cleaning the house if I weren't cutting apricots."

"You still have to help with the cooking," Mary Katherine countered. "This is extra work, and it's more taxing. I'm sure this is Mother Jorgensen's idea, not my husband's."

Unwilling to be drawn into a public discussion of Mrs. Jorgensen's faults, Elizabeth made no reply. On the opposite side of the table, the other two women pretended to be engrossed in their work, oblivious to the exchange.

When the entire surface of their table was covered with sliced apricots, they lifted the wooden tray and carried it from the shed to the truck, which would take the apricots to the sulfur house. Without pausing to rest, the other three women returned to the shed. Elizabeth hurried after them and helped place another long wooden tray on the sawhorses. In the few moments' wait before Marco brought them another box of apricots, Elizabeth flexed her wrists and fingers, worked the knots from her muscles, and ruefully realized she would probably be too sore to quilt that evening, and possibly for many evenings to come.

"Do we ever get a turn to pick the apricots?" she asked Mary Katherine, who smiled and told her she was lucky they didn't. The pickers had an even more difficult job, climbing up and down ladders and hauling forty-pound boxes of fruit in the hot sun. Just then, Lars pulled up in the wagon with another load of boxes. Elizabeth stifled a groan and picked up her knife.

All day long the pickers plucked sweet, ripe fruit from the trees for the women to cut, on and on, pausing only for lunch beneath the apricot trees. There the men and women mingled, friends greeted one another, laughing, talking, as if they were enjoying a picnic on a summer holiday. All too soon for Elizabeth they returned to work, chatting and gossiping about who had shared whose blanket in the shade and which young lady had brought what special treat in her lunch basket to share with which admirer. Since Elizabeth recognized few of the names that came up in conversation, she half listened to the talk while giving most of her attention to the task at hand. Although she had grown accustomed to the work, she still felt as if she had been thrown into the middle of an elaborate country dance in which everyone else knew the right places to spin and twirl and bow while all she could do was struggle to hear the caller over the band, doing the Charleston for all she was worth and hoping no one would notice.

By the third day, Elizabeth noted with some pride that no one who didn't know her would have been able to pick her out as the novice among the more accomplished cutters. While Oscar had not consented to grant her a punch card, the two beneficiaries of her labors must have felt either gratitude or pangs of conscience, for both brought Elizabeth gifts of food from their lunch baskets, delicacies like chicken pie and jars of preserves, which Elizabeth was clearly meant to take home rather than add to the picnic.

Elizabeth had assumed that the sulfur curing process was the last step in preserving the sliced apricots, but learned differently once the first trays were removed from the sulfur house. Local children joined the older harvest workers for the last task, carrying the large trays of cured apricots from the truck to a flat stretch of ground just south of the orchard. The trays were placed close together, with only enough space to walk single file between them, and left to dry in the sun for five or six days. During her infrequent breaks from cutting, Elizabeth enjoyed walking past the rows of plump, juicy cured apricots, breathing deeply of their sweet fragrance and admiring their bright orange hue. She admired the children, too, who were happy in their work but diligent, well aware of how essential they were to the success of the harvest. They reminded her of Henry and his siblings back at Two Bears Farm and of the Bergstrom children at Elm Creek Manor. Their work had been play to them, and they had been proud to contribute to the success of the farm.

One morning, Elizabeth was surprised to discover Marta and Lupita among the children arranging trays in the sun. Lupita was still too little to hold her own among the older children, but Marta kept her younger sister close and praised her efforts. Marta's smile was brighter than Elizabeth had ever seen it. Lupita was so happy she sometimes could not resist jumping up and down instead of remembering to carry her edge of the tray.

When Elizabeth mentioned seeing the Barclay girls, Mary Katherine seemed even more surprised than Elizabeth had been. "They've never helped with the harvest before, not since the Rodriguezes left the farm," she said, adding with an impish grin, "Maybe they need the extra cash to pay for John's car."

At lunchtime, Elizabeth discovered the truth. As she spread out her blanket in the shade of the apricot trees and unpacked her basket, she looked up at the sound of laughter to find Rosa seated on a blanket in the sunshine several yards away. Miguel lay in her lap, smiling up at Marta, who tickled him under the chin with a leafy twig from an apricot tree while Lupita and Ana dug into their picnic basket. Marta and Lupita had spent so much time in the sun that their hair had turned from dark brown to rich bronze.

As Elizabeth watched, Lars emerged from the orchard and crossed the grassy clearing, hastily finger-combing his thinning blond hair before replacing his hat. Elizabeth expected him to continue toward the house, where Mrs. Jorgensen had lunch ready for the immediate family and a few of the farmhands who preferred their usual table to a picnic blanket, but instead he paused at Rosa's blanket. She smiled up at him, they exchanged a few words, and Lupita jumped up to tug on his hand. Lars settled down on their blanket and smiled as he thanked Rosa for the leg of fried chicken she handed him. He almost dropped it as Lupita scrambled onto his lap. Rosa laughed, and Lars smiled warmly back. They sat so close together that their shoulders nearly touched.

"I hope John Barclay doesn't show up."

Elizabeth started at Henry's voice, but quickly turned to smile at him as he sat down beside her on the blanket. "He wouldn't like it," Elizabeth acknowledged. "He's a jealous man. He must not know they're here. I can't believe he would stand for it."

Henry glanced at the couple for a moment before deliberately turning away. "Lars better be careful," he said, reaching into the basket. "She's a married woman. It doesn't look right."

Henry disliked gossip, and Elizabeth knew that would be his last word on the subject. Still, she could not help observing Lars, Rosa, and the children as they enjoyed their picnic—and worrying about what others would think. Gossip and rumor already swirled around Rosa because of her children's mysterious illness, and although Lars had become a respected member of the community, he did not have a spotless past. They seemed oblivious to anything but their own happiness, unaware of the curious glances of their neighbors. Elizabeth, who had considered herself an expert in the art of gossip once upon a time, could imagine all too well the nature of their speculations: Could anyone remember seeing either Rosa or Lars so content in anyone else's company? Weren't they being rather bold, for two people who had once been in love? Wasn't it interesting how well the children took to Lars, who was not exactly known for his playful temperament?

At that moment, as Marta threw back her head and laughed at something Lars had said, her long, sun-bronzed hair slipped free of the red ribbon that had held it away from her face. As Rosa retied it, Elizabeth was suddenly struck by the realization that Ana had spent nearly as much time in the sun as Marta and Lupita had that summer, watching them play, and yet her hair was still the same dark hue as her mother's. Miguel, too, had hair so dark brown it was almost black.

Unbidden, an image of John Barclay swam to the surface of Elizabeth's thoughts—shouting at Lars to stay away from his family, his blue eyes snapping with anger as he snatched his hat to mop his brow. His hair was nearly as dark as his wife's.

It could mean nothing, Elizabeth told herself, but she could not make herself believe it.

As she had done every day of the apricot harvest, Elizabeth left the shed earlier than the other cutters so she could help Mrs. Jorgensen prepare a late supper for the family and finish other necessary tasks the work of the harvest had prevented Mrs. Jorgensen from completing. As she approached the yellow farmhouse, she spied an unfamiliar automobile parked near the carriage house. Three men, two in dark suits and one in a police officer's uniform, stood talking to Lars. They were too far away for Elizabeth to make out their words. Lars handed something wrapped in a handkerchief to one of the dark-suited men, they all shook hands, and the men climbed back into their automobile and drove away. Lars turned too suddenly for Elizabeth to pretend she had not been watching them. Annoyance clouded his face briefly, but he **offered** her a nod in greeting and strode back to the orchard **without a** word.

Elizabeth hurried on into the kitchen, where Mrs. Jorgensen set her to peeling a pile of carrots, freshly washed and glistening on the drainboard. What had Lars done to warrant a visit from the police? She could not believe he had committed any crime. It was not in his nature—unless he had begun drinking again, which was unbearable to contemplate. Had John Barclay, his only enemy, falsely accused him of something out of spite? Who were the other two men, and what had they taken from Lars?

Elizabeth took up her potato peeler and got to work. "Who were those men?" She knew Mrs. Jorgensen would have heard the unfamiliar car pull up to the carriage house.

"One is Tom Jeffries, the county sheriff," said Mrs. Jorgensen, quartering a chicken with a sharp cleaver. "The other two men aren't from around here. I don't know who they are. Why didn't you ask Lars?"

He had not given her a chance, but perhaps Mrs. Jorgensen knew that.

They worked in silence for several minutes. "May I ask you a question?" said Elizabeth, setting down her peeler.

Mrs. Jorgensen poured cooking oil into the frying pan and turned on the gas. "I suppose so."

"How many grandchildren do you have?"

For a moment, Mrs. Jorgensen froze, but she quickly resumed her work, and when she spoke, her voice was even. "What **an odd** sort of question. I think you know the answer."

"How many?"

Mrs. Jorgensen said nothing. The oil in the pan sizzled. She adjusted the gas and arranged chicken pieces in the pan with a pair of metal tongs, jerking her hand away as a spatter of oil touched skin. "Do you know anything about the language of flowers?" She quickly wiped the oil from the back of her wrist. "It's an old-fashioned belief that every flower has a symbolic meaning. Do you know what the apricot blossom is supposed to represent?"

Elizabeth shook her head, although Mrs. Jorgensen was not looking at her.

"Doubt. Perhaps in bygone days it meant doubt that a lover was true, but I think it could also act as a warning not to believe everything one sees, not to jump to conclusions based upon rumor and suspicion." Mrs. Jorgensen turned over the chicken pieces and set down the tongs. "The orchard was full of apricot blossoms in the spring. It was only a matter of time before they bore fruit. The soil may be rich, the rains ample and gentle, but if you sow mistrust, that is what you will harvest."

"John is dark-haired and Lars is fair," said Elizabeth. "Only two of Rosa's children have hair that lightens in the sun—Marta and Lupita. Rosa's children have been struck down by the same mysterious illness—all but two, Marta and Lupita. Mary Katherine once told me that one of John's sisters died in childhood after suffering an unknown sickness. Lars's siblings are healthy and strong."

At last Mrs. Jorgensen turned around. "I never took you for the sort to spread malicious rumors."

"I'm not," said Elizabeth. "I care about Rosa and her children. And Lars. I worry what John might do if he discovers he's been betrayed."

Mrs. Jorgensen gave a sharp laugh. "If *you* figured it out after knowing them for only a few short months, do you really believe John hasn't?"

Shocked into silence, Elizabeth could only stare at her. "Then why—"

"Why has John not accused Rosa of adultery? Why has he not cast her out?" Mrs. Jorgensen shook her head. "Only John knows that. I think he still loves her in his way—although love is perhaps the wrong word for it. He desires her. He covets her. He was willing to ignore what he did not want to see, because if he didn't, he would lose her."

"Lars and Rosa were lovers," said Elizabeth. It was not a question. "Rosa became pregnant with his child, but her parents had forbidden her to marry him. She was desperate to marry someone for the sake of her child and herself, and John was there—sober, a landowner, a man who claimed to love her."

"I don't know why liquor had such a hold on Lars," said Mrs. Jorgensen, an uncharacteristic ache in her voice. "My father was the same way. I'll never understand such men, not as long as I live. If only Lars had been able to stop drinking all those years ago, he and Rosa might have defied her parents and married. They might as well have. Rosa's obedience to her parents' demands gained her nothing. When Marta was born, two months earlier than expected but as perfect and healthy as only a full-term child could be, they knew Rosa had been pregnant when she married. The shame she had brought upon the family was so great they shunned her from that day forward."

"That's unfair," said Elizabeth. "What she did was wrong, but not unforgivable."

"Mr. and Mrs. Diaz were devout Catholics. Rosa had defied them, deceived them, and broken one of the strictest tenets of their religion. They believed she had committed a terrible sin. Worse yet, in their eyes, she was unrepentant. Her determination to conceal her sin was proof enough of that."

"But Marta was an innocent baby," Elizabeth protested. "Say what you will about how Rosa had disappointed her parents, how could the sight of their beautiful grandchild not move them to reconcile, regardless of the circumstances of her birth?"

The chicken began to smoke and spatter. With a start, Mrs. Jorgensen snatched the tongs and transferred the chicken from the frying pan to a serving platter. "I don't know that the Diazes ever saw Marta."

"What?"

"There was some talk around the valley that John had banned the Diazes from his property. Oscar heard it from their neighbor, a kindly soul who picked up their mail for years, until Rosa's father passed on, since they could no longer visit the post office."

"What did John have against Rosa's parents?" asked Elizabeth, bewildered. "They allowed him to marry Rosa, didn't they? And I myself have seen Carlos at the post office. He drove Henry and me there on our second day in the valley."

"Well, perhaps Carlos wasn't included in the ban. As for Rosa's parents, they believed John had relations with Rosa before their marriage, didn't they? From their point of view, he led their beloved daughter into sin. For all I know, it was their choice not to set foot on the Barclay farm, and John never banned them at all. I suppose that is a more plausible explanation."

Elizabeth did not agree. She could not believe the bright-eyed young bride gazing out warmly from the pages of Rosa's album could have transformed into a woman coldhearted enough to sever all ties with her only daughter. Rosa had spoken of her parents so lovingly, describing her father as a man who was always cheerful and laughing. She said she had grown up surrounded by love. If that was true, how could her mother and father have disowned her, even after she had broken their hearts?

"John must have suspected Marta was not his child," said Elizabeth.

"Suspected? I'm sure he knew it for an outright fact when she was born only seven months into their marriage. John Barclay is a man of many unadmirable qualities, but he is not stupid. He can count as well as the next man."

"Then he forgave Rosa. He forgave her, even when her parents did not."

"I don't know if he ever forgave her entirely. He certainly never forgave Lars. Accepting Marta as his own child was the price he had to pay to keep the woman he desired as his wife. He is a proud man, but I think he would have been content if Rosa had forgotten my son."

"But she didn't."

"For many years, I'm sure John was able to convince himself that she had. Everyone in the valley believed that Rosa chose sensibly when she married John instead of Lars, taking a sober man with a good living over a drunkard who had lost his farm. They have no reason to question her fidelity. If Rosa gave John reason, however, if he thought everyone knew she had betrayed him, exposed him to ridicule—then he would confront her. He would think he had no choice."

Mrs. Jorgensen's mouth was a grim line in the soft curves of her face, and Elizabeth knew they shared the same thought: Lupita's health, a blessing to be cherished by all who loved her, was to John nothing more than a sign that Rosa had betrayed him.

Mrs. Jorgensen gestured to the carrots. "Come. Let's finish. The others will be here soon."

Elizabeth picked up the peeler. "How long until John is forced to face the truth?"

"The other children took sick before the end of their fourth year," said Mrs. Jorgensen. "Lupita will be five in September."

For nearly a year, John Barclay had been watching his daughter, watching and waiting, torn between relief and rage. For nearly a year longer than should have been possible, Lupita had evaded the trap that had ensnared his other children. Lupita had thrived, her blossoming good health a mockery of John's willingness to overlook Rosa's sin and accept her as his wife. How much longer could he be expected to pretend, all for the sake of keeping an ungrateful wife who bore him only sickly children, who taunted him with the fruits of her infidelity?

But surely a man as suspicious as John Barclay would not have waited for Lupita's fifth year to doubt his wife's faithfulness. He must have been constantly vigilant all the years of their marriage, waiting for Rosa to betray him. In the forge of suspicion and mistrust, any love he might have had for his wife had turned to jealous cruelty. It was little wonder the grieving, heartsick woman had turned to her steadfast first love for comfort and solace.

"You were wrong to say that John forgave Rosa when her parents did not." Mrs. Jorgensen broke off at the sound of approaching voices just outside the window. The men had come in for a supper that was not yet prepared for them. "Mrs. Diaz's heart softened at the end. A friend of mine spotted her lingering out of sight in the back of the church at Ana's christening, and I myself saw her leave flowers on the graves of her grandchildren. She even approached me at the Arboles Grocery once and asked after Lars. That was shortly before her death, only a year before Lupita was born. Mrs. Diaz's death was such a shock. I have always suspected that she took her own life out of shame and remorse for forbidding Rosa to marry Lars. She wanted to make amends, I'm sure of it. If she had only lived a little time longer—"

The kitchen door swung open and the men trooped in, tired but in good spirits. Oscar declared that he had never seen such a bountiful harvest. Henry kissed Elizabeth on his way to the table, but his grin faded at the sight of her troubled expression. She smiled and patted his arm to assure him he had no need to worry, that she would explain later, when they were alone.

She urgently wanted to ask him if he, too, thought it was unfathomable that a mother—especially one known as a devout Catholic—would take her own life when reconciliation with her estranged daughter seemed imminent.

1917

Isabel watched the baptism from the vestibule of the church, shrouded in a dark shawl and veil. She crossed herself as the priest poured water over her newborn granddaughter's head, and again when he anointed her with oil. Her heart ached to see the emptiness in Rosa's eyes on a day that would have been joyous had it not come so soon after the death of her son.

As the ceremony ended, Isabel ducked into a shadowy alcove. Her disguise would not fool four-year-old Marta, who would surely call out a happy greeting and scamper down the aisle of the church to hug her grandmother the moment she spotted her. Hugs and kisses would have to wait until the next time Rosa could slip away from home and bring the children to meet Isabel on the mesa, a secluded spot with a breathtaking view of the canyon. Every week at the appointed time, Isabel went and waited, hoping Rosa would come. In recent months, the sudden illness and sudden death of Rosa's son and the last weeks of her pregnancy had kept her at home, and Isabel had walked home from the mesa discouraged and lonely. She resented her son-in-law for keeping her away from Rosa, but contrary to her heart's yearnings, she could not help blaming Rosa, as well. Why did Rosa not stand up to her husband? She had not learned such meek acceptance in her parents' house. Was it love that made Rosa so determined to please him?

Somehow Isabel could not believe it was so.

She watched, hidden in the alcove, as the family departed. John passed by first, escorting his mother, who beamed with proud satisfaction. She ought to be happy, that other grandmother, Isabel thought ungraciously. She possessed everything Isabel desired and because it came so easily to her, she could not have any sense of its true worth.

Marta trailed behind her, holding on to John's sister's hand, questioning her unhappily about something Isabel could not discern. Last of all came Rosa, carrying baby Ana. Isabel choked back a sob, longing to stretch out her arms to embrace her precious granddaughters. It was too painful to see them so close and not be able to speak to them, to hold them. She should not have come.

Suddenly, just as Rosa tugged a quilt over the baby's head and stepped from the warmth of the church into the cold November rain outside, a flash of white fell to the tile floor over her shoulder, like a dove descending.

Isabel waited until the door closed and the church grew still before stepping from her hiding place. She stooped over to pick up the fallen object, her fingers closing around soft satin. Ana's cap, trimmed in lace to match her baptismal gown. A gift from Rosa, an apology for all she had denied Isabel that day.

Years ago, Isabel would have been infuriated by the very idea that a baby's cap could compensate for the insult she had been forced to endure that morning, and so many other mornings since John had banished Isabel from his home. She never should have had to lurk in the back of the church at her granddaughter's baptism instead of sitting proudly in the first pew, as was a grandmother's right. But that was long ago. The years of waiting and hoping had drained her anger from her. Now all the spaces of her heart had room for was longing, and a fervent hope that someday John's resentment would abate and Isabel would no longer have to meet her daughter and grandchildren in secret.

She clutched the soft white satin cap and prayed.

Chapter Eleven

1925

After the apricot harvest, Elizabeth spent the summer evenings on the cabin's newly mended front porch, working on the quilts she had found in the old steamer trunk. Henry sat beside her, reading aloud from the newspaper or letters from home while she sewed. They sat together, talking quietly, content in each other's company, as the sun set behind the Santa Monica Mountains. Elizabeth imagined the fading daylight offering the valley below one last caress as it slipped behind the western hills, pulling a veil of darkness over the Norwegian Grade, then the Jorgensen farm, then the adobe where Rosa lived with her children, then Safari World, and last of all, the Grand Union Hotel. Then the sun disappeared behind the mountain range, and Elizabeth and Henry watched the stars appear, talking about the next day's work or reminiscing about summers in Pennsylvania—swimming in Elm Creek, riding the wooded trails that crisscrossed the valley, savoring the hint of autumn that came only at night, a gentle, wistful warning that summer could not endure forever.

Henry usually went to bed soon after the moon rose, and Elizabeth always joined him. If she could not sleep, she would leave the bed without disturbing her husband, light a lamp in the front room, and stay up to work on the quilts, mending torn seams, patching holes, replacing worn pieces with sturdy scraps, adding soft cotton batting to the places where the quilt had worn thin. When the top was whole and sound again, she restored the missing quilting stitches that had held top, batting, and lining together, following the tiny needle pricks left behind from the original threads. Some had broken over time; others Elizabeth had been forced to pick out in the act of mending. She followed her predecessor's patterns as closely as possible, even to the length of her stitches, so that her handiwork would blend in harmoniously with what had gone before.

She put her last stitch into the Road to Triumph Ranch quilt at the end of August, and when she finished, the hexagons no longer resembled wagon wheels that had broken and splintered on a hard road. They might roll on steadily for miles into the distance, even into an uncertain future.

Elizabeth washed the quilt, hung it to dry in a freshening breeze, and turned her attention to the Arboles Valley Star. On closer inspection, she became even more certain that it had rarely been used, or perhaps not at all. The binding around the edges, one of the first places signs of wear appeared on a quilt, had not rubbed to a threadbare thinness from use. She found no holes or tears aside from two places where a mouse had nibbled through the lining and removed some soft batting to make a nest elsewhere. What she had mistaken for stains was merely dust that came out in the first wash. The creases that she had attributed to the uneven shrinkage of the fabric and batting through many washings had disappeared during the months that the quilt had been draped over their bed instead of folded and crushed at the bottom of the steamer trunk. Curious, Elizabeth picked out a seam at the tip of one star and discovered that the fabric was the same shade from edge to edge. If the fabric had faded after the quilt was complete, the edges hidden within the seam would have been darker than the part in the center, which had been exposed to sunlight. The fading of the fabric must have occurred before the quiltmaker pieced her blocks, perhaps when the calico was still part of a favorite dress, worn by a child who played in the sunshine. As far as Elizabeth could tell, all of the damage to the quilt could have occurred while it was stored within the trunk.

Compared with the extensive restoration the older, homespun-and-wool quilt had required, repairing the Arboles Valley Star was a simple matter. Elizabeth replaced the missing batting and patched the holes. She replaced the stitches she had picked out to check for uneven fading of the fabric. Last of all, she studied an embroidered satin patch trimmed in lace appliquéd on the back of the quilt. Within the circle of rosebuds, the initials R.D. and L.J. were intertwined. There was no question in Elizabeth's mind whose names those letters represented, or who had made the quilt, or why.

She thought of her own floral Double Wedding Ring quilt, beautifully and lovingly made by the women of her family, and lost to her forever. She thought more wistfully of the Chimneys and Cornerstones quilt, sturdy and cheerful, delighting guests at the Grand Union Hotel. She could do without the quilts, as she certainly must learn to do, but what a comfort it would be to have them with her now, offering with their soft and gentle warmth the memory of love and the promise of happiness.

With one last, fond caress, she folded the quilts she had restored with such care, the quilts that were not truly hers. They had given her purpose and distraction in her loneliness, comfort and warmth in her need. Now it was time to pass them along to their rightful owner, whose need was so much greater.

❧

The next time Elizabeth made the mail run, on a cool, overcast day when the air tasted of the metallic tang of rain, she took the quilts with her, folded carefully and stacked on the backseat of Lars's car. When she arrived at the Barclay farm, no one was outside, neither in the fields nor beneath the orange trees, where she had grown accustomed to the sight of Marta and Lupita playing while Ana watched. A glance into the barn told her that John had gone off somewhere in the roadster. Suddenly anxious, she hurried to the adobe and knocked on the door, but her relief when Rosa answered was quickly tempered by concern. The haunted despair had returned to the mother's dark eyes, and her mouth was a tight knot of worry and pain.

Elizabeth's first thoughts were of the children. "What's wrong?"

"Nothing." Rosa quickly amended, "Nothing new. Nothing that has not been wrong for a very long time." She opened the door wider and beckoned Elizabeth inside. "Please come in while I get your letters."

Marta and Lupita played with dolls on the floor in the center of the room. They glanced up warily when she entered, but after recognizing her, they returned to their game. She did not see the other two children and assumed they were in bed. Days when they felt strong enough to get out of bed to play had become less frequent.

Rosa returned from the kitchen with a bundle of mail. Elizabeth took it, thanked her, and said, "I found something in the cabin that belongs to you."

While Rosa looked on, perplexed, Elizabeth took the mail to the car and returned with the quilts. She set the Arboles Valley Star quilt on the sofa and unfolded the Road to Triumph Ranch. Rosa's eyes widened as she reached out to take the bottom corners of the quilt, lifting them so the quilt unfurled between their hands. *"Dios mio,"* she breathed.

"It is your great-grandmother's, isn't it?" said Elizabeth. "I recognized it from the photograph you showed me."

"Without a doubt, it is hers." Rosa's gaze ran over the quilt as if she were drinking in the memories stitched into the cloth. "It is just as I remember it."

"Almost but not exactly," said Elizabeth apologetically. "It needed some mending. I matched the fabric as best as I could when I replaced worn pieces."

Rosa smiled. "Then it is even lovelier than I remember." She sat down in a rocking chair, draped the quilt across her lap, and ran her hand over it. "I remember my mother cuddling me in this quilt when I was a little girl no bigger than Lupita. My great-grandmother made it when she was a young bride-to-be in Texas. Her parents had arranged for her to marry my great-grandfather through a cousin who lived in Los Angeles. The first time she saw him was the day he came to San Antonio to bring her back to El Rancho Triunfo."

"Triumph Ranch," said Elizabeth.

"Yes, and for many years the name rang true. They raised barley and rye. One hundred head of cattle grazed where the sheep pasture and the apricot orchard stand today. But my family lost everything in a terrible drought, the worst ever to strike the Arboles Valley. Every farm in the valley suffered. Some families sold their land after the first summer without rain, but by the time my great-grandparents decided to put El Rancho Triunfo up for sale the following year, there were no buyers. My great-grandparents sold all the cattle to slaughterhouses rather than let them starve. They were thankful and relieved when Mrs. Jorgensen's grandfather bought the ranch and permitted them to remain on the land in exchange for their labor. The rains fell two months later. My great-grandparents never forgave themselves for not holding out a little while longer, for giving up too soon and accepting less than the land was truly worth."

"They never forgave the Jorgensens, either, or so I've heard."

"That is also true." Rosa glanced at the other quilt, almost forgotten on the sofa. Elizabeth unfolded it and held it up high by the corners so that only the bottom edge touched the floor. Rosa admired it politely, but she soon returned her gaze to her great-grandmother's quilt.

"I call this quilt the Arboles Valley Star," said Elizabeth, surprised by Rosa's reaction. She folded the quilt in half and draped it over the sofa. "I found it with your great-grandmother's. Don't you recognize it?"

"I've never seen it before," said Rosa. "I suppose I could look through the album and see if it appears in any of my family's photographs, but I've looked at them so many times. I think I would have recognized this quilt if it were in any of them. It seems too new for my great-grandmother's handiwork."

"I thought you had made it."

"Me?" Rosa shook her head. "Why would you think that?"

"Because of this."

Elizabeth turned the quilt over and showed Rosa the embroidered monogram on the square of lace-trimmed satin appliquéd to the back, the intertwined initials surrounded by a wreath of rosebuds. As if in a dream, Rosa touched the letters with her fingertips and pressed her other hand to her mouth. Her eyes widened in astonishment and, Elizabeth thought, confusion and anguish.

"What is it?" Elizabeth prompted her. "Do you remember the quilt now?"

"No." Rosa shook her head. "I've never seen this quilt, but I—I do know this embroidery. This is my mother's work. She made these stitches. And this satin and lace. It came from Ana's baptismal cap. But—why? And when?" Rosa swiftly turned the quilt over and studied the pieced stars, running her hands over the patches. Her long, slender fingers came to rest on a piece of ivory sateen. "This was from her wedding gown. I know it. And this—" She touched a triangle of pink floral calico. "This was from the dress Marta wore on her first day of school. But how did my mother come to have it? I don't understand." She threw Elizabeth a beseeching look. "Where did you find this quilt?"

"Both quilts were in an old steamer trunk in the cabin," said Elizabeth. "On the Jorgensen farm, where Henry and I live. Where your family once lived. I assumed your grandmother had forgotten the older quilt there when they moved out, but as for the newer—"

"Oh, no, no. They left nothing behind. The homespun-and-wool quilt was in my mother's home all my life. It never left her bed. But this star quilt . . ." Rosa looked from one quilt to the other in bewilderment. "My mother must have taken the quilts to the cabin and left them there. But I don't understand—" Suddenly Rosa grew very still. "She wanted me to have them. And she could not bring them to me here."

"Why not?"

"My husband would not allow my parents on his property, not even to visit their grandchildren. When I wanted to see my mother, we had to meet on the mesa. Once a week, when John went to pick up the mail from the train station, I would take the children to see her. You know the place."

"Rosa," said Elizabeth, gripped by a sudden fear. "The day your mother died—were you supposed to meet her on the mesa?"

"I was, but she didn't know that I could not come. A few days before, John had returned home with the mail and found me and the children gone. I—I had to tell him where we had been." A shadow of remembered pain crossed her features for a moment, and Elizabeth could imagine how she had been compelled to confess. "After that, he varied his schedule so I never knew when he would be gone or how soon he would return. I was never able to meet my mother again." She clutched her mother's quilt, her gaze far away. "I can't help but think of her waiting for me, waiting and waiting, every week without fail, hoping I would come. I cannot help but imagine her despair when I never appeared. Perhaps she thought she would never see her grandchildren again. Perhaps— perhaps I have been fooling myself all these years, telling myself her death was an accident."

Elizabeth's breath caught in her throat. "Perhaps you were."

Rosa looked up sharply and read the fear written on Elizabeth's face. "No. No. I know what you're thinking. I can't believe it."

But Elizabeth saw the doubt in her eyes. John had known that Rosa's mother waited for her daughter alone on the mesa on the days he traveled to the train station for the mail.

"Mami?" said Lupita fearfully.

With a start, Rosa turned to her daughters. "Marta, go and see if Miguel and Ana are still sleeping, would you, please?" she said. "Take Lupita with you."

Reluctantly, Marta did as she was told. She had barely left the room when outside, the roadster roared up the gravel road and braked hard. With preternatural calm, Rosa folded her mother's quilt, set it aside, and stood. She was on her feet when the door burst open and John stormed in.

"Where is that son of a bitch?" John's sharp gaze scanned the room, alighting on Elizabeth for a moment before moving on. "I know he's here."

"No one else is here," said Rosa. "Only Elizabeth."

John shoved Rosa aside and strode into the kitchen. Elizabeth heard the table overturn, glass shatter. John appeared in the doorway, his eyes ablaze with fury. "I saw his car."

"I drove it," said Elizabeth quickly. "I work for the Jorgensens."

"Did you come to help my dear wife plan the birthday party?" John addressed Elizabeth in a voice of acid. "Lupita turns five next week, did you know that?"

"I just came for the mail," said Elizabeth steadily.

John threw her a look of contempt and strode off toward the

children's room in the back of the adobe. Rosa drew in a shaky breath at the sound of a child's cry and gripped the back of the rocking chair so hard her knuckles turned white. Elizabeth put her arm around Rosa's shoulders and was startled when Rosa flinched in pain. She knew at once that John had not stopped hitting his wife; he had only become more discreet about where he left bruises.

Without warning John returned. Rosa drew back but not quickly enough to evade his grasp. He seized her by the shoulders and shook her. "Where is he?"

"I don't know," Rosa choked out. "He's not here."

Elizabeth tried to put herself between John and Rosa, but he knocked her to the floor. Instinctively she grabbed for the rocking chair as she fell, but her fingers slipped and her head struck the floor. Dazed, she tried to sit up, her head ringing with the sound of a fist striking flesh and Rosa crying out in pain. Then the door slammed, the roadster roared to life, and, but for Rosa's gasps as she fought for breath, silence.

"Are you all right?" said Elizabeth as she clutched the arm of the rocking chair and shakily pulled herself to her feet.

Rosa's face was a mess of tears and blood, but she nodded. "The children." She fled to the back of the adobe and returned moments later to report that they were unharmed. "John's going after Lars. I'm sure of it."

"You shouldn't be here when he returns," said Elizabeth. "Gather the children and come with me. You can stay in the cabin with me and Henry."

Rosa shook her head. "It's not safe. We'll have to pass John on the way."

"Then take a room at the Grand Union Hotel. Carlos will look after you."

"No," said Rosa, suddenly calm. "I know a better place. A place my husband fears."

The canyon. Elizabeth nodded. "Then take warm clothes and food. It looks like rain."

"I have to warn Lars. John keeps a pistol in the car."

"I'll warn Lars." Elizabeth hurried to the door, fully aware that John had a head start and a faster car. "Pack quickly. Take only what you need. John might double back at any time."

Rosa did not need the warning. Before the door closed behind her, Elizabeth heard Rosa call to Marta and Lupita to wake the other children.

The overcast sky had turned steel gray, mottled with charcoal. As Elizabeth turned onto the main road back to the Jorgensen farm, a steady, cold drizzle began to fall, but she dared not slow the car. She tried to remember what work assignments Oscar had given the men at breakfast that morning. If Lars was alone in the garage, waiting impatiently for Elizabeth's return as he usually did after her trips to the post office, he would have no chance. John would come upon him and kill him before Lars realized he was there. If Lars was in the pasture looking after the sheep or working in the orchard, he might see the roadster coming and have time to hide—but he would not know that he needed to hide.

Suddenly Elizabeth remembered. Lars was delivering the dried apricots to the packing house in Camarillo that day and was not expected back until close to suppertime. At that moment, he was probably driving the horse and wagon over the Norwegian Grade. Her relief at the realization that John would not cut down Lars in the garage was short-lived. John might lie in wait until Lars returned— or harm someone else when the object of his rage failed to appear.

She gunned the engine and raced for home.

She arrived at the Jorgensen farm in a driving rain stirred by strong gusts of wind from the west. The roadster was parked close to the house at the end of two rivers of mud the tires had cut through the front garden. John stood a few yards from the front door, brandishing a pistol and shouting up at the second-floor windows. Someone inside had drawn the curtains.

John spun around at the sound of her approach and leveled the pistol at Elizabeth. She slammed on the brake and flung herself down upon the seat just as the shot rang out. "Send him out," she heard John yell. "Send him out now or her blood is on his hands."

Elizabeth crouched out of sight, threw the car into reverse, and sped off blindly back the way she had come. Only when she reached the main road out of range of his pistol did she dare risk a glance over the dashboard. John had pursued her partway down the road, but he had given up. He shouted something unintelligible at her before turning and striding back to the house.

Her hands shook so badly she almost could not shut off the engine. Her thoughts raced. Mrs. Jorgensen was likely inside with Mary Katherine and the girls, but where were the men? Where was Henry? Surely Mrs. Jorgensen had called the police, but they were miles away, too far to help them now. All she could do was pray that they arrived in time to stop John before he killed someone—and if that failed, that Rosa would have enough time to get away with the children.

She would have to make sure Rosa had enough time.

Swallowing hard, she sat up, started the engine, and set the car in motion, creeping forward until she reached the driveway's narrowest point, thanking God for the downpour that drowned out the sound of the automobile. Slowly, so that she would not attract the attention of the madman shouting at the yellow farmhouse, she turned the wheel and maneuvered the car until it blocked access to the road. She shut down the engine again and crouched low in her seat, her gaze fixed on John, listening for sirens that did not come.

She almost screamed when the car door opened. "Slide over," a man's voice said in her ear.

It was Henry. Tears of relief filled her eyes as she flung her arms around him. "Where were you? Are you all right? Has he hurt anyone?"

"Not yet." Henry returned her embrace, but then gently freed himself. "Darling, I've got to get closer."

"What do you mean? What are you going to do?"

"I'm going to drive around back and get the women and girls out through the kitchen door. Oscar and Marco are waiting around the corner of the house to jump John if necessary."

"But he's armed."

"And sooner or later he's going to realize the Jorgensen women aren't, and he's going to break down the door and hurt someone." He kissed her quickly. "You've got to get out of the car."

"Henry—"

He kissed her again, a long, hard, almost painful kiss, then half led, half carried her from the car. "Stay in the ditch," he ordered as he slammed the door behind him and started the engine. "Keep your head down, no matter what."

She screamed his name and ran after the car until her foot slipped in the mud and she came down hard on her ankle. Pain shot up her right leg and she staggered to a halt, watching as Henry sped toward John. At the sound of the automobile, John turned and fired. The car swerved, struck a rock, and flipped over on its side. Cursing, soaked with rain, John approached the car, weapon leveled at the driver's door. Suddenly the door swung open and Henry dragged himself free of the wreckage. As John took aim, Henry ran at him, low and fast. A shot rang out as Henry tackled John and brought him to the ground.

"Henry!" Elizabeth screamed.

Limping, she ran toward the two still figures lying in the mud.

From behind the house sprinted Oscar and one of the hired hands. Oscar fell to his knees beside Henry and rolled him onto his back; the other man pinned John to the muddy ground and kicked the gun away.

From behind the thunder came the scream of sirens.

∽❧

1920

Isabel wanted to place the quilts in her daughter's arms, to see Rosa's face light up with happiness when she discovered how Isabel's heart had changed, but she did not know when Rosa would come again to the mesa. Isabel's message was too urgent to wait. She must insure that Rosa received the quilts soon, even if she would not see her mother again for a very long time.

Isabel rode on horseback to the Jorgensen farm, the quilts folded into a pack on the saddle behind her. No one would notice one lone woman among the throng of workers who had come for the apricot harvest.

She rode past the yellow farmhouse and over the hill to the cabin she had once called home. Many years had passed since she had last played on that front porch with her grandmother and baby sister, since she had last climbed the orange trees and picked the ripe, sweet fruit. Rosa had visited much more recently—of this, Isabel was certain. Where else could the young lovers have met? What better place than this, where Rosa knew her parents would never come?

Isabel dismounted and went inside, allowing herself only a moment's regret over the state of the home her mother and grandmother had once kept with such pride. She carried the quilts into the bedroom she and her parents had once shared. There she spotted a crate pushed against the window, more than large enough to accommodate the quilts. She removed the lid and discovered Lars's liquor stash. Disappointed, she replaced the lid. After all Lars had lost because of liquor, he should have smashed these bottles on the hard, dusty earth. When Lars drained the last of those bottles, would he then become the man her daughter needed? Could he ever be the man her daughter needed if the only reason he stopped drinking was because he had nothing left to drink?

Lars had so much left to prove before he would be worthy of her precious girl, her rose, but Isabel knew now she had been wrong not to allow him that chance. She only hoped it was not too late.

She went into her grandparents' old bedroom, where she found a dusty steamer trunk at the foot of a rusty bedstead with a sagging mattress, added to the room after her family's departure. Unbidden, images of her daughter embracing Lars upon the bed came to her, but she quickly closed her mind to such thoughts.

Inside the trunk she discovered an old blue-and-white checkered tablecloth and a candlewick bedspread, with ample room left over for the two quilts. She placed them gently inside and closed the lid. Either Rosa would discover them herself someday, or Lars would find them, recognize the initials Isabel had embroidered, and take them to Rosa.

Rosa would understand what the quilts meant, what Isabel could not say aloud.

Isabel could never tell her daughter to forsake her sacred wedding vows. Rosa had married a cruel man, the wrong man, but that made her promises before God no less binding. But when Rosa saw the quilt, the wedding quilt pieced from precious fabrics, she would know that Isabel would forgive her if she corrected a mistake made long ago, a mistake she never would have made if she had not feared losing her mother's love.

Isabel left the cabin, but hesitated on the porch and returned to her old bedroom. One by one she took the liquor bottles from the crate and emptied them out the window. Someone had to prod Lars down the road to sobriety. Rosa waited at the end of it, but she could not wait forever.

Isabel returned to her horse and set off on the road to the mesa. Today might be the day Rosa came. She would make excuses for John, but Isabel would not pretend to believe them anymore for the sake of her daughter's pride. Didn't Rosa know that every scathing word John spoke to her burned Isabel's ears as well? Didn't she know that every blow that fell upon Rosa left bruises on her mother's heart?

She waited at the edge of the canyon, breathing in the scent of wildflowers. Someday Rosa would come again, bringing the children, and Isabel would be waiting for them. She would not forsake her daughter a second time. Let weeks or months or years pass, Isabel would come to the mesa, undaunted, patient, awaiting the day her daughter would return to her.

Over the sound of the creek rushing through the canyon, Isabel heard a horse approaching. For a moment she was filled with joy and light, but the prayer of thanksgiving died on her lips at the sight of John Barclay crossing the mesa at a determined trot. His face was grim, his eyes dark with anger.

So. He knew where they met. Isabel had guessed as much the first day Rosa failed to appear.

She rose, brushed the grasses from her skirt, and faced him without fear. He would tell her Rosa was not coming, that she would never come. He would lie and say it was Rosa's choice. He would call Isabel a fool, a pathetic old woman, for clinging so desperately to futile hopes.

As John approached, Isabel prepared herself for what was to come. Let him say what he would. She would ignore his poison words. Her love for her daughter was stronger than his hate.

She had failed Rosa once, but never again.

Chapter Twelve

1925

Lars returned home a few hours after the police took John Barclay into custody. Elizabeth, riding with Henry to the hospital in the back of the makeshift ambulance, saw none of this. Only later, after the surgeon removed the bullet from Henry's shoulder and he had recovered enough for her to bring him home, did she learn that, upon hearing what had happened, Lars set the car upright and drove off toward the Barclay farm. The deputies searching the adobe for clues confirmed that Lars had spoken with them briefly, but left after determining Rosa and her children were not there.

That was the last time Lars Jorgensen was seen in the Arboles Valley.

Henry was still unconscious, recovering from surgery at the Oxnard General Hospital, when an investigator from the county came to take Elizabeth's statement. She told them about John's violent outburst and Rosa's plan to seek shelter in the canyon.

The investigator looked up sharply from his notepad. "The Salto Canyon?"

He seemed so apprehensive that Elizabeth quickly assured him that Rosa knew the canyon well—so well that Elizabeth assumed she must have known of a cave or other shelter from the rain, or she would not have kept the children outside overnight. Rosa was probably awaiting word that it was safe to come out from hiding. "Lars Jorgensen should go," she said. "Rosa trusts him."

The investigator nodded and jotted some notes. He did not tell her that Lars was missing. He also did not mention that the Salto Creek had overflowed its banks that day, or that a flash flood had swept through the canyon with a force strong enough to uproot trees and tear boulders from the canyon walls. He didn't want to upset her.

When the investigator finished with Elizabeth, he radioed the county sheriff. Two deputies found John Barclay's team and wagon on the mesa where Elizabeth had told them to look. Later that week, a child's rag doll was pulled from the mud two miles downstream of the canyon's edge where Isabel Rodriguez Diaz had fallen to her death. Rosa and her four children were presumed drowned. Their bodies were never recovered.

In the course of searching the Barclay farm for evidence to explain John's assault on the Jorgensen home, the police discovered two large crates buried in straw in the hayloft. Inside were a stash of small arms, a valise full of cash, and more than fifty gallons of contraband liquor in bottles that matched the one Lars Jorgensen had turned in to the Feds during the apricot harvest. They had been tracking Mob activity in southern California for years, but until Lars's tip, they had lacked proof that the Mob had enlisted the services of local farmers in their illegal liquor and weapons activities. Thanks to Lars, they were on the track of some highly placed figures in organized crime, and hoped soon to be able to put some of them away for good.

Privately, the Feds agreed that they didn't blame Lars for disappearing. He'd have to be a fool not to lie low for the rest of his life, now that he had made himself an enemy of the Mob. For all they knew, the Mob had already found him, and his bones were bleaching in the Mojave Desert.

John served two years in prison on federal racketeering charges. Carlos looked after his farm while he was away, although no one thought it was out of love for his brother-in-law. Carlos refused to believe that his sister, nieces, and nephew had drowned. Someday they would return and he would not allow their home to fall to ruin in the meantime. The post office moved to a small building next to the Arboles Grocery. Since no one else wanted the job, Carlos took over as postmaster.

Three weeks after John was released from prison, a hiker discovered his body at the bottom of Salto Canyon. The coroner concluded that he had jumped to his death. Rumors sped through the Arboles Valley like a brushfire in summer. Some people thought he had killed himself out of grief for the loss of his wife and children. Others noted that with his postmaster job gone and his ties to organized crime severed, John had realized he would actually have to work for a living again, and he just couldn't take it. A few people whispered that he had not intended to take his own life but that he had fallen to his death after fleeing in terror from the ghost of Isabel Rodriguez Diaz. Older women in the valley, the friends of Isabel's youth, knew such a thing was impossible but found a certain satisfaction in the tale.

The years passed. Carlos maintained the adobe and the outbuildings out of respect for his sister's memory, but he allowed the native grasses and scrub to take over the fields. No farmer could ride past the old Barclay place without shaking his head and thinking that it was a shame to let so many fertile acres go to waste. Developers, eyeing the land hungrily, felt the same way. When Carlos would not accept any price for the farm, saying that it was not his to sell, they became determined to work around him. They cornered every government official with any possible influence over land issues and insisted the government should sell that abandoned farm near the canyon. It was a race pitting one developer against another to find someone in authority who would agree the city, state, or county owned the land and could make a deal. But the developers' efforts proved futile. There was no mortgage on the land, so the developers could not anticipate a bank foreclosure. The property taxes were being paid regularly, so the government had no reason to interfere. If the developers wanted the land so badly, they should take the matter up with John and Rosa Barclay's heirs.

The developers gave up in frustration. They had already approached Carlos and had been turned away. But they could wait. He obviously was not much of a farmer. He would change his mind someday when he finally realized his sister wasn't coming back. Every man came upon hard times sooner or later, and someday he would be glad to have money in the bank.

1933

Elizabeth sat at the kitchen table in the cabin, counting out bills and change. At last she had enough money saved to buy back the Chimneys and Cornerstones quilt from Mrs. Diegel, but now that she did, she could not help thinking of other, more sensible uses for the money. There would be doctor bills when the baby came. Little Thomas outgrew clothes almost as quickly as she could sew them. Eleanor would need new shoes and school supplies in the fall. It seemed frivolous to spend so much on a quilt she did not truly need. She had pieced other quilts for the family, quilts that equaled the Chimneys and Cornerstones in beauty and warmth. As much as she longed for her quilt, she had managed to do without it for eight years. She could wait a few years more.

She sighed softly, bound the roll of bills with a rubber band, and returned the money to the coffee can. To think she had once teased Henry for refusing to put his money in a bank. His mistrust had spared them from losing everything after the stock market crashed and the banks failed. The Jorgensens had lost thousands, but the Nelsons had not lost a dime.

Henry looked up from his seat on the floor in front of the fireplace, where he and Thomas were engrossed in a game involving toy fire trucks and a wooden elephant. "Don't tell me you've changed your mind."

"I can't justify the expense," she said. "As soon as I spend this money, a better use for it will appear. It always does."

He couldn't deny it. They both knew how many times through the years one emergency or another had forced them to nearly deplete their savings. Slowly they would build it up again, just in time for the next crisis. They managed to stay afloat, and in those troubled times they were grateful for that much, but they could never quite get ahead. Henry assured Elizabeth that better times were coming, and Elizabeth wanted to believe him, but she feared better times would not come soon enough. Not for them, and not for the migrant families who had abandoned Dust Bowl farms for the promise of work in the Arboles Valley. Almost daily, Oscar Jorgensen had to turn a carload of hungry, exhausted people away with nothing more than dried apricots to eat and milk for the children. Even during the apricot harvest, there were more workers than jobs on the farm.

"Go ahead and ransom your quilt," said Henry. "You've waited long enough. Consider it an early birthday present."

Elizabeth smiled, but said, "After all these years, it might be worn to tatters."

"You can mend it."

"Yes, but the money will still be gone. Times are hard. We don't know how much longer the Jorgensens will be able to keep you on." They had already been forced to let Elizabeth go, but except for the loss of wages and Mary Katherine's daily company, she did not mind. She was content to tend her own garden, keep her own house, and care for her children.

Henry grinned. "Oscar would never fire me and you know it."

Of course she knew it. Henry had taken over Lars's responsibilities upon his disappearance nearly eight years before. Elizabeth could not imagine how the Jorgensens would manage without Henry. His job was as secure as any job could be.

"If the quilt is worn out," she said, "maybe I can talk Mrs. Diegel into setting a lower price."

"That's the spirit." Henry came to her and kissed her on both cheeks. "So beautiful and yet so shrewd."

The next afternoon, Annalise agreed to babysit the children while Elizabeth went into town. First she stopped by the post office to send a letter to her parents and collect the mail. Cousin Sylvia had sent her a postcard from the World's Fair in Chicago, where she had apparently spent most of her time at the Sears exhibition hall admiring the winners of a national quilt contest. She and her sister had collaborated on an entry, but they had been eliminated at the regional level, not a bad showing for two teenage girls. "My mother would have loved this show," Sylvia had written. "If she were still with us, and if she had entered one of her quilts, she would have won first place."

Sylvia's wistful note decided the matter for Elizabeth. Her beloved aunt Eleanor was gone. So was Grandma Bergstrom. The quilts the Bergstrom women made were becoming increasingly rare and precious with each passing year. Extravagance or not, she wanted her quilt back.

"Carlos," she asked, "do you have any advice for someone on her way to haggle with Mrs. Diegel over the price of a used quilt?"

"Remind her that the quilt has lost value since you sold it to her, new," Carlos said dryly. He had resigned as the handyman of the Grand Union Hotel to become the full-time postmaster after the post office expanded to accommodate the growing population of the Arboles Valley. "Mention the limited market for used quilts. She catered to those developer types for so many years, that's language she'll understand." He hesitated, struggling with conflicting loyalties. "I don't think you'll have much trouble getting her to lower her price. She . . . could use the money."

Elizabeth thanked him and continued on to the Grand Union Hotel. She had not visited in several years, not since Henry treated her to supper in the dining room to celebrate their fifth anniversary. She had heard that the hotel had fallen on hard times after Mrs. Diegel's favorite developers went bankrupt after the stock market crash, but she was still startled to find peeling paint on the eaves and weeds overtaking the once meticulously kept front garden. Inside, the lobby was as neat and tidy as ever, the bar even more crowded with imbibers than in more prosperous days. Elizabeth could guess how Mrs. Diegel had managed to eke out a living after overnight guests became scarce. She only hoped that for her sake, Mrs. Diegel kept her own still and had not become involved with what might euphemistically be described as an outside supplier. Elizabeth knew all too well what happened to people who became tangled up with that lot.

She found Mrs. Diegel in the kitchen stirring a pot of chicken stew. The cook was nowhere to be seen, but a girl a few years older than Annalise stood at the sideboard peeling apples for pie. Mrs. Diegel greeted Elizabeth like an old friend and offered her a glass of lemonade. Elizabeth gladly accepted and pulled up a stool so they could talk while Mrs. Diegel worked.

"Did you hear the big news?" Mrs. Diegel asked before Elizabeth could bring up the quilt. "Hoot Gibson is coming to the

Arboles Valley to shoot a new picture. It's called *Raging Gulch*. They're going to film most of the outdoor scenes on the mesa and in the Salto Canyon."

"Is that so?"

Mrs. Diegel's sharp gaze did not miss a thing. "Now, I know you lost a friend in that canyon, but you can't hold that against Hoot Gibson. The canyon is a great setting for a movie. It might even bring more tourists back to the valley."

"I suppose you're right."

"That's not the best part. They've decided to use the Grand Union for many of the indoor scenes. Lucky for me, they chose this place based upon some old photographs George Hanneman has hanging on the wall in his office at Safari World. If they had gone to the trouble to see it for themselves, they might have chosen the Conejo Lodge instead." She shook her head and frowned. "I have to spruce this place up before the production crew arrives next month, but where I'm going to find the money to buy paint or hire a painter, I have no idea."

Elizabeth smiled. "I have an idea how you could make some extra cash."

They haggled over the price for a time, but eventually Mrs. Diegel admitted that she needed new paint more than an old quilt, and she accepted Elizabeth's fair offer. Elizabeth waited in the lobby while the innkeeper went to fetch the quilt, climbing the stairs slowly and grasping the smooth oak banister for support. Until that moment, Elizabeth had not realized how much Mrs. Diegel had aged in the past few years, her shoulders stooped as if weighed down by worry. It saddened Elizabeth to know that not even the crafty and indomitable Mrs. Diegel could evade the hard times that had struck them all.

Before long, Mrs. Diegel returned downstairs with the quilt, which was in better condition than Elizabeth had hoped. The colors had faded somewhat, the binding was worn, but Elizabeth found no stains, no holes or tears. Not that it would have mattered. She was so glad to hold her quilt again after so many years that half the batting could have been hanging out of popped seams and she would not have regretted her purchase.

She bade Mrs. Diegel good-bye and was nearly at the door when the older woman called her back. "I recall you once had a hankering to be in the pictures," Mrs. Diegel said. "When the producers contacted me about shooting at the Grand Union, they mentioned that they would be looking for local folks to fill in the scene. I don't expect you would have any lines, but it might be good for a laugh, and a small paycheck, and who knows what else? You might impress the director and be on your way to bigger and better things."

Once, that news would have thrilled her. Once, Elizabeth would have seized any chance for even the smallest, nonspeaking role in any film. But Mrs. Diegel was not the only one who had aged beyond her years since the Depression had begun. Elizabeth knew she was no longer the lovely, bright-eyed girl who had come to the Arboles Valley with her new husband and the boundless hopes and expectations of youth. If she were to enter that dance hall at Venice Beach today, a farmhand's wife in a homemade calico dress, she knew no movie director would think to give her his card—even if she weren't seven months pregnant with her third child. By the time Hoot Gibson came to the valley, directors and producers in tow, Elizabeth would have a new baby in her arms and too much to do to consider reviving her old dreams of stardom.

"Thanks for letting me know," she told Mrs. Diegel, knowing she would not audition for a part. She was content with the role she had already won. Her children were joyful and healthy. She loved and was beloved. She had a home and friends. She needed nothing else.

Elizabeth drove back to the Jorgensen farm to return Oscar's car—a 1926 Model T Ford he had bought to replace the one that had vanished along with Lars—and to collect Eleanor and Thomas from Annalise. As she pulled up to the garage, she spotted an unfamiliar car parked near the house. Curious, she glanced in through the kitchen window as she went around back to search for the children, but she saw no one. Either the guest was with Oscar in the barley fields or Mrs. Jorgensen was entertaining in the front parlor.

She found the children in the garden with Annalise, helping her pull weeds. The young woman was infinitely patient with them, willingly pointing out over and over again the difference between carrot tops and weeds. Thomas looked up first and toddled over to Elizabeth with a fistful of grass, dirt still clinging to the roots. "Look," he crowed. "Weeds!"

Elizabeth awkwardly stooped to pick him up, keeping his fat little legs clear of her belly. "What a good little farmer you're turning out to be," she praised him. To Annalise, she said, "How were they?"

"Perfect little angels, as always."

Eleanor beamed at her. She admired the older girl and drank up her praise. The same words from any other source never seemed to satisfy her in quite the same way.

Elizabeth indicated the yellow farmhouse with a nod. "Who's visiting?"

"I don't know." Annalise rose and brushed dirt from her shins. She wore dungarees instead of skirts, in keeping with the recent fashion among young women her age in the valley, much to her grandmother's chagrin. "He can't be from around here or I'd know him."

Elizabeth wasn't convinced. So many housing developments had sprung up around them that no one knew everyone who lived in the Arboles Valley anymore.

"The man came to see Daddy," Eleanor piped up.

Elizabeth smiled at her sweet, golden-haired girl. "Why would you say that, darling?"

"It's true," said Annalise. "Nana sent Margaret running to fetch him from the orchard a few minutes after the man arrived."

A tremor of uneasiness stirred within Elizabeth. "What sort of business would anyone have with Henry?"

Annalise shrugged. "I could watch the kids while you go find out."

Elizabeth nodded, handed Thomas to her, and strode back to the house as quickly as her ample belly would allow. Although she no longer worked for the Jorgensens, she had been nearly part of the family so long that she entered through the kitchen door without knocking, as they would have expected her to do. She found Mrs. Jorgensen, Oscar, Henry, and another man seated in the formal parlor with teacups and cookies close at hand. They all looked up when she appeared in the doorway. The men rose and Mrs. Jorgensen beckoned her inside. "Come, Elizabeth," she said. "Sit down. This gentlemen has some interesting news for you."

Her heart leaped into her throat even as she noted that Mrs. Jorgensen had said *interesting,* not *unfortunate,* and that Henry's expression was a mix of surprise and doubt, but not alarm. She took a deep breath and sat down as Mrs. Jorgensen introduced the visitor as Horace Tomilson from the law firm of Tomilson, Hanks, and Dunbar of San Francisco.

"You're a long way from home," said Elizabeth nervously. Mrs. Jorgensen pressed a cup of tea into her hands.

"Only a commission of a sensitive nature would have induced me to travel so far," he admitted. "My clients, Mr. and Mrs. Nils Ottesen of Sonoma County, own a parcel of land not far from here. I believe they bought the land intending to farm it, but the vineyard on their property up north has thrived, so they have decided to remain there. They would like to put the land up for sale, and they thought you and your husband might be prospective buyers."

Elizabeth regarded him in disbelief. How would a vintner from hundreds of miles away know anything about her and Henry? They must have her confused with some other Nelsons, a much wealthier Nelson family with ties to the real estate business. "What land?" she asked, stalling for time. "How much?"

"He's talking about the Barclay farm," said Henry.

"Five dollars an acre," added Mr. Tomilson.

Elizabeth looked around the circle of faces. "This must be some kind of a joke."

"That's what I thought," said Henry, who had good reason to be suspicious. "Five dollars an acre is practically giving it away. Developers have been salivating over that land for years. These Ottesens could make a small fortune off that land."

"If it's theirs to sell," said Elizabeth.

"I assure you, it's all very legal." Mr. Tomilson opened his briefcase and showed them a host of documents with official seals and stamps indicating that the parcel of land formerly known as the Barclay farm belonged free and clear to the Ottesens. He presented a notarized copy of the title as well as several receipts indicating that the Ottesens had paid the property taxes on the farm for the past four years.

But Elizabeth had been taken in by such documents before. She set her cup of tea aside and began to rise. "Thank you for coming," she said tightly. "But my husband and I never heard of Nils Ottesen and we know better than to buy land that isn't really for sale."

"Mrs. Ottesen thought you might say that," he replied. "She asked me to make sure you saw this."

He took a page from the sheaf of documents and placed it in her hands. Elizabeth read it over and found it to be a bill of sale transferring the Barclay farm from Mr. and Mrs. John Barclay to Mr. and Mrs. Nils Ottesen for a modest sum of one hundred dollars.

"You'll see this land has a history of selling for less than what it is worth," remarked Mr. Tomilson.

What interested Elizabeth more was the date stamped on the document. She wondered if Mr. Tomilson realized that John Barclay had signed and dated the bill of sale in Sonoma County at the same time he was also imprisoned in the Ventura County jail.

She looked to Henry. He gave her an almost imperceptible nod, which told her he realized it, even if the lawyer did not.

Mr. Tomilson peered at her over the rims of his glasses. "I'm surprised that you don't remember the Ottesens. She told me that you had once done her a great kindness, helped her in her most desperate hour, when all others had turned their backs upon her. She wants this land to belong to you, even if it means suffering a financial loss herself. I advised her against this, of course, but she insisted. She's quite a remarkable woman."

"I think I remember her," said Elizabeth. "Tell me, what does she look like?"

"Oh, she's quite lovely. Slender, tall, long dark hair—some Spanish blood, perhaps."

"And her husband?" Mrs. Jorgensen broke in. "What about him?"

Mr. Tomilson shrugged, smiling. "Well, he's rather tall and thin and sunburned. Losing his hair. I'm sure he's a fine man, but not the sort that I would have thought capable of plucking such a lovely Spanish rose. Forgive me—I'm not being forward, I'm merely quoting him. I've overheard him call his wife his Spanish rose. Perhaps that's his secret. Romantic words?"

"Yes, he's quite a poet," said Oscar dryly, adding, "or so it seems."

Elizabeth calculated quickly. One hundred acres at five dollars an acre was five hundred dollars, or 480 more than she and Henry had left after ransoming the quilt. "Please give Mrs. Ottesen our thanks," said Elizabeth. "As much as we appreciate their generous offer, I'm afraid we can't afford it."

"In that case, I'm authorized to hire you and your husband to run the Ottesens' farm in their absence."

Elizabeth stared at him. "What?" said Henry.

"They're willing to offer very generous terms. In exchange for farming the land, maintaining the property, and paying the property taxes, the Ottesens will give you a modest salary and let you keep any profits you earn from whatever crops you decide to raise."

"This can't be real," murmured Elizabeth.

"There are a couple of conditions," said Mr. Tomilson, taking a page from his briefcase. "The first is that you send the Ottesens a quarterly payment of twenty-five dollars, which will be put toward the five-hundred-dollar purchase price. All payments will be made through my office. In five years, the title will be transferred over to you."

"What's the second condition?" asked Henry.

Mr. Tomilson frowned at the page as if he considered the request rather odd and was almost too embarrassed to mention it. "They want you to rename the farm 'Triumph Ranch.' "

Elizabeth laughed aloud.

"Legally, once the title is in your name, you can call the farm anything you like," Mr. Tomilson hastened to add. "Surely you can live with an unusual name for a few short years."

"No, no. The name is perfect." Elizabeth reached out her hand to Henry. "What do you think, sweetheart? How does 'Triumph Ranch' sound to you?"

"It sounds perfect." Elizabeth knew he meant too perfect. "What's the catch?"

Mr. Tomilson began gathering up his papers. "There is no catch, simply an offer and your decision, which I await. Eagerly."

"What happens to the farm if we decline?" asked Elizabeth. "I imagine the same offer would be made to her brother."

Mr. Tomilson regarded her curiously. "Whose brother?"

"Mrs. Ottesen's, of course."

"Mrs. Ottesen has no brothers or sisters." He glanced at his notes. "She does have six children, however. Six healthy children who are seen once a year by a skilled physician whether they need to or not. She wanted me to make sure you knew that."

"Six?" said Mrs. Jorgensen in wonder. "My heavens."

Henry had not forgotten Elizabeth's question. "What happens to the land if we don't take their offer?"

"In that case, I have been authorized to put it up for auction between three respected land developers."

"You'll find no such creature," said Mrs. Jorgensen sharply. "I can't believe that—what was his name now? That this Nils Ottesen intends for that beautiful, arable land to become a housing development." She looked from Elizabeth to Henry, rapping a finger upon the table for emphasis so hard she made the teapot rattle. "He's obviously trying to force your hand, and I say—let him!"

Oscar shifted in his seat. "Don't I get any say in this matter?"

"No, son, you don't," said Mrs. Jorgensen. "You're Henry's employer, not his father."

"Even so," said Henry, "I value your opinion."

Elizabeth waited to hear what he would say. Oscar Jorgensen knew the valley better than anyone. He knew about the probability of devastating drought, crop failure, and plunging prices for food that made it barely more profitable to farm than to let the land grow fallow. But he also loved the land, felt the rhythm of the seasons in his blood, and would always respect those who could do the same.

"I say, take the offer before they change their minds," Oscar declared. "You'll never get land in the Arboles Valley at that price ever again."

Henry grinned. "I thought you were going to try to talk me out of leaving because you need me too much."

"I considered that, but I figured you wouldn't listen."

Henry stood, took Elizabeth's hands in his, and pulled her to her feet. "Darling—"

"You don't have to talk me into it," she said. "Yes. A hundred times yes. Once for each acre."

The matter was settled quickly. Within a month, the Nelsons moved from the cabin to the adobe home on Triumph Ranch. Eleanor and Thomas played in the shade of the orange trees as Rosa's children had before them. Since it was too late for spring planting, Henry agreed to work for the Jorgensens through the apricot harvest. In the meantime, he planned for the next season.

As she awaited the birth of her baby, Elizabeth sorted through the belongings the Barclays had been forced to leave so abruptly. The furniture was well made and in good condition, far sturdier and more comfortable than what she and Henry had grown accustomed to in the cabin. The kitchen was fully furnished with all the dishes, pots, pans, and tools a farm wife could ever need. Many items of a more personal nature had been abandoned, too, and Elizabeth could not touch them without thinking of Rosa's desperate flight to the canyon. How had she decided what to take and what to leave? What in that last moment had become most precious to her?

She bid a last farewell to her absent friend as she put away Rosa's belongings to make room for her own. Some things she packed up to give to Carlos, whom she felt would be glad for mementos of his sister, nieces, and nephews. Other things—toys, dolls, clothing—she saved for her own children. She was sure Rosa would have given them freely, generously, just as she had the land and the home.

But what she searched for most was the photograph album and the portraits Rosa had shown her of the first quilters of Triumph Ranch. She longed to hold her children on her lap and show them the women who had lived in their old cabin, just as she now told them about the children who had once lived in their adobe.

She never found the album. Nor did she find the quilts the women had made, stitching their hopes and prayers into the fabric, the patterns of their unspoken regrets and unanswered questions like fingerprints upon the cloth. Elizabeth knew the quilts had once comforted frightened children hiding in a canyon, and that they now graced a loving home on a vineyard where a happy family rejoiced in everyday moments—fresh strawberries for breakfast, a hair ribbon, a game of tag, a bedtime story.

Elizabeth knew the quilters of Triumph Ranch, past and present, rejoiced in their happiness.

A Conversation with
Jennifer Chiaverini

❧

Q: The Quilter's Homecoming *follows the adventures of Elizabeth (Bergstrom) Nelson, a character who appeared in your earlier novels,* The Quilter's Legacy *and* The Christmas Quilt. *What drew you to writing a novel about Elizabeth's experiences as a newlywed in California?*

A: When I was in high school, my family moved to Thousand Oaks, California, a city in the Conejo Valley about forty-five miles north of Los Angeles. My first real job was working as a page at the Thousand Oaks Library, which is where I met Patricia A. Allen, a renowned local historian. I was one of many pages and I'm sure she didn't even know my name, but she made quite an impression on me. As a sixteen-year-old, I was fascinated by the idea that a place that seemed so new had such a rich history. I checked out all of Ms. Allen's books from the library and learned a great deal from them. I also listened to co-workers who had lived in the region for many decades and had witnessed its transformation from a farming town and occasional outdoor movie set to a growing residential community.

Those stories lingered in my memory all these years, germinating, awaiting a story. Some locations and events in the fictional Arboles Valley will seem very familiar to people who know Thousand Oaks, but *The Quilter's Homecoming* is not meant to be a history of the Conejo Valley.

Q: How do you decide which quilts and patterns to include in which novels?

A: The quilts my characters make are never arbitrary. They are not included as an afterthought or to provide set decoration, but are as important to my characters as real quilts are to the quilters who make them.

Sometimes a quilt will play an important role as a narrative device. In *The Quilter's Apprentice*, a sampler quilt serves as a useful instructional project as an older woman teaches a young friend how to quilt, but the patterns of the different blocks also evoke stories from the elder woman's childhood and life as a young bride on the World War II homefront. In *Round Robin*, a round robin quilt allowed me to tell the story from different characters' perspectives, in which the quilt's center block was passed around the circle of friends and each contributed her border. In *The Quilter's Homecoming*, the two quilts Elizabeth discovers in a cabin on Triumph Ranch hold an important clue to a family's history. As Elizabeth searches for the rightful owner of the quilts, she uncovers long-buried secrets that, once exposed, force those around her to face conflicts hidden in their own pasts.

Often I will use a quilt to provide insight into a particular character's personality or past. You can tell a lot about a quilter from the style of quilts she makes, the techniques she uses, her color and fabric palettes, and whether she finishes quilts or has a closet full of UFOs (Unfinished Fabric Objects). My characters are no exception.

Q: *In the course of the expansion of the American West, how common were fraudulent land deals of the kind that Henry and Elizabeth Nelson encounter with Triumph Ranch?*

A: Unfortunately, fraudulent land deals were quite common. Often con artists would sell deeds to property they did not own, and often they chose land that belonged to Native Americans.

Q: *At least initially, Elizabeth and Henry's misfortune in California does not make them grow closer as newlyweds. Why don't they turn to each other for solace?*

A: They respond to their crisis differently because only Henry realizes just how dire their circumstances are. Elizabeth believes that all they have to do is endure their present situation long enough to earn the train fare home, where their initial embarrassment will fade over time as they take their rightful places on the family farm. Henry hasn't told Elizabeth that he sold his share of the farm to his brothers in order to purchase Triumph Ranch. He knows they can't return to Pennsylvania. He is ashamed that he was duped and he can't bring himself to confess his failure to the wife he adores. Sadly, instead of trusting Elizabeth, he becomes more remote as he struggles to earn a living and confess the truth. For her part, Elizabeth, used to being adored by many admirers, doesn't know what to make of his behavior. They weren't expecting their marriage to be tested so soon, and they have no family or friends nearby to guide them.

Q: You have said that you began writing about quilting and quilters because you know something about both. Can you briefly describe your experiences?

A: Beginning writers are always advised to "write what you know." Since I knew about quilters—their quirks, their inside jokes, their disputes and their generosity, their quarrels and their kindnesses—the lives of quilters became a natural subject for me. I also wanted to pay tribute to the quilters of ages past who preserved and handed down their traditions through the generations.

When I first began writing about quilters, I had two audiences in mind. The first included my quilter friends, whom I thought might enjoy reading about contemporary women like themselves with problems and dreams like their own, overcoming obstacles in their lives by taking strength from their own moral courage and the support of faithful friends. I also believed quilters would appreciate a depiction of modern quilters and quilt making, free of the usual stereotypes that clutter far too much writing on the subject.

But I also intended to write for nonquilters, to give them some insight into the quilting world, so that they might better understand how passionate we quilters are about our art and why we love it so. I wanted them to take away from my books a greater understanding of how quilting is a wonderful creative outlet that can draw you into a wider community of talented, welcoming quilters who support and encourage one another. Perhaps more important, I wanted them to discover how quilting can bring together people from different generations, races, religions, and socioeconomic backgrounds into a patchwork of friendship.

Q: What's your next project?

A: I'm pleased to announce that my readers won't have to wait long for the next Elm Creek Quilts novel. A second holiday story, *The New Year's Quilt*, will be published by Simon & Schuster in November 2007. I return to contemporary Elm Creek Manor in this story, which begins as Sylvia and Andrew set out on their honeymoon after their Christmas Eve wedding.

SIMON & SCHUSTER

PROUDLY PRESENTS

The Winding Ways Quilt

Turn the page for a preview of
The Winding Ways Quilt ...

Sylvia

Sylvia woke to a gentle breeze and birdsong beyond the open window. Sitting up in bed and stretching, she saw clouds in the eastern sky, pink with the new light of dawn. Andrew had risen earlier, without waking her, but she knew there was only one place her husband could be at that hour on a Sunday morning.

She dressed in a light sweater and slacks and went to join her husband, pausing at the top of the grand oak staircase to savor the brief, reverential stillness that descended upon Elm Creek Manor on Sunday mornings. In a few hours, the gray stone artists' retreat would bustle and hum with the sounds of dozens of eager quilters arriving for a week of quilting, friendship, and fun, but for the moment, Sylvia, Andrew, and the manor's other three permanent residents had the estate all to themselves.

After descending the staircase, grasping a banister worn smooth from the hands of generations, Sylvia crossed the black marble floor of the front foyer and turned to walk down the older west wing of the manor, built by her great-grandfather in 1858. She brushed the wall lightly with her fingertips, wondering what her great-grandparents would think of the changes their descendants had brought to the farm they had founded, nestled in the fertile Elm Creek Valley in central Pennsylvania.

Voices and the smell of frying sausages drifted to her from the kitchen at the end of the hall. Sarah would be at the stove, no doubt, preparing breakfast for five, but who kept her company? Her husband, Matt, most likely, although usually he was too busy with his caretaker's duties to linger in the kitchen. Perhaps Sarah's best friend and fellow Elm Creek Quilter, Summer, had finished her daily yoga routine early and had decided to lend a hand, taking advantage of the opportunity to contribute more vegetarian options to the meal.

"Good morning," Sylvia sang out as she entered the kitchen, but she stopped short at the sight of Sarah sitting on a bench and resting her head in her arms on the kitchen table. Her husband attended the stove, a pink calico apron tied around his waist.

"Morning," Matt said, throwing her a grin over his shoulder and raising a spatula in salute. Sarah managed to lift her head long enough to give Sylvia a pale smile. Then she groaned and let her head drop onto her arms again, her long, reddish brown ponytail falling onto an open package of saltine crackers beside her on the table.

"Goodness, Sarah. Are you ill?" Sylvia sat down on the opposite bench, brushed Sarah's ponytail away from the food, and felt her forehead. Sylvia detected no trace of fever, thank goodness, but the younger woman clearly was not well.

"I'll be all right." Sarah's voice wavered feebly, belying her words. "I think I finally understand why Summer won't eat meat. I never realized how awful it smells."

Sylvia thought breakfast smelled delicious, but she knew better than to discuss food with someone suffering from a stomach bug. "Perhaps you should go back to bed, dear. Matthew seems to have everything well in hand, and you wouldn't want to pass on whatever you have to our guests during registration."

At the stove, Matt choked back a laugh. "I don't think we have to worry about any of them taking home this particular souvenir."

"We can't be too careful."

"I'll be all right in a moment." Sarah pushed herself to her feet. "It's my turn to fix breakfast and I'm not going to shirk my duty."

"Shirk away, honey," said Matt. "I have everything under control."

"Beginning today, we'll have a professional chef on staff again," Sylvia reminded her. "Anna's planning a cold buffet for lunch, but supper will be a gourmet feast. She phoned me with the menu. Mushroom and rosemary soup, salmon en croute, some kind of eggplant cassoulet that Summer is sure to love, and chocolate mousse for dessert. Best of all, no more kitchen duty for the rest of us!"

"I can't wait," Sarah croaked, then pressed her lips together and hurried from the room.

"She'll be fine," said Matt when Sylvia rose to go after her. "Don't worry. Just give her a minute, and she'll be back here scrambling eggs."

Sylvia wasn't so sure, but she put on a pot of coffee and offered to mix up a batch of biscuits. Just as she was about to dust her hands with flour to knead the dough, Sarah returned, looking remarkably better. She insisted on taking over, and when the younger couple overruled Sylvia's protests, she left them to their work. She filled two travel mugs with coffee—cream and sugar for her, sugar only for Andrew—and carried them out the back door and down four steps to the rear parking lot.

Outside the air was cool from the night and misty, dew fresh on the grass. Insects chirped and buzzed and darted in the sunlight shafting through the forest canopy, the elms barely stirring in the still air. Sylvia knew the day ahead would be warm and humid, but the gray stone walls of Elm Creek Manor would keep their arriving guests cool and comfortable—as long as she reminded Sarah to open all the windows and keep plenty of lemonade on ice.

With a mug in each hand, Sylvia crossed the bridge over Elm Creek without spilling a single drop. Andrew's favorite fishing spot, a large, round, flat rock on the creek bank beneath a willow tree, had been her favorite secluded hideaway as a child. Whenever she had needed time alone to think or to cool her temper after an argument with her sister, she had stolen away to the willow and the rock. The musical burbling of the creek never failed to soothe her, and sometimes even now, a woman grown, she favored the private spot for quiet contemplation.

But she was happy to share it with her dear Andrew.

She knew better than to scare away the fish by calling out to him when she spied him through the willow branches, that faded, worn fishing cap on his head, a tackle box on the rock by his side. She approached quietly, but her footfalls alerted him when she was still several yards away. He glanced over his shoulder, and his face lit up at the sight of her. "There's my girl," he said, his voice low. Shifting his fishing rod to one hand, he patted the rock beside him.

Sylvia gladly took the offered seat, handed him his coffee, and rested her head upon his shoulder as he drew her closer. "Anything biting?"

"No keepers. Not like you." He sipped his coffee and nodded to show it was just the way he liked it. "You're definitely a keeper."

"I'm glad to know you don't plan to throw me back."

"Not on your life."

She smiled, and they sat in companionable silence, watching minnows draw close to the hook and dart away into the shadows. "Sarah and Matt have breakfast cooking," Sylvia remarked. "Sarah seems to be under the weather."

Andrew grinned. "She's not sick. She's just sick of cooking."

"No, that's not it. I urged her to return to bed, but she flatly refused." Sarah wasn't a shirker. If anything, she worked herself too hard. "But I think we'll all be happy when Anna Del Maso joins our staff today. We've been without a real chef for too long."

"If those cookies she brought to her job interview are any indication, she's going to be a great addition to the staff."

"I couldn't agree more. If she can make a simple sugar cookie taste that delicious, I can't wait to see what she'll do for Judy's going-away party." Sylvia sighed and sipped her coffee. "I only wish it weren't necessary."

"Judy couldn't turn down such a great offer from an Ivy League school."

"Of course not. I wouldn't expect her to. But I'll miss her very much."

"That's only natural. She'll miss you Elm Creek Quilters, too."

"She's one of our founding members," said Sylvia, steadying a quaver in her voice. "It's difficult to believe this is her last week." The Elm Creek Quilters were fortunate that one of their new hires, Gretchen Hartley, was willing to start right away. Although Gretchen and Judy had very different quilting styles, adjusting the course offerings was a minor inconvenience compared to the upheaval of canceling classes altogether. At least the rest of their staff would remain through the rest of the season, but then . . . "We won't have Summer for much longer, either."

"I thought she was staying through the end of September."

"That's what she says now, but I'm sure once camp wraps up for the season, she'll be eager to move to Chicago before the fall quarter begins."

"What about her boyfriend? Won't she want to stick around in Waterford for him?"

"I'm not so sure about that. She's more likely to delay her departure for her mother than for Jeremy."

Andrew chuckled. "Gwen's so proud of her, I wouldn't be surprised if she drove Summer to Chicago and walked her to class on the first day."

Sylvia smiled at the image of Gwen in a brightly colored gypsy skirt and beaded necklaces escorting her red-faced, twenty-eight-year-old daughter to her first graduate school symposium. "Gwen might do exactly that, if she didn't have her own students to worry about. And if Summer wouldn't faint away from embarrassment."

"Summer doesn't seem the fainting type."

"No, I suppose you're right." It was far more likely that the spirited young woman would welcome her mother's companionship. Gwen and Summer were very close, and Sylvia was so happy for them both, so proud of Summer's accomplishments and her prospects, that Sylvia could almost forget to regret her leaving them.

Almost.

Andrew finished his coffee, drew in his fishing line, and began packing his gear. "Do you think you'll finish your quilt in time?" he asked.

"Unfortunately, no. The grand unveiling I had planned for Judy's going-away party will have to wait."

"Think of it this way." Andrew squeezed her hand in sympathy and helped her to her feet. "Now we'll have an excuse to visit Judy in Philadelphia. A quilt that special ought to be delivered in person."

Sylvia nodded, but the thought of a future visit was small consolation. She had worked on the quilts all summer in secret, tracing the templates on the back of her favorite fabrics, carefully cutting the pieces, pinning and sewing each curve by hand.

Winding Ways. The pattern's name was as evocative as the design was lovely. A mosaic of overlapping circles and intertwining curves, the circles would appear only if the quiltmaker created a careful balance of dark and light hues, if she harmonized the colors and gave contrast its pride of place. Such was the harmony and balance of the Elm Creek Quilters, whose friendship had been tested by time and conflict. In the years ahead, it would face the test of distance, as well. The quilt—or quilts, rather—that Sylvia was making would capture the spirit of that friendship, the necessary journeys that sometimes led one woman far from the embrace of her beloved friends.

"When I think of all the winding ways the path of my life has followed," Sylvia said as she and Andrew strolled arm-in-arm back to the manor, "I believe it's a miracle that I ended up back in this beautiful place, surrounded by so much love and friendship. I could have followed my winding ways anywhere, and yet here I am, exactly where I am meant to be."

She would have to trust that Judy's and Summer's own winding ways would lead them to joy and fulfillment. They both deserved happiness in abundance.

"My favorite winding path is the Pennsylvania Toll Road," remarked Andrew.

Sylvia laughed, her melancholy momentarily forgotten. "Why is that?"

"Because it brought me back to Elm Creek Manor, and to you."